The Knight Of Gwynne

Vol. 1

by

Charles James Lever

Double 9
BOOKS

The Knight Of Gwynne
Vol. 1
by Charles James Lever

ISBN: 978-93-62769-78-7

Published by

DOUBLE 9 BOOKS

2/13-B, Ansari Road
Daryaganj, New Delhi – 110002
info@double9books.com
www.double9books.com
Tel. 011-40042856

ABOUT THE AUTHOR

Charles James Lever was an Irish author and storyteller who lived from August 31, 1806 to June 1, 1872. Anthony Trollope said that Lever's books were like his conversations. Lever was born on Amiens Street in Dublin. He was the second son of architect and builder James Lever and went to special schools. He had many adventures at Trinity College, Dublin, from 1823 to 1828. It was there that he got his medical degree in 1831. Some of the stories of his books are based on these experiences. The character of Frank Webber in the book Charles O'Malley was based on Robert Boyle, a friend from college who later became a priest. Lever and Boyle made extra money by singing original songs in the streets of Dublin. They also pulled off a lot of other jokes, which Lever wrote about in more detail in his books O'Malley, Con Cregan, and Lord Kilgobbin. Before he really started studying medicine, Lever went to Canada on an emigrant ship as an untrained surgeon. He has used some of what he learned in Con Cregan, Arthur O'Leary, and Roland Cashel. When he got to Canada, he went into the woods and joined a Native American group. But he had to leave because his life was in danger, just like his character Bagenal Daly did in his book The Knight of Gwynne.

CONTENTS

PREFACE

I wrote this story in the Tyrol. The accident of my residence there was in this wise: I had travelled about the Continent for a considerable time in company with my family with my own horses. Our carriage was a large and comfortable calèche, and our team, four horses; the leaders of which, well-bred and thriving-looking, served as saddle horses when needed.

There was something very gypsy-like in this roving, uncertain existence, that had no positive bent or limit, and left every choice of place an open question, that gave me intense enjoyment. It opened to me views of Continental life, scenery, people and habits I should certainly never have attained to by other modes of travel.

Not only were our journeys necessarily short each day, but we frequently sojourned in little villages, and out-of-the-world spots, where, if pleased by the place itself, and the accommodation afforded, we would linger on for days, having at our disposal the total liberty of our time, and all our nearest belongings around us.

In the course of these rambles we had arrived at the town of Bregenz, on the Lake of Constance; where the innkeeper, to whom I was known, accosted me with all the easy freedom of his calling, and half-jestingly alluded to my mode of travelling as a most unsatisfactory and wasteful way of life, which could never turn out profitably to myself or to mine. From the window where we were standing as we talked, I could descry the tall summit of an ancient castle, or schloss, about two miles away; and rather to divert my antagonist from his argument than with any more serious purpose, I laughingly told my host, if he could secure me such a fine old chateau as that I then looked at, I should stable my nags and rest where I was. On the following day, thinking of nothing less than my late conversation, the host entered my room to assure me that he had been over to the castle, had seen the baron, and learned that he would have no objection to lease me his chateau, provided I took it for a fixed term, and with all its accessories, not only of furniture but cows and farm requisites. One of my horses, accidentally pricked in shoeing, had obliged me at the moment to delay a day or two at the inn, and for want of better to do, though without the most remote intention of becoming a tenant of the castle, I yielded so far to my host's solicitation,— to walk over and see it.

If the building itself was far from faultless it was spacious and convenient, and its position on a low hill in the middle of a lawn finer than anything I can convey; the four sides of the schloss commanding four distinct and perfectly dissimilar views. By the north it looked over a wooded plain, on which stood the Convent of Mehreran; and beyond this, the broad expanse of the Lake of Constance. The south opened a view towards the Upper Rhine, and the valley that led to the Via Mala. On the east you saw the Gebhardsberg and its chapel, and the lovely orchards that bordered Bregenz; while to the west rose the magnificent Lenten and the range of the Swiss Alps,—their summits lost in the clouds.

I was so enchanted by the glorious panorama around me, and so carried away by the thought of a life of quiet labor and rest in such a spot, that after hearing a very specious account of the varied economies I should secure by this choice of a residence, and the resources I should have in excursions on all sides, that I actually contracted to take the chateau, and became master of the Rieden Schloss from that day.

Having thus explained by what chance I came to pitch my home in this little-visited spot, I have no mind to dwell further on my Tyrol experiences than as they concern the story which I wrote there.

If the scene in which I was living, the dress of the peasants, the daily ways and interests had been my prompters, I could not have addressed myself to an Irish theme; but long before I had come to settle at Predeislarg, when wandering amongst the Rhine villages, on the vine-clad slopes of the Bergstrasse, I had been turning over in my mind the Union period of Ireland as the era for a story. It was a time essentially rich in the men we are proud of as a people, and peculiarly abounding in traits of self-denial and devotion which, in the corruption of a few, have been totally lost sight of; the very patriotism of the time having been stigmatized as factious opposition, or unreasoning resistance to wiser counsels. That nearly every man of ability in the land was against the Minister, that not only all the intellect of Ireland, but all the high spirit of its squirearchy, and the generous impulses of its people, were opposed to the Union,—there is no denying. If eloquent appeal and powerful argument could have saved a nation, Henry Grattan or Plunkett would not have spoken in vain; but the measure was decreed before it was debated, and the annexation of Ireland was made a Cabinet decision before it came to Irishmen to discuss it.

I had no presumption to imagine I could throw any new light on the history of the period, or illustrate the story of the measure by any novel details; but I thought it would not be uninteresting to sketch the era itself; what aspect society presented; how the country gentleman of the time bore himself in the midst of solicitations and temptings the most urgent and insidious; what, in fact, was the character of that man whom no national misfortunes could subdue, no Ministerial blandishments corrupt; of him, in short, that an authority with little bias to the land of his birth has called, — *The First Gentleman of Europe.*

I know well, I feel too acutely, how inadequately I have pictured what I desired to paint; but even now, after the interval of years, I look back on my poor attempt with the satisfaction of one whose aim was not ignoble. A longer and deeper experience of life has succeeded to the time since I wrote this story, but in no land nor amongst any people have I ever found the type of what we love to emblematize by the word Gentleman, so distinctly marked out as in the educated and travelled Irishman of that period. The same unswerving fidelity of friendship, the same courageous devotion to a cause, the same haughty contempt for all that was mean or unworthy; these, with the lighter accessories of genial temperament, joyous disposition, and a chivalrous respect for women, made up what I had at least in my mind when I tried to present to my readers my Knight of Gwynne.

That my character of him was not altogether ideal, I can give no better proof than the fact that during the course of the publication I received several letters from persons unknown to me, asking whether I had not drawn my portrait from this or that original, several concurring in the belief that I had taken as my model The Knight of Kerry, whose qualities, I am well assured, fully warranted the suspicion.

For my attempt to paint the social habits of-the period, I had but to draw on my memory. In my boyish days I had heard much of that day, and was familiar with most of the names of its distinguished men. Anecdotes of Henry Grattan, Flood, Parsons, Ponsonby, and Curran jostled in my mind with stories of their immediate successors, the Bushes and the Plunketts, whose fame has come down to the very day we live in. As a boy, it was my fortune to listen to the narratives of the men who had been actors in the events of that exciting era, and who could even show me in modern Dublin the scenes where memorable events occurred, and not unfrequently the very houses where celebrated convivialities occurred. And thus from Drogheda Street, the modern Sackville Street, where the beaux of the day lounged in all their bravery, to the Circular road, where a long file of carriages, six in hand, evidenced the luxury and tone of display of the capital. I was deeply imbued with the features of the time, and ransacked the old newspapers and magazines with a zest which only great familiarity with the names of the leading characters could have inspired.

Though I have many regrets on the same score, there is no period of my life in which I have the same sorrow for not having kept some sort of note-book, instead of trusting to a memory most fatally unretentive and uncertain. Through this omission I have lost traces of innumerable epigrams, and *jeux d'esprit* of a time that abounded in such effusions, and even where my memory has occasionally relieved the effort, I have forgotten the author. To give an instance, the witty lines, —

> *"With a name that is borrowed, a title that 's bought,*
>
> *Sir William would fain be a gentleman thought;*
>
> *His wit is but cunning, his courage but vapor,*
>
> *His pride is but money, his money but paper:"* —

which, wrongfully attributed to a political leader in the Irish house, were in reality written by Lovel Edgeworth on the well-known Sir William Gladowes, who became Lord Newcomen; and the verse was not only poetry but prophecy, for in his bankruptcy some years afterwards the sarcasm became fact, — "his money was but paper."

This circumstance of the authorship was communicated to me by Miss Maria Edgeworth, whose letter was my first step in acquaintance with her, and gave me a pleasure and a pride which long years have not been able to obliterate.

I remember in that letter her having told me how she was in the habit of reading my story aloud to the audience of her nephews and nieces; a simple announcement that imparted such a glow of proud delight to me, that I can yet recall the courage with which I resumed the writing of my tale, and the hope it suggested of my being able one day to win a place of honor amongst those who, like herself, had selected Irish traits as the characteristics to adorn fiction.

For Con Heffernan I had an original. For Bagenal Daly, too, I was not without a model. His sister is purely imaginary, but that she is not unreal I am bold enough to hope, since several have assured me that they know where I found my type. In my brief sketch of Lord Castlereagh I was not, I need scarcely say, much aided by the journals and pamphlets of the time, where his character and conduct were ruthlessly and most falsely assailed. It was my fortune, however, to have possessed the close intimacy of one who had acted as his private secretary, and whose abilities have since raised him to high station and great employment; and from him I came to know the real nature of one of the ablest statesmen of his age, as he was one of the most attractive companions, and most accomplished gentlemen. I have no vain pretence to believe that by my weak and unfinished sketch I have in any way vindicated the Minister who carried the Union against the attacks of his opponents, but I have tried at least to represent him such as he was in the society of his intimates; his gay and cheerful temperament, his frank nature, and what least the world is disposed to concede to him, his sincere belief in the honesty of men whose convictions were adverse to him, and who could not be won over to his opinions.

I have not tried to conceal the gross corruption of an era which remains to us as a national shame, but I would wish to lay stress on the fact that not a few resisted offers and temptations, which to men struggling with humble fortune, and linked for life with the fate of the weaker country, must redound to their high credit. All the nobler their conduct, as around them on every side were the great names of the land trafficking for title and place, and shamelessly demanding office for their friends and relatives as the price of their own adhesion.

For that degree of intimacy which I have represented as existing between Bagenal Daly and Freney the robber, I have been once or twice reprehended as conveying a false and unreal view of the relations of the time; but the knowledge I myself had of Freney, his habits and his exploits, were given to me by a well-known and highly-connected Irish gentleman, who represented a county in the Irish Parliament, and was a man of unblemished honor, conspicuous alike in station and ability. And there is still, and once the trait existed more remarkably in Ireland, a wonderful sympathy between all classes and conditions of people: so that the old stories and traditions that amuse the crouching listener round the hearth of the cottage, find their way into luxurious drawing-rooms; and by their means a brotherhood of sentiment was maintained between the highest class in the land and the humblest peasant who labored for his daily bread.

I tried to display the effect of this strange teaching on the mind of a cultivated gentleman when describing the Knight of Gwynne. I endeavored to show the "Irishry" of his nature was no other than the play of those qualities by which he appreciated his countrymen and was appreciated by them. So powerful is this sympathy, and so strong the sense of national humor through all classes of the people, that each is able to entertain a topic from the same point of view as his neighbor, and the subtle *équivoque* in the polished witticism that amuses the gentleman is never lost on the untutored ear of the unlettered peasant. Is there any other land of which one can say as much?

If this great feature of attractiveness pertains to the country and adds to its adaptiveness as the subject of fiction, I cannot but feel that to un-Irish ears it is necessary to make an explanation which will serve to show that which would elsewhere imply a certain blending of station and condition, is here but a proof of that widespread understanding by which, however divided by race, tradition, and religion, we are always able to appeal to certain sympathies and dispositions in common, and feel the tie of a common country.

At the period in which I have placed this story the rivalry between the two nations was, with all its violence, by no means ungenerous. No contemptuous estimate of Irishmen formed the theme of English journalism; and between the educated men of both countries there was scarcely a jealousy that the character which political contest assumed later on, changed much of this spirit and dyed nationalities with an amount of virulence which, with all its faults and all its shortcomings, we do not find in the times of the Knight of Gwynne.

CHARLES LEVER.

Trieste, 1872.

CHAPTER I
A FIRESIDE GROUP

It was exactly forty-five years ago that a group, consisting of three persons, drew their chairs around the fire of a handsome dinner-room in Merrion Square, Dublin. The brilliantly lighted apartment, the table still cumbered with decanters and dessert, and the sideboard resplendent with a gorgeous service of plate, showed that the preparations had been made for a much larger party, the last of whom had just taken his departure.

Of the three who now drew near the cheerful blaze, more intent, as it seemed, on confidential intercourse than the pleasures of the table, he who occupied the centre was a tall and singularly handsome man, of some six or seven-and-twenty years of age. His features, perfectly classical in their regularity, conveyed the impression of one of a cold and haughty temperament, unmoved by sudden impulse, but animated by a spirit daringly ambitious. His dress was in the height of the then mode, and he wore it with the air of a man of fashion and elegance.

This was Lord Castlereagh, the youthful Secretary for Ireland, one whose career was then opening with every promise of future distinction.

At his right hand sat, or rather lounged, in all the carelessness of habitual indolence, a young man some years his junior, his dark complexion and eyes, his aquiline features, and short, thin upper lip almost resembling a Spanish face.

His dress was the uniform of the Foot Guards,—a costume which well became him, and set off to the fullest advantage a figure of perfect symmetry. A manner of careless inattention in which he indulged, contrasted strongly with the quick impatience of his dark glances and the eager rapidity of his utterance when momentarily excited; for the Honorable Dick Forester was only cool by training, and not by temperament, and, at the time we speak of, his worldly education was scarcely more than well begun.

The third figure—strikingly unlike the other two—was a man of fifty or thereabouts, short and plethoric. His features, rosy and sensual, were lit up by two gray eyes whose twinkle was an incessant provocative to laughter. The mouth was, however, the great index to his character. It was large and full, the under lip slightly projecting,—a circumstance perhaps acquired in the long habit of a life where the tasting function had been actively employed; for Con Heffernan was a gourmand of the first water, and the most critical judge of a vintage the island could boast. Two fingers of either hand were inserted in the capacious pockets of a white vest, while, his head jauntily leaning to one side, he sat the very ideal of self-satisfied ease and contentment. The *aplomb*—why should there be a French word for an English quality?—he possessed was not the vulgar ease of a presuming or underbred man,—far from it; it was the impress of certain gifts which gave him an acknowledged superiority in the society he moved in. He was shrewd, without over-caution; he was ready-witted, but never rash; he possessed that rare combination of quick intelligence with strong powers of judgment; and, above all, he knew men, or at least such specimens of the race as came before him in a varied life, well and thoroughly.

If he had a weak point in his character, it was a love of popularity,—not that vulgar mob-worship which some men court and seek after; no, it was the estimation of his own class and set he desired to obtain. He was proud of his social position, and nervously sensitive in whatever might prejudice or endanger it. His enemies—and Con was too able a man not to have made some—said that his low origin was the secret of his nature; that his ambiguous position in society demanded exertions uncalled for from others less equivocally circumstanced; and that Mr. Heffernan was, in secret, very far from esteeming the high and titled associates with whom his daily life brought him in contact. If this were the case, he was assuredly a consummate actor. No man ever went through a longer or more searching trial unscathed, nor could an expression be quoted, or an act mentioned, in which he derogated, even for a moment, from the habits of "his order."

"You never did the thing better in your life, my Lord," said Con, as the door closed upon the last departing guest. "You hit off Jack Massy to perfection; and as for Watson, though he said nothing at the time, I 'll wager my roan cob against Deane Moore's hackney—long odds, I fancy—that you find him at the Treasury to-morrow morning, with a sly request for five minutes' private conversation."

"I'm of your mind, Heffernan. I saw that he took the bait,—indeed, to do the gentlemen justice, they are all open to conviction."

"You surely cannot blame them," said Con, "if they take a more conciliating view of your Lordship's opinions when assisted by such claret as this: this is old '72, if I mistake not."

"They sold it to me as such; but I own to you I'm the poorest connoisseur in the world as regards wine. Some one remarked this evening that the '95 was richer in bouquet."

"It was Edward Harvey, my Lord. I heard him; but that was the year he got his baronetcy, and he thinks the sun never shone so brightly before; his father was selling Balbriggan stockings when this grape was ripening, and now, the son has more than one foot on the steps of the peerage." This was said with a short, quick glance beneath the eyelids, and evidently more as a feeler than with any strong conviction of its accuracy.

"No Government can afford to neglect its supporters, and the acknowledgments must be proportioned to the sacrifices, as well as to the abilities of the individuals who second it."

"By Jove! if these gentlemen are in the market," said Forester, who broke silence for the first time, "I don't wonder at their price being a high one; in consenting to the 'Union,' they are virtually voting their own annihilation."

"By no means," said the Secretary, calmly; "the field open to their ambition is imperial, and not provincial; the English Parliament will form an arena for the display of ability as wide surely as this of Dublin. Men of note and capacity will not be less rewarded: the losers will be the small talkers, county squires of noisy politics, and crafty lawyers of no principles; they will, perhaps, be obliged to remain at home and look after their own affairs; but will the country be the worse for that, while the advantages to trade and commerce are inconceivable?"

"I agree with you there," said Con; "we are likely to increase our exports, by sending every clever fellow out of the country."

"Why not, if the market be a better one?"

"Would n't you spare us a few luxuries for home consumption?" said Con, as he smacked his lips and looked at his glass through the candle.

His Lordship paid no attention to the remark, but, taking a small tablet from his waistcoat-pocket, seemed to study its contents. "Are we certain of Cuffe; is he pledged to us, Heffernan?"

"Yes, my Lord, he has no help for it; we are sure of him; he owes the Crown eleven thousand pounds, and says the only ambition he possesses is to make the debt twelve, and never pay it."

"What of that canting fellow from the North,—New-land?"

"He accepts your terms conditionally, my Lord," said Con, with a sly roll of his eye. "If the arguments are equal to your liberality, he will vote for you; but as yet he does not *see* the advantages of a Union."

"Not *see* them!" said Lord Castlereagh, with a look of irony; "why did you not let him look at them from your own windows, Heffernan? The view is enchanting for the Barrack Department."

"The poor man is short-sighted," said Con, with a sigh, "and never could stretch his vision beyond the Custom House."

"Be it so, in the devil's name; a commissioner more or less shall never, stop us!"

"What a set of rascals," muttered Forester between his teeth, as he tossed off a bumper to swallow his indignation.

"Well, Forester, what of your mission? Have you heard from your friend Darcy?"

"Yes; I have his note here. He cannot come over just now, but he has given me an introduction to his father, and pledges himself I shall be well received."

"What Darcy is that?" said Heffernan.

"The Knight of Gwynne," said his Lordship; "do you know him?"

"I believe, my Lord, there is not a gentleman in Ireland who could not say yes to that question; while west of the Shannon, Maurice Darcy is a name to swear by."

"We want such a man much," said the Secretary, in a low, distinct utterance; "some well-known leader of public opinion is of great value just now. How does he vote usually? I don't see his name in the divisions."

"Oh, he rarely comes up to town, never liked Parliament; but when he did attend the House, he usually sat with the Opposition, but, without linking himself to party, spoke and voted independently, and, strange to say, made considerable impression by conduct which in any other man would have proved an utter failure."

"Did he speak well, then?"

"For the first five minutes you could think of nothing but his look and appearance; he was the handsomest man in the House, a little too particular, perhaps, in dress, but never finical; as he went on, however, the easy fluency of his language, the grace and elegance of his style, and the frank openness of his statements, carried his hearers with him; and many who were guarded enough against the practised power of the great speakers were entrapped by the unstudied, manly tone of the Knight of Gwynne. You say truly, he would be a great card in your hands at this time."

"We must have him at his own price, if he has one. Is he rich?"

"He has an immense estate, but, as I hear, greatly encumbered; but don't think of money with him, that will never do."

"What's the bait, then? Does he care for rank? Has he any children grown up?"

"One son and one daughter are all his family; and as for title, I don't think that he 'd exchange that of Knight of Gwynne for a Dukedom. His son is a lieutenant in the Guards."

"Yes; and the best fellow in the regiment," broke in Forester. "In every quality of a high-spirited gentleman, Lionel Darcy has no superior."

"The better deserving of rapid promotion," said his Lordship, smiling significantly.

"I should be sorry to offer it to him at the expense of his father's principles," said Forester.

"Very little fear of your having to do so," said Heffernan, quickly; "the Knight would be no easy purchase."

"You must see him, however, Dick." said the Secretary; "there is no reason why he should not be with us on grounds of conviction. He is a man of enlightened and liberal mind, and surely will not think the worse of a measure because its advocates are in a position to serve his son's interests."

"If that topic be kept very studiously out of sight, it were all the more prudent," said Con, dryly.

"Of course; Forester will pay his visit, and only advert to the matter with caution and delicacy. To gain him to our side is a circumstance of so much moment that I say *carte blanche* for the terms."

"I knew the time that a foxhound would have been a higher bribe than a blue ribbon with honest Maurice; but it's many years since we met, now, and Heaven knows what changes time may have wrought in him. A smile and a soft speech from a pretty woman, or a bold exploit of some hare-brained fellow, were sure to find favor with him, when he would have heard flattery from the lips of royalty without pride or emotion."

"His colleague in the county is with us; has he any influence over the Knight?"

"Far from it. Mr. Hickman O'Reilly is the last man in the world to have weight with Maurice Darcy, and if it be your intention to make O'Reilly a peer, you could have taken no readier method to arm the Knight against you. No, no; if you really are bent on having him, leave all thought of a purchase aside; let Forester, as the friend and brother officer of young

Darcy, go down to Gwynne, make himself as agreeable to the Knight as may be, and when he has one foot on the carriage-step at his departure, turn sharply round, and say, 'Won't you vote with us, Knight?' What between surprise and courtesy, he may be taken too short for reflection, and if he say but 'Yes,' ever so low, he's yours. That's *my* advice to you. It may seem a poor chance, but I fairly own I see no better one."

"I should have thought rank might be acceptable in such a quarter," said the Secretary, proudly.

"He has it, my Lord,—at least as much as would win all the respect any rank could confer; and besides, these new peerages have no prestige in their favor yet a while; we must wait for another generation. This claret is perfect now, but I should not say it were quite so delicate in flavor the first year it was bottled. The squibs and epigrams on the new promotions are remembered where the blazons of the Heralds' College are forgotten; that unlucky banker, for instance, that you made a Viscount the other day, both his character and his credit have suffered for it."

"What was that you allude to?—an epigram, was it?"

"Yes, very short, but scarcely sweet. Here it is:—

"*'With a name that is borrowed, a title that's bought,—'*

you, remember, my Lord, how true both allegations are,—

"'With a name that is borrow'd, a title that's bought, Sir William would fain be a gentleman thought; While his Wit is mere cunning, his Courage but vapor, His Pride is but money, his Money but paper.'"

"Very severe, certainly," said his Lordship, in the same calm tone he ever spoke. "Not your lines, Mr. Heffernan?"

"No, my Lord; a greater than Con Heffernan indited these,—one who did not scruple to reply to yourself in the House in an imitation of your own inimitable manner."

"Oh, I know whom you mean,—a very witty person indeed," said the Secretary, smiling; "and if we were to be laughed out of office, he might lead the Opposition. But these are very business-like, matter-of-fact days we 're fallen upon. The cabinet that can give away blue ribbons may afford to be indifferent to small jokers. But to revert to matters more immediate: you must start at once, Forester, for the West, see the Knight, and do whatever you can to bring him towards us. I say *carte blanche* for the terms; I only wish our other elevations to the peerage had half the pretension he has; and, whatever our friend Mr. Heffernan may say, I opine to the mere matter of compact, which says, so much for so much."

"Here's success to the mission, however its negotiations incline," said Heffernan, as he drained off his glass and rose to depart. "We shall see you again within ten days or a fortnight, I suppose?"

"Oh, certainly; I'll not linger in that wild district an hour longer than I must." And so, with good night and good wishes, the party separated, — Forester to make his preparations for a journey which, in those days, was looked on as something formidable.

CHAPTER II
A TRAVELLING ACQUAINTANCE

Whatever the merits or demerits of the great question, the legislative union between England and Ireland,—and assuredly we have neither the temptation of duty nor inclination to discuss such here,—the means employed by Ministers to carry the measure through Parliament were in the last degree disgraceful. Never was bribery practised with more open effrontery, never did corruption display itself with more daring indifference to public opinion; the Treasury office was an open mart, where votes were purchased, and men sold their country, delighted, as a candid member of the party confessed,—delighted "to have a country to sell."

The ardor of a political career, like the passion for the chase, would seem in its high excitement to still many compunctious murmurings of conscience which in calmer moments could not fail to be heard and acknowledged: the desire to succeed, that ever-present impulse to win, steels the heart against impressions which, under less pressing excitements, had been most painful to endure; and, in this way, honorable and high-minded men have often stooped to acts which, with calmer judgment to guide them, they would have rejected with indignation.

Such was Dick Forester's position at the moment. An aide-de-camp on the staff of the Viceroy, a near relative of the Secretary, he was intrusted with many secret and delicate negotiations, affairs in which, had he been a third party, he would have as scrupulously condemned the tempter as the tempted; the active zeal of agency allayed, however, all such qualms of conscience, and every momentary pang of remorse was swallowed up in the ardor for success.

Few men will deny in the abstract the cruelty of many field-sports they persist in following; fewer still abandon them on such scruples; and while Forester felt half ashamed to himself of the functions committed to him, he would have been sorely disappointed if he had been passed over in the selection of his relative's political adherents.

Of this nature were some of Dick Forester's reflections as he posted along towards the West; nor was the scene through which he journeyed suggestive of pleasanter thoughts. If any of our readers should perchance be acquainted with that dreary line of country which lies along the great western road of Ireland, they will not feel surprised if the traveller's impressions of the land were not of the brightest or fairest. The least reflective of mortals cannot pass through a dreary and poverty-stricken district without imbibing some of the melancholy which broods over the place. Forester was by no means such, and felt deeply and sincerely for the misery he witnessed on every hand, and was in the very crisis of some most patriotic scheme of benevolence, when his carriage arrived in front of the little inn of Kilbeggan. Resisting, without much violence to his inclinations, the civil request of the landlord to alight, he leaned back to resume the broken thread of his lucubrations, while fresh horses were put to. How long he thus waited, or what progress his benign devices accomplished in the mean while, this true history is unable to record; enough if we say that when he next became aware of the incidents then actually happening around him, he discovered that his carriage was standing fast in the same place as at the moment of his arrival, and the rain falling in torrents, as before.

To let down the glass and call out to the postilions was a very natural act; to do so with the addition of certain expletives not commonly used in good society, was not an extraordinary one. Forester did both; but he might have spared his eloquence and his indignation, for the postilions were both in the stable, and his servant agreeably occupied in the bar over the comforts of a smoking tumbler of punch. The merciful schemes so late the uppermost object of his thoughts were routed in a moment, and, vowing intentions of a very different purport to the whole household, he opened the door and sprang out. Dark as the night was, he could see that there were no horses to the carriage, and, with redoubled anger at the delay, he strode into the inn.

"Holloa, I say—house here! Linwood! Where the devil is the fellow?"

"Here, sir," cried a smart-looking London servant, as he sprang from the bar with his eyes bolting out of his head from the heat of the last mouthful, swallowed in a second. "I've been a trying for horses, sir; but they've never got 'em, though they 've been promising to let us have a pair this half-hour."

"No horses! Do you mean that they've not got a pair of posters in a town like this?"

"Yes, indeed, sir," interposed a dirty waiter in a nankeen jacket; for the landlord was too indignant at the rejection of his proposal to appear again, "we've four pair, besides a mare in foal; but there's a deal of business on the line this week past, and there's a gentleman in the parlor now has taken four of them."

"Taken four! Has he more than one carriage?"

"No, sir, a light chariot it is; but he likes to go fast."

"And so do I—when I can," muttered Forester, the last words being an addition almost independent of him. "Could n't you tell him that there's a gentleman here very much pressed to push on, and would take it as a great favor if he'd divide the team?"

"To be sure, sir, I'll go and speak to him," said the waiter, as he hurried away on the errand.

"I see how it is, sir," said Linwood, who, with true servant dexterity, thought to turn his master's anger into any other channel than towards himself, "they wants to get you to stop the night here."

"Confound this trickery! I'll pay what they please for the horses, only let us have them.—Well, waiter, what does he say?"

"He says, sir," said the waiter, endeavoring to suppress a laugh, "if you 'll come in and join him at supper, you shall have whatever you like."

"Join him at supper! No, no; I'm hurried, I'm anxious to get forward, and not the least hungry besides."

"Hadn't you better speak a word to him, anyhow?" said the waiter, half opening the parlor door. And Forester, accepting the suggestion, entered.

In the little low-ceilinged apartment of the small inn, at a table very amply and as temptingly covered, sat a large and, for his age, singularly handsome man. A forehead both high and broad surmounted two clear blue eyes, whose brilliancy seemed to defy the wear of time; regular and handsome teeth; and a complexion the very type of health appeared to vouch for a strength of constitution rare at his advanced age. His dress was the green coat so commonly worn by country gentlemen, with leather breeches and boots, nor, though the season was winter, did he appear to have any great-coat, or other defence against the weather. He was heaping some turf upon the fire as Forester entered, and, laughingly interrupting the operation, he stood up and bowed courteously.

"I have taken a great liberty, sir, first, to suppose that any man at this hour of the night is not the worse for something to eat and drink; and, secondly, that he might have no objection to partake of either in my company." Forester was not exactly prepared for a manner so palpably that of the best society, and, at once repressing every sign of his former impatience, replied by apologizing for a request which might inconvenience the granter. "Let me help you to this grouse-pie, and fill yourself a glass of sherry; and by the time you have taken some refreshment, the horses will be put to. I am most happy to offer you a seat."

"I am afraid there is a mistake somewhere," said Forester, half timidly. "I heard you had engaged the only four horses here, and as my carriage is without, my request was to obtain two if you—"

"But why not come with me? I 'm pressed, and must be up, if possible, before morning. Remember, we are forty-eight miles from Dublin."

"Dublin! But I'm going the very opposite road. I'm for Westport."

"Oh, by Jove! that is different. What a stupid fellow the waiter is! Never mind; sit down. Let us have a glass of wine together. You shall have two of the horses. Old Wilkins must only make his spurs supply the place of the leaders."

There was a hearty good-nature in every accent of the old man's voice, and Forester drew his chair to the table, by no means sorry to spend some time longer in his company.

There is a kind of conversation sacred to the occupations of the table,—a mixture of the culinary and the social, the gustatory with the agreeable. And the stranger led the way to this, with the art of an accomplished proficient, and while recommending the good things to Forester's attention, contrived to season their enjoyment by a tone at once pleasing and cordial.

"I could have sworn you were hungry," said he, laughing, as Forester helped himself for the second time to the grouse-pie. "I know you did not expect so appetizing a supper in such a place; but Rickards has always something in the larder for an old acquaintance, and I have been travelling this road close upon sixty years now."

"And a dreary way it is," said Forester, "except for this most agreeable incident. I never came so many miles before with so little to interest me."

"Very true; it is a flat, monotonous-looking country, and poor besides; but nothing like what I remember it as a boy."

"You surely do not mean that the people were ever worse off than they seem now to be?"

"Ay, a hundred times worse off. They may be rack-rented and over-taxed in some instances now,—not as many as you would suppose, after all,—but then, they were held in actual slavery, nearly famished, and all but naked; no roads, no markets; subject to the caprice of the landowners on every occasion in life, and the faction fights—those barbarous vestiges of a rude time—kept up and encouraged by those who should have set the better example of mutual charity and good feeling. These unhappy practices have not disappeared, but they are far less frequent than formerly; and however the confession may seem to you a sad one, to me there is a pride in saying, Ireland is improving."

"It is hard to conceive a people more miserably off than these," said Forester, with a sigh.

"So they seem to your eyes; but let me remark that there is a transition state between rude barbarism and civilization which always appears more miserable than either; habits of life which suggest wants that can rarely, if ever, be supplied. The struggle between poverty and the desire for better, is a bitter conflict, and such is the actual condition of this people. You are young enough to witness the fruits of the reformation; I am too old ever to hope to see them, but I feel assured that the day is coming."

"I like your theory well; it has Hope for its ally," said Forester, as he gazed on the benevolent features of the old squire.

"It has even better, sir, it has truth; and hence it is that the peasantry, as they approach nearer to the capital,—the seat of civilization,—have fewest of those traits that please or attract strangers; they are in the transition state I speak of; while down in *my* wild country, you can see them in their native freshness, reckless and improvident, but light-hearted and happy."

"Where may the country be you speak of, sir?" said Forester.

"The Far West, beside the Atlantic. You have heard of Mayo?"

"Oh, that is my destination at this moment; I am going beyond Westport, to visit one of the chieftains there. I have not the honor to know him, but I conclude that his style of living and habits will not be a bad specimen of the gentry customs generally."

"I know that neighborhood tolerably well. May I ask the name of your future host?"

"The Knight of Gwynne is his title—Mr. Darcy—"

"Oh! an old acquaintance,—I may almost say an old friend of mine," said the other, smiling. "And so you are going to pass some time at Gywnne?"

"A week or so; I scarcely think I can spare more."

"They 'll call that a very inhospitable visit at Gwynne, sir; the Knight's guests rarely stay less than a month. I have just left it, and there were some there who had been since the beginning of the partridge-shooting, and not the least welcome of the party."

"I am sorry I had not the good fortune to meet you there," said Forester.

"Make your visit a fortnight, and I 'll join you, then," said the old man, gayly. "I 'm going up to town to settle a wager,—a foolish excursion, you 'll say, at my time of life; but it's too late to mend."

"The horses is put to, sir," said the waiter, announcing the fact for something like the fourth time, without being attended to.

"Well, then, it is time to start. Am I to take it as a pledge that I shall find you at Gwynne this day fortnight?"

"I cannot answer for my host," said Forester, laughing.

"Oh! old Darcy is sure to ask you to stay. By the way, would you permit me to trouble you with five lines to a friend who is now stopping there?"

"Of course; I shall be but too happy to be of any service to you."

The old gentleman sat down, and, tearing a leaf from a capacious pocket-book, wrote a few hurried lines, which, having folded and sealed, he addressed, "Bagenal Daly, Esquire, Gwynne Abbey."

"There, that's my commission; pray add my service to the Knight himself, when you see him."

"Permit me to ask, how shall I designate his friend?"

"Oh! I forgot, you don't know me," said he, laughing. "I have half a mind to leave the identification with your own descriptive powers."

"I'd wager five guineas I could make the portrait a resemblance."

"Done, then; I take the bet," said the other; "and I promise you, on the word of a gentleman, I am known to every visitor in the house."

Each laughed heartily at the drollery of such a wager, and, with many a profession of the pleasure a future meeting would afford to both, they parted, less like casual acquaintances than as old and intimate friends.

CHAPTER III
GWYNNE ABBEY

When Forester parted with his chance companion at Kilbeggan, he pursued his way without meeting a single incident worth recording; nor, although he travelled with all the speed of posters, aided by the persuasive power of additional half-crowns, shall we ask of our reader to accompany him, but, at one bound, cross the whole island, and stand with us on the margin of that glorious sheet of water which, begirt with mountains and studded with its hundred islands, is known as Clue Bay.

At the southern extremity of the bay rises the great mountain of Croagh Patrick, its summit nearly five thousand feet above the sea; on the side next the ocean, it is bold and precipitous, crag rising above crag in succession, and not even the track of a mountain goat visible on the dangerous surface; landward, however, a gentle slope descends about the lower third of the mountain, and imperceptibly is lost in the rich and swelling landscape beneath. Here, sheltered from the western gales, and favored by the fertility of the soil, the trees are seen to attain a girth and height rarely met with elsewhere, while they preserve their foliage to a much later period than in other parts of the country.

The ruins of an ancient church, whose very walls are washed by the Atlantic, show that the luxuriant richness of the spot was known in times past. They who founded these goodly edifices were no mean judges of the resources of the land, and the rich woods and blossoming orchards that still shelter their ruined shrines evidence with what correctness they selected their resting-places.

The coast-road which leads from Westport skirts along the edge of the bay, and is diversified by many a pretty cottage whose trellised walls and rose-covered porches vouch for the mildness of the climate, and are in summer resorted to as bathing-lodges by numbers from the inland counties. The high-road has, however, a grander destiny than to such humble, though picturesque, dwellings, for it suddenly ceases at the gate of an immense demesne, whose boundary wall may be seen stretching away for miles, and at last is traced high up the mountain side, where it forms the enclosure of a deer park.

Two square and massive towers connected by an arch form the gateway, and though ivy and honeysuckle have covered many an architectural device which once were looked on with pride, a massive armorial escutcheon in yellow stone forms the key of the arch, while two leopards supporting a crown, with the motto, "Ne la touchez pas!" proclaim the territory of the Knight of Gwynne.

Within, an avenue wide enough for a high-road led through a park of great extent, dotted with trees single or in groups, and bounded by a vast wood, whose waving tops were seen for miles of distance. If a landscape-gardener would have deplored with uplifted hands the glorious opportunities of embellishment which neglect or ignorance had suffered to lie undeveloped within these grounds, a true lover of scenery would have felt delighted at the wild and picturesque beauty around him, as, sometimes, the road would dip into a deep glade, where the overhanging banks were clothed with the dog-rose and the sweet-brier, still and hushed to every sound save the song of the thrush or the not less sweet ripple of the little stream that murmured past; and again, emerging from the shade, it wound along some height whence the great mountain might be seen, or, between the dark foliage, the blue surface of the sea, swelling and heaving with ever-restless motion. All the elements of great picturesque beauty were here, and in that glorious profusion with which nature alone diffuses her wealth,— the mountain, the forest, and the ocean, the greensward, the pebbly shore, the great rocks, the banks blue with the violet and the veronica,—and all diversified and contrasted to produce effects the most novel and enchanting.

Many a road and many a pathway led through these woods and valleys, some grass-grown, as though disused, others bearing the track of recent wheels, still, as you went, the hares and the rabbits felt no terror, the wood-pigeon sat upon the branch above your head, nor was scared at your approach; for though the Knight was a passionate lover of sport, it was his fancy to preserve the demesne intact, nor would he suffer a shot to be fired within its precincts. These may seem small and insignificant matters to record, but they added indescribably to the charms of the spot, completing, as they did, the ideas of tranquillity and peace suggested by the scene.

The approach was of some miles in extent, not needlessly prolonged by every device of sweep and winding, but in reality proceeding by its nearest way to the house, which, for the advantage of a view over the sea, was situated on the slope of the mountain. Nor was the building unworthy of its proud position: originally an abbey, its architecture still displayed the elaborate embellishment which characterized the erections of the latter part of the sixteenth century.

A long façade, interrupted at intervals by square towers, formed the front, the roof consisting of a succession of tall and pointed gables, in each of which some good saint stood enshrined in stone; the windows, throughout this long extent, were surmounted by pediments and figures not rudely chiselled, but with high pretension as works of art, and evidencing both taste and skill in the designer; while the great entrance was a miracle of tracery and carving, the rich architraves retreating one within another to the full depth of twelve feet, such being the thickness of the external wall.

Spacious and imposing as this great mass of building appeared at first sight, it formed but a fragment of the whole, and was in reality but the side of a great quadrangle, the approach to which led through one of the large towers, defended by fosse and drawbridge, while overhead the iron spikes of a massive portcullis might be seen; for the Abbot of Gwynne had been a "puissance" in days long past, and had his servitors in steel, as well as his followers in sackcloth. This road, which was excessively steep and difficult of access, was yet that by which carriages were accustomed to approach the house; for the stables occupied one entire wing of the quadrangle, the servants, of whom there were a goodly company, holding possession of the suite of rooms overhead, once the ancient dormitory of the monks of Gwynne.

In the middle of the courtyard was a large fountain, over which an effigy of St. Francis had formerly stood; but the saint had unhappily been used as a lay figure whereupon to brush hunting-coats and soiled leathers, and gradually his proportions had suffered grievous injury, till at last nothing remained of him save the legs, which were still profaned as a saddle-tree; for grooms and stable-boys are irreverent in their notions, and, probably, deemed it no disgrace for a saint to carry such honorable trappings.

The appearance of the abbey from within was even more picturesque than when seen from the outside, each side of the quadrangle displaying a different era and style of architecture; for they had been built with long intervals of time between them, and one wing, a low, two-storied range, with jail-like windows and a small, narrow portal, bore, on a three-cornered stone, the date 1304.

We shall not ask of our readers to accompany us further in our dry description, nor even cast a glance up at that myriad of strange beasts which, in dark gray stone, are frowning or grinning, or leaping or rearing, from every angle and corner of the building,—a strange company, whose representatives in real life it would puzzle the zoologist to produce; but there they were, some with a coat-of-arms between their paws, some supporting an ornamental capital, and others actually, as it seemed, cutting their uncouth capers out of pure idleness.

At the back of the abbey, and terraced on the mountain side, lay a perfect wilderness of flower-gardens and fishponds, amid which a taste more profane than that of the founders had erected sundry summer-houses in rockwork, hermitages without hermits, and shrines without worshippers, but all moss-grown, and old enough to make them objects of curiosity, while some afforded glorious points of view over the distant bay and the rich valley where stands the picturesque town of Westport.

The interior of this noble edifice was worthy of its appearance from without. Independent of the ample accommodation for a great household, there was a suite of state apartments running along the entire front and part of one wing, and these were fitted up and furnished with a luxury and costliness that would not have disgraced a royal palace. Here were seen velvet hangings and rich tapestries upon the walls, floors inlaid with tulip and sandal-wood, windows of richly stained glass threw a mysterious and mellow light over richly carved furniture, the triumphs of that art which the Netherlands once boasted; cabinets, curiously inlaid with silver and tortoiseshell, many of them gifts of distinguished donors, few without their associations of story; while one chamber, the ancient hall of audience, was hung round with armor and weapons, the trophies of long-buried ancestors, the proud memorials of a noble line; dark suits of Milan mail, or richly inlaid cuirasses of Spanish workmanship, with great two-handed swords and battle-axes, and, stranger still, weapons of Eastern mould and fashion, for more than one of the house had fought against the Turks, and crossed his broadsword with the scimitar.

There were objects rare and curious enough within these walls to stay and linger over; but even if we dared to take such a liberty with our reader, our duty would not permit the dalliance, and it is to a very different part of the building, and one destined for far other uses, that we must now for a brief space conduct him.

In a small chamber of the ground-floor, whose curiously groined roof and richly stained window showed that its occupancy had once been held by those in station above the common, now sat two persons at a well-garnished table, while before them, on the wide hearth, blazed a cheerful fire of bog deal. On either side of the fireplace was a niche, in which formerly some saintly effigy had stood, but now—such are Time's chances—an earthenware pitcher, with a pewter lid, decorated each, of whose contents the boon companions drank jovially to each other. One of these was a short, fat old fellow of nigh eighty years; his bowed legs and wide round shoulders the still surviving signs of great personal strength in days gone by; his hair, white as snow, was carefully brushed back from his forehead, and tied into "queue" behind. Old as he was, the features were intelligent and pleasing, the hale and hearty expression of good health and good temper animated them when he spoke, nor were the words the less mellow to an Irish ear that they smacked of the "sweet south," for Tate Sullivan was a Kerry man, and possessed in full measure the attributes of that pleasant kingdom; he was courteous and obliging, faithful in his affections, and if a bit hasty in temper, the very first to discover and correct it. His failing was the national one, — the proneness to conceal a truth if its disclosure were disagreeable: he could not bring himself to bear bad tidings; and this tendency had so grown with years that few who knew his weakness could trust any version of a fact from his lips without making due allowance for blarney.

For eight-and-forty years he had been a butler in the Knight's family, and his reverence for his master went on increasing with his years; in his eyes he was the happy concentration of every good quality of humanity, nor could he bring himself to believe that his like would ever come again.

Opposite to him sat one as unlike him in form and appearance as he was in reality by character: a gaunt, thin, hollow-cheeked man of sixty-six or seven, rueful and sad-looking, with a greenish gray complexion, and a head of short, close gray hair, cut horseshoe fashion over the temples, his long thin nose, pointed chin, and his cold green eye only wanted the additional test of his accent to pronounce him from the North. So it was, Sandy M'Grane was from Antrim, and a keener specimen of the "cold countrie" need not have been looked for.

His dress was a wide-skirted, deep-cuffed brown coat, profusely studded with large silver buttons richly crested, one sleeve of which, armless and empty, was attached to his breast; a dark-crimson waistcoat, edged with silver lace, descended below the hips; black leather breeches and high black boots,—a strange costume, uniting in some respects the attributes of in-door life and the road. On the high back of his oaken chair hung a wide-brimmed felt hat and a black leather belt, from which a short straight sword depended, the invariable companion of his journeys; for Sandy had travelled in strange lands, where protective police were unknown, and his master, Mr. Bagenal Daly, was one who ever preferred his own administration of criminal law, when the occasion required such, to the slower process of impartial justice.

Meagre and fleshless as he looked, he was possessed of great personal strength, and it needed no acute physiognomist to pronounce, from the character of his head and features, that courage had not been omitted among the ingredients of his nature.

A word of explanation may be necessary as to how a western gentleman, as Bagenal Daly was, should have attached to his person for some forty years a native of a distant county, and one all whose habits and sympathies seemed so little in unison with his own part of the country. Short as the story is, we should not feel warranted in obtruding it on our readers if it did not to a certain extent serve to illustrate the characters of both master and man.

Mr. Daly when a very young man chanced to make an excursion to the northern part of the island, the principal object of which was to see the Giant's Causeway, and the scenery in the neighborhood. The visit was undertaken with little foresight or precaution, and happened at the very time of the year when severe gales from the north and west prevail, and a heavy sea breaks along that iron-bound coast. Having come so far to see the spot, he was unwilling to be baulked in his object; but still, the guides and boatmen of the neighborhood refused to venture out, and, notwithstanding the most tempting offers, would not risk their lives by an enterprise so full of danger.

Daly's ardor for the expedition seemed to increase as the difficulty to its accomplishment grew greater, and he endeavored, now by profuse offers of money, now by taunting allusions to their want of courage, to stimulate the men to accompany him; when, at last, a tall, hard-featured young fellow stood forward and offered, if Daly himself would pull an oar, to go along with him. Overjoyed at his success, Daly agreed to the proposal; and although a heavy sea was then running, and the coast for miles was covered with fragments of a wreck, the skiff was Boon launched, and stood out to sea.

"I'll ga wi'ye to the twa caves and Dunluce; but I 'll no engage to ga to Carrig-a-rede," said Sandy, as the sea broke in masses on the bow, and fell in torrents over them.

After about an hour's rowing, during which the boat several times narrowly escaped being swamped, and was already more than half full of water, they arrived off the great cave, and could see the boiling surf as, sent back with force, it issued beneath the rock, with a music louder than thunder, while from the great cliffs overhead the water poured in a thick shower, as each receding wave left a part behind it.

"The cobble" (so is the boat termed there) "is aye drawing in to shore," said Sandy; "I trow we 'd better pull back, noo."

"Not till we 've seen Carrig-a-rede, surely," said Daly, on whom danger acted like the most exciting of all stimulants.

"Ye may go there by yersel," said Sandy, "when ye put me ashore; I tauld you, I 'd no ga so far."

"Come, come, it's no time to flinch now," said Daly; "turn her head about, and lean down to your oar."

"I 'll no do it," said Sandy, "nor will I let you either." And as he spoke, he leaned forward to take the oar from Daly's hand. The young man, irritated at the attempt, rudely repulsed him, and Sandy, whose temper, if not as violent, was at least as determined, grappled with him at once.

"You'll upset the boat—curse the fellow!" said Daly, who now found that he had met his match in point of strength and daring.

"Let go the oar, man," cried Sandy, savagely.

"Never," said Daly, with a violent effort to free his hands.

"Then swim for it, if ye like better," said Sandy; and, placing one foot on the gunwale, he gave a tremendous push, and the next instant they were both struggling in the sea. For a long time they continued, almost side by side, to buffet the dark water; but at last Daly began to falter, his efforts became more labored, and his strength seemed failing; Sandy turned his head, and seized him in the very struggle that precedes sinking. They were still far from shore, but the hardy Northern never hesitated; he held him by the arm, and after a long and desperate effort succeeded in gaining the land.

"Ye got a bra wetting for your pains, anyhow," said Sandy; "but I 'm no the best off either: I 'll never see the cobble mair."

Such were the first words Bagenal Daly heard when consciousness returned to him; the rest of the story is soon told. Daly took Sandy into his service, not without all due thought and consideration on the latter's part, for he owned a small fishing-hut, for which he expected and received due compensation, as well as for the cobble and the damage to his habiliments by salt water,—all matters of which, as they were left to his own uncontrolled valuation, he was well satisfied with the arrangement; and thus began a companionship which had lasted to the very moment we have presented him to our readers.

It is but fair to say that in all this time no one had ever heard from Sandy's lips one syllable of the adventure we have related, nor did he ever, in the remotest degree, allude to it in intercourse with his master. Sandy was little disposed to descant either on the life or the character of his master; the Scotch element of caution was mingled strongly through his nature, and he preferred any other topic of conversation than such as led to domestic events. Whether that he was less on his guard on this evening, or that, esteeming Tate's perceptions at no very high rate, so it is, he talked more freely and unadvisedly than was his wont.

"Ye hae a bra berth o' it here, Maister Sullivan," said he, as he smacked his lips after the smoking compound, whose odor pronounced it mulled port; "I maun say, that a man wha has seen a good deal of life might do far war' than settle down in a snug little nook like this; maybe, ye hae no journeyed far in your time either."

"Indeed, 'tis true for you, Mr. M'Grane, I had not the opportunities you had of seeing the world, and the strange people in foreign parts; they tell me you was in Jericho, and Jerusalem, and Gibraltar."

"Further than that, Maister Sullivan. I hae been in very curious places wi' Mr. Daly; this day nine years we were in the Rocky Mountains, among the Red Indians."

"The Red Indians! blood alive! them was dangerous neighbors."

"Not in our case. My master was a chief among them, I was the doctor of the tribe,—the 'Great Mystery Man,' they cau'd me; my master's name was the 'Howling Wind.'"

"Sorra doubt, but it was not a bad one,—listen to him now;" and Tate lifted his hand to enforce silence, while a cheer loud and sonorous rang out, and floated in rich cadence along the arched corridors of the old abbey; "'tis singing he is," added Tate, lower, while he opened the door to listen.

"That's no a sang, that's the war-cry of the Manhattas," said Sandy, gravely.

"The saints be praised it's no worse!" remarked Tate, with pious horror in every feature. "I thought he was going to raise the divil. And who was the man-haters, Mr. M'Grane?" added he, meekly.

"A vara fine set o' people; a leetle fond o' killing and eating their neighbors, but friendly and ceevil to strangers; I hae a wife amang them mysel."

"A wife! Is she a Christian, then?"

"Nae muck le o' that, but a douce, good-humored lassie for a' that."

"And she'sa black?"

"Na, na; she was a rich copper tint, something deeper than my waistcoat here, but she had twa yellow streaks over her forehead, and the tip o' her nose was blue."

"The mother of Heaven be near us! she was a beauty, by all accounts."

"Ay, that she was; the best-looking squaw of the tribe, and rare handy wi' a hatchet."

"Divil fear her," muttered Tate, between his teeth. "And what was her name, now?"

"Her name was Orroawaccanaboo, the 'Jumping Wild Cat.'"

"Oh, holy Moses!" exclaimed Tate, unable any longer to subdue his feelings, "I would n't be her husband for a mine of goold."

"You are no sae far wrong there, my auld chap," said Sandy, without showing any displeasure at this burst of feeling.

"And Mr. Daly, had he another—of these craytures?" said Tate, who felt scruples in applying the epithet of the Church in such a predicament.

"He had twa," said Sandy, "forbye anein the mountains, that was too auld to come down; puir lone body, she was unco' fond of a child's head and shoulders wi' fish gravy!"

"To ate it! Do you mane for ating, Mr. M'Grane?"

"Ay, just so; butchers' shops is no sae plenty down in them parts. But what's that! dinna ye hear a ringing o' the bell at the gate there?"

"I hear nothing, I can think of nothing! sorra bit! with the thought of that ould baste in my head, bad luck to her!" exclaimed Tate, ruefully. "A child's head and shoulders! Sure enough, that's the bell, and them that's ringing it knows the way, too." And with these words Tate lighted his lantern and issued forth to the gate tower, the keys of which were each night deposited in his care.

As the massive gates fell back, four splashed and heated horses drew forward a calèche, from which, disengaging himself with speed, Dick Forester descended, and endeavored, as well as the darkness would permit, to survey the great pile of building around him.

"Coming to stop, yer honor?" said Tate, courteously uncovering his white head.

"Yes. Will you present these letters and this card to your master?"

"I must show you your room first,—that's my orders always.—Tim, bring up this luggage to 27.—Will yer honor have supper in the hall, or in your own dressing-room?"

There is nothing more decisive as to the general tone of hospitality pervading any house than the manner of the servants towards strangers; and thus, few and simple as the old butler's words were, they were amply sufficient to satisfy Forester that his reception would be a kindly one, even though less ably accredited than by Lionel Darcy's introduction; and he followed Tate Sullivan with the pleasant consciousness that he was to lay his head beneath a friendly roof.

"Never mind the supper," said he; "a good night's rest is what I stand most in need of. Show me to my room, and to-morrow I 'll pay my respects to the Knight."

"This way then, sir," said Tate, entering a large hall, and leading the way up a wide oak staircase, at the top of which was a corridor of immense extent. Turning short at the head of this, Tate opened a small empanelled door, and with a gesture of caution moved forwards. Forester followed, not a little curious to know the meaning of the precaution, and at the same instant the loud sounds of merry voices laughing and talking reached him, but from what quarter he could not guess, when, suddenly, his guide drew back a heavy cloth curtain, and he perceived that they were traversing a long gallery, which ran along the entire length of a great room, in the lower part of which a large company was assembled. So sudden and unexpected was the sight that Forester started with amazement, and stood uncertain whether to advance or retire, while Tate Sullivan, as if enjoying his surprise, leaned his hands on his knees and stared steadily at him.

The scene below was indeed enough to warrant his astonishment. In the great hail, which had once been the refectory of the abbey, a party of about thirty gentlemen were now seated around a table covered with drinking vessels of every shape and material, as the tastes of the guests inclined their potations. Claret, in great glass jugs holding the quantity of two or three ordinary bottles; port, in huge square decanters, both being drunk from the wood, as was the fashion of the day; large china bowls of mulled wine, in which the oranges and limes floated fragrantly; and here and there a great measure made of wood and hooped with silver, called the "mether," contained the native beverage in all its simplicity, and supplied the hard drinker with the liquor he preferred to all,—"poteen." The guests were no less various than the good things of which they partook. Old, young, and middle-aged; some men stamped with the air and seeming of the very highest class; others as undeniably drawn from the ranks of the mere country squire; a few were dressed in all the accuracy of dinner costume; some wore the well-known livery of Daly's Club, and others were in the easy negligence of morning dress; while, scattered up and down, could be seen the red coat of a hunter, whose splashed and stained scarlet spoke rather for the daring than the dandyism of its wearer. But conspicuous above all was a figure who, on an elevated seat, sat at the head of the table and presided over the entertainment. He was a tall—a very tall—and powerfully built man, whose age might have been guessed at anything, from five-and-forty to seventy; for though his frame and figure indicated few touches of time, his seared and wrinkled forehead boded advanced life. His head was long and narrow, and had been entirely bald, were it not for a single stripe of coal-black hair which grew down the very middle of it, and came to a point on the forehead, looking exactly like the scalplock of an Indian warrior. The features were long and melancholy in expression,—a character increased by a drooping moustache of black hair, the points of which descended below the chin. His eyes were black as a raven's wing, and glanced with all the brilliancy and quickness of youth, while the incessant motion of his arched eyebrows gave to their expression a character of almost demoniac intelligence. His voice was low and sonorous, and, although unmistakably Irish in accent, occasionally lapsed into traits which might be called foreign, for no one that knew him would have accused him of the vice of affectation. His dress was a claret-colored coat edged with narrow silver lace, and a vest of white satin, over which, by a blue ribbon, hung the medal of a foreign order; white satin breeches and silk stockings, with shoes fastened by large diamond buckles, completed a costume which well became a figure that had lost nothing of its pretension to shapeliness and symmetry. His hands, though remarkably large and bony, were scrupulously white and cared for, and more than one ring of great value ornamented his huge and massive fingers. Altogether, he was one whom the least critical would have pronounced not of the common herd of humanity, and yet whose character was by no means so easy to guess at from external traits.

Amid all the tumult and confusion of the scene, his influence seemed felt everywhere, and his rich, solemn tones could be heard high above the crash and din around. As Forester stood and leaned over the balcony, the noise seemed to have reached its utmost; one of the company—a short, square, bull-faced little squire—being interrupted in a song by some of the party, while others—the greater number—equally loud, called on him to proceed. It was one of the slang ditties of the time,—a lyric suggested by that topic which furnished matter for pamphlets and speeches and songs, dinners, debates, and even duels,—the Union.

"Go on, Bodkin; go on, man! You never were in better voice in your life," mingled with, "No, no; why introduce any party topic here?"— with a murmured remark: "It's unfair, too. Hickman O'Reilly is with the Government."

The tumult, which, without being angry, increased every moment, was at last stilled by the voice of the chairman, saying,—

"If the song have a moral, Bodkin—"

"It has, I pledge my honor it has, your 'Grandeur.'" said Bodkin.

"Then finish it. Silence there, gentlemen." And Bodkin resumed his chant:—

> "'Trust me, Squire,' the dark man cried,
> 'I 'll follow close and mind you,
> Nor however high the fence you ride,
> I 'll ever be far behind you.'
>
> "And true to his word, like a gentleman
> He rode, there 'a no denying;
> And though full twenty miles they ran,
> He took all his ditches flying.
>
> "The night now came, and down they sat,
> And the Squire drank while he was able;
> But though glass for glass the dark man took,
> He left him under the table.
>
> "When morning broke, the Squire's brains,
> Though racking, were still much clearer.
> 'I know you well,' said he to his guest,
> 'Now that I see you nearer.

"'You 've play'd me a d — —d scurvy trick:
Come, what have I lost — don't tease me.
Is it my soul?' 'Not at all,' says Nick;
'Just vote for the Union, to please me.'"

Amid the loud hurrahs and the louder laughter that fol-lowed this rude chant Forester hurried on to his room, fully convinced that his mission was not altogether so promising as he anticipated.

Undeniable in every respect as was the accommodation of his bed-chamber, Forester lay awake half the night, the singular circumstances in which he found himself occupied his thoughts, while at intervals came the swelling sounds of some loud cheers from the party below, whose boisterous gayety seemed to continue without interruption.

CHAPTER IV
THE DINNER-PARTY

It was late on the following day when Forester awoke, nor was it for some time that he could satisfy himself how far he had been an actor, or a mere spectator in the scene he had witnessed the preceding night. The room and the guests were vividly impressed upon his memory, and the excitement of the party, so different in its character from anything he had seen in his own country, convinced him that the sea, narrow as it was, separated two races very unlike in temperament.

What success should he have in this, his first, mission? was the question ever rising to his mind; how should he acquit himself among persons to whose habits of life, thought, and expression he felt himself an utter stranger? Little as he had seen of the party, that little showed him that the anti-Union feeling was in the ascendant, and that, if a stray convert to the Ministerial doctrines was here and there to be found, he was rather ashamed of his new convictions than resolute to uphold and defend them. From these thoughts he wandered on to others, about the characters of the party, and principally of the host himself, who in every respect was unlike his anticipations. He opened his friend Lionel's letter, and was surprised to find how filial affection had blinded his judgment,—keen enough when exercised without the trammels of prejudice. "If this," thought he, "be a fair specimen of Lionel's portrait-painting, I must take care to form no high-flown expectations of his mother and sister; and as he calls one somewhat haughty and reserved in manner, and the other a blending of maternal pride with a dash of his father's wilful but happy temperament, I take it for granted that Lady Eleanor is a cold, disagreeable old lady, and her daughter Helen a union of petted vanity and capriciousness, pretty much what my good friend Lionel himself was when he joined us, but what he had the good sense to cease to be very soon after."

Having satisfied himself that he fairly estimated the ladies of the house, he set himself, with all the ingenuity of true speculation, to account for the traits of character he had so good-naturedly conferred on them. "Living in a remote, half-civilized neighborhood," thought he, "without any intercourse save with some country squires and their wives and daughters, they have learned, naturally enough, to feel their own superiority to those about them; and possessing a place with such claims to respect from association, as well as from its actual condition, they, like all people who have few equals and no superiors, give themselves a license to think and act independent of the world's prescription, and become, consequently, very intolerable to every one unaccustomed to acknowledge their sovereignty. I heartily wish Lionel had left these worthy people to my own unassisted appreciation of them; his flourish of trumpets has sadly spoiled the effect of the scene for me;" and with this not over gracious reflection he proceeded to dress for the day.

"The squire has been twice at the door this morning, sir," said Lin wood, as he arranged the dressing apparatus on the table; "he would not let me awake you, however, and at last said, 'Present my cordial respects to Mr. Forester, and say, that if he should like to ride with the hounds, he'll find a horse ready for him, and a servant who will show him the way.'"

"And are they out already?" said Forester.

"Yes, sir, gone two hours ago; they breakfasted at eight, and I heard a whipper-in say they 'd twelve miles to go to the first cover."

"Why, it appeared to me that they were up all night."

"They broke up at four, sir, and except two gentlemen that are gone over to Westport on business, but to be back for dinner, they're all mounted to-day."

"And what is the dinner-hour, Linwood?"

"Six, sir, to the minute."

"And it's now only eleven," said Forester to himself, with a wearied sigh; "how am I to get through the rest of the day? Are the ladies in the drawing-room, Linwood?"

"Ladies! no, sir; there are no ladies in the house as I hear of."

"So much the better, then," thought his master; "passive endurance is better any day than active boredom, and with all respect for Lady Eleanor and her daughter, I 'd rather believe them such as Lionel paints them, than have the less flattering impression nearer acquaintance would as certainly leave behind it."

"The old butler wishes to know if you will breakfast in the library, sir?" asked Linwood.

"Yes, that will do admirably; delighted I am to hear there is such a thing here," muttered he; for already he had suffered the disappointment the host's appearance had caused him to tinge all his thoughts with bitterness, and make him regard his visit as an act of purgatorial endurance.

In a large and well-furnished library, with a projecting window offering a view over the entire of Clue Bay, Forester found a small breakfast-table laid beside the fireplace. From the aspect of comfort in everything around, to the elegance of the little service of Dresden, with its accompaniment of ancient silver, the most fastidious critic would not have withheld his praise, and the young Englishman fell into a puzzled revery how so much of taste for the refinements of daily life could consort with the strange specimen of society he had witnessed the preceding evening. The book-shelves, too, in all their later acquisitions, exhibited judgment in the works selected, and as Forester ran his eye over the titles, he was more than ever at fault to reconcile such readings with such habits. On the tables lay scattered the latest of those political pamphlets which the great contested question of the day evoked, many of them ably and powerfully written, and abounding in strong sarcasm; of these, the greater number were attacks on the meditated Union; some of them, too, bore pencil-marks and annotations, from which Forester collected that the Knight's party leanings were by no means to the Government side of the question.

"It will be hard, however," thought he, "but some inducement may be found to tempt a man whose house and habits evidence such a taste for enjoyment; he must have ambitions of one kind or other, and if not for himself, his son, at least, must enter into his calculations. Your ascetic or your anchorite may be difficult to treat with, but show me the man with a good cook, a good stable, a good cellar, and the odds are there is a lurking void somewhere in his heart, to discover which is to have the mastery over him forever." Such were the conclusions the young aide-de-camp came to after long and mature thought, nor were they very unnatural in one whose short experience of life had shown him few, if any, exceptions to his theory. He deemed it possible, besides, that, although the Knight's politics should incline to the side of Opposition, there might be no very determined or decided objection to the plans of Government, and that, while proof against the temptations of vulgar bribery, he might be won over by the flatteries and seductions of which a Ministry can always be the dispensers. To open the negotiation with this view was then the great object with Forester, to sound the depth of the prejudices with which he had to deal, to examine their bearings and importance, to avoid even to ruffle the slightest of national susceptibilities, and to make it appear that, while Government could have little doubt of the justice of their own views, they would not permit a possibility of misconstruction to interfere with the certainty of securing the adhesion of one so eminent and influential as the Knight of Gwynne.

The old adage has commemorated the facility of that arithmetic which consists in reckoning "without one's host," and there are few men of warm and generous temperament who have not fallen, some time or other, into the error. Forester was certainly not the exception; and so thoroughly was he imbued with the spirit of his mission, and so completely captivated by the force of his own argument, that he walked up and down the ample apartment, repeating aloud, in broken and disjointed sentences, some of those irrefutable positions and plausible inducements by which he speculated on success. It was already the dusk of the evening, the short hours of a wintry day had hurried to a close, and, except where the bright glare of the wood fire was reflected on the polished oaken floor, all was shrouded in shadow within that spacious library. Now pushing aside some great deep-cushioned chair, now removing from his path the projecting end of a table, Forester succeeded in clearing a space in which, as he walked, he occasionally gave vent to such reflections as these:—

"The necessities of the Empire, growing power and influence of England, demand a consolidation of her interests and her efforts—this only to be effected by the Act of Union—an English Parliament, the real seat of legislation, and, as such, the suitable position for you, Sir Knight, whose importance will now increase with the sphere in which you exercise your abilities. I do not venture," said he, aloud, and with a voice attuned to its most persuasive accents,—"I do not venture to discuss with you a question in which your opportunities and judgment have given you every advantage over me; I would merely direct your attention to those points on which my relative, Lord Castlereagh, founds the hopes of obtaining your support, and those views by which, in the success of the measure, a more extended field of utility will open before you. If I do not speak more fully on the gratitude which the Ministry will feel for your co-operation, and the pledges they are most ready and willing to advance, it is because I know—that is, I am certain that you—in fact, it is the conviction that—in short—"

"In short, it is because bribery is an ugly theme, sir, and, like a bad picture, only comes out the worse the more varnish you lay on it." These words, uttered in a low, solemn voice from a corner of the apartment, actually stunned Forester, who now stood peering through the gloom to where the indistinct figure of a man was seen seated in the recess of a large chair.

"Excuse me, Captain Forester," said he, rising, and coming forward with his hand out; "but it has so seldom been my fortune to hear any argument in defence of this measure that I could not bring myself to interrupt you before. Let me, however, perform a more pleasing task, in bidding you welcome to Gwynne Abbey. You slept well, I trust, for I left you in a happy unconsciousness of this world and its cares." It required all Forester's tact to subdue the uncomfortable sensations his surprise excited, and receive the proffered welcome with becoming cordiality. But in this he soon succeeded, not less from his own efforts than from the easy and familiar tone of the speaker. "I have to thank you for a very pleasant note you were kind enough to bring me," continued he, as he seated himself beside the fire. "And how have you left Dublin? Is the popular excitement as great as some weeks ago? or are the people beginning to see that they have nothing to say to a measure which, like venison and turtle, is a luxury only to be discussed by their betters?"

"I should say that there is more of moderation in the tone of all parties of late," said Forester, diffidently, for he felt all the awkwardness of alluding to a topic in which his own game had been so palpably discovered.

"In that case, your friends have gained the victory. Patriotism, as we call it in Ireland, requires to be fed by mob adulation; and when the 'canaille' get hoarse, their idols walk over to the Treasury benches.—But there's the bell to dress; and I may as well tell you that we are the models of punctuality in this house, and you have only fifteen minutes for your toilet." With these words the old gentleman arose and strode out of the room, while Forester hastened, on his side, to prepare for the dinner-hour.

When the aide-de-camp had accomplished his dressing, he found the party at table, where a vacant place was left for himself at the right hand of the host.

"We gave you three minutes' grace, Captain Forester. I knew a candidate lose his election in the county by very little more,"—and here he dropped his voice to a whisper, only audible to Forester,—"and I'd rather contract to keep the peace in a menagerie full of tigers than hold in check the passions of twenty hungry fox-hunters while waiting for dinner."

Forester cast his eyes over the table, and thought he perceived that his delay had not prepossessed the company in his favor. The glances which met his own round the board bore an expression of very unmistakable dissatisfaction, and although the conversation was free and unrestrained, he felt all the awkwardness of his position.

There was at the time we speak of—has it quite disappeared even yet?—a very prevalent notion in most Irish circles that Englishmen in general, and English officials in particular, assumed airs of superiority over the natives of the country, treating them as very subordinate persons in all the relations in which good-breeding and social intercourse are concerned; and this impression, whether well or ill founded, induced many to suspect intentional insult in those chance occurrences which arise out of thoughtlessness and want of memory.

If the party now assembled manifested any portion of this feeling, it was not sufficient to interrupt the flow of conversation, which took its course in channels the most various and dissimilar. The individuals were intimate, or, at least, familiar with each other, and, through all the topics of hunting, farming, politics, and horse-racing, ran a tone of free and easy raillery that kept a laugh moving up and down the table, or occasionally occupying it entirely. The little chill which marked Forester's first entrance into the room wore off soon, and ere the dinner was over he had drunk wine with nearly every man of the party, and accepted invitations to hunt, course, and shoot in at least a dozen different quarters. Lionel Darcy's friend, as he was soon known to be, was speedily made the object of every attention and civility among the younger members of the company, while even the older and less susceptible reserved their judgments on one they had at first received with some distrust.

Forester had seen in the capital some specimens of those hard-drinking habits which characterized the period, but was still unprepared for the determined and resolute devotion to the bottle which at once succeeded to the dinner. The claret-jugs coursed round the table with a rapidity that seemed sleight of hand, and few refrained from filling a bumper every time. With all his determination to preserve a cool head and a calm judgment, Forester felt that, what between the noisy tumult of the scene, the fumes of wine, and the still more intoxicating excitement of this exaggerated conviviality, he could listen to tales of miraculous performances in the hunting-field, or feats of strength and activity more than mortal, with a degree of belief, or, at least, sufferance, he could scarcely have summoned a few hours earlier.

If wine expands the heart, it has a similar influence on the credulity; and belief, when divested of the trammels of cool judgment, takes a flight which even imagination might envy. It was in a frame of mind reduced to something like this, amid the loud voices of some, the louder laughter of others, strange and absurd bets as eagerly accepted as proffered, that he became suddenly mindful of his own wager made with the stranger at Kilbeggan, and the result of which he had pledged himself to test at the very first opportunity.

No sooner had he mentioned the fact than the interests of the company, directed before into so many different channels, became centred upon the circumstance, and questions and inquiries were rapidly poured in upon him to explain the exact nature of the wager, which in the then hallucination of the party was not an over-easy task.

"You are to describe the stranger, Captain Forester, and we are to guess his name: that I take it is the substance of the bet," said a thin-faced, dark-eyed man, with a soft silkiness of accent very unlike the others. This was Mr. Hickman O'Reilly, member for the county, and colleague of "the Knight" himself.

"Yes, that is exactly what I mean. If my portrait be recognized, I've won my bet."

"May I ask another question?" said Mr. O'Reilly. "Are we to pronounce only from the evidence before us, or are we at liberty to guess the party from other circumstances known to ourselves?"

"Of course, from the evidence only," interrupted a red-faced man of about five-and-thirty, with an air and manner which boded no small reliance on his own opinion; then, mimicking the solemnity of a judge, he addressed the assembled party thus: "The gentlemen of the jury will dismiss from their minds everything they may hear touching the case outside this court, and base their verdict solely on the testimony they shall now hear." These few words were delivered in a pompous and snuffling tone, and, it was easy to see, from the laughter they excited, were an accurate imitation of some one well known to the company.

Mr. Alexander MacDonough was, however, a tolerably successful mimic, and had practised as an attorney until the death of an uncle enabled him to exercise his abilities in the not less crafty calling of a squireen gentleman; he was admitted by a kind of special favor into the best county society, for no other reason, as it seemed, than that it never occurred to any one to exclude him. He was a capital horseman, never turned from a fence in his life, and a noted shot with the pistol, in which his prowess had been more than once tried on "the ground." Probably, however, these qualities would scarcely have procured him acceptance where he now sat, if it were not that he was looked upon as the necessary accompaniment of Mr. Hickman O'Reilly and his son Beecham, not indeed to illustrate their virtues and display their good gifts, but as a species of moral blister, irritating and maddening them eternally.

They had both more money and ambition than MacDonough, had taken higher and wider views of life, and were strenuously working up from the slough of a plebeian origin to the high and dry soil of patrician security. To them, MacDonough was a perfect curse; he was what sailors call "a point of departure," everlastingly reminding them of the spot from which they had sailed, and tauntingly hinting how, with all their canvas spread, they had scarcely gained blue water.

Of the O'Reillys a few words are necessary. Three generations were still living, each depicting most strikingly the gradations by which successful thrift and industry transmute the man of humble position into the influential grade of an estated gentleman: the grandfather was an apothecary of Loughrea; the son, an agent, a money-lender, and an M. P.; and the grandson, an Etonian and a fellow-commoner of Balliol, emerging into life with the prospect of a great estate, unencumbered with debt, considerable county influence, and, not least of all, the *ricochet* of that favor with which the Government regarded his pliant parent.

To all of these, MacDonough was insupportable, nor was there any visible escape from the insolent familiarity of his manner. Flattery had been tried in vain; all their blandishments could do nothing with one who well knew that his own acceptance into society depended on his powers of annoying; if not performing the part of torturer, he had no share in the piece; a quarrel with him was equally out of the question, for even supposing such an appeal safe,—which it was very far from being,—it would have reflected most disadvantageously on the O'Reillys to have been mixed up in altercation with a man so much beneath themselves as Alexander MacDonough of "The Tenement;" for such, in slang phrase, did he designate his country residence.

Let us now return from this long but indispensable digression to the subject which suggested it.

So many questions were put, explanations demanded, doubts suggested, and advices thrown out to Forester that it was not until after a considerable lapse of time he was enabled to commence his description of the unknown traveller, nor even then was he suffered to proceed without interruption, a demand being made by MacDonough that the absent individual was entitled to counsel, who should look after his interests, and, if necessary, cross-examine the evidence. All this was done in that style of comic seriousness to which Forester was so little accustomed that, what with the effect of wine, heat, and noise, combined with the well-assumed gravity of the party, he really forgot the absurdity of the whole affair, and became as eager and attentive as though the event were one of deep importance.

It was at last decided that MacDonough should act as counsel for the unknown, and the company should vote separately, each writing down on a slip of paper their impression of the individual designated, the result being tested by the majority in favor of any one person.

"Gentlemen of the jury," said the host, in a voice of deep solemnity, "you will hear and well weigh the evidence before you touching this case, and decide with truth and conscience on its merits; so fill a bumper and let us begin. Make your statement, Captain Forester."

The sudden silence succeeding to the tumultuous uproar, the directed gaze of so many eager faces, and the evident attention with which his statement was awaited, conspired to make Forester nervous and uneasy; nor was it without something of an effort that he began the recital of his adventure at Kilbeggan. Warming as he proceeded, he told of the accident by which his acquaintance with the unknown traveller was opened, and at length, having given so much of preliminary, entered upon the description of the individual.

Whatever Forester's own impression of the stranger, he soon felt how very difficult a task portrait-painting was, and how very unlike was his representation of the individual in question. The sure way to fail in any untried career is to suspect a failure; this he soon discovered, and cut short a most imperfect description by abruptly saying, "If you guess him now, gentlemen, I acknowledge the merit is far more in *your* perspicuity than in *my* powers of description."

"Only a few questions before you leave the table, sir," said MacDonough, addressing him with the mock sternness of a cross-examining barrister. "You said the unknown was gifted with a most courteous and prepossessing manner: pray what is the exact meaning of your phrase? for we uncouth inhabitants of a remote region have very imperfect notions on such subjects. My friend Dan Mahon here would call any man agreeable who could drink fourteen tumblers, and not forget the whiskey in mixing the fifteenth; Tom Callaghan, on the other hand, would test his breeding by what he knew of a wether or a 'short-horn;' Giles, my neighbor here, would ask, Did he lend you any money? and Mr. Hickman O'Reilly would whisper a hope that he came of an old family."

The leer by which these words were accompanied gave them an impertinence even greater than their simple signification; but however coarse the sarcasm, it suited well the excited tone of the party, who laughed loud and vociferously as he uttered it.

Strange as he was to the party, Forester saw that the allusion had a personal application, and was very far from relishing a pleasantry whose whole merit was its coarseness; he therefore answered in a tone of rather haughty import, "The person I met, sir, was a gentleman; and the word, so far as I know, has an easy signification, at least to all who have had opportunities to learn it."

"I have no doubt of that, Captain Forester," replied MacDonough; "but if we divided the house on it here, some of us might differ about the definition. Your neighbor there, Mr. Beecham O'Reilly, thinks his own countrymen very far down in the scale."

"A low fellow,—nobody pays attention to him," muttered young O'Reilly in Forester's ear, as, with a cheek pale as death, he affected to seem totally indifferent to the continued insolence of his tormentor.

"I beg your pardon, Mr. Beecham O'Reilly," interposed MacDonough, with a significant smile, "but your observation was, I think, meant to apply to me."

The young man made no answer, but proceeded to fill his glass with claret, while his hand trembled so much that he spilled the wine about the table. Forester stared at him, expecting each instant to hear his reply to this appeal; but not a word escaped him, nor did he even look towards the quarter from which the taunt proceeded.

"Didn't I tell you so, sir?" exclaimed MacDonough, with a triumphant laugh. "There are various descriptions of gentlemen: some are contented with qualities of home growth, and satisfied to act, think, and deport themselves like their neighbors; others travel for this improvement, and bring back habits and customs that seem strange in their own country; now, I don't doubt but in England that young gentleman would be thought all that was spirited and honorable."

"I have nothing to say to that, sir!" replied Forester, sternly; "but if you would like to hear the opinion my fellow-countrymen would have of yourself, I could perhaps favor you."

"Stop, stop! where are you hurrying to? No more of this nonsense," cried the host, who had suddenly caught the last few words, while conversing with a person on his left.

"I beg your pardon most humbly, sir," said MacDonough, whose faced was flushed with passion, and whose lip trembled, notwithstanding all his efforts to seem calm and collected, "but the gentleman was about to communicate a trait of English society. I know you misunderstood him."

"Perhaps so," said the host; "what was it, Captain Forester? I believe I did not hear you quite accurately."

"A very simple fact, sir," said Forester, coolly, "and one that can scarcely astonish Mr. MacDonough to hear."

"And which is—?" said MacDonough, affecting a bland smile.

"Perhaps you 'd ask for a definition, if I employ a single word."

"Not this time," said MacDonough, still smiling in the same way.

"You are right, sir, it would be affectation to do so; for though you may feel very natural doubts about what constitutes a gentleman, you ought to be pretty sure what makes a blackguard."

The words seemed to fall like a shell in the company; one burst of tumultuous uproar broke forth, voices in every tone and accent of eagerness and excitement, when suddenly the host cried out, "Lock the doors; no man leaves the room till this matter is settled; there shall be no quarrelling beneath this roof so long as Bagenal Daly sits here for his friend."

The caution came too late—MacDonough was gone.

CHAPTER V
AN AFTER-DINNER STORY

The unhappy event which so suddenly interrupted the conviviality of the party scarcely made a more than momentary impression. Altercations which ended most seriously were neither rare nor remarkable at the dinner-tables of the country gentlemen, and if the present instance caused an unusual interest, it was only because one of the parties was an Englishman.

As for Forester himself, his first burst of anger over, he forgot all in his astonishment that the host was not "the Knight" himself, but only his representative and friend, Bagenal Daly.

"Come, Captain Forester," said he, "I owe you an *amende* for the mystification I have practised upon you. You shall have it. Your travelling acquaintance at Kilbeggan was the 'Knight of Gwynne;' and the few lines he sent through your hands contained an earnest desire that your stay here might be sufficiently prolonged to admit of his meeting you at his return."

"I shall be extremely sorry," said Forester, in a low voice, "if anything that has occurred to-night shall deprive me of that pleasure."

"No, no—nothing of the kind," said Daly, with a significant nod of his head. "Leave that to me." Then, raising his voice, he added: "What do you say to that claret, Conolly?"

"I agree with you," replied a rosy-cheeked old squire in a hunting-dress, "it 's too old,—there's little spirit left in it."

"Quite true, Tom. Wine has its dotage, like the rest of us. All that the best can do is to keep longest; and, after all, we scarcely can complain of the vintage that has a taste of its once flavor at our age. It's a long time since we were schoolfellows."

"It is not an hour less than—"

"Stop, Tom,—no more of that. Of all scores to go back upon, that of years past is the saddest."

"By Jove! I don't think so," said the hearty old squire, as he tossed off a bumper. "I never remember riding better than I did to-day. Ask Beecham O'Reilly there which of us was first over the double ditch at the red barn."

"You forget, sir," said the young gentleman referred to, "that I was on an English-bred mare, and she doesn't understand these fences."

"Faith, she wasn't worse off, in that respect, than the man on her back," said old Conolly, with a hearty chuckle. "If to look before you leap be wisdom, you ought to be the shrewdest fellow in the country."

"Beecham, I believe, keeps a good place in Northamptonshire," said his father, half proudly.

"Another argument in favor of the Union, I suppose," whispered a guest in Conolly's ear.

"Well, well," sighed the old squire, "when I was a young man, we 'd have thought of bringing over a dromedary from Asia as soon as an English horse to cross the country with."

"Dick French was the only one I ever heard of backing a dromedary," said a fat old farmer-like man, from the end of the table.

"How was that, Martin?" said Daly, with a look that showed he either knew the story or anticipated something good.

"And by all accounts, it 's the devil to ride," resumed the old fellow; "now it's the head down and the loins up, and then a roll to one side, and then to the other, and a twist in the small of your back, as if it were coming in two. Oh, by the good day! Dick gave me as bad as a stitch in the side just telling me about it."

"But where did he get his experience, Martin? I never heard of it before," said Daly.

"He was a fortnight in Egypt, sir," said the old farmer. "He was in a frigate, or a man-of-war of one kind or another, off—the devil a one o' me knows well where it was, but there was a consul there, a son of one of his father's tenants—indeed, ould French got him the place from the Government—and when he found out that Dick was on board the ship, what does he do but writes him an invitation to pass a week or ten days with him at his house, and that he 'd show him some sport. 'We 've elegant hunting,' says he; 'not foxes or hares, but a big bird, bigger nor a goose, they call—'By my conscience, I 'll forget my own name next, for I heard Dick tell the story at least twenty times."

"Was it an ostrich?" said Tom.

"No; nor an oyster either, Mr. Conolly," said the old fellow, who thought the question was meant to quiz him.

"'T was an ibis, Martin," cried Daly,—"an ibis."

"The devil a doubt of it,—that's the name. A crayture with legs as long as Mr. Beecham O'Reilly's, and a way of going—half-flying, half-walking—almost impossible to catch; and they hunt him on dromedaries. Dick liked the notion well, and as he was a favorite on board, he got lave for three days to go on shore and have his fun; though the captain said, at parting, 'It's not many dromedaries you'll see, Dick, for the Pasha has them all up the country at this time.' This was true enough; sorra a bit of a camel or dromedary could be seen for miles round. But however it was, the consul kept his word, and had one for Dick the next morning,—a great strapping baste, all covered with trappings of one kind or other; elegant shawls and little hearthrugs all over him.

"The others were mounted on mules or asses, any way they could, and away they went to look after the goose—the 'ibis,' I mean. Well, to be short with it, they came up with one on the bank of the river, and soon gave chase; he was a fine strong fellow, and well able to run. I wish you heard Dick tell this part of it; never was there such sport in the world, blazing away all together as fast as they could prime and load, at one time at the goose, more times at each other; the mules kicking, the asses braying, and Dick cantering about on his dromedary, upsetting every one near him, and shouting like mad. At last he pinned the goose up in a narrow corner among some old walls, and Dick thought he 'd have the brush; but sorra step the dromedary would stir; he spurred and kicked, and beat away with a stick as hard as he could, but it was all no good,—it was the carpets maybe, that saved him; for there he stood fast, just for all the world as if he was made of stone.

"Dick pulled out a pistol and fired a shot in his ear, but all to no use; he minded it no more than before. 'Bad luck to you for a baste,' says Dick, 'what ails you at all—are you going to die on me? Get along now.' The divil receave the step I 'll go till I get some spirits and wather!' says the dromedary, 'for I 'm clean smothered with them b———y blankets;' and with them same words the head of the baste fell off, and Dick saw the consul's own man wiping the perspiration off his face, and blowing like a porpoise. 'How the divil the hind legs bears it I can't think,' says he; 'for I 'm nigh dead, though I had a taste of fresh air.'

"The murther was out, gentlemen, for ye see the consul could n't get a raal dromedary, and was obliged to make one out of a Christian and a black fellow he had for a cook, and sure enough in the beginning of the day Dick says he went like a clipper; 'twas doubling after the goose destroyed him."

Whether the true tale had or had not been familiar to most of the company before, it produced the effect Bagenal Daly desired, by at first creating a hearty roar of laughter, and then, as seems the consequence in all cases of miraculous narrative, set several others upon recounting stories of equal credibility. Daly encouraged this new turn of conversation with all the art of one who knew how to lead men's thoughts into a particular channel without exciting suspicion of his intentions by either abruptness or over zeal: to any ordinary observer, indeed, he would have now appeared a mere enjoyer of the scene, and not the spirit who gave it guidance and direction.

In this way passed the hours long after midnight, when, one by one, the guests retired to their rooms; Forester remaining at the table in compliance with a signal which Daly had made him, until at length Hickman O'Reilly stood up to go, the last of all, save Daly and the young guardsman.

Passing round the table, he leaned over Forester's chair, and in a low, cautious whisper, said, "You have put down the greatest bully in this country, Captain Forester; do not spoil your victory by being drawn into a disreputable quarrel! Good night, gentlemen both," said he, aloud, and with a polite bow left the room.

"What was that he whispered?" said Daly, as the door closed and they were left alone together.

Forester repeated the words.

"Ah, I guessed why he sat so late; he sees the game clearly enough. You, sir, have taken up the glaive that was thrown down for his son's acceptance, and he knows the consequence—clever fellow that he is! Had you been less prompt, Beecham's poltroonery might have escaped notice; and even now, if you were to decline a meeting—"

"But I have no intention of doing any such thing."

"Of course, I never supposed you had; but were you to be swayed by wrong counsels and do so, Master Beecham would be saved even yet. Well,

well, I am sorry, Captain Forester, you should have met such a reception amongst us, and my friend Darcy will be deeply grieved at it. However, we have other occupation now than vain regret, so to bed as fast as you can, and to sleep; the morning is not very far off, and we shall have some one from MacDonough here by daybreak."

With a cordial shake-hands, like men who already knew and felt kindly towards each other, they separated for the night.

While Forester was thus sensible of the manliness and straightforward resolution that marked Bagenal Daly's character, he was very far from feeling satisfied with the position in which he found himself placed. A duel under any circumstances is scarcely an agreeable incident in one's life; but a meeting whose origin is at a drinking-bout, and where the antagonist is a noted fire-eater, and by that very reputation discreditable, is still a great aggravation of the evil.

To have embroiled himself in a quarrel of this kind would, he well knew, greatly prejudice him in the estimation of his cold-tempered relative, Lord Castlereagh, who would not readily forgive an indiscretion that should mar his own political views. As he sat in his dressing-room revolving such unpleasant reflections, there came a gentle tap at the door; he had but time to say, "Come in," when Mr. Hickman O'Reilly entered.

"Will you excuse this intrusion, Captain Forester?" said he, with an accent in which the blandest courtesy was mingled with a well-affected cordiality; "but I really could not lay my head on a pillow in tranquillity until I had seen and spoken to you in confidence. This foolish altercation—"

"Oh, pray don't let that give you a moment's uneasiness! I believe I understand the position the gentleman you allude to occupies in your country society: that license is accorded him, and freedoms taken with him, not habitually the case in the world at large."

"You are quite right, your views are strictly accurate. MacDonough is a low fellow of very small fortune, no family,—indeed, what pretension he has to associate with the gentry I am unable to guess, nor would you have ever seen him under this roof had the Knight been at home; Mr. Daly, however, who, being an old schoolfellow and friend of Darcy's, does the honors here in his absence, is rather indiscriminate in his hospitalities. You may have remarked around the table some singular-looking guests,—in fact, he not only invites the whole hunting-field, but half the farmers over whose ground we've ridden, and, were it not that they have sense and shame enough to see their own place with truer eyes, we should have an election mob here every day of the week; but this is not exactly the topic which led to my intruding upon you. I wished, in the first place, to rest assured that you had no intention of noticing the man's impertinence, or of accepting any provocation on his part; in fact, were he admissible to such a privilege, my son Beecham would have at once taken the whole upon himself, it being more properly his quarrel than yours."

Forester, with all his efforts, was unable to repress a slight smile at these words. O'Reilly noticed it, and colored up, while he added: "Beecham, however, knew the impossibility of such a course,—in fact, Captain Forester, I may venture to say, without any danger of being misunderstood by you, that my son has imbibed more correct notions of the world and its habits at *your* side of St. George's Channel than could have fallen to him had his education been merely Irish."

This compliment, if well meant, was scarcely very successful, for Forester bit his lip impatiently, but never made any answer. Whether O'Reilly perceived the cause of this, or that, like a skilful painter, he knew when to take his brush off the canvas, he arose at once and said, "I leave you, then, with a mind much relieved. I feared that a mistaken estimate of MacDonough's claims in society, and probably some hot-brained counsels of Mr. Bagenal Daly—"

"You are quite in error there; let me assure you, sir, his view of the matter is exactly my own," interrupted Forester, calmly.

"I am delighted to hear it, and have now only one request: will you favor us with a few days' visit at Mount O'Reilly? I may say, without vanity, that my son is more likely to be a suitable companion to you than the company here may afford; we 've some good shooting and—"

"I must not suffer you to finish the catalogue of temptations," said Forester, smiling courteously; "my hours are numbered already, and I must be back in Dublin within a few days."

"Beecham will be sorely disappointed; in fact, we came back here to-day for no other reason than to meet you at dinner. Daly told us of your arrival. May we hope to see you at another opportunity? are your engagements formed for Christmas yet?"

"I believe so,—Dorsetshire, I think," muttered Forester, with a tone that plainly indicated a desire to cushion the subject at once; and Mr. O'Reilly, with a ready tact, accepted the hint, and, wishing him a most cordial goodnight, departed.

CHAPTER VI
A MESSAGE

While Forester slept soundly and without a dream, his long, light breathing scarce audible within the quiet chamber, a glance within the room of Bagenal Daly would have shown that, whatever the consequences of the past night's troubles, he, at least, was not likely to be taken unprepared. On the table in the middle of the apartment two wax candles burned, two others, as yet unlighted, stood ready on the chimney-piece, a pistol case lay open, displaying the weapons, whose trim and orderly appearance denoted recent care, a fact attested by certain cloths and flannels which lay about; a mould for bullets, and about a dozen newly-cast balls most carefully filed and rubbed smooth with sandpaper, were flanked by a small case of surgical instruments, with an ample supply of lint and ligatures such as are used to secure bleeding vessels, in the use of which few unprofessional persons could vie with Bagenal Daly. A few sheets of paper lay also there, on which appeared some recent writing; and in a large, deep armchair, ready dressed for the day, sat Daly himself, sound asleep; one arm hung listlessly over the chair, the other was supported in the breast of his waistcoat. The strong, stern features, unrelaxed by repose, had the same impassive expression of cold defiance as when awake, and if his lips muttered, the accents were not less determined and firm than in his moments of self-possession. He awoke from time to time and looked at his watch, and once threw open the sash, and held out his hand to ascertain if it were raining; but these interruptions did not interfere with his rest, for, the minute after, he slept as soundly as before. Nor was he the only one within that house who counted the hours thus anxiously. A lantern in the stable beamed brightly, showing three horses ready saddled, the bridles on the neck of each, and ready at a moment's notice to be bitted; while pacing slowly to and fro, like a sentinel on his post, was the tall figure of Sandy M'Grane, wrapped in a long cloth cloak, and his head covered by a cap, whose shape and material spoke of a far-off land and wild companionship; for it was the skin of a black fox, and the workmanship the product of a squaw's fair fingers.

Sandy's patrol was occasionally extended to the gateway, where he usually halted for a few seconds to listen, and then resumed his path as leisurely as before. At last, he remained somewhat longer at the gate, and bent his head more cautiously to hear; then, noiselessly unbarring and unlocking the door, he leaned out. To an ear less practised than his own the silence would have been complete. Not so with Sandy, whose perceptions had received the last finish of an Indian education. He retired hastily, and, approaching that part of the court beneath his master's window, gave a long, low whistle. The next moment the casement was opened, and Daly's head appeared.

"What now, Sandy? It is but a quarter past five."

"It may be so; but there's a horse coming fast up the lower road."

"Listen again, and try if you hear it still."

Sandy did so, and was back in a few moments. "He's crossing the bridge at 'the elms' now, and will be here in less than three minutes more."

"Watch the gate, then—let there be no noise—and come up by the back stairs." With these words Daly closed the sash, and Sandy returned to his post.

Ere many minutes elapsed, the door of Mr. Daly's chamber was opened, and Sandy announced Major Hackett of Brough. As Bagenal Daly rose to meet him, an expression of more than ordinary sternness was stamped upon his bold features.

"Your servant informed me that I should find you in readiness to receive me, Mr. Bagenal Daly," said the Major, a coarse-looking, carbuncled-face man of about forty; "but perhaps the object of my visit would be better accomplished if I could have a few minutes' conversation with a Captain Forester who is here."

"If you can show me no sufficient cause to the contrary, sir," replied Daly, proudly, "I shall act for him on this occasion."

"I beg pardon," said Hackett, smiling dubiously. "The business I came upon induced me to suspect that, at your time of life—"

"Go on, sir,—finish your speech," said Daly, with' a fixed and steady stare which, very far from reassuring, seemed only to increase the Major's confusion.

"After all, Mr. Daly," resumed he, more hurriedly, "I have nothing whatever to do with that. My duty is to convey a message from Mr. Alexander MacDonough to a gentleman named Forester, here. If you will accept the proposition, and assist in the necessary arrangements—"

"We are ready, sir,—quite ready. One of the consequences of admitting dubious acquaintances to the intimacy of the table is such a case as the present. I was guilty of one fault in this respect, but I shall show you I was not unprepared for what might follow it." And as he spoke he threw open the window and called out, "Sandy! awaken Captain Forester. I suppose you are ready, Major Hackett, with your friend?"

"Yes, sir. Mr. MacDonough expects us at Cluan Point."

"And bridle the horses, Sandy," continued Daly, speaking from the window.

"I conclude, from what I see," said Hackett, "that your friend is not only decided against offering an apology for his offence, but desirous of a meeting."

"Who said so, sir?—or what right have you to suppose that any gentleman of good family and good prospects should indulge such an unnatural caprice as to wish to risk character and life in a quarrel with Mr. Alexander MacDonough?"

"Circumstanced as that gentleman is at this moment, your observations are unsuitable, sir," replied the Major.

"So they are," said Daly, hastily; "or, rather, so they would have been, if not provoked by your remark. But, hang me! if I think it signifies much; if it were not that some of our country neighbors were good-natured enough to treat this same Mr. MacDonough on terms of equality before, I 'd have advised Captain Forester not to mind him. *My* maxim is, there are always low fellows enough to shoot one another, and never come trespassing among the manors of their betters."

"I must confess myself unprepared, sir, to hear language like this," said Hackett, sternly.

"Not a whit more than I feel at seeing myself negotiating a meeting with a man turned out of the army with disgrace," said Daly, as his face grew purple with anger. "Were it not that I would not risk a hint of dishonor on this young Englishman's fame, I 'd never interchange three words with Major Hackett."

"You shall answer for this, sir, and speedily too, by G——d!" said Hackett, moving towards the door.

Daly burst into an insolent laugh, and said, "Your friend waits us at Cluan?" The other bowed. "Well, within an hour we'll be there also," continued the old man; and Hackett retired without adding a syllable.

"We 've about five miles to ride, Captain Forester," said Daly, as they issued forth beneath the deeply arched gate of the abbey; "but the road is a mountain one, and will not admit of fast riding. A fine old place it is," said he, as, halting his horse, he bestowed a gaze of admiration on the venerable building, now dimly visible in the gray of the breaking dawn. "The pious founders little dreamt of men leaving its portals on such an errand as ours." Then, suddenly, with a changed voice, he added, "Men are the same in every age and country; what our ancestors did in steel breastplates, we do now in broadcloth; the law, as they call it, must always be subservient to human passions, and the judge and the jury come too late, since their function is penalty, and not prevention."

"But surely you do not think the world was better in the times when might was right?" said Forester.

"The system worked better than we suspect," said the old man, gravely; "there was such a thing as public opinion among men in those days, although its exponents were neither pamphlets nor scurrilous newspapers. The unjust and the cruel were held in reprobation, and the good and the charitable had a fame as pure, although their deeds were not trumpeted aloud or graven on marble. Believe me, sir, we are not by any means so much wiser or better than those who went before us, and even if we were both, we certainly are not happier. This eternal warfare, this hand to hand and foot to foot straggle for rank, apd wealth, and power, that goes on amongst us now, had no existence then, when a man's destiny was carved out for him, and he was all but powerless to alter or control it."

"That alone was no small evil," said Forester, interrupting him; "the humbly born and the lowly were debarred from all the prizes of life, no matter how great their deserts or how shining their abilities."

"Every rank and class had wherewithal to supply its own requirements," answered Daly, proudly, "and the menial had more time to indulge affection for his master, when removed from the temptation to rival him. That strong bond of attachment has all but disappeared from amongst us." As he spoke, he turned in his saddle and called out, "Can we cross the sands now, or is the tide making, Sandy?"

"It's no just making yet," said the servant, cautiously; "but when the breakers are so heavy off the Point, it's aye safer to keep the road."

"The road be it, then," muttered Daly to himself; "men never are so chary of life as when about to risk it."

The observation, although not intended, reached Forester's ears, and he smiled and said, "Naturally enough, perhaps we ought not to be too exacting with fortune."

Daly turned suddenly round, and, after a brief pause, asked, "What skill have you with the pistol?"

"When the mark is a shilling I can hit it, three times out of four, at twenty paces; but I never fired at a man."

"That does make a difference," said Daly, musingly; "nothing short of an arrant coward could look calmly on a fellow-creature while he pointed a loaded pistol at his heart. A brave man will always have self-possession enough to feel the misery of his position. Had the feat been one of vengeance, and not of love, Tell had never hit the apple, sir. But there, — is not that a fire yonder?"

"Yes, I see a red glare through the mist."

"There's a fire on Cluan Point," said Sandy, riding up to his master's side; "I trow it's a signal."

"Ah! meant to quicken us, perhaps; some fear of being surprised," said Daly, hastily; "let us move on faster." And they spurred their horses to a sharp trot as they descended the gentle slope, which, projecting far out to sea, formed the promontory of Cluan.

It was at this moment the glorious panorama of Clue Bay broke forth before Forester's astonished eyes. He looked with rapture on that spacious sheet of water, which, in all the majesty of the great ocean, came heaving and swelling against the rocky coast, or pouring its flood of foam through the narrow channels between the islands. Of these, the diversity seemed endless, some rich and verdant, teeming with abundance and dotted with cottages; others, less fertile, were covered with sheep or goats; while some, rugged and barren, frowned gloomily amid the watery waste, and one, far out to sea, a bold and lofty cliff, showed a faint twinkling star upon its side, the light for the homeward-bound ships over the Atlantic.

"That's Clare Island yonder," said Bagenal Daly, as he observed the direction of Forester's gaze; "I must show you the great cliff there. What say you if we go to-morrow?"

"To-morrow!" repeated Forester, smiling faintly; "perhaps so."

CHAPTER VII
A MOTHER AND DAUGHTER

When speaking of Gwynne Abbey to our readers, we omitted to mention a very beautiful portion of the structure,—a small building which adjoined the chapel, and went, for some reason or other, by name of the "Sub-Prior's house." More recent in date than the other parts of the abbey, it seemed as if here the architect had expended his skill in showing of how much ornament and decoration the Gothic was capable. The stone selected was of that pinkish hue that is seen in many of the cathedrals in the North of England,—a material peculiarly favorable to the labors of the chisel, and when protected from the rude influence of weather possessing qualities of great endurance. This building was surrounded on three sides by a flower-garden, which descended by successive terraces to the edge of a small river pursuing its course to the sea, into which it emerged about a mile distant. A very unmindful observer would have been struck at once with the aspect of greater care and cultivation bestowed here than on other portions of the abbey grounds. The trim and orderly appearance of everything, from the flowering shrubs that mingled their blossoms with the rich tracery of the architraves, to the bright gravel of the walks, denoted attention, while flowers of rare beauty, and plants of foreign growth, were seen blending their odors with the wild heaths that shed their perfume from the mountain side. The brilliant beauty of the spot was, indeed, heightened by the wild and rugged grandeur of the scene, like a diamond glittering brighter amid the dark dross of the mine.

On the side nearest to the bay, and with a view extending to the far-off Island of Achill, an apartment opened by three large windows, the upper compartments of which exhibited armorial bearings in stained glass. If the view without presented a scene of the most grand and varied loveliness, within this chamber art seemed to have vied in presenting objects the most strange and beautiful. It was furnished in all the gorgeous taste of the time of Louis XV. The ceiling, a deep mass of carving relieved by gold, presented masses of fruit and flowers fantastically interwoven, and hanging, as though suspended, above the head. The walls were covered with cabinet pictures of great price, the very frames objects of wonder and admiration. Large vases of Dresden and Sèvres porcelain stood on brackets of massive silver, and one great cabinet of ebony, inlaid with gold and tortoiseshell, displayed an inscription that showed it was a present from the great Louis XIV. himself.

It is not, however, to linger over the objects of rare and costly excellence which here abounded that we have conducted our reader to this chamber, and whither we would beg of him to accompany us about two hours later than the events we have narrated in our last chapter.

At a breakfast-table whose equipage was, in price and elegance, in exact keeping with all around, were two ladies. The elder of the two was advanced in life, and although her hair was perfectly white, her regular features and finely pencilled brow bore, even yet, great marks of beauty. If the expression of the face was haughty, it was so without anything of severity; it was a look of pride that denoted rather a conscious sense of position and its duties, than any selfish assumption of personal importance. Habitual delicacy of health contributed to strengthen this expression, lending to it a character which, to an incautious observer, might convey the notion of weariness or ennui. The tones of her voice were low and measured, and perfectly devoid of any peculiar accent. If to those more familiar with the cordial familiarity of Irish manner, Lady Eleanor Darcy might seem cold and frigid, such as knew more of the world at large, and were more conversant with the general habits of society, could detect, through all the seeming impassive-ness of her air, that desire to please, that anxiety to make a favorable impression, which marked the character of one who in early life had been the beauty of her circle. Even now, as she lay back indolently within the deep recess of a cushioned chair, her attitude evinced a gracefulness and ease which long habit seemed to have identified with her nature.

At the opposite side of the table, and busy in the preparation of the breakfast, stood a young girl whose age could not have been more than eighteen. So striking was the resemblance between them that the least acute of physiognomists must have pronounced her the daughter. She was dressed with remarkable simplicity; but not all the absence of ornament could detract from the first impression her appearance conveyed, that she was one of birth and station. Her beauty was of that character which, although attributed peculiarly to the Celtic race, seems strangely enough to present its most striking examples among the Anglo-Irish. Rich auburn hair, the color varying from dark brown to a deep golden hue as the light falls more or less strongly on it, was braided over a brow of classic beauty; her eyes were of blue, that deep color which, in speaking or in moments of excitement, looks like dark hazel or even black; these were fringed with long dark lashes which habitually hung heavily over the eyes, giving them a character of sleepy, almost indolent, beauty. The rest of her features, in unison with these, were of that Greek mould which our historians attribute to the Phoenician origin of our people,—a character by no means rare to be seen to this day among the peasantry. If the mild and gentle indications of womanly delicacy were told in every lineament of her face, there were traits of decision and determination when she spoke not less evident. From her mother she inherited the placid tenderness of English manner, while from her father her nature imbibed the joyous animation and buoyant light-heartedness of the Irish character.

"And there are but two letters, Mamma," said Helen, "in the bag this morning?"

"But two," said Lady Eleanor; "one of them from Lionel."

"Oh, from Lionel!" cried the young girl, eagerly; "let me see it."

"Read this first," said Lady Eleanor, as she handed across the table a letter bearing a large seal impressed with an Earl's coronet; "if I mistake not very much, Helen, that's my cousin Lord Netherby's writing; but what eventful circumstance could have caused his affectionate remembrance of me, after something nigh twenty years' silence, is beyond my power of divination."

Helen Darcy well knew that the theme on which her mother now touched was the sorest subject on her mind, and, however anxiously she might, under other circumstances, have pressed for a sight of her brother's letter, she controlled all appearance of the wish, and opened the other without speaking.

"It is dated from Carlton House, Mamma, the 2d— — —"

"He is in waiting, I suppose," said Lady Eleanor, calmly; and Helen began.

"'My dear cousin—'"

"Ah! so he remembers the relationship at least," muttered the old lady to herself.

"'My dear cousin, it would be a sad abuse of the small space a letter affords, to inquire into the cause of our long silence; faults on both sides might explain much of it. I was never a brilliant correspondent, you were always an indolent one; if I wrote stupid letters, you sent me very brief answers; and if you at last grew weary of giving gold for brass, I can scarcely reproach you for stopping the exchange. Still, at the risk of remaining unanswered, once more—'"

"This is intolerable," broke in Lady Eleanor; "he never replied to the letter in which I asked him to be your godfather."

"'Still, at the risk of remaining unanswered, once more I must throw myself on your mercy. In the selfishness of age,—don't forget, my dear coz, I am eleven years your senior,—in the selfishness of age—'"

The old lady smiled dubiously at these words, and Helen read on:—

"'I desire to draw closer around me those ties of kindred and family which, however we may affect to think lightly of, all our experiences in life tend to strengthen and support. Yes, my dear Eleanor, we are the only two remaining of all those light-hearted boys and bright-eyed girls that once played upon the terrace at Netherby. Poor Harry, your old sweetheart at Eton, fell at Mysore. Dudley, with ability for anything, would not wait patiently for the crowning honors of his career, took a judgeship in Madras, and he, too, sleeps in the land of the stranger! And our sweet Catherine! your only rival amongst us, how short-lived was her triumph!—for so the world called her marriage with the Margrave: she died of a broken heart at two-and-twenty! I know not why I have called up these sad memories, except it be in the hope that, as desolation deals heavily around us, we may draw more closely to each other.'"

Lady Eleanor concealed her face with her handkerchief, and Helen, who had gradually dropped her voice as she read, stopped altogether at these words.

"Read on, dear," said the old lady, in a tone whose firmness was slightly shaken.

"'A heart more worldly than yours, my dear Eleanor, would exclaim that the *parti* was unequal,—that I, grown old and childless, with few friends left, and no ambitions to strive for, stood in far more need of *your* affectionate regard, than you, blessed with every tie to existence, did of *mine*; and the verdict would be a just one, for, by the law of that Nemesis we all feel more or less, even in this world, *you*, whom we deemed rash and imprudent, have alone amongst us secured the prize of that happiness we each sought by such different paths.'"

A heavy sigh that broke from her mother made Helen cease reading, but at a motion of her hand she resumed: "'For all our sakes, then, my dear cousin, only remember so much of the past as brings back pleasant memories. Make my peace with your kind-hearted husband. If I can forgive *him* all the pangs of jealousy he inflicted on *me*, *he* may well pardon any slight transgressions on *my* part, and Lionel, too.—But, first, tell me how have I offended my young kinsman? I have twice endeavored to make his acquaintance, but in vain. Two very cold and chilling answers to my invitations to Netherby are all I have been able to obtain from him: the first was a plea of duty, which I could easily have arranged; but the second note was too plain to be mistaken: "I'll none of you," was the tone of every line of it. But I will not be so easily repulsed: I am determined to know him, and, more still, determined that he shall know me. If you knew, my dear Eleanor, how proudly my heart beat at hearing his Royal Highness speak of him!—he had seen him at Hounslow at a review. It was a slight incident, but I am certain your son never told it, and so I must. Lionel, in passing with his company, forgot to lower the regimental flag before the Prince, on which Lord Maxwell, the colonel, the most passionate man in England, rode up, and said something in an angry tone. "I beg pardon, Colonel," said the Prince, "if I interfere with the details of duty, but I have remarked that young officer before, and, trust me, he 'll come off 'with flying colors,' on more occasions than the present." The *mot* was slight, but the flattery was perfect; indeed, there is not another man in the kingdom can compete with his Royal Highness on this ground. Fascination is the only word that can express the charm of his manner. To bring Lionel more particularly under the Prince's notice, has long been a favorite scheme of mine; and I may say, without arrogance, that my opportunities are not inferior to most men's in this respect; I am an old courtier now,—no small boast for one who still retains his share of favor. If the son have any of his father's gifts, his success with the Prince is certain. The manner of the highly-bred Irish gentleman has been already pronounced by his Royal Highness as the type of what manner should be, and, with your assistance, I have little doubt of seeing Lionel appointed on the staff, here.

"'Now, I must hazard my reputation a little, and ask what is the name of your second boy, and what is he doing?'"

Helen burst into a fit of laughter at these words, nor could Lady Eleanor's chagrin prevent her joining in the emotion.

"This, he shall certainly have an answer to," said the old lady, recovering her self-possession and her pride; "he shall hear that my second boy is called Helen."

"After all, Mamma, is it not very kind of him to remember even so much?"

"I remember even more, Helen," interrupted Lady Eleanor; "and no great kindness in the act either."

"Shall I read all the possible and impossible chances of pushing my fortune in the Army or Navy, Mamma?" said Helen, archly, "for I see that his Lordship is most profuse in offers for my advancement,—nay, if I have a clerical vocation, here is a living actually waiting my acceptance."

"Let us rather look for something that may explain the riddle, my dear," said Lady Eleanor, taking the letter in her own hand, while she lightly skimmed over the last page. "No, I can find no clew to it here—Stay, what have we in this corner?—'Politically speaking, there is no news here; indeed, in that respect, *your* side of the Channel engrosses all the interest; the great question of the "Union" still occupies all attention. Virtually, *we* know the ministry have the majority, but there will be still a very respectable fight, to amuse the world withal. How does the Knight vote? With us, I hope and trust, for although I may tell you, in confidence, the result is certain, his support would be very grateful to the Government, and, while he himself can afford to smile at ministerial flatteries, Lionel is a young fellow whom rapid promotion would well become, and who would speedily distinguish himself, if the occasion were favorable. At all events, let the Knight not vote *against* the minister; this would be a crime never to be forgiven, and personally offensive to his Royal Highness; and I trust Darcy is too good a sportsman to prefer riding the last horse, even should he not wish to mount the winner.'"

Here the letter concluded, amid protestations of regard most affectionately worded, and warm wishes for a renewal of intimacy, only to cease with life. Across this was written, with a different ink, and in a hurried hand: "I have this moment seen Mr. Pitt; the Knight's vote is very important. He may make any terms he pleases,—Pitt spoke of a peerage; but I suppose that would not be thought advisable. Let me hear *your* opinion. Lionel has been gazetted to a company this morning, *en attendant* better."

Lady Eleanor, who had read these last lines to herself, here laid down the letter without speaking, while the slight flush of her cheek and the increased brilliancy of her eyes showed that her feelings were deeply and powerfully excited.

"Well, Mamma, have you found the solution to this mystery?" said Helen, as she gazed with affectionate solicitude on her mother's features.

"How unchangeable a thing is nature!" muttered Lady Eleanor, unconsciously, aloud; "that boy was a crafty tuft-hunter at Eton."

"Of whom are you speaking, Mamma?"

"Lord Netherby, my dear, who would seem to have cultivated his natural gift with great success; but," added she, after a pause, and in a voice scarcely above a whisper, "I am scarcely as easy a dupe now as when he persuaded me to take ash-berries in exchange for cherries. Let us hear what Lionel says."

"As usual, Mamma, four lines in each page, and the last a blank," said Helen, laughing:—"'My dear mother, what blandishments have you been throwing over the War Office? They have just given me my company, which, by the ordinary rules of the service, I had no pretension to hope for, these five years to come! Our colonel, too, a perfect Tartar, overwhelms me with civilities, and promises me a leave of absence on the first vacancy. Have you seen Forester, of ours? and how do you like him? A little cold or so at first, but *you* will not dislike that. His riding will please my father. Get him to sing, if you can; his taste and voice are both first-rate. Your worthy relative, Lord Netherby, bores me with invitations to his houses, town and country. I say "No;" but he won't be denied. Was he not rude, or indifferent, or something or other, once upon a time, to the ancient house of Darcy? Give me the *consigne*, I pray you, for I hear he has the best cock-shooting in England; and let my virtue, if possible, be rewarded by a little indulgence. Tell Helen they are all giving up powder here, and wear their hair as she does; but not one of them half as good-looking.

Yours, as ever,

Lionel Darcy.

Hounslow, January 1st, 1800'"

"Is that Sullivan, there?" said Lady Eleanor, as her daughter finished the reading of this brief epistle. "What does he mean by staring so at the window? The old man seems to have lost his senses!"

"Ochone arie! ochone! ochone!" cried Tate, wringing his hands with the gestures of violent grief, as he moved up and down before the windows.

"What has happened, Tate?" said Helen, as she threw open the sash to address him.

"Ochone! he's kilt—he's murthered—cut down like a daisy in a May morning. And he, the iligant, fine young man!"

"Whom do you mean? Speak plainly, Sullivan," said the commanding voice of Lady Eleanor. "What is it?"

"'Tis the young officer from England, my lady, that came down the night before last to see the master. Oh, murther! murther! if his honor was here, the sorra bit of this grief we 'd have to-day—ochone!"

"Well, go on," said his mistress, sternly.

"And if he came down for joy, 't is sorrow he supped for it,' the young crayture! They soon finished him."

"Once for all, sir, speak out plainly, and say what has occurred."

"It's Mr. Bagenal Daly done it all, my lady,—divil a one of me cares who hears me say it. He's a cruel man, ould as he is. He made him fight a duel, the darling young man,—the 'moral' of Master Lionel himself; and now he's kilt—ochone! ochone!"

"Can this dreadful story be true, Helen?" said Lady Eleanor, as the faint color left her features. "Call Margaret; or, stay—Sullivan, is Mr. Daly here?"

"That he is, never fear him. He's looking at his morning's work—he's in the room where they carried the corpse; and the fine corpse it is."

"Go tell Mr. Daly that Lady Eleanor desires to see him at once."

"Go, and lose no time, Tate," said Helen, as, almost fainting with terror, she half pushed the old man on his errand.

The mother and daughter sat silently gazing on each other for several minutes, terror and dismay depicted in the face of each, nor were they conscious of the lapse of time, when the door opening presented Mr. Bagenal Daly before them. He was dressed in his usual suit of dark brown, and with all his accustomed neatness. His long cravat, which, edged with deep lace, hung negligently over his waistcoat, was spotless in color and accurate in every fold, while his massive features were devoid of the slightest signs of emotion or excitement.

For an instant Lady Eleanor was deceived by all these evidences of tranquillity, but a glance at old Tate's face, as he stood near the door, assured her that from such signs she had nothing to hope. Twice had Mr. Bagenal Daly performed his courteous salutations, which, in the etiquette of a past time, he made separately to each lady, and still Lady Eleanor had not summoned courage to address him. At last he said,—

"Have I been mistaken, and must I apologize for a visit at an hour so unseemly? But I heard that your Ladyship wished to see me."

"Quite true, Mr. Daly," interrupted Lady Eleanor, her habitual tact supplying a courage her heart was far from feeling. "Will you be seated? Leave the room, Sullivan. My daughter and I," continued she, speaking with increased rapidity, to cover the emotion of the moment, "have just heard something of a dreadful event which is said to have occurred this morning. Old Sullivan so often exaggerates that we indulge the hope that there may be little or no foundation for the story. Is it true, sir, there has been a duel fought near this?" Her voice grew fainter as she spoke, and at last became a mere whisper.

"Yes, madam," replied Daly, with an air of perfect calmness. "Two gentlemen met this morning at Cluan Point, and both were wounded."

"Neither of them killed?"

"Wounded, madam," reiterated Daly, as if correcting a misconstruction.

"Are the wounds deemed dangerous, sir?"

"Mr. MacDonough's, madam, is not so. The inconvenience of using his left hand on any similar occasion, in future, will be probably the extent of the mishap. The other gentleman has not been equally fortunate,—his life is in peril." Mr. Daly paused for a second, and then, perceiving that Lady Eleanor still awaited a further explanation, added, with gravity, "When taking his position on the ground, madam, instead of standing half-front, as I took pains to point out to him, Captain Forester—"

"Forester!—is that his name, sir?" interrupted Helen, as, in a hand trembling with terror, she held out Lionel's letter towards her mother.

"A friend of my son's,—is he in the same regiment with Lionel?" asked Lady Eleanor, eagerly.

Daly bowed, and answered, "The same, madam."

A low, faint sigh broke from Lady Eleanor, and, covering her eyes with her hand, she sat for some moments without speaking.

"Has any one seen him, sir?" asked Helen, suddenly, and in a voice that showed energy of character had the mastery over every feeling of grief,—"is there a surgeon with him?"

"No, Miss Darcy," said Daly, with a certain haughtiness of manner. "I believe, however, that, although not a professional person, my knowledge of a gunshot wound is scarcely inferior to most men's. I have sent in two directions for a surgeon; meanwhile, with my servant's aid, I have succeeded in extracting the ball—I beg pardon, ladies, I think I heard the noise of wheels; it is probably the doctor." And, with a deep bow and a measured step, Mr. Bagenal Daly withdrew, leaving Lady Eleanor and her daughter speechless, between grief and terror.

CHAPTER VIII
THE "HEAD" OF A FAMILY

When Bagenal Daly reached the courtyard, he was disappointed at finding that, instead of the surgeon whose arrival was so anxiously looked for, the visitor was no other than old Dr. Hickman, the father of Hickman O'Reilly, M. P. for the county, and grandfather of that very promising young gentleman slightly presented to our reader in an early chapter.

If the acorn be a very humble origin for the stately oak of the forest, assuredly Peter Hickman, formerly of Loughrea, "Apothecary and Surgeon," was the most unpretending source for the high and mighty house of O'Reilly. More strictly speaking, the process was only a "graft," and it is but justice to him to say, that of this fact no one was more thoroughly convinced than old Peter himself. Industry and thrift had combined to render him tolerably well off in the world, when the death of a brother who had sought his fortunes in the East—when fortunes were to be found in that region—put him in possession of something above two hundred thousand pounds. Even before this event, he had been known as a shrewd contriver of small speculations, a safe investor of little capital, was conversant, from the habits of his professional life, with the private circumstances of every family of the country where money was wanting, and where repayment was sure; the very temperament of his patients suggested to him the knowledge by which he guided his operations, and he could bring his skill as a medical man into his service, and study his creditors with the eye of a physiologist. When this great accession of wealth so suddenly occurred, far from communicating his good fortune to his friends and neighbors, he merely gave out that poor Tom had left him "his little savings," "though God knows, in that faraway country, if he'd ever see any of it." His guarded caution on the subject, and the steady persistence with which he maintained his former mode of life, gave credence to the story, and the utmost estimate of his wealth would not have gone beyond being a snug old fellow "that might give up his business any day." This was, however, the very last thing in his thoughts; the title of "Doctor," so courteously bestowed in Ireland on the humbler walks of medicine, was a "letter of marque" enabling him to cruise in latitudes otherwise inaccessible. Any moneyed embarrassment of the country gentry, any severe pressure to be averted by an opportune loan or the sale of landed property, was speedily made available by him as a call to see whether "the cough was easier;" or "how was the gouty ankle;" if the "mistress was getting better of the nerves," "and the children gaining strength by the camomile." And in this way he made one species of gain subservient to another, while his character for kindness and benevolence was the theme of the whole neighborhood.

For several years long he pursued this course without deviating, and in that space had become the owner of estated property to a very great extent, not only in his own, but in three neighboring counties. How much longer he might have persisted in growing rich by stealth it is difficult to say, when accident compelled him to change his *tactique*. A very large property had been twice put up for sale in the county Mayo, under the will of its late owner, the trustees being empowered to make a great reduction in the price to any purchaser of the whole,—a condition which, from the great value of the estates, seemed of little avail, no single individual being supposed able to make such a purchase.

At last, and as a final effort to comply with the wishes of the testator, the estate was offered at ten thousand pounds below the original demand, when a bidder made his appearance, the offer was accepted, and the apothecary of Lough-rea became the owner of one of the most flourishing properties of the West, with influence sufficient to return a member for the county.

The murder was now out, and the next act was to build a handsome but unpretentious dwelling-house on a part of the estate, to which he removed with his son, a widower with one child. The ancient family of O'Reilly had been the owners of the property, and the name was still retained to grace the new demesne, which was called Mount O'Reilly, while Tom Hickman became Hickman O'Reilly, under the plea of some relationship to the defunct,—a point which gained little credence in the county, and drew from Bagenal Daly the remark "that he trusted that they had a better title to the acres than the arms of the O'Reillys." When old Peter had made this great spring, he would gladly have retired to Loughrea once more, and pursued his old habits; but, like a blackleg who has accidentally discovered his skill at the game, no one would play with him again, and so he was fain to put up with his changed condition, and be a "gentleman," as he called it, in spite of himself.

He it was who, under the pretence of a friendly call to see the Knight, now drove into the courtyard of Gwynne Abbey. His equipage was a small four-wheeled chair close to the ground, and drawn by a rough mountain pony which, in size and shape, closely resembled a water-dog. The owner of this unpretending conveyance was a very diminutive, thin old man, with a long, almost transparent nose, the tip of which was of a raspberry red; a stiff queue, formed of his wiry gray hair carefully brushed back, even from the temples, made a graceful curve on his back, or occasionally appeared in front of his left shoulder. His voice was a feeble treble, with a tremulous quiver through all he said, while he usually finished each sentence with a faint effort content with his opinion; and this, on remarkable occasions, at a laugh, a kind of acknowledgment to himself that he was would be followed by the monosyllable "ay,"—a word which, brief as it was, struck terror into many a heart, intimating, as it did, that old Peter had just satisfied himself that he had made a good bargain, and that the other party was "done."

The most remarkable circumstance of his appearance was his mode of walking, and even here was displayed his wonted ingenuity. A partial paralysis had for some years affected his limbs, and particularly the muscles which raise and flex the legs; to obviate this infirmity, he fastened a cord with a loop to either foot, and by drawing them up alternately he was enabled to move forward, at a slow pace, to be sure, and in a manner it was rather difficult to witness for the first time with becoming gravity. This was more remarkable when he endeavored to get on faster, for then the flexion, a process which required a little time, was either imperfectly performed or altogether omitted, and consequently he remained stationary, and only hopped from one leg to the other after the fashion of a stage procession. His dress was a rusty black coat with a standing collar, black shorts, and white cotton stockings, over which the short black gaiters reached half way up the leg; on the present occasion he also wore a spencer of light gray cloth, as the day was cold and frosty, and his hat was fastened under his chin by a ribbon.

"And so he is n't at home, Tate," said he, as he sat whipping the pony from habit,—a process which the beast seemed to regard with a contemptuous indifference.

"No, Docther," for by this title the old man was always addressed by preference, "the Knight's up in Dublin; he went on Monday last."

"And this is the seventh of the month," muttered the other to himself. "Faith, he takes it easy, anyhow! And you don't know when he'll be home?"

"The sorra know I know, Docther; 't is maybe to-night he 'd come— maybe to-morrow—maybe it would be three weeks or a month; and it's not but we want him badly this day, if it was God's will he was here!" These words were uttered in a tone that Tate intended should provoke further questioning, for he was most eager to tell of the duel and its consequences; but the "doctor" never noticed them, but merely muttered a short "Ay."

"How do you do, Hickman?" cried out the deep voice of Bagenal Daly at the same moment. "You did n't chance to see Mulville on the road, did you?"

"How d'ye do, Mister Daly? I hope I see you well. I did n't meet Dr. Mulville this morning,—is there anything that's wrong here? Who is it that's ill?"

"A young fellow, a stranger, who has been burning powder with Mr. MacDonough up at Cluan, and has been hit under the rib here."

"Well, well, what folly it is, and all about nothing, I 'll engage."

"So your grandson would tell you," said Daly, sternly; "for if he felt it to be anything, this quarrel should have been his."

"Faix, and I'm glad he left it alone," said the other, complacently; "'t is little good comes of the same fighting. I 'll be eighty-five if I live to March next, and I never drew sword nor trigger yet against any man."

"One reason for which forbearance is, sir, that you thereby escaped a similar casualty to yourself. A laudable prudence, and likely to become a family virtue."

The old doctor felt all the severity of this taunt against his grandson, but he merely gave one of his half-subdued laughs, and said, in a low voice, "Did you get a note from me, about a fortnight ago? Ay!"

"I received one from your attorney," said Daly, carelessly, "and I threw it into the fire without reading it."

"That was hasty, that was rash, Mr. Daly," resumed the other, calmly; "it was about the bond for the four thousand six hundred—"

"D——n me if I care what was the object of it! I happened to have some weightier things to think of than usury and compound interest, as I, indeed, have at this moment. By the by, if you have not forgotten the old craft, come in and see this poor fellow. I 'm much mistaken, or his time will be but short."

"Ay, ay, that's a debt there's no escaping!" muttered the old man, combining his vein of moralizing with a sly sarcasm at Daly, while he began the complicated series of manouvres by which he usually effected his descent from the pony carriage.

In the large library, and on a bed hastily brought down for the purpose, lay Forester, his dress disordered, and his features devoid of all color. The glazed expression of his eye, and his pallid, half-parted lips showed that he was suffering from great loss of blood, for, unhappily, Mr. Daly's surgery had not succeeded in arresting this symptom. His breathing was short and irregular, and in the convulsive movement of his fingers might be seen the evidence of acute suffering. At the side of the bed, calm, motionless, and self-possessed, with an air as stern as a soldier at his post, stood Sandy M'Grane; he had been ordered by his master to maintain a perfect silence, and to avoid, if possible, even a reply to Forester's questions, should he speak to him. The failure of the first few efforts on Forester's part to obtain an infraction of this rule ended in his submitting to his destiny, and supplying by signs the want of speech; in this way he had just succeeded in procuring a drink of water, when Daly entered, followed by Hickman. As with slow and noiseless steps they came forward, Forester turned his head, and, catching a glance of the mechanism by which old Peter regulated his progression, he burst into a fit of uncontrollable laughter.

"Ye mauna do it, ye mauna do it, sir," said Sandy, sternly; "ye are lying in a pool of blood this minute, and it's no time for a hearty laugh. Ech! ech! sir," continued he, turning towards his master, "if we had that salve the Delawares used to put on their wounds, I wadna say but we 'd stap it yet."

By this time old Peter had laid his hand on the sick man's wrist, and, with a large watch laid before him on the bed, was counting his pulse aloud.

"It's a hundred and fifty," said he, in a whisper, which, although intended for Daly's ear, was overheard by Forester; "but it's thin as a thread, and looks like inward bleeding."

"What's to be done, then? have you anything to advise?" said Daly, almost savagely.

"Very little," said Hickman, with a malignant grin, "except writing to his friends. I know nothing else to serve him."

A brief shudder passed over Daly's stern features, rather like the momentary sense of cold than proceeding from any mental emotion, and then he said, "I spoke to you as a doctor, sir; and I ask you again, is there nothing can be done for him?"

"Well, well, we might plug up the wound, to be sure, and give him a little wine, for he's sinking fast. I 've got a case of instruments and some lint in the gig—never go without the tools, Mr. Daly—there's no knowing when one may meet a little accident like this."

"In Heaven's name, then, lose no time!" said Daly. "Whatever you can do, do it at once."

The tone of command in which he spoke seemed to act like a charm on the old doctor, for he turned at once to hobble from the room.

"My servant will bring what you want," said Daly, impatiently.

"No, no," said Peter, shaking his head, "I have them under lock and key in the driving-box; there's no one opens that but myself."

Daly turned away with a muttered execration at the miser's suspicions, and then, fixing his eyes steadily on Sandy's face, he gave a short and significant nod. The servant instinctively looked after the doctor; then, slowly moving across the floor, the nod was repeated, and Sandy, wheeling round, made three strides, and, catching the old man round the body with his remaining arm, carried him out of the room with the same indifference to his struggles or his cries as a nurse would bestow on a misbehaving urchin.

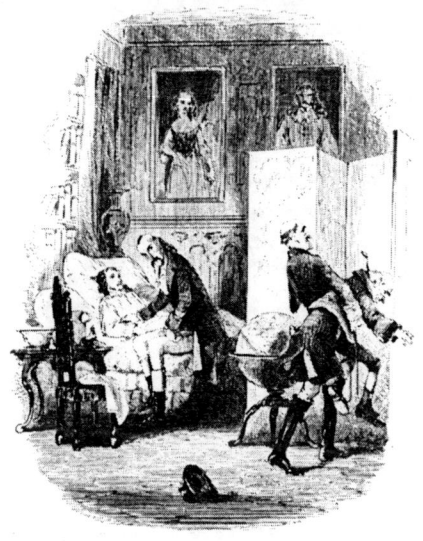

Sandy, McGrane carpulet the doctor.

When Sandy deposited his burden beside the pony-carriage, old Peter's passion had reached its climax, and assuredly, if the will could have prompted the act, he would have stamped as roundly as he swore.

"It's an awfu' thing," observed Sandy, quaintly, "to see an auld carle, wi' his twa legs in the grave, blaspheming that gate; but come awa', tak' your gimcracks, and let's get back again, or, by the saul of my body, I 'll pit you in the fountain!"

Reasoning on that excellent principle of analogy, that what had happened might happen again even in a worse form, old Hickman unlocked the box and delivered into Sandy's hands a black leather case, bearing as many signs of long years and service as his own.

"Let me walk I let me walk!" cried he, in a supplicating tone.

"Av you ca' it walking," said Sandy, grimly; "but it's mair, far mair, like the step o' a goose than a Christian man."

What success might have attended Peter's request it is difficult to say, for at this moment the noise of a horse was heard galloping up the avenue, and, immediately after, Mulville, the surgeon sent for by Mr. Daly, entered the courtyard. Without deigning a look towards Hickman, or paying even the slightest attention to his urgent demands for the restoration of his pocket-case, Sandy seized Mulville by the arm and hurried him away to the house.

The newly arrived doctor was an army surgeon, and proceeded, with all the readiness experience had taught him, to examine Forester's wound; while Sandy, to save time, opened old Hickman's case on the bed, and arranged the instruments.

"Look here, Mr. Daly," said the doctor, as he drew some lint from the antiquated leather pocket, — "look here, and see how our old friend practises the art of medicine." He took up, as he spoke, a roll of paper, and held it towards Daly: it was a packet of bill stamps of various value, for old Peter could never suffer himself to be taken short, and was always provided with the ready means of transacting money affairs with his patients.

"Here's my d——d old bond," said Daly, laughing, as he drew forth a much-crumpled and time-discolored parchment; "I'd venture to say the man would deserve well of his country who would throw this confounded pocket-book, and its whole contents, into that fire."

"Ye maybe want some o' the tools yet," said Sandy, dryly, for, taking his master's observations in the light of a command, he was about to commit the case and the paper to the flames.

"Take care! take care!" said Mulville, in a whisper; "it might be a felony."

"It's devilish little Sandy would care what name they would give it," replied Daly; "he 'd put the owner on the top of them, and burn all together, on a very brief hint;" then, lowering his voice, he added, "What's his chance?"

"The chance of every young fellow of two or three-and-twenty to live through what would kill any man of my time of life. With good care and quiet, but quiet above all, he may rub through it. We must leave him now."

"You 'll remain here," said Daly; "you 'll not quit this, I hope?"

"For a day or two at least, I 'll not leave him." And with this satisfactory assurance Daly closed the door, leaving Sandy on guard over the patient.

"Here's your case of instruments, Hickman," said Daly, as the old doctor sat motionless in his gig, awaiting their reappearance; for, in his dread of further violence, he had preferred thus patiently to await their return, than venture once more into the company of Sandy M'Grane. "We 've robbed you of nothing except some lint; and," added he in a whisper to Muiville, "I very much doubt if that case were ever opened and closed before with so slight an offence against the laws of property."

Old Hickman by this time had opened the pocket-book, and was busily engaged inspecting its contents.

"Ay, that's the bond!" said Daly, laughing; "you may well think how small the chance of repayment is, when I did not think it worth while burning it."

"It will be paid in good time," said Hickman, in a low cackle, "and the interest too, maybe—ay!" And with sundry admonitions from the whip, and successive chucks of the rein, the old pony threw up his head, shook his tail crossly, and, with a step almost as measured as that of his master, moved slowly out of the courtyard.

"So much for our century and our civilization!" said Daly, as he looked after him; "the old miser that goes there has more power over our country and its gentry than ever a feudal chief wielded in the days of vassalage."

CHAPTER IX
"DALY'S"

It was upon one of the very coldest evenings of the memorably severe January of 1800 that the doors of Daly's Club House were besieged by carriages of every shape and description: some brilliant in all the lustre of a perfect equipage; others more plainly denoting the country gentleman or the professional man; and others, again, the chance occupants of the various coach-stands, displayed every variety of that now extinct family whose members went under the denominations of "whiskeys," "jingles," and "noddies."

A heavy fall of sleet, accompanied with a cutting north wind, did not prevent the assemblage of a considerable crowd, who, by the strange sympathy of gregarious curiosity, were drawn up in front of the building, satisfied to think that something unusual, of what nature they knew not, was going forward within, and content to gaze on the brilliant glare of the lustres as seen through the drawn curtains, and mark the shadowy outlines of figures as they passed and repassed continually.

Leaving the mob, for it was in reality such, to speculate on the cause of this extraordinary gathering, we shall at once proceed up the ample stair and enter the great saloon of the Club, which, opening by eight windows upon College Green, formed the conversation-room of the members.

Here were now assembled between three and four hundred persons, gathered in groups and knots, and talking with all the eagerness some engrossing topic could suggest. In dress, air, and manner they seemed to represent sections of every social circle of the capital: some, in full Castle costume, had just escaped from the table of the Viceroy; others, in military uniform or the dress of the Club, contrasted with coats of country squires or the even more ungainly quaintness of the lawyers' costume. They were of every age, from the young man emerging into life, to the old frequenter of the Club, who had occupied his own place and chair for half a century, and in manner and style as various, many preserving the courteous observances of the old school in all its polished urbanity, and the younger part of the company exhibiting the traits of a more independent, but certainly less graceful, politeness. Happily for the social enjoyments of the time, political leanings had not contributed their bitterness to private life, and men of opinions the most opposite, and party connections most antagonistic, were here met, willing to lay aside for a season the arms of encounter, or to use them with only the sportive pleasantry of a polished wit. If this manly spirit of mutual forbearance did not characterize the very last debates of the Irish Parliament, it may in a great measure be attributed to the nature of that influence by which the measure of the Union was carried; for bribery not only corrupted the venal, but it soured and irritated the men who rejected its seductions; and in this wise a difference was created between the two parties, wider and more irreconcilable than all which political animosity or mere party dislike could effect.

On the present occasion, however, the animating spirit of the assemblage seemed to partake of nothing less than a feature of political acrimony; and amid the chance phrases which met the ear, and the hearty bursts of laughter that every moment broke forth, it was easy to collect that no question of a party nature occupied their attention.

At the end of the room a group of some twenty persons stood or sat around a chair in which a thin elderly gentleman was seated, his fine and delicately marked features far more unequivocally proclaiming rank than even the glittering star he wore on his breast. Without being in reality very old, Lord Drogheda seemed so, for, partly from delicacy of health, and partly, as some affirmed, from an affectation of age (a more frequent thing than is expected), he had contracted a stoop, and walked with every sign of debility.

"Well, gentlemen, how does time go?" said he, with an easy smile. "Are we not near the hour?"

"Yes; it wants but eleven minutes of ten now, my Lord," said one of the group. "Do you mean to hold him sharp to time?"

"Egad, I should think so," interrupted a red-whiskered squire, in splashed top-boots. "I've ridden in from Kildare to-night to see the match, and I protest against any put-off."

Lord Drogheda turned his eyes towards the speaker with a look in which mildness was so marked, it could not be called reproof, but it evidently confused him, as he added, "Of course, if the gentlemen who have heavy wagers on it are content I must be also."

"I, for one, say 'sharp time,'" cried out a dapperly dressed young fellow, with an open pocket-book in his hand; "play or pay is the only rule in these cases."

"I 've backed my Lord at eight to ten, in hundreds," said another, "and certainly I 'll claim my bet if the Knight is one minute late."

"Then you have just three to decide that question," said one at his side. "My watch is with the Post-office."

"Quite, time enough left to order my carriage," said Lord Drogheda, rising with an energy very different from his ordinary indolent habit. "If the Knight of Gwynne should be accidentally delayed, gentlemen, I, for my part, prefer being also absent. It will then be a matter of some difficulty for the parties betting to say who is the delinquent." He took his hat as he spoke, and was moving through the crowd, when a sudden cheer from without was heard, and then, almost the instant after, a confused sound of acclamation as the Knight of Gwynne entered, leaning on the arm of Con Heffernan. Making his way with difficulty through the crowd of welcoming friends and acquaintances, the Knight approached the end of the room where Lord Drogheda now awaited him, standing.

"Not late, my Lord, though very near it," said he, extending his hand. "If I should apologize, however, I have an excuse you will not reject,—Con Heffernan's Burgundy is hard to part with."

"Very true, Knight," said his Lordship, smiling. "With a friend one sees so seldom, a little dalliance is most pardonable."

This sarcasm was met by a ready laugh, for Heffernan was better known as a guest at other tables than a host at his own; nor did he, at whose expense the jest was made, refrain from joining in the mirth, while he added,—

"The Burgundy, like one of your Lordship's *bons mots*, is perhaps appreciated the more highly because of its rarity."

"Very true, Heffernan," replied Lord Drogheda; "we should keep our wit and wine only for our best friends."

"Faith, then," whispered the red-whiskered squire who spoke before, "if the liquor does not gain more by keeping than the wit, I'd recommend Con to drink it off a little faster."

"Or, better still," interposed the Knight, "only give it to those who understand its flavor. But we are, if I mistake not, losing very valuable time. What say you to the small room off the library, or will your Lordship remain here?"

"Here, if equally agreeable to you. We are both of us too old in the harness to care much for being surrounded by spectators."

"Is it true, Con," said a friend in Heffernan's ear, "that Darcy has laid fifty thousand on this party?"

"I believe you are rather under than over the mark," whispered Heffernan. "The wager has been off and on these last eight or ten years. It was made at Hutchinson's one evening when we all had drunk a good deal of wine. At first, whist was talked of; but Drogheda objected to Darcy's naming Vicars as his partner."

"More fool he! Vicars is a first-rate player, but confoundedly unlucky."

"Be that as it may, they fixed on piquet as the game, and, if accounts be true, all the better for Darcy. They say he has beaten the best players in France."

"And what is really the stake? One hears so many absurd versions of it."

"The Ballydermot property."

"The whole of it?"

"Every acre, with the demesne, house, plate, pictures, carriages, wine, — begad! I 'm not sure if the livery servants are not included, —against fifty thousand pounds. You know Drogheda has lent him a very large sum on a mortgage of that property already, and this will make the thing about double or quits."

"Well, Heffernan," cried the Knight, "are you making your book there? When you've quite finished, let me have a pinch of that excellent snuff of yours."

"Why not try mine?" said Lord Drogheda, pushing a magnificently jewelled box, containing a miniature, across the table.

"'T would be a bad augury, my Lord," said Darcy, laughing. "If I remember aright, you won this handsome box from the Duke de Richelieu."

"Ah! you know that story, then?"

"I was present at the time, and remember the circumstance perfectly. The King was leaning over the Duke's chair, watching the game—"

"Quite true. The Duke affected not to know that his Majesty was there, and when he placed the box on the table, cried, 'A thousand louis against the portrait of the King!' There was no declining such a wager at such a moment, although, intrinsically, the box was not worth half the sum. I accepted, and won it."

"And the Duke then offered to give you twice the money for it back again?"

"He did so, and I refused. I shall not readily forget the sweet, sad smile of the King as he tapped the wily courtier on the shoulder, and said, 'Ah!

Monsieur le Duc, do you only value your King when you've lost him?' They were prophetic words! Well, well! we 've got upon a sorrowful theme; let's change it."

"Here are the cards, at last," said the Knight, taking a sealed packet from the waiter's hand, and breaking it open on the table. "Now, Heffernan, order me a glass of claret negus, and take care that no one comes to worry us with news of the House."

"It's a sugar bill, or a new clause in the Corporation Act, or something of that kind, they 're working at," said Lord Drogheda, negligently.

"No, my Lord," interposed Heffernan, slyly, "it's a bill to permit your Lordship's nephew to hold the living of Ardragh with his deanery."

"All right and proper," said his Lordship, endeavoring to hide a rising flush on his cheek by an opportune laugh. "Tom is a capital fellow, and a good parson too."

"And ought never to omit the prayer for the Parliament!" muttered Heffernan, loud enough to be heard by the bystanders, who relished the allusion heartily.

"The deal is with you, Knight," said Lord Drogheda, pushing the cards across the table.

The moment afterwards, a pin could not have fallen unheard in that crowded assembly. Even they who were not themselves bettors felt the deepest interest in the game where the stake was so great, and all who could set value on skill and address were curious to watch the progress of the contest. Not a word was spoken on either side as the cards fell upon the table, and although many of the bystanders displayed looks of more eager anxiety, the players showed by their intentness how strenuously each struggled for the victory.

After the lapse of about half an hour, a low, murmuring noise spread through the room, and the news was circulated that the first game was over, and the Knight was the winner. The players, however, were silent as before, and the deal went over without a word.

"One moment, my Lord," said Darcy, as he gently interposed his hand to prevent Lord Drogheda taking up his cards,—"a single moment. You will call me faint-hearted for it, but I do not care. I beseech you, let the party cease here. It is a great favor; but as I could not ask it if I had lost the game, give me, I pray, so much of advantage for my good luck."

"You forget, Knight, that I, as a loser, could not accede to your proposal; what would be said of any man who, with such a stake at issue, accepted an offer like this?"

"My dear Lord, don't you think that you and I might afford to have our actions canvassed, and yet be very little afraid of criticism?" said Darcy, proudly.

"No, no, my dear Darcy, I really could not do this; besides, you must concede something to mortified vanity. Now, I am anxious to have my revenge."

"Be it so, my Lord," said the Knight, with a sigh, and the game began.

The looks and glances which were interchanged by those about during this brief colloquy showed how little sympathy there was felt with the generosity of either side. The bettors had set their hearts on gain, and cared little for the feelings of the players.

"You see he was right," whispered the red-whiskered squire to his neighbor; "my Lord has won the game in one hand." And so it was; in less than five minutes the party was over.

"Now for the conqueror," cried the Knight of Gwynne, who, somewhat nettled at a success which seemed to lessen the generous character of his own proposal, dealt the cards hastily, as if anxious to conclude.

"Now, Darcy, we have a better opportunity," said Lord Drogheda, smiling; "what say you to draw stakes as we stand?"

"Willingly, most willingly, my Lord. If a bad cause saps courage, I have reason to be low at heart. This foolish wager has cost me the loss of three nights' sleep, and if you are content—"

"But are these gentlemen here satisfied?" said Lord Drogheda; and an almost universal cry of "No" was the reply.

"Then if we are to play for the bystanders, my Lord, let us not delay them," said the Knight, as he took up his cards and began to arrange them.

"Darcy has it, by Jove!—the game is his," was muttered from one to another in the crowd behind his chair, and the report, gaining currency, was soon circulated in the larger room without.

"Have you anything heavy on it, Con?" said a fashionably dressed man to Heffernan, who endeavored to force his way through the crowd to where the Knight sat.

"Look at Heffernan!" said another. "They say he never bets; but mark the excitement of his face now!"

"What is it, Heffernan?" said the Knight, as the other leaned over his chair and tried to whisper something in his ear. "Is that a queen, my Lord? In that case I believe the game is mine.—What is it, Heffernan?" and he bent his ear to listen; then, suddenly dashing the cards upon the table, cried out, "Great Heaven! is this true?—the young fellow I met at Kilbeggan?"

"The same," whispered Heffernan, rapidly; "a brother officer of your son Lionel's—a cousin of Lord Castle-reagh's—a fine, dashing fellow, too."

"Where is he wounded?" asked Darcy, eagerly.

"Finish your game—I must tell you all about it," said Heffernan, folding up a letter which he had taken from his pocket a few minutes before.

"Your pardon, my Lord," said Darcy, with a look full of agitation; "I have just heard very bad news.—I play the knave." A murmur ran through the crowd behind him.

"You meant the king, I know, Knight," said Lord Drogheda, restoring the card to his hand as he spoke, but a loud expression of dissatisfaction arose from those at his side.

"You are right, my Lord, I did intend the king," said the Knight; "but these gentlemen insist upon the knave, and, if you'll permit me, I'll play it."

The whole fortune of the game hung upon the card, and, after a brief struggle, the Knight was beaten.

"Even so, my Lord," said the Knight, smiling calmly, "you have beaten me against luck; Fortune will not do everything. The Roman satirist goes even further, and says she can do nothing." He rose as he said these words, and looked around for Heffernan.

"If you want Con Heffernan, Knight," said one of the party, "I think he has gone down to the House."

"The very man," said Darcy. "Good-night, my Lord,—good-night, gentlemen all."

"I did not believe that anything could shake Darcy's nerve, but he certainly played that game ill," said a bystander.

"Heffernan could tell us more about it," said another; "rely on it, Master Con and the devil knew why that knave was played."

CHAPTER X
AN INTRIGUE DETECTED

Of all the evil influences which swayed the destinies of Ireland in latter days, none can compare, in extent of importance, with the fatal taste for prodigality that characterized the habits of the gentry. Reckless, wasteful extravagance, in every detail of life, suggested modes of acting and thinking at variance with all individual and, consequently, all national prosperity. Hospitality was pushed to profusion, liberality became a spendthrift habit. The good and the bad qualities of the Irish temperament alike contributed to this passion; there was the wish to please, the desire to receive courteously, and entertain with splendor within doors, and to appear with proportionate magnificence without.

A proud sense of what they deemed befitting their station induced the gentry to vie in expenditure with the richly endowed officials of the Government, and the very thought of prudence or foresight in matters of expense would have been stigmatized as a meanness by those who believed they were sustaining the honor of their country while sapping the foundation of its prosperity.

If we have little to plead in defence or in palliation of such habits, we can at least affirm that in many cases they were practised with a taste and elegance that shed lustre over the period. Unlike the vulgar displays of newly acquired wealth, they exhibited in a striking light the generous and high-spirited features of the native character, which deemed that nothing could be too good for the guest, nor any expenditure for his entertainment either too costly or too difficult. The fatal facility of Irish nature, and the still more ruinous influence of example, hurried men along on this road to ruin; and as political prospects grew darker, a reckless indifference to the future succeeded, in which little care was taken for the morrow, until, at last, thoughtless extravagance became a habit, and moneyed difficulties the lot of almost every family of Ireland.

That a gentry so embarrassed, and with such prospects of ruin before them, should have been easy victims to Ministerial seduction, is far less surprising than that so many were to be seen who could prefer their integrity to the rich bribes of Government patronage; and it is a redeeming feature of the day that amid all the lavish and heedless course of prodigality and excess there were some who could face poverty with stouter hearts than they could endure the stigma of gilded corruption: nor is it the history of every Parliament that can say as much.

Let us leave this theme, even at the hazard of being misunderstood, for the moment, by our reader, and turn to the Knight of Gwynne, who now was seated at his breakfast in a large parlor of his house in Henrietta Street. Sad and deserted as it seems now, this was in those days the choice residence of Irish aristocracy, and the names of peers and baronets on every door told of a class which, now, should be sought for in scattered fragments among the distant cities of the Continent.

The Knight was reading the morning papers, in which, amid the fashionable news, was an account of his own wager with Lord Drogheda, when a carriage drove up hastily to the door, and, immediately after, the loud summons of a footman resounded through the street.

While the Knight was yet wondering who this early visitor should prove, the servant announced Mr. Con Heffernan.

"The very man I wished to see," cried Darcy, eagerly; "tell me all about this unfortunate business. But, first of all, is he out of danger?"

"Quite safe. I understand, for a time, it was a very doubtful thing; Daly's surgery, it would seem, rather increased the hazard. He began searching for the ball regardless of the bleeding, and the young fellow was very near sinking under loss of blood."

"The whole affair was his doing!" said the Knight, impatiently. "How Mr. MacDonough could have found himself at *my* table is more than I can well imagine; that when he got there, something like this would follow, does not surprise me. Daly is really too bad. Well, well, I hoped to have set off for the abbey to-day, but I must stay here, I find; Drogheda is kind enough to let me redeem Ballydermot, and I must see Gleeson about it. It's rather a heavy blow just now."

"I am afraid I am not altogether blameless," said Heffernan, timidly. "I ought not to have mentioned that unlucky business till the game was over; but I thought your nerve was proof against anything."

"So it was, Heffernan," said the Knight, laughing, "some five-and-twenty years ago; but this shattered wreck has little remains of the old three-decker. I should have won that game."

"It's all past and over now, so never think more about it."

"Yes, I should have won the game. Drogheda saw my advantage: he went on with the very suit in my hand, and when he reached over for his snuff-box, his hand trembled like in an ague-fit."

"Come, don't let the thing dwell in your mind. There is another and a heavier game to play, and you 're certain to win there, if you do but like it."

"I don't clearly understand you," said Darcy, doubtingly.

"I'll be explicit enough, then," said Heffernan, taking a chair and seating himself directly in front of the Knight. "You know the position of the Government at this moment. They have secured a safe and certain majority,—the 'Union' is carried. When I say 'carried,' I mean that there is not a doubt on any reasonable mind but that the bill will pass. The lists show a majority of seven, perhaps eight, for the Ministry; and if they had but one in their favor, Pitt is determined to go through with it. Now, we all very well know how this has been done. Our people have behaved infamously, disgracefully,—there's no mincing the matter. You heard of Fox—?"

"No. What of him?"

"He has just accepted the escheatorship of—I forget what or where, but he vacates his seat to make room for Courtenay."

"Sam Courtenay?—Scrub, as we used to call him?"

"Scrub,—exactly so. Well, he comes in for Roscommon, and is to have a place under the new commission of twelve hundred a year. But to go back to what I was saying: Castlereagh has bought these fellows at his price or their own; some were dear enough, some were cheap. Barton, for instance, takes it out in Castle dinners, and has sold his birthright for the Viceroy's venison."

"May good digestion wait on appetite!" repeated Darcy, laughing.

"Well, let's not waste more time on them, but come to what I mean. Castlereagh wants to know how you mean to vote: some have told him you would be on his side; others, myself among the number, say the reverse. In fact, little as you may think about the matter, heavy bets are laid at this moment on the question, and—But I won't mention names; enough if I say a friend of ours—an old friend, too—has a thousand on it."

The Knight tapped his snuff-box calmly, and with his blandest smile begged Heffernan to proceed.

"Faith! I 've nearly told all I had to say. Every one well knows that, whatever decision you come to, it will be unbiassed by everything save your own conscientious sense of right; and as arguments are pretty nearly equal on the question,—for, in truth, after having heard and read most of what has been written or spoken on the point,—I'm regularly nonplussed on which side to see the advantage. The real question seems to be, Can we go on as we are?"

"I think not," observed the Knight, gravely. "A Parliament which has exhibited its venality so openly can have little pretension to public confidence."

"The very remark I made myself," cried Heffernan, triumphantly.

"The men who sell themselves to-day to the Crown will, if need be, sell themselves to-morrow to the mob."

"My own words, by Jove!—my very words."

"A dependent Parliament, attempting separate and independent legislation, means an absurdity."

"There is no other name for it," cried Heffernan, in ecstasy.

"I have known Ireland for something more than half a century now," said the Knight, with a touch of melancholy in his voice, "and yet never before saw so much of social disorder as at present, and perhaps we are only at the beginning of it. The scenes we have witnessed in France have been more bloody and more cruel, but they will leave less permanent results behind them than our own revolution; for such, after all, it is. The property of the country is changing hands, the old aristocracy are dying out, if not dead; their new successors have neither any hold on the affection of the people, nor a bond of union with each other. See what will come of it; the old game of feudalism will be tried by these men of yesterday, and the peasantry, whose reverence for birth is a religion, will turn on them, and the time is not very distant, perhaps, when the men who would not harm the landlord's dog will have little reverence for the landlord's self."

"You have drawn a sad picture," said Heffernan, either feeling or affecting to feel the truthfulness of the Knight's delineation.

"Our share in the ruin," said the Knight, rising, and pacing the room with rapid strides,—"our share is not undeserved. We had a distinct and defined duty to perform, and we neglected it; instead of extending civilization, we were the messengers of barbarism among the people."

"Your own estates, I have heard, are a refutation of your theory," interposed Heffernan, insinuatingly.

"My estates—" repeated the Knight; and then, stopping suddenly, with a changed voice, he said, "Heffernan, we have got into a long and very unprofitable theme; let us try back, if we can, and see whence we started: we were talking of the Union."

"Just so," said Heffernan, not sorry to resume the subject which induced his visit.

"I have determined not to vote on the measure," said the Knight, solemnly; "my reasons for the course I adopt I hope to be able to justify when the proper time arrives; meanwhile, it will prevent unnecessary speculation, and equally unnecessary solicitation, if I tell you frankly what I mean to do. Such is my present resolve."

The word "solicitation" fell from the Knight's lips with such a peculiar expression that Heffernan at once saw his own game was detected, and, like a clever tactician, resolved to make the best of his forced position.

"You have been frank with me, Knight; I'll not be less candid with *you*, I came here to convey to you a distinct offer from the Government,—not of any personal favor or advantage, *that*, they well knew, you would reject,—but, in the event of your support, to take any suggestion you might make on the new Bill into their serious and favorable consideration; to advise with you how, in short, the measure might be made to meet your views, and, so to say, admit you into conclave with the Cabinet."

"All this is very flattering," said the Knight, with a smile of evident satisfaction, "but I scarcely see how the opinions of a very humble country gentleman can weigh in the grave councils of a Government."

"The best proof is the fact itself," replied Heffernan, artfully. "Were I to tell you of other reasons, you might suspect me of an intention to canvass your support on very different grounds."

"I confess I'm in the dark; explain yourself more fully."

"This is a day for sincerity," said Heffernan, smiling, "and so, here it is: the Prince has taken a special liking to your son Lionel, and has given him his company."

"His company! I never heard of it."

"Strange enough that he should not have written to you on the subject, but the fact is unquestionable; and, as I was saying, he is a frequent guest at Carlton House, and admitted into the choice circle of his Royal Highness's parties: if, in the freedom of that intimacy with which he is honored by the Prince, the question should have arisen, how his father meant to vote, the fact was not surprising, no more than that Captain Darcy should have replied—"

"Lionel never pledged himself to control *my* vote, depend upon that, Mr. Heffernan," said the Knight, reddening.

"Nor did I say so," interposed Heffernan. "Hear me out: your son is reported to have answered, 'My father's family have been too trained in loyalty, sire, not to give their voice for what they believe the best interests of the empire: your Royal Highness may doubt his judgment, his honor will, I am certain, never be called in question.' The Prince laughed good-naturedly, and said, 'Enough, Darcy,—quite enough; it will give me great satisfaction to think as highly of the father as I do of the son; there is a vacancy on the staff, and I can offer you the post of an extra aide-de-camp.'"

"This is very good news,—the best I've heard for many a day, Heffernan; and for its accuracy—"

"Lord Castlereagh is the guarantee," added Heffernan, hastily; "I had it from his own lips."

"I'll wait on him this morning. I can at least express my gratitude for his Royal Highness's kindness to my boy."

"You'll not have far to go," said Heffernan, smiling.

"How so?—what do you mean?"

"Lord Castlereagh is at the door this moment in that carriage;" and Hefifernan pointed to the chariot which, with its blinds closely drawn, stood before the street door.

The Knight moved hastily towards the door, and then, turning suddenly, burst into a hearty laugh,—a laugh so racy and full of enjoyment that Heffernan himself joined in it, without knowing wherefore.

"You are a clever fellow, Hefifernan!" said the Knight, as he lay back in a deep-cushioned chair, and wiped his eyes, now streaming with tears of laughter, — "a devilish clever fellow! The whole affair reminds me of poor Jack Morris."

"Faith! I don't see your meaning," said Hefifernan, half fearful that all was not right.

"You knew Jack, — we all knew him. Well, poor Morris was going home one night, — from the theatre, I believe it was, — but, just as he reached Ely Place, he saw, by the light of a lamp, a gentlemanlike fellow trying to make out an address on a letter, and endeavoring, as well as he could, to spell out the words by the uncertain light. 'Devilish provoking!' said the stranger, half aloud; 'I wrote it myself, and yet cannot read a word of it.' 'Can I be of any service?' said Jack. Poor fellow! he was always ready for anything kind or good-natured. 'Thank you,' said the other; 'but I 'm a stranger in Dublin, — only arrived this evening from Liverpool, — and cannot remember the name or the street of my hotel, although I noted both down on this letter.' 'Show it to me,' said Jack, taking the document. But although he held it every way, and tried all manner of guesses, he never could hit on the name the stranger wanted. 'Never mind,' said Jack; 'don't bother yourself about it. Come home with, me and have an oyster, — I 'll give you a bed; 't will be time enough after breakfast to-morrow to hunt out the hotel.' To make short of it, the stranger complied; after all the natural expressions of gratitude and shame, home they went, supped, finished two bottles of claret, and chatted away till past two o'clock. 'You 'd like to get to bed, I see,' said Jack, as the stranger seemed growing somewhat drowsy, and so he rang the bell and ordered the servant to show the gentleman to his room. 'And, Martin,' said he, 'take care that everything is comfortable, and be sure you have a nightcap.' 'Oh! I 've a nightcap myself,' said the stranger, pulling one, neatly folded, out of his coat pocket. 'Have you, by G—d!' said Jack. 'If you have, then, you 'll not sleep here. A man that's so ready for a contingency has generally some hand in contriving it.' And so he put him out of doors, and never saw more of him. Eh, Heffernan, was Jack right?" And again the old man broke into a hearty laugh, in which Heffernan, notwithstanding his discomfiture, could not refrain from participating. "Well," said he, as he arose to leave the room, "I feel twenty years younger for that hearty laugh. It reminds me of the jolly days we used to have long ago, with Price Godfrey and Bagenal Daly. By the way, where is Bagenal now, and what is he doing?"

"Pretty much what he always was doing, — mischief and devilment," said the Knight, half angrily.

"Is he still the member for Old-Castle? I forget what fate the petition had."

"The fate of the counsel that undertook it is easily remembered," said the Knight. "Bagenal called him out for daring to take such a liberty with a man who had represented the borough for thirty years, and shot him in the hip. 'You shall have a plumper, by Jove,' said Bagenal; and he gave him one. Men grew shy of the case afterwards, and it was dropped, and so Bagenal still represents the place. Good-by, Heffernan; don't forget Jack Morris." And so saying, the Knight took leave of his visitor, and returned to his chair at the breakfast-table.

CHAPTER XI
THE KNIGHT AND HIS AGENT

The news of Lionel's promotion, and the flattering notice which the Prince had taken of him, made the Knight very indifferent about his heavy loss of the preceding evening. It was, to be sure, an immense sum; but as Gleeson was arranging his affairs, it was only "raising" so much more, and thus preventing the estate from leaving the family. Such was his own very mode of settling the matter in his own mind, nor did he bestow more time on the consideration than enabled him to arrive at this satisfactory conclusion.

If ever there was an agent designed to compensate for the easy, careless habits of such a principal, it was Mr. Gleeson, or, as he was universally known in the world of that day, "Honest Tom Gleeson." In him seemed concentrated all those peculiar gifts which made up the perfect man of business. He was cautious, painstaking, and methodical; of a temper which nothing could ruffle, and with a patience no provocation could exhaust; punctual as a clock, neither precipitate nor dilatory, he appeared prompt to the slow, and seemed almost tardy to the hasty man.

In the management of several large estates—he might have had many more if he would have accepted the charge—Mr. Gleeson had amassed a considerable fortune; but so devotedly did he attach himself to the interests of his employers, so thoroughly identify their fortunes with his own, that he gave little time to the cares of his immediate property. By his skill and intelligence many country gentlemen had emerged from embarrassments that threatened to engulf their entire fortunes; and his aid in a difficulty was looked upon as a certain guarantee of success. It was not very surprising if a man endowed with qualities like these should have usurped something of ascendency over his employers. To a certain extent their destiny lay in his hands. Of the difficulties by which they were pressed he alone knew either the nature or amount, while by what straits these should be overcome none but himself could offer a suggestion. If in all his dealings the most strict regard to honor was observable, so did he seem also inexhaustible in his contrivances to rescue an embarrassed or encumbered estate. There was often the greatest difficulty in securing his services, solicitation and interest were even required to engage him; but once retained, he applied his energies to the task, and with such zeal and acuteness that it was said no case, however desperate, had yet failed in his hands.

For several years past he had managed all the Knight's estates; and such was the complication and entanglement of the property, loaded with mortgages and rent-charges, embarrassed with dowries and annuities, that nothing short of his admirable skill could have supported the means of that expensive and wasteful mode of life which the Knight insisted on pursuing, and all restriction on which he deemed unfitting his station. If Gleeson represented the urgent necessity of retrenchment, the very word was enough to cut short the negotiation; until, at last, the agent was fain to rest content with the fruits of good management, and merely venture from time to time on a cautious suggestion regarding the immense expense of the Knight's household.

With all his guardedness and care, these representations were not always safe; for though the Knight would sometimes meet them with some jocular or witty reply, or some bantering allusion to the agent's taste for money-getting, at other times he would receive the advice with impatience or ill-humor, so that, at last, Gleeson limited all complaints on this score to his letters to Lady Eleanor, with whom he maintained a close and confidential correspondence.

This reserve on Gleeson's part had its effects on the Knight, who felt a proportionate delicacy in avowing any act of extravagance that should demand a fresh call for money, and thus embarrass the negotiation by which the agent was endeavoring to extricate the property.

If Darcy felt the loss of the preceding night, it was far more from the necessity of avowing it to Gleeson than from the amount of the money, considerable as it was; and he, therefore, set out to call upon him, in a frame of mind far less at ease than he desired to persuade himself he enjoyed.

Mr. Gleeson lived about three miles from Dublin, so that the Knight had abundant time to meditate as he went along, and think over the interview that awaited him. His revery was only broken by a sudden change from the high-road to the noiseless quiet of the neat avenue which led up to the house.

Mr. Gleeson's abode had been an ancient manor-house in the Gwynne family, a building of such antiquity as to date from the time of the Knights Templars; and though once a favored residence of the Darcys, had, from the circumstances of a dreadful crime committed beneath its roof,—the murder of a servant by his master,—been at first deserted, and subsequently utterly neglected by the owners, so that at last it fell into ruin and decay. The roof was partly fallen in, the windows shattered and broken, the rich ceilings rotten and discolored with damp; it presented an aspect of desolation, when Mr. Gleeson proposed to take it on lease. Nor was the ruin only within doors, but without; the ornamental planting had been torn up, or used as firewood; the gardens pillaged and overrun with cattle; and the large trees—among which were some rare and remarkable ones—were lopped and torn by the country people, who trespassed and committed their depredations without fear or impediment. Now, however, the whole aspect was changed; the same spirit of order that exercised its happy influence in the management of distant properties had arrested the progress of destruction here, and, happily, in sufficient time to preserve some of the features which, in days past, had made this the most beautiful seat in the county.

It was not without a feeling of astonishment that the Knight surveyed the change. An interval of twelve years—for such had been the length of time since he was last there—had worked magic in all around. Clumps had sprung up into ornamental groups, saplings become graceful trees, sickly evergreens that leaned their frail stems against a stake were now richly leaved hollies or fragrant laurustinas; and the marshy pond, that seemed stagnant with rank grass and duckweed, was a clear lake fed by a silvery cascade which descended in quaint but graceful terraces from the very end of the neat lawn.

In Darcy's eyes, the only fault was the excessive neatness perceptible in everything; the very gravel seemed to shine with a peculiar lustre, the alleys were swept clean, not even a withered leaf was suffered to disfigure them, while the shrubs had an air of trim propriety, like the self-satisfied air of a Sunday citizen.

The brilliant lustre of the heavy brass knocker, the white and spotless flags of the stone hall, and the immaculate accuracy of the staid footman who opened the door, were types of the prevailing tastes and habits of the proprietor. A mere glance at the orderly arrangement of Mr. Gleeson's study would have confirmed the impression of his strict notions and regularity of discipline: not a book was out of place; the boxes, labelled with high and titled names, were ranged with a drill-like precision upon the shelves; the very letters that lay in the baskets beside the table fell with an attention to staid decorum becoming the rigid habits of the place.

The Knight had some minutes to bestow in contemplation of these objects before Gleeson entered; he had only that morning arrived from a distant journey, and was dressing when the Knight was announced. With a bland, soft manner, and an air compounded of diffidence and self-importance, Mr. Gleeson made his approaches.

"You have anticipated me, sir," said he, placing a chair for the Knight; "I had ordered the carriage to call upon you. May I beg you to excuse the question, but my anxiety will not permit me to defer it: there is no truth, or very little, I trust, in the paragraph I've just read in Carrick's paper—"

"About a party at piquet with Lord Drogheda?" interrupted Darcy.

"The same."

"Every word of it correct, Gleeson," said the Knight, who, notwithstanding the occasion, could not control the temptation to laugh at the terrified expression of the agent's face.

"But surely the sum was exaggerated; the paper says, the lands and demesne of Ballydermot, with the house, furniture, plate, wine, equipage, garden utensils—"

"I'm not sure that we mentioned the watering-pots," said Darcy, smiling; "but the wine hogsheads are certainly included."

"A rental of clear three thousand four hundred and seventy-eight pounds, odd shillings, on a lease of lives renewable forever—pepercorn fine!" exclaimed Gleeson, closing his eyes, and folding his hands upon his breast, like a martyr resigning himself to the torture.

"So much for going on spades without the head of the suit!" observed the Knight; "and yet any man might have made the same blunder; and then, Heffernan, with his interruption,—altogether, Gleeson, the whole was mismanaged sadly."

"The greater, part of the land tithe free," moaned Gleeson to himself; "it was a grant from the Crown to your ancestor, Everard Darcy."

"If it was the king gave it, Gleeson, it was the queen lost it."

"The lands of Corrabeg, Dunragheedaghan, and Muscarooney, let at fifteen shillings an acre, with a right to cut turf on the Derryslattery bog! not to speak of Knocksadowd! lost, and no redemption!"

"Yes, Gleeson, that's the point I'm coming to; there is a proviso in favor of redemption, whenever your grief will permit you to hear it."

Gleeson gave a brief cough, blew his nose with considerable energy, and with an air of submissive sorrow apologized for yielding to his feelings. "I have been so many years, sir, the guardian—if I may so say—of that property that I cannot think of being severed from its interests without deep, very deep, regret."

"By Jove! Gleeson, so do I! you have no monopoly of the sorrow, believe me. I acknowledge, readily, the full extent of my culpability. This foolish bet came to pass at a dinner at Hutchison's,—it was the crowning point of a bragging conversation about play,—and Drogheda, it seems, booked it, though I totally forgot all about it. I'm certain he never intended to push the wager on me, but when reminded of it, of course I had nothing else for it but to express my readiness to meet him. I must say he behaved nobly all through; and even when Heffer-nan's stupid interruption had somewhat ruffled my nerves, he begged I would reconsider the card—he saw I had made a mistake—very handsome that!—his backers, I assure you, did not seem as much disposed to extend the courtesy. I relieved their minds, however, I stood by my play, and—"

"And lost an estate of three thousand—"

"Quite correct; I'm sure no man knows the rental better. And now, let us see how to keep it in the family."

The stare of amazement with which Gleeson heard these words might have met a proposition far more extravagant still, and he repeated the speech to himself, as if weighing every syllable in a balance.

"Yes, Gleeson, that was exactly what I said; now that we are engaged in liquidating, let us proceed with the good work. If I have given you enlarged occasion for the exercise of your abilities, I'm only acting like Peter Henessy,—old Peter, that held the mill at Brown's Barn."

The agent looked up with an expression in which all interest to learn the precedent alluded to was lost in astonishment at the levity of a man who could jest at such a moment.

"I see you never heard it, and, as the lawyers say, the rule will apply. I'll tell it to you. When Peter was dying, he sent for old Rush of the Priory to give him absolution; he would not have the parish priest, for he was a 'hard man,' as Peter said, with little compassion for human weakness, never loved pork nor 'poteen,' but seemed to have a relish for fasts and vigils. 'Rush will do,' said he to all the family applications in favor of the other,—'I 'll have Father Rush;' and so he had, and Rush came, and they were four hours at it, for Peter had a long score of reminiscences to bring up, and it was not without considerable difficulty, it is said, that Rush could apply the remedies of the Church to the various infractions of the old sinner. At last, however, it was arranged, and Peter lay back in bed very tired and fatigued; for, I assure you, Gleeson, whatever you may think of it, confessing one's iniquities is excessively wearying to the spirits. 'Is it all right, Father?' said he, as the good priest counted over the roll of ragged bank-notes that were to be devoted to the purchase of different masses and offerings. 'It will do well,' said Rush; 'make your mind easy, your peace is made now.' 'And are you sure it's quite safe?' said Peter; 'a pound more or less is nothing now compared to—what you know,'—for Peter was polite, and followed the poet's counsel. "'Tis safe and sure both,' said Rush; 'I have the whole of the sins under my thumb now, and don't fret yourself.' 'Take another thirty shillings then, Father,' said he, pushing the note over to him, 'and let Whaley have the two barrels of seed oats—the smut is in them, and they 're not worth sixpence; but, when we are at it, Father, dear, let us do the thing complete: what signifies a trifle like that among the rest?' Such was Peter's philosophy, Gleeson, and, if not very laudable as he applied it, it would seem to suit our present emergency remarkably well."

Gleeson vouchsafed but a very sickly smile as the Knight finished, and, taking up a bundle of papers from the table, proceeded to search for something amongst them.

"This loss was most inopportune, sir—"

"No doubt of it, Gleeson; it were far better had I won my wager," said the Knight, half testily; but the agent, scarce noticing the interruption, went on:—

"Mr. Lionel has drawn on me for seven hundred, and so late as Wednesday last I was obliged to meet a bill of his amounting to twelve hundred and eighty pounds. Thus, you will perceive that he has this year overdrawn his allowance considerably. He seems to have been as unlucky as yourself, sir."

Soft and silky as the accents were, there was a tincture of sarcasm in the way these words were uttered that did not escape Darcy's notice; but he made no reply, and appeared to listen attentively as the other resumed:—

"Then, the expenses of the abbey have been enormous this year; you would scarcely credit the outlay for the hunting establishment; and, as I learn from Lady Eleanor that you rarely, if ever, take the field yourself—"

"Never mind that, Gleeson," broke in the Knight, suddenly. "I 'll not sell a horse or part with a dog amongst them. My income must well be able to afford me the luxuries I have always been used to. I 'm not to be told that, with a rental of eighteen thousand a year—"

"A rental, sir, I grant you," said Gleeson, interrupting him; "you said quite correctly,—the rental is even more than you stated; but consider the charges on that rental,—the heavy sums raised on mortgages, the debt incurred by building, the two contested elections, your losses on the turf: these make sad inroads in the amount of your income."

"I tell you frankly, Gleeson," said the Knight, starting up and pacing the room with hasty steps, "I 've neither head nor patience for details of this kind. I was induced to believe that my embarrassments, such as they are, were in course of liquidation; that by raising two hundred and fifty thousand pounds at four-and-a-half, or even five per cent, we should be enabled to clear off the heavy debts, for which we are paying ten, twelve, — ay, by Jove! I believe fifteen per cent."

"Upon my word, I believe you do not exaggerate," said Gleeson, in a conciliating accent. "Hickman's bond, though nominally bearing six per cent, is actually treble that sum. He holds 'The Grove' at the rent of a cottier's tenure, and with the right of cutting timber in Clon-a-gauve wood, — a right he is by no means chary of exercising."

"That must be stopped, and at once," broke in Darcy, with a heightened color. "The old man is actually making a clearing of the whole mountain side; the last time I was up there, Lionel and I counted two hundred and eighteen trees marked for the hatchet. I ordered Finn not to permit one of them to be touched; to go with a message from me to Hickman, saying that there was a wide difference between cutting timber for farm purposes and carrying on a trade in rivalry with the Baltic. Oaks of twenty, eighty, ay, a hundred and fifty years' growth, the finest trees on the property, were among those I counted."

"And did he desist, sir?" asked Gleeson, with a half cunning look.

"Did he? — what a question you ask me! By Heavens! if he barked a sapling in that wood after my warning, I 'd have sent the Derrahinchy boys down to his place, and they would not have left a twig standing on his cockney territory. Devilish lucky he 'd be if they stopped there, and left him a house to shelter him."

"He's a very unsafe enemy, sir," observed Gleeson, timidly.

"By Jove! Gleeson, I think you are bent on driving me distracted this morning. You have hit upon perhaps the only theme on which I cannot control my irritability, and I beg of you, once and for all, to change it."

"I should never have alluded to Mr. Hickman, sir, but that I wished to remark to you that he is in a position which requires all our watchfulness; he has within the last three weeks bought up Drake's mortgage, and also Belson's bond for seventeen thousand, and, I know from a source of unquestionable accuracy, is at this moment negotiating for the purchase of

Martin Hamilton's bond, amounting to twenty-one thousand more; so that, in fact, with the exception of that small debt to Batty and Rowe, he will remain the sole creditor."

"The sole creditor!" exclaimed Darcy, growing pale as marble,—"Peter Hickman the sole creditor!"

"To be sure, this privilege he will not long enjoy," said Gleeson, with a degree of alacrity he had not assumed before; "when our arrangements are perfected with the London house of Bicknell and Jervis, we can pay off Hickman at once; he shall have a check for the whole amount the very same day."

"And how soon may we hope for this happy event, Gleeson?" cried the Knight, recovering his wonted voice and manner.

"It will not be distant now, sir; one of the deeds is ready at this moment, or at least will be to-morrow. On your signing it, we shall have some very trifling delays, and the money can be forthcoming by the end of the next week. The other will be perfected and compared by Wednesday week."

"So that within three weeks, or a month at furthest, Gieeson, we shall have cut the cable with the old pirate?"

"Three weeks, I trust, will see all finished; that is, if this affair of Ballydermot does not interfere."

"It shall not do so," cried the Knight, resolutely; "let it go. Drogheda is a gentleman at least, and if our old acres are to fall into other hands, let their possessor have blood in his veins, and he will not tyrannize over the people; but Hickman—"

"Very right, sir, Hickman might foreclose on the 24th of this month."

"Gieeson, no more of this; I 'm not equal to it," said the Knight, faintly; and he sat down with a wearied sigh, and covered his face with his hands. The emotion, painful as it was, passed over soon, and the Knight, with a voice calm and measured as before, said, "You will take care, Gieeson, that my son's bills are provided for; London is an expensive place, and particularly for a young fellow situated like Lionel; you may venture on a gentle—mind, a very gentle—remonstrance respecting his repeated calls for money; hint something about arrangements just pending, which require a little more prudence than usual. Do it cautiously, Gieeson; be very guarded. I remember when I was a young fellow being driven to the Jews by an old agent of my grandfather's; he wrote me a regular homily on thrift and economy, and to show I had benefited by the lesson, I went straightway and raised a loan at something very like sixty per cent."

"You may rely upon my prudence, sir," said Gieeson. "I think I can promise that Mr. Lionel will not take offence at my freedom. May I say Tuesday to wait on you with the deeds,—Tuesday morning?"

"Of course, whenever you appoint, I 'll be ready. I hoped to have left town this week; but these are too important matters to bear postponement. Tuesday, then, be it." And with a friendly shake-hands, they parted,— Gleeson, to the duties of his laborious life; the Knight, with a mind less at ease than was his wont, but still bearing no trace of discomposure on his manly and handsome countenance.

CHAPTER XII
A FIRST VISIT

"Whenever Captain Forester is quite able to bear the fatigue, Sullivan, — mind that you say 'quite able,' — it will give me much pleasure to receive him."

Such was the answer Lady Eleanor Darcy returned to a polite message from the young officer, expressing his desire to visit Lady Eleanor and thank her for the unwearied kindness she had bestowed on him during his illness.

Lady Eleanor and her daughter were seated in the same chamber in which they have already been introduced to the reader. It was towards the close of a dark and gloomy day, the air heavy and overcast towards the land, while, over the sea, masses of black, misshapen cloud were drifted along hurriedly, the presage of a coming storm. The pine wood blazed brightly on the wide hearth, and threw its mellow lustre over the antique carvings and the porcelain ornaments of the chamber, contrasting the glow of in-door comfort with the bleak and cheerless look of all without, where the crashing noise of breaking branches mingled with the yet sadder sound of the swollen torrent from the mountain.

It may be remarked that persons who have lived much on the seaside, and near a coast abounding in difficulties or dangers, are far more susceptible of the influences of weather than those who pass their lives inland. Storm and shipwreck become, in a measure, inseparably associated. The loud beating of the waves upon the rocky shore, the deafening thunder of the swollen breakers, speak with a voice to *their* hearts, full of most meaning terror. The moaning accents of the spent wind, and the wailing cry of the petrel, awake thoughts of those who journey over "the great waters," amid perils more dreadful than all of man's devising.

Partly from these causes, partly from influences of a different kind, both mother and daughter felt unusually sad and depressed, and had sat for a long interval without speaking, when Forester's message was delivered, requesting leave to pay his personal respects.

Had the visit been one of mere ceremony, Lady Eleanor would have declined it at once; her thoughts were wandering far away, engrossed by topics of dear and painful interest, and she would not have constrained herself to change their current and direction for an ordinary matter of conventional intercourse. But this was a different case; it was her son Lionel's friend, his chosen companion among his brother officers, the guest, too, who, wounded and almost dying beneath her roof, had been a charge of intense anxiety to her for weeks past.

"There is something strange, Helen, is there not, in this notion of acquaintanceship with one we have never seen; but now, after weeks of watching and inquiry, after nights of anxiety and days of care, I feel as if I ought to be very intimate with this same friend of Lionel's."

"It is more for that very reason, Mamma, and simply because he is Lionel's friend."

"No, my dear child, not so; it is the tie that binds us to all for whom we have felt interested, and in whose sorrows we have taken a share. Lionel has doubtless many friends in his regiment, and yet it is very unlikely any of them would cause me even a momentary impatience to see and know what they are like."

"And do you confess to such in the present case?" said Helen, smiling.

"I own it, I have a strange feeling of half curiosity, and should be disappointed if the real Captain Forester does not come up to the standard of the ideal one."

"Captain Forester, my Lady," said Sullivan, as he threw open the door of the apartment, and, with a step which all his efforts could not render firm, and a frame greatly reduced by suffering, he entered. So little was he prepared for the appearance of the ladies who now stood to receive him, that, despite his habitual tact, a slight expression of surprise marked his features, and a heightened color dyed his cheek as he saluted them in turn.

With an air which perfectly blended kindliness and grace, Lady Eleanor held out her hand, and said, "My daughter, Captain Forester;" and then, pointing to a chair beside her own, begged of him to be seated. The unaccustomed exertion, the feeling of surprise, and the nervous irritability of convalescence, all conspired to make Forester ill at ease, and it was with a low, faint sigh he sank into the chair.

"I had hoped, madam," said he, in a weak and tremulous accent,—"I had hoped to be able to speak my gratitude to you,—to express at least some portion of what I feel for kindness to which I owe my life; but the greatness of the obligation would seem too much for such strength as mine. I must leave it to my mother to say how deeply your kindness has affected us."

The accents in which these few words were uttered, particularly that which marked the mention of his mother, seemed to strike a chord in Lady Eleanor's heart, and her hand trembled as she took from Forester a sealed letter which he withdrew from another.

"Julia Wallincourt," said Lady Eleanor, unconsciously reading half aloud the signature on the envelope of the letter.

"My mother, madam," said Forester, bowing.

"The Countess of Wallincourt!" exclaimed Lady Eleanor, with a heightened color and a look of excited and even anxious import.

"Yes, madam, the widowed Countess of the Earl of Wallincourt, late Ambassador at Madrid; am I to have the happiness of hearing that my mother is known to you?"

"I had, sir, the pleasure,—the honor of meeting Lady Julia D'Esterre; to have enjoyed that pleasure, even once, is quite enough never to forget it." Then, turning to her daughter, she added: "You have often heard me speak of Lady Julia's beauty, Helen; she was certainly the most lovely person I ever saw, but the charm of her appearance was even inferior to the fascination of her manner."

"She retains it all, madam," cried Forester, as his eyes sparkled with enthusiastic delight; "she has lost nothing of that power of captivating; and as for beauty, I confess I know nothing higher in that quality than what conveys elevation of sentiment, with purity and tenderness of heart: this she possesses still."

"And your elder brother, Captain Forester?" inquired Lady Eleanor, with a manner intended to express interest, but in reality meant to direct the conversation into another channel.

"He is in Spain still, madam; he was Secretary of the Embassy when my father died, and replaced him in the mission."

There was a pause, a long and chilling silence, after these words, that each party felt embarrassing, and yet were unable to break; at last Forester, turning towards Helen, asked "when she had heard from her brother?"

"Not for some days past," replied she; "but Lionel is such an irregular correspondent, we think nothing of his long intervals of silence. You have heard of his promotion, perhaps?"

"No; pray let me learn the good news."

"He has got his company. Some very unexpected—I might say, from Lionel's account, some very inexplicable—piece of good fortune has aided his advancement, and he now writes himself, greatly to his own delight, it would appear, Captain Darcy."

"His Royal Highness the Prince of Wales," said Lady Eleanor, with a look of pride, "has been pleased to notice my son, and has appointed him an extra aide-de-camp."

"Indeed!" cried Forester; "I am rejoiced at it, with all my heart. I always thought, if the Prince were to know him, he 'd be charmed with his agreeability. Lionel has the very qualities that win their way at Carlton House: buoyant spirit, courtly address, tact equal to any emergency,—all these are his; and the Prince likes to see handsome fellows about his Court. I am overjoyed at this piece of intelligence."

There was a hearty frankness with which he spoke this that captivated both mother and daughter.

There are few more winning traits of human nature than the unaffected, heartfelt admiration of one young man for the qualities and endowments of another, and never are they more likely to meet appreciation than when exhibited in presence of the mother of the lauded one. And thus the simple expression of Forester's delight at his friend's advancement went further to exalt himself in the good graces of Lady Eleanor than the display of any powers of pleasing, however ingeniously or artfully exercised.

As through the openings of a dense wood we come unexpectedly upon a view of a wide tract of country, unfolding features of landscape unthought of and unlooked for, so occasionally doth it happen that, in conversation, a chance allusion, a mere word, will develop sources of interest buried up to that very moment, and display themes of mutual enjoyment which were unknown before. This was now the case. Lionel's name, which evoked the mother's pride and the sister's affection, called also into play the generous warmth of Forester's attachment to him.

Thus pleasantly glided on the hours, and none remarked how time was passing, or even heeded the howling storm that raged without, while anecdotes and traits of Lionel were recorded, and comments passed upon his character and temper such as a friend might utter and a mother love to hear.

At last Forester rose. More than once during the interview a consciousness crossed his mind that he was outstaying the ordinary limits of a visit; but at each moment some observation of Lady Eleanor or her daughter, or some newly remembered incident in Lionel's career, would occur, and delay his departure. At last he stood up, and, warned by the thickening darkness of how time had sped, was endeavoring to mutter some words of apology, when Lady Eleanor interrupted him with,—

"Pray do not let us suppose you felt the hours too long, Captain Forester; the theme you selected will always make my daughter and myself insensible to the lapse of time. If I did not fear we should be trespassing on both your kindness and health together, I should venture to request you would dine with us."

Forester's sparkling eyes and flushed cheek replied to the invitation before he had words to say how gladly he accepted it.

"I feel more reconciled to making this request, sir," said Lady Eleanor, "because in your present state of weakness you cannot enjoy the society of a pleasanter party, and it is a fortunate thing that you can combine a prudent action with a kind one."

Forester appreciated the flattery of the remark, and, with a broken acknowledgment of its import, moved towards the door.

"No, no," said Lady Eleanor, "pray don't think of dressing; you have all the privilege of an invalid, and a—friend also."

The pause which preceded the word brought a slight blush into her cheek, but when it was uttered, she seemed to have resumed her self-possession.

"We shall leave you now with the newspapers, which I suppose you are longing to look at, and join you at the dinner-table." And as she spoke, she took her daughter's arm and passed into an adjoining room, leaving Forester in one of those pleasant reveries which so often break in upon the hours of returning health, and compensate for all the sufferings of a sick-bed.

"How strange and how unceasing are the anomalies of Irish life!" thought he, as he sat alone, ruminating on the past. "Splendor, poverty, elevation of sentiment, savage ferocity, delicacy the most refined, barbarism the most revolting, pass before the mind's eye in the quick succession of the objects in a magic lantern. Here, in these few weeks, what characters and incidents have been revealed to me! and how invariably have I found myself wrong in every effort to decipher them! Nor are the indications of mind and temper in themselves so very singular, as the fact of meeting them under circumstances and in situations so unlikely. For instance, who would have expected to see a Lady Eleanor Darcy here, in this wild region, with all the polished grace and dignity of manner the best circles alone possess; and her daughter, haughtier, perhaps, than the mother, more reserved, more timid it may be, and yet with all the elegance of a Court in every gesture and every movement. Lionel told me she was handsome,—he might have said downright beautiful. Where were these, fascinations nurtured and cultivated? Is it here, on the margin of this lonely bay, amid scenes of reckless dissipation?"

Of this kind were his musings; nor, amid them all, did one thought obtrude of the cause which threw him first into such companionship, nor of that mission, to discharge which was the end and object of his coming.

CHAPTER XIII
A TREATY REJECTED

Forester's recovery was slow, at least so his friends in the capital thought it, for to each letter requiring to know when he might be expected back again, the one reply forever was returned, "As soon as he felt able to leave Gwynne Abbey." Nor was the answer, perhaps, injudiciously couched.

From the evening of his first introduction to Lady Eleanor and her daughter, his visits were frequent, sometimes occupying the entire morning, and always prolonged far into the night. Never did an intimacy make more rapid progress; so many tastes and so many topics were in common to all, for while the ladies had profited by reading and study in matters which he had little cultivated, yet the groundwork of an early good education enabled him to join in discussions, and take part in conversation which both interested at the time, and suggested improvement afterward; and if Lady Eleanor knew less of the late events which formed the staple of London small-talk, she was well informed on the characters and passages of the early portion of the reign, which gave all the charm of a history to reminiscences purely personal.

With the wits and distinguished men of that day she had lived in great intimacy, and felt a pride in contrasting the displays of intellectual wealth, so common then, with the flatter and more prosaic habita since introduced into society. "Eccentricities and absurdities," she would say, "have replaced in the world the more brilliant exhibitions of cultivated and gifted minds, and I must confess to preferring the social qualities of Horace Walpole to the exaggerations of Bagenal Daly, or the ludicrous caprices of Buck Whaley."

"I think Mr. Daly charming, for my part," said Helen, laughing. "I'm certain that he is a miracle of truth, as he is of adventure; if everything he relates is not strictly accurate and matter of fact, it is because the real is always inferior to the ideal. The things *ought* to have happened as he states."

"It is, at least, *ben trovato*," broke in Forester; "yet I go further, and place perfect confidence in his narratives, and truly I have heard some strange ones in our morning rides together."

"I suspected as much," said Lady Eleanor, "a new listener is such a boon to him; so, then, you have heard how he carried away the Infanta of Spain, compelled the Elector of Saxony to take off his boots, made the Doge of Venice drunk, and instructed the Pasha of Trebizond in the mysteries of an Irish jig."

"Not a word of these have I heard as yet."

"Indeed! then what, in all mercy, has he been talking of,—India, China, or North America, perhaps?"

"Still less; he has never wandered from Ireland and Irish life, and I must say, as far as adventure and incident are concerned, it would have been quite unnecessary for him to have strayed beyond it."

"You are perfectly right there," said Lady Eleanor, with some seriousness in the tone; "our home anomalies may shame all foreign wonders: he himself could scarcely find his parallel in any land."

"He has a sincere affection for Lionel, Mamma," said Helen, in an accent of deprecating meaning.

"And that very same regard gave the bias to Lionel's taste for every species of absurdity! Believe me, Helen, Irish blood is too stimulating an ingredient to enter into a family oftener than once in four generations. Mr. Daly's has been unadulterated for centuries, and the consequence is, that, although neither deficient in strong sense or quick perception, he acts always on the impulse that precedes judgment, and both his generosity and his injustice outrun the mark."

"I love that same rash temperament," said Helen, flushing as she spoke; "it is a fine thing to see so much of warm and generous nature survive all that he must have seen of the littleness of mankind."

"There! Captain Forester, there! Have I not reason on my side? You thought me very unjust towards poor Mr. Daly,—I know you did; but it demands all my watchfulness to prevent him being equally the model for my daughter, as he is for my son's imitation."

"There are traits in his character any might well be proud to imitate," said Helen, warmly; "his life has been a series of generous, single-minded actions; and," added she, archly "if Mamma thinks it prudent and safe to warn her children against some of Mr. Daly's eccentricities, no one is more ready to acknowledge his real worth than she is."

"Helen is right," said Lady Eleanor; "if we could always be certain that Mr. Daly's imitators would copy the truly great features of his character, we might forgive them falling into his weaknesses; and now, can any one tell me why we have not seen him for some days past? He is in the Abbey?"

"Yes, we rode out together yesterday morning to look at the wreck near the Sound of Achill; strange enough, I only learned from a chance remark of one of the sailors that Daly had been in the boat, the night before, that took the people off the wreck."

"So like him!" exclaimed Helen, with enthusiasm.

"He is angry with me, I know he is," said Lady Eleanor, musingly. "I asked his advice respecting the answer I should send to a certain letter, and then rejected the counsel. He would have forgiven me had I run counter to his opinions without asking; but when I called him into consultation, the offence became a grave one."

"I declare, Mamma, I side with him; his arguments were clear, strong, and unanswerable, and the best proof of it is, you have never had the courage to follow your own determination since you listened to him."

"I have a great mind to choose an umpire between us. What say you, Captain Forester, will you hear the case? Helen shall take Mr. Daly's side; I will make my own statement."

"It's a novel idea," said Helen, laughing, "that the umpire should be selected by one of the litigating parties."

"Then you doubt my impartiality, Miss Darcy?"

"If I am to accept you as a judge, I 'll not prejudice the Court against myself, by avowing my opinions of it," said she, archly.

"When I spoke of your arbitration, Captain Forester," said Lady Eleanor, "I really meant fairly, for upon all the topics we have discussed together, politics, or anything bordering on political opinions, have never come uppermost; and, up to this moment, I have not the slightest notion what are your political leanings, Whig or Tory."

"So the point in dispute is a political one?" asked Forester, cautiously.

"Not exactly," interposed Helen; "the policy of a certain reply to a certain demand is the question at issue; but the advice of any party in the matter might be tinged by his party leanings, if he have any."

"If I judge Captain Forester aright, he has troubled his head very little about party squabbles," said Lady Eleanor; "and in any case, he can scarcely take a deep interest in a question which is almost peculiarly Irish."

Forester bowed,—partly in pretended acquiescence of this speech, partly to conceal a deep flush that mounted suddenly to his cheek; for he felt by no means pleased at a remark that might be held to reflect on his political knowledge.

"Be thou the judge, then," said Lady Eleanor. "And, first of all, read that letter." And she took from her work-box her cousin Lord Netherby's letter, and handed it to Forester.

"I reserve my right to dispute that document being evidence," said Helen, laughing; "nor is there any proof of the handwriting being Lord Netherby's. Mamma herself acknowledges she has not heard from him for nearly twenty years."

This cunning speech, meant to intimate the precise relation of the two parties, was understood at once by Forester, who could with difficulty control a smile, although Lady Eleanor looked far from pleased.

There was now a pause, while Forester read over the long letter with due attention, somewhat puzzled to conceive to what particular portion of it the matter in dispute referred.

"You have not read the postscript," said Helen, as she saw him folding the letter, without remarking the few concluding lines.

Forester twice read over the passage alluded to, and at once whatever had been mysterious or difficult was revealed before him. Lord Netherby's wily temptation was made manifest, not the less palpably, perhaps, because the reader was himself involved in the very same scheme.

"You have now seen my cousin's letter," said Lady Eleanor, "and the whole question is whether the reply should be limited to a suitable acknowledgment of its kind expressions, and a grateful sense of the Prince's condescension, or should convey—"

"Mamma means," interrupted Helen, laughingly,—"Mamma means, that we might also avow our sincere gratitude for the rich temptation offered in requital of my father's vote on the 'nion.'"

"No minister would dare to make such a proposition to the Knight of Gwynne," said Lady Eleanor, haughtily.

"Ministers are very enterprising nowadays, Mamma," rejoined Helen; "I have never heard any one speak of Mr. Pitt's cowardice, and Lord Castlereagh has had courage to invite old Mr. Hickman to dinner!"

Forester would gladly have acknowledged his relationship to the Secretary, but the moment seemed unpropitious, and the avowal would have had the semblance of a rebuke; so he covered his confusion by a laugh, and said nothing.

"We can scarcely contemn the hardihood of a Government that has made Crofton a bishop, and Hawes a general," said Helen, with a flashing eye and a lip curled in superciliousness. "Nothing short of a profound reliance on the piety of the Church and the bravery of the Army would support such a policy as that!"

Lady Eleanor seemed provoked at the hardy tone of Helen's speech; but the mother's look was proud, as she gazed on the brilliant expression of her daughter's beauty, now heightened by the excitement of the moment.

"Is it not possible, Miss Darcy," said Forester, in a voice at once timid and insinuating, — "is it not possible that the measure contemplated by the Government may have results so beneficial as to more than compensate for evils like these?"

"A Jesuit, or a Tory, or both," cried Helen. "Mamma, you have chosen your umpire most judiciously; his is exactly the impartiality needed."

"Nay, but hear me out," cried the young officer, whose cheek was crimsoned with shame. "If the measure be a good one, — well, let me beg the question, if it be a good one—and yet, the time for propounding it is either inopportune or unfortunate, and, consequently, the support it might claim on its own merits be withheld either from prejudice, party connection, or any similar cause, — you would not call a ministry culpable who should anticipate the happy working of a judicious Act, by securing the assistance of those whose convictions are easily won over, in preference to the slower process of convincing the men of more upright and honest intentions."

"You have begged so much in the commencement, and assumed so much in the conclusion, sir, that I am at a loss to which end of your speech to address my answer; but I will say this much: it is but sorry evidence of a measure's goodness when it can only meet with the approval of the venal. I don't prize the beauty so highly that is only recognized by the blind man."

"Distorted vision, Miss Darcy, may lead to impressions more erroneous than even blindness."

"I may have the infirmity you speak of," said she, quickly, "but assuredly I'll not wear Government spectacles to correct it."

If Forester was surprised at finding a young lady so deeply interested in a political question, he was still more so on hearing the tone of determination she spoke in, and would gladly, had he known how, have given the conversation a less serious turn.

"We have been all the time forgetting the real question at issue," said Lady Eleanor. "I 'm sure I never intended to listen to a discussion on the merits or demerits of the Union, on which you both grow so eloquent; will you then kindly return to whence we started, and advise me as to the reply to this letter."

"I do not perceive any remarkable difficulty, madam," said Forester, addressing himself exclusively to Lady Eleanor. "The Knight of Gwynne has doubtless strong opinions on this question; they are either in favor of, or adverse to, the Government views: if the former, your reply is easy and most satisfactory; if the latter, perhaps he would condescend to explain the nature of his objections, to state whether it be to anything in the detail of the measure he is adverse to, or to the principle of the Bill itself. A declaration like this will open a door to negotiation, without the slightest imputation on either side. A minister may well afford to offer his reasons for any line of policy to one as eminent in station and ability as the Knight of Gwynne, and I trust I am not indiscreet in assuming that the Knight would not be derogating from that station in listening to, and canvassing, such explanations."

"Lord Castlereagh, 'aut—-,'" said Helen, starting up from her seat, and making a low courtesy before Forester, who, feeling himself in a measure detected, blushed till his face became scarlet.

"My dear Helen, at this rate we shall never—But what is this?—who have we here?"

This sudden exclamation was caused by the appearance of a small four-wheeled carriage drawn up at the gate of the flower-garden, from which old Hickman's voice could now be heard, inquiring if Lady Eleanor were at home.

"Yes, Sullivan," said she, with a sigh, "and order luncheon." Then, as the servant left the room, she added, "I am always better pleased when the visits of that family are paid by the old gentleman, whom I prefer to the son or the grandson. They are better performers, I admit, but he is an actor of nature's own making."

"Do you know him, Captain Forester?" asked Helen.

But, before he could reply, the door was opened, and Sullivan announced, by his ancient title, "Doctor Hickman."

Strange and grotesque as in every respect he looked, the venerable character of old age secured him a respectful, almost a cordial, reception; and as Lady Eleanor advanced to him, there was that urbanity and courtesy in her manner which are so nearly allied to the expression of actual esteem. It was true, there was little in the old man's nature to elicit such feelings towards him; he was a grasping miser, covetousness and money-getting filled up his heart, and every avenue leading to it. The passion for gain had alone given the interest to his life, and developed into activity any intelligence he possessed. While his son valued wealth as the only stepping-stone to a position of eminence and rank, old Hickman loved riches for their own sake. The bank was, in his estimation, the fountain of all honor, and a strong credit there better than all the reputation the world could confer. These were harsh traits. But then he was old; long years of infirmity were bringing him each hour closer to the time when the passion of his existence must be abandoned; and a feeling of pity was excited at the sight of that withered, careworn face, to which the insensate cravings of avarice lent an unnatural look of shrewdness and intelligence.

"What a cold morning for your drive, Mr. Hickman," said Lady Eleanor, kindly. "Captain Forester, may I ask you to stir the fire? Mr. Hickman— Captain Forester."

"Ah, Miss Helen, beautiful as ever!" exclaimed the old man, as, with a look of real admiration, he gazed on Miss Darcy. "I don't know how it is, Lady Eleanor, but the young ladies never dressed so becomingly formerly. Captain Forester, your humble servant; I'm glad to see you about again,— indeed, I did n't think it very likely once that you'd ever leave the library on your own feet; Mac-Donough 's a dead shot they tell me—ay, ay!"

"I hope your friends at 'The Grove' are well, sir?" said Lady Eleanor, desirous of interrupting a topic she saw to be particularly distressing to Forester.

"No, indeed, my Lady; my son Bob—Mr. Hickman O'Reilly, I mean— God forgive me, I'm sure they take trouble enough to teach me that name—he's got a kind of a water-brash, what we call a pyrosis. I tell him it's the French dishes he eats for dinner, things he never was brought op to, concoctions of lemon juice, and cloves, and saffron, and garlic, in meat roasted—no, but stewed into chips."

"You prefer our national cookery, Mr. Hickman?"

"Yes, my Lady, with the gravy in it; the crag-end,—if your Ladyship knows what's the crag-end of a—"

"Indeed, Mr. Hickman," said Lady Eleanor, smiling, "I'm deplorably ignorant about everything that concerns the household. Helen affects to be very deep in these matters; but I suspect it is only a superficial knowledge, got up to amuse the Knight."

"I beg, Mamma, you will not infer any such reproach on my skill in *menage*. Papa called my *omelette à la curé* perfect."

"I should like to hear Mr. Hickman's judgment on it," said Lady Eleanor, with a sly smile.

"If it's a plain joint, my Lady, boiled or roasted, without spices or devilment in it, but just the way Providence intended—"

"May I ask, sir, how you suppose Providence intended to recommend any particular kind of cookery?" said Helen, seriously.

"Whatever is most natural, most simple, the easiest to do," stammered out Hickman, not over pleased at being asked for an explanation.

"Then the Cossack ranks first in the art," exclaimed Forester; "for nothing can be more simple or easier than to take a slice of a live ox and hang it up in the sun for ten or fifteen minutes."

"Them's barbarians," said Hickman, with an emphasis that made the listeners find it no easy task to keep down a laugh.

"Luncheon, my Lady," said old Tate Sullivan, as with a reverential bow he opened the folding-doors into a small breakfast parlor, where an exquisitely served table was laid out.

"Practice before precept, Mr. Hickman," said Lady Eleanor; "will you join us at luncheon, where I hope you may find something to your liking?"

As the old man seated himself at the table, his eye ranged over the cabinet pictures that covered the walls, the richly chased silver on the table, and the massive wine-coolers that stood on the sideboard, with an eye whose brilliancy betokened far more the covetous taste of the miser than the pleased expression of mere connoisseurship; nor could he recall himself from their admiration to hear Forester's twice-repeated question as to what he would eat.

"'T is elegant fine plate, no doubt of it," muttered he, below his breath; "and the pictures may be worth as much more—ay!"

The last monosyllable was the only part of his speech audible, and being interpreted by Forester as a reply to his request, he at once helped the old gentleman to a very highly seasoned French dish before him.

"Eh! what's this?" said Hickman, as he surveyed his plate with unfeigned astonishment; "if I did n't see it laid down on your Ladyship's table, I 'd swear it was a bit of Galway marble."

"It's a *gélatine truffée*, Mr. Hickman," said Forester, who was well aware of its merits.

"Be it so, in the name of God!" said Hickman, with resignation, as though to say that any one who could eat it might take the trouble to learn the name. "Ay, my Lady, that 's what I like, a slice of Kerry beef,—a beast made for man's eating."

"Mr. Hickman's pony is more of an epicure than his master," said Forester, as he arose from his chair and moved towards the glass-door that opened on the garden; "he has just eaten the top of your lemon-tree."

"And by way of dessert, he is now cropping my japonica," cried Helen, as she sprang from the room to rescue her favorite plant. Forester followed her, and Lady Eleanor was left alone with the doctor.

"Now, my Lady, that I have the opportunity,—and sure it was luck gave it to me,—would you give me the favor of a little private conversation?"

"If the matter be on business, Mr. Hickman, I must frankly own I should prefer your addressing yourself to the Knight; he will be home early next week."

"It is—and it is not, my Lady—but, there! they're coming back, now, and it is too late;" and so he heaved a heavy sigh, and lay back in his chair, as though worn out and disappointed.

"Well, then, in the library, Mr. Hickman," said Lady Eleanor, compassionately, "when you've eaten some luncheon."

"No more, my Lady; 'tis elegant fine beef as ever I tasted, and the gravy in it, but I'm not hungry now."

Lady Eleanor, without a guess as to what might form the subject of his communication, perceived that he was agitated and anxious; and so, requesting Forester and her daughter to continue their luncheon, she added: "And I have something to tell Mr. Hickman, if he will give five minutes of his company in the next room."

Taking a chair near the fire, Lady Eleanor motioned to the doctor to be seated; but the old man was so engaged in admiring the room and its furniture that he seemed insensible to all else. As his eye wandered over the many objects of taste and luxury on every side, his lips muttered unceasingly, but the sound was inarticulate.

"I cannot pledge myself that we shall remain long uninterrupted, Mr. Hickman," said Lady Eleanor, "so pray lose no time in the communication you have to make."

"I humbly ask pardon, my Lady," said the old man, in a voice of deep humility; "I'm old and feeble now, and my senses none of the clearest, — but sure it's time for them to be worn out; ninety-one I'll be, if I live to Lady-day." It was his habit to exaggerate his age; besides, there was a tremulous pathos in his accents to which Lady Eleanor was far from feeling insensible, and she awaited in silence what was to follow.

"Well, well," sighed the old man, "if I succeed in this, the last act of my long life, I'm well content to go whenever the Lord pleases." And so saying, he took from his coat-pocket the ominous-looking old leather case to which we have already alluded, and searched for some time amid its contents. "Ay! here it is—that is it—it is only a memorandum, my Lady, but it will show what I mean." And he handed the paper to Lady Eleanor.

It was some time before she had arranged her spectacles and adjusted herself to peruse the document; but before she had concluded, her hand trembled violently, and all color forsook her cheek. Meanwhile; the doctor sat with his filmy eyes directed towards her, as if watching the working of his spell; and when the paper fell from her fingers, he uttered a low "Ay," as though to say his success was certain.

"Two hundred thousand pounds!" exclaimed she, with a shudder; "this cannot be true."

"It is all true, my Lady, and so is this too;" and he took from his hat a newspaper and presented it to her.

"The Ballydermot property! The whole estate lost at cards! This is a calumny, sir,—the libellous impertinence of a newspaper paragraphist. I'll not believe it."

"'T's true, notwithstanding, my Lady. Harvey Dawson was there himself, and saw it all; and as for the other, the deeds and mortgages are at this moment in the hands of my son's solicitor."

"And this may be foreclosed —"

"On the 24th, at noon, my Lady," continued Hickman, as he folded the memorandum and replaced it in his pocket-book.

"Well, sir," said she, as, with a great effort to master her emotion, she addressed him in a steady and even commanding voice, "the next thing is to learn what are your intentions respecting this debt? You have not purchased all these various liabilities of my husband's without some definite object. Speak it out—what is it? Has Mr. Hickman O'Reilly's ambition increased so rapidly that he desires to date his letters from Gwynne Abbey?"

"The Saints forbid it, my Lady," said the old man, with a pious horror. "I 'd never come here this day on such an errand as that. If it was not to propose what was agreeable, you 'd not see me here—"

"Well, sir, what is the proposition? Let me hear it at once, for my patience never bears much dallying with."

"I am coming to it, my Lady," muttered Hickman, who already felt really ashamed at the deep emotion his news evoked. "There are two ways of doing it—" A gesture of impatience from Lady Eleanor stopped him, but, after a brief pause, he resumed: "Bear with me, my Lady. Old age and infirmity are always prolix; but I'll do my best."

It would be as unfair a trial of the reader's endurance as it proved to Lady Eleanor's, were we to relate the slow steps by which Mr. Hickman announced his plan, the substance of which, divested of all his own circumlocution and occasional interruptions, was simply this: a promise had been made by Lord Castlereagh to Hickman O'Reilly that if, through his influence, exercised by means of moneyed arrangements or otherwise, the Knight of Gwynne would vote with the Government on the "Union," he should be elevated to the Peerage, an object which, however inconsiderable in the old man's esteem, both his son and grandson had set their hearts upon. For this service they, in requital, would extend the loan to another period of seven years, stipulating only for some trifling advantages regarding the right of cutting timber, some coast fisheries, and other matters to be mentioned afterwards,—points which, although evidently of minor importance, were recapitulated by the old man with a circumstantial minuteness.

It was only by a powerful effort that Lady Eleanor could control her rising indignation at this proposal, while the very thought of Hickman O'Reilly as a Peer, and member of that proud "Order" of which her own haughty family formed a part, was an insult almost beyond endurance.

"Go on, sir," said she, with a forced composure which deceived old Hickman completely, and made him suppose that his negotiation was proceeding favorably.

"I'm sure, my Lady, it's little satisfaction all this grandeur would give me. I'd rather be twenty years younger, and in the back parlor of my old shop at Loughrea than the first peer in the kingdom."

"Ambition is not your failing, then, sir," said she, with a glance which, to one more quick-sighted, would have conveyed the full measure of her scorn.

"That it is n't, my Lady; but they insist upon it."

"And is the Peerage to be enriched by the enrolment of your name among its members? I thought, sir, it was your son."

"Bob — Mr. Hickman, I mean — suggests that I should be the first lord in the family, my Lady, because then Beecham's title won't seem so new when it comes to him. 'T is the only use they can make of me now — ay!" and the word was accented with a venomous sharpness that told the secret anger he had himself awakened by his remark.

"The Knight of Gwynne," said Lady Eleanor, proudly, "has often regretted to me the few opportunities he had embraced through life of serving his country; I have no doubt, sir, when he hears your proposal, that he will rejoice at this occasion of making an *amende*. I will write to him by this post. Is there anything more you wish to add, Mr. Hickman?" said she, as, having risen from her chair, she perceived that the old man remained seated.

"Yes, indeed, my Lady, there is, and I don't think I'd have the heart for it, if it was n't your Ladyship's kindness about the other business; and even now, maybe, it would take you by surprise."

"You can scarcely do that, sir, after what I have just listened to," said she, with a smile.

"Well, there's no use in going round about the bush, and this is what I mean. We thought there might be a difficulty, perhaps, about the vote; that the Knight might have promised his friends, or said something or other how he'd go, and would n't be able to get out of it so easily, so we saw another way of serving his views about the money. You see, my Lady, we considered it all well amongst us."

"We should feel deeply grateful, sir, to know how far this family has occupied your kind solicitude. But proceed."

"If the Knight does n't like to vote with the Government, of course there is no use in Bob doing it; so he'll be a Patriot, my Lady, — and why not? Ha! ha! ha! they'll be breaking the windows all over Dublin, and he may as well save the glass! — ay!"

"Forgive me, sir, if I cannot see how this has any reference to my family."

"I'm coming to it—coming fast, my Lady. We were thinking then how we could help the Knight, and do a good turn to ourselves; and the way we hit upon was this: to reduce the interest on the whole debt to five per cent, make a settlement of half the amount on Miss Darcy, and then, if the young lady had no objection to my grandson, Beecham—"

"Stop, sir," said Lady Eleanor; "I never could suppose you meant to offend me intentionally,—I cannot permit of your doing so through inadvertence or ignorance. I will therefore request that this conversation may cease. Age has many privileges, Mr. Hickman, but there are some it can never confer: one of these is the right to insult a lady and—a mother."

The last words were sobbed rather than spoken: affection and pride, both outraged together, almost choked her utterance, and Lady Eleanor sat down trembling in every limb, while the old man, only half conscious of the emotion he had evoked, peered at her in stolid amazement through his spectacles.

Any one who knew nothing of old Hickman's character might well have pitied his perplexity at that moment; doubts of every kind and sort passed through his mind as rapidly as his timeworn faculties permitted, and at last he settled down into the conviction that Lady Eleanor might have thought his demand respecting fortune too exorbitant, although not deeming the proposition, in other respects, ineligible. To this conclusion the habits of his own mind insensibly disposed him.

"Ay, my Lady," said he, after a pause, "'tis a deal of money, no doubt; but it won't be going out of the family, and that's more than could be said if you refuse the offer."

"Sir!" exclaimed Lady Eleanor, in a tone that to any one less obtusely endowed would have been an appeal not requiring repetition; but the old man had only senses for his own views, and went on:—

"They tell me that Mr. Lionel is just as free with his money as his father; throws it out with both hands, horse-racing and high play, and every extravagance he can think of. Well, and if that's true, my Lady, sure it 's well worth while to think that you 'll have a decent house to put your head under when your daughter's married to Beecham. He has no wasteful ways, but can look after the main chance as well as any boy ever I seen. This notion about Miss Helen is the only thing like expense I ever knew him take up, and sure"—here he dropped his voice to soliloquy—"sure, maybe, that same will pay well, after all—ay!"

"My head! my head is bursting with blood," sighed Lady Eleanor; but the last words alone reached Hickman's ears.

"Ay! blood's a fine thing, no doubt of it, but, faith, it won't pay interest on a mortgage; nor I never heard of it staying the execution of a writ! 'T is little good blood I had in my veins, and yet I contrived to scrape a trifle together notwithstanding—ay!"

"I do not feel myself very well, Mr. Hickman," said Lady Eleanor; "may I request you will send my daughter to me, and excuse me if I wish you a good morning."

"Shall I hint anything to the young lady about what we were saying?" said he, in a tone of most confidential import.

"At your peril, sir!" said Lady Eleanor, with a look that at once seemed to transfix him; and the old man, muttering his adieu, hobbled from the room, while Lady Eleanor leaned back in her chair, overcome by the conflict of her emotions.

"Is he gone?" said Lady Eleanor, faintly, as her daughter entered.

"Yes, Mamma; but are you ill? You look dreadfully pale and agitated."

"Wearied—fatigued, my dear, nothing more. Tell Captain Forester I must release him from his engagement to us to-day; I cannot come to dinner." And, so saying, she covered her eyes with her hand, and seemed lost in deep thought.

CHAPTER XIV
"THE MECHANISM OP CORRUPTION"

"Well, Heffernan," said Lord Castlereagh, as they sat over their wine alone in a small dining-room of the Secretary's Lodge,—"well, even with Hackett, we shall be run close. I don't fancy the thought of another division so nearly matched; our fellows don't see the honor of a Thermopylae."

"Very true, my Lord; and the desertions are numerous, as they always will be when men receive the bounty before they are enlisted."

"Yes; but what would you do? We make a man a Commissioner or a sinecurist for his vote,—he vacates his seat on taking office; and, instead of standing the brunt of another election, coolly says, 'That, differing as he must do from his constituents on an important measure, he restores the trust they had committed into his hands—'"

"'He hopes unsullied,'—don't forget that, my Lord."

"Yes,—'he hopes unsullied,—and prefers to retire from the active career of politics, carrying with him the esteem and regard of his former friends, rather than endanger their good opinion by supporting measures to which they are conscientiously opposed.'"

"Felicitous conjuncture, that unites patriotism and profit!" exclaimed Heffernan. "Happy man, that can draw tears from the Mob, and two thousand a year from the Treasury!"

"And yet I see no remedy for it," sighed the Secretary.

"There is one, notwithstanding; but it demands considerable address and skill. You have always been too solicitous about the estimation of the men you bought were held in,—always thinking of what would be said and thought of them. You pushed the system so far that the fellows themselves caught up the delusion, and began to fancy they had characters to lose. All this was wrong,—radically, thoroughly wrong. When the butcher smears a red streak round a lamb's neck,—we call it 'raddling' in Ireland, my Lord,— any child knows he 's destined for the knife; now, when you 'raddled' your flock, you wanted the world to believe you were going to make pets of them, and you said as much, and so often that the beasts themselves believed it, and began cutting their gambols accordingly. Why not have paraded them openly to the shambles? It was their bleating you wanted, and nothing else."

"You forget, Heffernan, how many men would have refused our offers if we had not made a show, at least, of respect for their scruples."

"I don't think so, my Lord; you offered a bonus on prudery, and hence you met nothing but coyness. I'd have taken another line with them."

"And what might that be?" asked Lord Castlereagh, eagerly.

"Compromise them," said Heffernan, sternly. "I never knew the man yet, nor woman either, that you could n't place in such a position of entanglement that every effort to go right should seem a struggle to do wrong; and *vice versa*. You don't agree with me! Well, my Lord, I ask you if, in your experience of public men, you have ever met one less likely to be captured in this way than my friend Darcy?"

"From what I have seen and heard of the Knight of Gwynne, I acknowledge his character has all those elements of frankness and candor which should except him from such an embarrassment."

"Well, he 's in the net already," said Heffernan, rubbing his hands gleefully.

"Why, you told me he refused to join us, and actually saw through your negotiation."

"So he did, and, in return for his keen-sightedness, I 've compromised him with his party,—you did n't perceive it, but the trick succeeded to perfection. When the Knight told me that he would not vote on the Union, or any measure pertaining to it, I waited for Ponsonby's motion, and made Holmes and Dawson spread the rumor at Daly's and through town that Darcy was to speak on the division, well knowing he would not rise. About eleven o'clock, just as Toler sat down, Prendergast got up to reply, but there was a shout of 'Darcy! Darcy!' and Prendergast resumed his seat amid great confusion. At that moment I left the bench beside you, and walked over to Darcy's side of the House, and whispered a few words in his ear—an invitation to sup, I believe it was; but while he was answering me, I nodded towards you, and, as I went down the steps, muttered loud enough to be heard, 'All right!' Every eye was turned at once towards him, and he, having no intention of speaking, nor having made any preparation, felt both confused and amazed, and left the House about five minutes afterwards, while Prendergast was bungling out his tiresome reply. Before Darcy reached the Club House, the report was current that he was bought, and old Gillespie was circumstantially recounting how that his title was 'Lord Darcy in England,'—'Baron Gwynne in that part of the United Kingdom called Ireland.'"

"Not even success, Heffernan," said the Secretary, with an air of severity, — "not even success will excuse a trick of this kind."

Heffernan looked steadily towards him, as if he half doubted the sincerity of the speech; it seemed something above or beyond his comprehension.

"Yes," said Lord Castlereagh, "you heard me quite correctly. I repeat it, advantages obtained in this fashion are too dearly purchased."

"What an admirable actor John Kemble is, my Lord," said Heffernan, with a quiet smile; "don't you think so?"

Lord Castlereagh nodded his assent: the transition was too abrupt to please him, and he appeared to suspect that it concealed some other object than that of changing the topic.

"Kemble," continued Heffernan, while he sipped his wine carelessly, — " Kemble is, I suspect strongly, the greatest actor we have ever had on the English stage. Have you seen him in 'Macbeth'?"

"Several times, and always with renewed pleasure," said the Secretary, gradually recovering from his reserve.

"What a force of passion he throws into the part! How terrible he makes the conflict between a great purpose and a weak nature! Do you remember his horror at the murderers who come to tell of Banquo's death? The sight of their bloody hands shocks him as though they were not the evidences of his own success."

Lord Castlereagh's calm countenance became for a second crimson, and his lip trembled with struggling indignation; and then, as if subduing the temptation of anger, he broke into a low, easy laugh, and with an imitation at Kemble's manner, called out, "There 's blood upon thy face!"

"Talking of a bloody hand, my Lord," said Heffernan, at once resuming his former easy jocularity, "reminds me of that Mr. Hickman, or Hickman O'Reilly, as the fashion is to call him: is he to have the baronetcy?"

"Not, certainly, if we can secure him without it."

"And I think we ought. It should be quite sufficient remuneration for a man like him to vote with the Government; his father became a Protestant because it was the gentlemanly faith; and I don't see why the son should not choose his politics on the same principle. Have you ever asked him to dinner, my Lord?"

"Yes, and his father, too. I have had the three generations, but I rather fear the party did not go off well. I had not in those days, Heffernan, the benefit of your admirable counsels, and picked my company unwisely."

"A great mistake with such men as these," said Heffernan, oracularly; "the guests should have been the cream of your Lordship's noble acquaintance. I 'd have had an Earl and a Marquis at either side of each of them; I 'd have turned their heads with noble names, and pelted them with the Peerage the whole time of dinner; when he had taken wine with a chamberlain and some lords-in-waiting, if your Lordship would only address him, in a voice loud enough to be heard, as 'O'Reilly,' referring to him on a point of sporting etiquette or country gentleman's life, I think you might spare the baronetage the honor of his alliance. Do you think, on a proper representation, and with due securities against the repetition of the offence, the chancellor would let himself be called 'Clare'? only for once, remember,—because I 'm satisfied, if this could be arranged, O'Reilly is yours."

"I 'd rather depute you to ask the question," said Lord Castlereagh, laughing; "assuredly I 'll not do so myself. But when do these people come to town?—to-morrow or next day, I suppose."

"On Friday next they will all be here. Old Hickman comes up to receive something like two hundred and twenty thousand pounds,—for Darcy has raised the money to pay off the incumbrances,—the son is coming for the debate, and the grandson is to be balloted for at Daly's."

"You have made yourself master of all their arrangements, Heffernan: may I ask if they afford you any clew to assisting us in our object?"

"When can you give a dinner, my Lord?" said the other.

"Any day after Wednesday,—nay, Wednesday itself; I might easily get off Brooke's dinner for that day."

"The sooner the better; time is of great consequence now. Shall we say Wednesday?"

"Be it so; now for the party."

"A small one: selectness is the type of cordiality. The invitation must be verbal, done in your own admirable way: 'Don't be late, gentlemen, for Beerhaven and Drogheda are to meet you, and you know they scold if the soup suffers,'—something in that style. Now let us see who are our men."

"Begin with Beerhaven and Drogheda, they are sure cards."

"Well, then, Massey Hamilton,—but he's only a commoner,—to be sure his uncle's a Duke, but, confound him, he never talks of him! I might draw him out about the Highlands and deer-stalking, and the Christmas revels at Clanchattagan; he 's three—Kilgoff four; he 's first-rate, and will discuss his noble descent till his carriage is announced. Loughdooner, five—"

"He's another bore, Heffernan."

"I know he is, my Lord; but he has seven daughters, and will consequently make up to young Beecham, who is a great prize in the wheel matrimonial. We shall want a Bishop to say grace; I think Dunmore is the man: he is the last of your Lordship's making, and can't refuse a short invitation."

"Six, and the three Hickmans nine, and ourselves eleven; now for the twelfth—"

"Darcy, of course," said Heffernan; "he must be asked, and, if possible, induced to come; Hickman O'Reilly will be far more easily managed if we make him suppose that we have already secured Darcy ourselves."

"He'll decline, Heffernan; depend upon it, he'll not come."

"You think he saw through my *ruse* in the House,—not a bit of it; he is the least suspecting man in Ireland, and I'll make that very circumstance the reason of his coming. Hint to him that rumor says he is coquetting with the Government, and he'll go any lengths to brave public opinion by confronting it,—that's Darcy, or I'm much mistaken in my man; and, to say truth, my Lord, it's an error I rarely fall into." A smile of self-satisfaction lit up Heffernan's features as he spoke; for, like many cunning people, his weak point was vanity.

"You may call me as a witness to character whenever you please," said Lord Castlereagh, who, in indulging the self-glorification of the other, was now taking his own revenge; "you certainly knew Upton better than I did."

"Depend upon it," said Heffernan, as he leaned back in his chair and delivered his words in a tone of authority,—"depend upon it, the great events of life never betray the man, it is the small, every-day dropping occurrences both make and mar him. I made Upton my friend for life by missing a woodcock he aimed at; *he* brought down the bird, and I bagged the sportsman. Ah, my Lord, the real science of life is knowing how to be gracefully in the wrong; how to make those slips that reflect on your own prudence, by exhibiting the superior wisdom of your acquaintances. Of the men who compassionate your folly or deplore your weakness, you may borrow money, from the fellows who envy your abilities and extol your capacity, you'll never get sixpence."

"How came it, Heffernan, that you never took office?" said Lord Castlereagh, suddenly, as if the idea forced itself abruptly upon him.

"I'll tell you, my Lord," replied Heffernan, speaking in a lower tone, and as if imparting a deep secret, "they could not spare me—that's the real fact—they could not spare me. Reflect, for a moment, what kind of thing the

Government of Ireland is; see the difficulty, nay, the impossibility, of any set of men arriving here fresh from England being able to find out their way, or make any guess at the leading characters about them: every retiring official likes to embarrass his successor,—that's all natural and fair; then, what a mass of blunders and mistakes await the newly come Viceroy or Secretary! In the midst of the bleak expanse of pathless waste I was the sign-post. The new players, who took up the cards when the game was half over, could know nothing of what trumps were in, or what tricks were taken. I was there to tell them all; they soon saw that I could do this; and they also saw that I wanted nothing from any party."

"That must be confessed on every hand, Heffernan. Never was support more generous and independent than yours! and the subject reminds me of a namesake, and, as I hear, a nephew of yours, the Reverend Joshua Heffernan,—is not that the name?"

"It is, my Lord, my nephew; but I'm not aware of having asked anything for him; I never—"

"But I did, Heffernan, and I do. He shall have the living of Drumslade; I spoke to the Lord-Lieutenant about it yesterday. There is a hitch somewhere, but we'll get over it."

"What may be the obstacle you allude to?" said Heffernan, with more anxiety than he wished to evince.

"Lord Killgobbin says the presentation was promised to his brother, for his influence over Rochfort."

"Not a bit of it, my Lord. It was I secured Rochfort. The case was this. He is separated from his wife, Lady Mary, who had a life annuity chargeable on Rochfort's pension from the Ordnance. Cook enabled me to get him twelve thousand pounds on the secret service list, provided he surrendered the pension. Rochfort was only too happy to do so, because it would spite his wife; and the next Gazette announced 'that the member for Dun raven had declared his intention of voting with the Government, but, to prevent even the breath of slander on his motives, had surrendered his retiring pension as a Store-keeper-General.' There never was a finer theme for editorial panegyric, and in good sooth your Lordship's press made the most of it. What a patriot!"

"What a scoundrel!" muttered Lord Castlereagh; and it would have puzzled a listener, had there been one, to say on whom the epithet was conferred.

"As for Killgobbin or his brother having influence over Rochfort, it's all absurd. Why, my Lord, it was that same brother married Rochfort to Lady Mary."

"That is conclusive," said Lord Castlereagh, laughing.

"Faith, I think so," rejoined Heffernan; "if you do recover after being hanged, I don't see that you want to make a friend of the fellow that pinioned your hands in the 'press-room.' If there's no other reason against Jos's promotion than this—"

"If there were, I 'd endeavor to overcome it," said Lord Castlereagh. "Won't you take more wine? Pray let's have another bottle."

"No more, my Lord; it's only in such safe company I ever drink so freely," said Heffernan, laughing, as he rose to say, "Good-night."

"You 'll take measures for Wednesday, then; that is agreed upon?"

"All settled," said Heffernan, as he left the room. "Good-bye."

"There's a building debt on that same living of seventeen hundred pounds," said Lord Castlereagh, musing; "I'll easily satisfy Killgobbin that we mean to do better for his brother."

"Take office, indeed!" muttered Heffernan, as he lay back in his carriage; "there 's something better than that,—governing the men that hold office, holding the reins, pocketing the fare, and never paying the breakage when the coach upsets. No, no, my Lord, you are a clever fellow for your years, but you must live longer before you measure Con Heffernan."

CHAPTER XV
THE KNIGHT'S NOTIONS OF FINANCE

Heffernan's calculations were all correct, and the Knight accepted Lord Castlereagh's invitation, simply because rumor attributed to him an alliance with the Government "It is a pity," said he, laughing, "so much good calumny should have so little to feed upon; so here goes to give it something."

Darcy had as little time as inclination to waste on the topic, as the whole interval was occupied in law business with Gleeson, who arrived each morning with a chariot full of parchments, and almost worried the Knight to death by reciting deeds and indentures, to one word of which throughout he could not pay the least attention. He affected to listen, however, as he saw how much Gleeson desired it, and he wrote his name everywhere and to everything he was asked.

"By Jove!" cried he, at last, "I could have run through the whole estate with less fatigue of mind or body than it has cost me to keep a hold of it."

Through all the arrangements, there was but one point on which he felt anxious, and the same question recurred at every moment, "This cannot compromise Lionel in any way?—this will lead to no future charge upon the estate after my death?" Indeed, he would not consent to any plan which in the slightest degree affected his son's interests, being determined that whatever his extravagances, the penalty should end with himself.

While these matters were progressing, old Hickman studiously avoided meeting the Knight; a sense of his discomfiture at the abbey—a fact he supposed must have reached Darcy's ears—and the conviction that his long-cherished game to obtain the property was seen through, abashed the old man, and led him to affect illness when the Knight called.

A pleasant letter which the post had brought from Lionel routed every other consideration from Darcy's mind. His son was coming over to see him, and bringing three or four of his brother officers to have a peep at "the West," and a few days' hunting with the Knight's pack. Every line of this letter glowed with buoyancy and high spirits; schemes for amusement alternating with the anticipated amazement of his English friends at the style of living they were to witness at Gwynne Abbey.

"We shall have but eight days with you, my leave from the Prince will go no further," wrote he; "but I know well how much may be done in that short space. Above all, secure Daly; I wish our fellows to see him particularly. I do not ask about the stable, because I know the horses are always in condition; but let Dan give the black horse plenty of work every day; and if the brown mare we got from Mulloch can be ridden by any one, she must have a saddle on her now. We hope to have four days' hunting; and let the woodcocks take care of themselves in the intervals, for we are bent on massacre."

The postscript was brief, but it surprised Darcy more than all the rest.

"Only think of my spending four days last week down in Essex with a worthy kinsman of my mother's, Lord Netherby: a splendid place, glorious shooting, and the best greyhounds I ever saw run. He understands everything but horses; but I have taken on me to enlighten him a little, and have sent down four grays from Guildfords' yesterday,—better than any we have in the Prince's stables; he is a fine fellow, though I did n't like him at first; a great courtier in his way, but *au fond* warm-hearted and generous. Keep my secret from my mother, but he intends coming over with us. Adieu! dear father. Look to Forester, don't let him run away before we arrive. Cut Dublin and its confounded politics. Netherby says the ministers have an immense majority,—the less reason for swelling or decreasing it.

"Yours ever,

"Lionel Darcy."

"And so our trusty and well-beloved cousin of Netherby is coming to visit us," said the Knight, musing. "Well, Lionel, I confess myself half of your mind. I did not like him at first: the better impression is yet to come. In any case, let us receive him suitably; and, fortunately, here's Gleeson to help the arrangement—Well, Gleeson, I hope matters are making some progress. Are we to see the last of these parchments soon? Here's a letter from my son. Read it, and you 'll see I must get back to 'the West' at once."

Gleeson perused the letter, and when he had finished, returned it into the Knight's hand without speaking.

"Can we conclude this week?" asked Darcy.

"There are several points yet, sir, of great difficulty. Some I have already submitted for counsel's opinion; one in particular, as regards the serving the notice of repayment: there would appear to be a doubt on this head."

"There can be none in reality," said Darcy, hastily. "I have Hickman's letter, in his own handwriting, averring his readiness to release the mortgage at any day."

"Is the document witnessed, and on a stamp?" asked Gleeson, cautiously.

"Of course it is not. Those are scarcely the forms of a note between two private gentlemen."

"It might be of use in equity, no doubt," muttered Gleeson, "or before a jury; but we have no time for these considerations now. The Attorney-General thinks—"

"Never mind the Attorney-General. Have we the money to repay? Well, does Hickman refuse to accept it?"

"He has not been asked as yet, sir," said Gleeson, whose business notions were not a little ruffled by this abrupt mode of procedure.

"And, in Heaven's name, Gleeson! why pester yourself and me with overcoming obstacles that may never arise? Wait on Hickman at once,— to-day. Tell him we are prepared, and desirous of paying off these incumbrances. If he objects, hear his objection."

"He will refer me to his solicitor, sir,—Mr. Kennedy, of Hume Street,—a very respectable man, no higher in the profession, but I may remark, in confidence, one who has no objection to a suit in equity or a trial at bar. It is not money Hickman wants, sir. He is perfectly satisfied with his security."

"What the devil is it, then? He's not Shylock, is he?" said Darcy, laughing.

"Not very unlike, perhaps, sir; but in the present instance, it is your influence with the Government he desires."

"But I have none, Gleeson,—actually none. No man knows that better than you do. I could not make a gauger or a tide-waiter to-morrow."

"But you might, sir,—you might make a peer of the realm if you wished it. Hickman knows this; and whatever scruples *you* might have in adopting the necessary steps, *his* conscience could never recognize them as worthy a moment's consideration."

"This is a topic I 'll scarcely discuss with him," said the Knight, proudly. "I never, so far as I know, promised to pay a percentage in my principles as well as in my gold. Mr. Hickman has a fair claim on the one; on the other, neither he nor any other man shall make an unjust demand. I am not of Christie Ford's mind," added he, laughingly. "He says, Gleeson, that if the English are bent on taking away *our* Parliament, the only revenge we have left is to spoil *their* peerage. This is but a sorry theme to joke upon, after all; and, to come back, what say you to trying my plan? I am to meet the old fellow at dinner, on Wednesday next, at Lord Castlereagh's."

"Indeed, sir!" said Gleeson, with a mixture of surprise and agitation greatly disproportioned to the intelligence.

"Yes. Why does that astonish you? The Secretary is too shrewd to neglect such men as these; they are the rising influences of Ireland."

Gleeson muttered a half assent; but evidently too much occupied with his own reflections to pay due attention to the Knight's remark, continued to himself, "on Wednesday!" then added aloud, "On Monday he is to be in Kildare. He told me he would remain there to receive his rents, and on Wednesday return to town. I believe, sir, there may be good counsel in your words. I 'll try on Monday. I 'll follow him down to Kildare, and as the papers relative to the abbey property are all in readiness, I'll endeavor to conclude that at once. So you are to meet at dinner?"

"That same dinner-party seems to puzzle you," said the Knight, smiling.

"No, not at all, sir," replied Gleeson, hurriedly. "You were desirous of getting home next week to meet Mr. Lionel—Captain Darcy I must call him; if this arrangement can be made, there will be no difficulty in your return. But of course you will not leave town before it is completed."

The Knight pledged himself to be guided by his man of business in all respects; but when they parted, he could not conceal from himself that Gleeson's agitated and troubled manner, so very unlike his usual calm deportment, boded difficulties and embarrassments which to his own eyes were invisible.

CHAPTER XVI
A HURRIED VISIT

It was on a severe night, with frequent gusts of stormy wind shaking the doors and window-frames, or carrying along the drifted flakes of snow with which the air was charged, that Lady Eleanor, her daughter, and Forester, were seated round the fire. All the appliances of indoor comfort by which they were surrounded seemed insufficient to dispel a sense of sadness that pervaded the little party. Conversation flowed not as it was wont, in its pleasant current, diverging here and there as fancy or caprice suggested; the sentences were few and brief, the pauses between them long and frequent; a feeling of awkwardness, too, mingled with the gloom, for, at intervals, each would make an endeavor to relieve the weariness of time, and in the effort show a consciousness of constraint.

Lady Eleanor lay back in her deep chair, and, with half-closed lids, seemed lost in thought. Helen was working at her embroidery, and, apparently, diligently too, although a shrewd observer might have remarked on the slow progress the work was making, and how inevitably her balls of colored worsted seemed bent on entanglement; while Forester sat silently gazing on the wood fire, and watching the bright sparks as they flitted and danced above the red flame; his brow was clouded, and his look sorrowful; not without reason, perhaps: it was to be his last evening at the abbey; the last of those hours of happiness which seemed all the fairer when about to part with them forever.

Lady Eleanor seemed grieved at his approaching departure. From the habit of his mind, and the nature of his education, he was more companionable to her than Lionel.

She saw in him many qualities of high and sterling value, and even in his prejudices she could trace back several of those traits which marked her own youth, when, in the pride of her English breeding, she would tolerate no deviation from the habits of her own country. It was true, many of these notions had given way since his residence at the abbey; many of his opinions had undergone modification or change, but still he was distinctively English.

Helen, who possessed no standard by which to measure such prejudices, was far less indulgent towards them; her joyous, happy nature—the heirloom of her father's house—led her rather to jest than argue on these topics, and she contrasted the less apt and ready apprehension of Forester with the native quickness of her brother Lionel, disadvantageous to the former. She was sorry, too, that he was going; more so, because his society was so pleasing to her mother, and that before him, Lady Eleanor exerted herself in a way which eventually reacted favorably on her own health and spirits. Further than this, her interest in him was weak.

Not so Forester: he was hopelessly, inextricably, in love, not the less so that he would not acknowledge it to himself; far more so because he had made no impression on the object of his passion. There is a period in every story of affection when the flame grows the brighter because unreflected, and seems the more concentrated because unreturned. Forester was in this precise stage of the malady; he was as much piqued by the indifference as fascinated by the charms of Helen Darcy. The very exertions he made for victory stimulated his own passion; while, in her efforts to interest or amuse him, he could not help feeling the evidence of her indifference to him.

We have said that the conversation was broken and interrupted; at length it almost ceased altogether, a stray remark of Lady Eleanor's, followed by a short reply from Forester, alone breaking the silence. Nor were these always very pertinent, inasmuch as the young aide-de-camp occasionally answered his own reflections, and not the queries of his hostess.

"An interesting time in Dublin, no doubt," said Lady Eleanor, half talking to herself; "for though the forces are unequal, and victory and defeat predestined, there will be a struggle still."

"Yes, madam, a brief one," answered Forester, dreamily, comprehending only a part of her remark.

"A brief and a vain one," echoed Lady Eleanor.

"Say, rather, a glorious one," interposed Helen; "the last cheer of a sinking crew!"

Forester looked up, startled into attention by the energy of these few words.

"I should say so too, Helen," remarked her mother, "if they were not accessory to their own misfortunes."

"Nay, nay, Mamma, you must not remember their failings in their hour of distress; there is a noble-hearted minority untainted yet."

"There will be a majority of eighteen," said Forester, whose thoughts were wandering away, while he endeavored to address himself to what he believed they were saying; nor was he aware of his error till aroused by the laughter of Lady Eleanor and her daughter.

"Eighteen!" reiterated he, solemnly.

"How few!" remarked Lady Eleanor, almost scornfully.

"You should say, how costly, Mamma!" exclaimed Helen. "These gentlemen are as precious from their price as their rarity!"

"That is scarcely fair, Miss Darcy," said Forester, at once recalled to himself by the tone of mockery she spoke in; "many adopted the views of Government, after duly weighing every consideration of the measure: some, to my own knowledge, resisted offers of great personal advantage, and Lord Castlereagh was not aware of their adhesion—"

"Till he had them *en poche*, I suppose," said Helen, sarcastically; "just as you have been pleased to do with my ball of yellow worsted, and for which I shall be thankful if you will restore it to me."

Forester blushed deeply, as he drew from his coat-pocket the worsted, which in a moment of abstraction he had lifted from the ground, and thrust into his pocket, without knowing.

Had any moderately shrewd observer witnessed his confusion, and her enjoyment of it, he would easily have understood the precise relation of the two parties to each other. Forester's absence of mind betrayed his engaged affection as palpably as Helen's laughter did her own indifference.

Lady Eleanor did not remark either; her thoughts still rested on the topic of which they had spoken, for it was a subject of no inconsiderable difficulty to her. Whatever her sense of indignant contempt for the bribed adherents of the Ministry, her convictions always inclined to these measures, whose origin was from her native country; her predilections were strongly English; not only her happiest days had been passed there, but she was constantly contrasting the position they would have occupied and sustained in that favored land, against the wasteful and purposeless extravagance of their life in Ireland.

Was it too late to amend? was the question ever rising to her mind, now if even yet the Knight should be induced to adopt the more ambitious course? Every accidental circumstance seemed favorable to the notion: the Government craving his support; her own relatives, influential as they were from rank and station, soliciting it; the Prince himself according favors which could no more be rejected than acknowledged ungraciously.

"What a career for Lionel! What a future for Helen!" such were reflections that would press themselves upon her, but to whose disentanglement her mind suggested no remedy.

"'Tis Mr. Daly, my Lady," said Tate, for something like the fourth time, without being attended to. "'T is Mr. Daly wants leave to visit you."

"Mr. Bagenal Daly, Mamma, wishes to know if you'll receive him?"

"Mr. Daly is exactly the kind of person to suggest this impracticable line of policy," said Lady Eleanor, with half-closed eyes; for the name alone had struck her, and she had not heard what was said.

"My dear Mamma," said Helen, rising, and leaning over her chair, "it is a visit he proposes; nothing so very impracticable in that, I hope!" and then, at a gesture from her mother, continued to Tate, "Lady Eleanor will be very happy to see Mr. Daly."

Lady Eleanor had scarcely aroused herself from her revery when Bagenal Daly entered. His manner was stately, perhaps somewhat colder than usual, and he took his seat with an air of formal politeness.

"I have come, my Lady," said he, slowly, "to learn if I can be of any service in the capital; unexpected news has just reached me, requiring my immediate departure for Dublin."

"Not to-night, sir, I hope; it is very severe, and likely, I fear, to continue so."

"To-night, madam, within an hour, I expect to be on the road."

"Could you defer a little longer, and we may be fellow-travellers," said Forester; "I was to start to-morrow morning, but my packing can soon be made."

"I should hope," said Lady Eleanor, smiling, "that you will not leave us unprotected, gentlemen, and that one, at least, will remain here." This speech, apparently addressed to both, was specially intended for Forester, whose cheek tingled with a flush of pleasure as he heard it.

"I have no doubt, madam, that Captain Forester, whose age and profession are more in accordance with gallantry, will respond to your desire."

"If I could really fancy that I was not yielding to my own wishes only," stammered out Forester.

"Nay, I make it a request."

"There, sir, how happy to be entreated to what one's wishes incline them," added Daly; "you may go through a deal of life without being twice so fortunate. I should apologize for so brief a notice of my departure, Lady Eleanor, but the intelligence I have received is pressing." Here he dropped his voice to a whisper. "The Ministers have hurried forward their bill, and I shall scarcely be in time for the second reading."

"All accounts agree in saying that the Government majority is certain," observed Lady Eleanor, calmly.

"It is to be feared, madam, that such rumors are well founded, but the party who form the forlorn hope have their devoirs also."

"I am a very indifferent politician, Mr. Daly, but it strikes me that a body so manifestly corrupt, give the strongest possible reasons for their own destruction."

"Were they all so, madam, I should join in the sentiment as freely as you utter it," replied Daly, proudly; "but it is a heavy sentence that would condemn the whole crew because there was a mutiny in the steerage; besides, these rights and privileges are held only in trust; no man can in honor or justice vote away that of which he is only the temporary occupant; forgive me, I beg, for daring to discuss the topic, but I thought the Knight had made you a convert to his own opinions."

"We have never spoken on the subject, Mr. Daly," replied Lady Eleanor, coldly; "the Knight dislikes the intrusion of a political matter within the circle of his family, and for that reason, perhaps," added she, with a smile, "my daughter and myself feel for it all the temptation of a forbidden pleasure."

"Oh, yes!" exclaimed Helen, who heard the last few words of her mother's speech, "I am as violent a partisan as Mr. Daly could ask for; indeed, I am not certain if all my doctrines are not of his own teaching; I fear the Premier, distrust the Cabinet, and put no faith in the Secretary for Ireland; is not that the first article of our creed?—nay, nay, fear was no part of your instruction."

"And yet I have fears, my dear Helen, and very great fears just now," said Daly in a low whisper, only audible by herself, and she turned her full and beaming eyes upon him for an explanation. As if anxious to escape the interrogatory, Daly arose hastily. "I must crave your indulgence for an abrupt leave-taking, Lady Eleanor," said he, approaching, as he kissed the hand held out to him; "I shall be able to tell the Knight that I left you both well, and under safe protection. Captain Forester, adieu; you need no admonition of mine respecting your charge;" and, with a low and courtly salute, he departed.

"Rely upon it, Captain Forester, he's bent on mischief now. I never saw him particularly mild and quiet in his manner that it was not the prelude to some desperate ebullition," said Lady Eleanor.

"He is the very strangest of all mortals."

"Say, the most single-minded and straightforward," interposed Helen, "and I 'll agree with you."

"When men of strong minds and ambitious views are curbed and held in within the petty sphere of a small social circle, they are, to my thinking, intolerable. It is making a drawing-room pet of a tiger; every step he takes upsets a vase or smashes a jar. You smile at my simile."

"I 'm sure it's a most happy one," said Forester, continuing.

"I enter a dissent," cried Helen, playfully. "He's a tiger, if you will, with his foes, but in all the relations of private life, gentleness itself; for my part, I can imagine no more pleasing contrast to the modern code of manners than Mr. Bagenal Daly."

"There, Captain Forester, if you would win Miss Darcy's favor, you have now the model for your imitation."

Forester's face flushed, and he appeared overwhelmed with confusion, while Helen went on with her embroidery, tranquil as before.

"I believe," resumed Lady Eleanor, — "I believe, after all, I am unjust to him; but much may be forgiven me for being so; he has made my son a wild, thoughtless boy, and my daughter—"

"No indiscretions, Mamma," cried Helen, holding up her hand.

"Well, he has made my daughter *telle que vous la voyez*."

Forester was too well bred to venture on a word of flattery or compliment, but his glowing color and sparkling eyes spoke his admiration.

Lady Eleanor's quick glance remarked this; and, as if the thought had never occurred before, she seemed amazed, either at the fact or at her own previous inattention.

"Let us finish that second volume you were reading, Captain Forester," said she, glad to cut short the discussion. And, without a word, he took the book and began to read.

CHAPTER XVII
BAGENAL DALY'S JOURNEY TO DUBLIN

It is not our desire to practise any mystery with our reader, nor would the present occasion warrant such. Mr. Daly's hurried departure for Dublin was caused by the receipt of tidings which had that morning reached him, conveying the startling intelligence that his friend the Knight had accepted terms from the Government, and pledged himself to support their favored measure.

It was a time when men were accustomed to witness the most flagrant breaches of honor and good faith. No station was too high to be above the reach of this reproach, no position too humble not to make its possessor a mark for corruption. It was an epidemic of dishonesty, and people ceased to wonder as they heard of each new victim to the malady.

Bagenal Daly well knew that no man could be more exempt from an imputation of this nature than the Knight of Gwynne: every act of his life, every sentiment he professed, every trait of his character, flatly contradicted the supposition. But he also knew that though Darcy was unassailable by all the temptations of bribery, come in what shape they might, that his frank and generous spirit would expose him to the stratagems and devices of a wily and insidious party, and that if, by any accident, an expression should fall from him in all the freedom of convivial enjoyment that could be tortured into even the resemblance of a pledge, he well knew that his friend would deem any sacrifice of personal feeling light in the balance, rather than not adhere to it.

Resolved not to lose a moment, he despatched Sandy to order horses along the line, and having passed the remainder of the day in the preparations for his departure, he left the abbey before midnight. A less determined traveller might have hesitated on setting out on such a night: the long menacing storm had at length burst forth, and the air resounded with a chaos of noise, amid which the roaring breakers and the crash of falling trees were uppermost; with difficulty the horses were enabled to keep their feet, as the sea washed heavily over the wall and deluged the road, while at intervals the fallen timber obstructed the way and delayed his progress.

Difficulty was, however, the most enjoyable stimulant to Daly's nature; he loved an obstacle as other men enjoy a pleasure, and, as he grew older, so far from yielding to the indolence of years, his hardy spirit seemed to revel in the thought that amid dangers and perils his whole life had been passed, yet never had he suffered himself to be a beaten enemy.

The whole of that night, and all the following day, the violence of the storm was unabated; uprooted trees and wrecked villages met his eye as he passed, while, in the larger towns, the houses were strongly barred and shuttered, and scarcely one living thing to be seen through the streets. Nothing short of the united influence of bribery and intimidation could procure horses in such a season, and had any messenger of less sturdy pretensions than honest Sandy been despatched to order them, they would have been flatly refused. Bagenal Daly and his man were, however, too well known in that part of Ireland to make such a course advisable, and though postboys and ostlers condoled together, the signal of Daly's appearance silenced every thought of opposition, and the words, "I 'm ready!" were an order to dash forward none dared to disobey.

So had it continued until he reached Moate, where he found a message from Sandy, informing him that no horses could be procured, and that he must bring on those from Athlone the entire way to Kilbeggan.

"You hear me," cried Daly to the astonished postboy, who for the last two miles had spared neither whip nor spur, in the glad anticipation of a speedy shelter,—"you hear me. To Kilbeggan."

"Oh, begorra! that's impossible, yer honor. If it was the month of May, and the road was a bowling-green, the bastes couldn't do it."

"Go on!" cried Daly, shutting up the glass, and throwing himself back in the chaise.

But the postboy only buttoned up the collar of his coat around his face, thrust his whip into his boot, and, drawing his sleeves over his hands, sat a perfect picture of fatalism.

"I say, go on!" shouted Daly, as he lowered the front window of the chaise.

A low muttering from the driver, still impassive as before, was all the reply, and at the same instant a sharp report was heard, and a pistol bullet whizzed beside his hat.

"Will you go *now?*" cried Bagenal Daly, as he levelled another weapon on the window; but no second entreaty was necessary, and, with his bead bent down almost to the mane, and with a mingled cry for mercy and imprecation together, he drove the spurs into his jaded beast, and whipped with all his might through the almost deserted town. With the despairing energy of one who felt his life was in peril, the wretched postboy hurried madly forward, urging the tired animals up the hills, and caring neither for rut nor hollow on his onward course, till at length, blown and exhausted, the animals came to a dead stand, and, with heaving flanks and outstretched forelegs, refused to budge a step farther.

"There!" cried the postboy, as, dropping from the saddle, he fell on his knees upon the road, "shoot, and be d — — —d to you; I can do no more."

The terrified expression of the fellow's face as the lamp of the chaise threw its light upon him, seemed to change the current of Daly's thoughts, for he laughed loud and heartily as he looked upon him.

"Come, come," said he, good-humoredly, "is not that Kilbeggan where I see the lights yonder?"

"Sorra bit of it," sighed the other, "it is only Horseleap."

"Well, push on to Horseleap; perhaps they 've horses there."

"Begorra! you might as well look for black tay in a bog-hole; 't is a poor 'shebeen' is the only thing in the village;" and, so saying, he took the bridle on his arm, and walked along before the horses, who, with drooping heads, tottered after at a foot pace.

About half an hour of such travelling brought Daly in front of a miserable cabin, over the door of which a creaking sign proclaimed accommodation for man and beast. To the partial truth of this statement the bright glare of a fire that shone between the chinks of the shutters bore witness, and, disengaging himself from the chaise, Daly knocked loudly for admission. There are few less conciliating sounds to the ears of a hot-tempered man than those hesitating whispers which, while exposed to a storm himself, he hears deliberating on the question of his admission. Such were the mutterings Daly now listened to, and to which he was about to reply by forcing his entrance, when the door was opened by a man in the dress of a peasant, who somewhat sulkily demanded what he wanted.

"Horses, if you have them, to reach Kilbeggan," said Daly, "and if you have not, a good fire and shelter until they can be procured;" and as he spoke, he pushed past the man, and entered the room from which the blazing light proceeded.

With his back to the fire, and hands thrust carelessly into the pockets of his coat, stood a man of eight-and-thirty or forty years of age; in dress, air, and appearance he might have been taken for a country horse-dealer; and so, indeed, his well-worn top-boots and green coat, cut in jockey fashion, seemed to bespeak him. He was rather under the middle size, but powerfully built, his wide chest, long arms, and bowed legs all indicating the possession of that strength which is never the accompaniment of more perfect symmetry.

Although Daly's appearance unquestionably proclaimed his class in life, the other exhibited no mark of deference or respect to him as he entered, but maintained his position with the same easy indifference as at first.

"You make yourself at home here, good friend, if one might judge from the way you knocked at the door," said he, addressing Daly with a look whose easy familiarity was itself an impertinence.

"I have yet to learn," said Daly, sternly, "that a gentleman must practise any peculiar ceremony when seeking the shelter of a 'shebeen,' not to speak of the right by which such as you address me as your good friend."

An insolent laugh, that Daly fancied was re-echoed by some one without, was the first reply to this speech; when, after a few minutes, the man added, "I see you 're a stranger in these parts."

"If I had not been so, the chance is I should have taught you somewhat better manners before this time. Move aside, sir, and let me see the fire."

But the other never budged in the slightest, standing in the same easy posture as before.

Daly's dark face grew darker, and his heavy brows met in a deep frown, while, with a spring that showed no touch of time in his strong frame, he bounded forward and seized the man by the collar. Few men were Daly's equals in point of strength; but although he with whom he now grappled made no resistance whatever, Daly never stirred him from the spot, to which he seemed fast and firmly rooted.

"Well, that's enough of it!" said the fellow, as with a rough jerk he freed himself from the grasp, and sent Daly several paces back into the room.

"Not so!" cried Daly, whose passion now boiled over, and, drawing a pistol from his bosom, he levelled it at him. Quick as the motion was, the other was equally ready, for his hand now presented a similar weapon at Daly's head.

"Move aside, or—"

A coarse, insulting laugh drowned Daly's words, and he pulled the trigger; but the pistol snapped without exploding.

"There it is, now," cried the fellow, rudely; "luck's against you, old boy, so you 'd better keep yourself cool and easy;" and with these words he uncocked the weapon and replaced it in his bosom. Daly watched the moment, and with a bound placed himself beside him, when, bringing his leg in front, he caught the man round the middle, and hurled him headlong on the ground.

He fell as if he had been shot; but, rolling over, he leaned upon his elbow and looked up, without the slightest sign of passion or even excitement on his features.

"I 'd know that trip in a thousand; begad, you 're Bagenal Daly, and nobody else!"

Although not a little surprised at the recognition, Daly suffered no sign of astonishment to escape him, but drew his chair to the fire, and stretched out his legs before the blaze. Meanwhile, the other, having arisen, leaned over the back of a chair, and stared at him steadfastly.

"I am as glad as a hundred-pound note, now, you did n't provoke me to lay a hand on you, Mr. Daly," said he, slowly, and in a voice not devoid of a touch of feeling; "'t is n't often I bear malice, but I 'd never forgive myself the longest day I 'd live."

Daly turned his eyes towards him, and, for some minutes, they continued to look at each other without speaking.

"I see you don't remember me, sir," said the stranger, at length; "but I 've a better memory, and a better reason to have it besides: you saved my life once."

"Saved your life!" repeated Daly, thoughtfully; "I 've not the slightest recollection of ever having seen you before."

"It's all true I 'm telling, for all that," replied the other; "and although it happened above five-and-twenty years since, I'm not much changed, they tell me, in look or appearance." He paused at these words, as if to give Daly time to recognize him; but the effort seemed in vain, as, after along and patient scrutiny, Daly said, "No, I cannot remember you."

"Let me see, then," said the man, "if I can't refresh your memory. Were you in Dublin in the winter of '75?"

"Yes; I had a house in Stephen's Green—"

"And used to drive four black thoroughbreds without winkers?"

"It's clear that *you* know me, at least," said Daly; "go on."

"Well, sir, do you remember, it was about a week before Christmas, that Captain Burke Fitzsimon was robbed of a pair of pistols in the guard-room of the Upper Castle Yard, in noonday, ay, and tied with his own sash to the guard-bed?"

"By Jove! I do. He was regularly laughed out of the regiment."

"Faix, and many that laughed at him mightn't have behaved a deal better than he did," replied the other, with a dogged sternness in his manner. He became silent after these words, and appeared deeply sunk in meditation, when suddenly he drew two splendidly chased pistols from his bosom, and held them out to Daly as he said, "There they are, and as good as they are handsome, true at thirty paces, and never fail."

Daly gazed alternately from the pistols to their owner, but never uttered a word.

"That same day," resumed the man, "you were walking down the quay near the end of Watling Street, when there was a cry of 'Stop thief!—stop him!—a hundred guineas to the man that takes him!' and shortly after a man crossed the quay, pursued closely by several people, one of them, and the foremost, being Tom Lambert, the constable, the strongest man, they said, of his day, in Ireland. The fellow that ran could beat them all, and was doing it too, when, just as he had gained Bloody Bridge, he saw a child on the pathway all covered with blood, and a bulldog standing over him, worrying him—"

"I have it all," said Daly, interrupting him; "'tis as fresh before me as if it happened yesterday. The robber stopped to save the child, and, seizing the bulldog by the throat, hurled him over the wall into the Liffey. Lambert, as you call him, had by this time come close up, and was within two yards of the man, when I, feeling compassion for a fellow that could be generous at such a moment, laid my hand on the constable's arm to stop him; he struck me; but if he did, he had his reward, for I threw him over the hip on the crown of his head, and he had a brain fever after it that almost brought him to death's door. And where were you all this time, and what were you doing?"

"I was down Barrack Street, across the park, and near Knockmaroon Gate, before they could find a door to stretch Tom Lambert on."

"You!" said Daly, staring at him; "why, it was Freney, they told me, performed that exploit for a wager."

"So it was, sir," said the man, standing up and crossing his arms, not without something of pride in his look,—"I'm Freney."

Daly arose and gazed at the man with all that curious scrutiny one bestows upon some remarkable object, measuring his strong, athletic frame with the eye of a connoisseur, and, as it were, calculating the physical resources of so powerful a figure.

"You see, sir," said the robber, at last, "I was right when I told you that you saved my life: there were thirteen indictments hanging over my head that day, and if I 'd been taken they 'd have hanged me as round as a turnip."

"You owe it to yourself," said Daly; "had you not stopped for the child, it was just as likely that I 'd have tripped you up myself."

"'Tis a feeling I never could get over," said the robber; "'twas a little boy, about the same age as that, that saved the Kells coach the night I stopped it near Dangan. And now, sir, let me ask you what in the world brought you into the village of Horseleap? For I am sure," added he with a laugh, "it was never to look after me."

"You are right there, friend; I'm on my way up to town to be present at the debate in Parliament on the Union,—a question that has its interest for yourself too."

"How so, sir?" said the other, curiously.

"Plainly enough, man; if they carry the Union, they'll not leave a man worth robbing in the island. You 'll have to take to an honest calling, Freney,—turn cattle-drover. By the way, they tell me you 're a good judge of a horse."

"Except yourself, there's not a better in the island; and if you 've no objection, I 'll mount and keep you company as far as Maynooth, where you 'll easily get horses—and it will be broad daylight by that time—to bring you into Dublin."

"I accept the offer willingly. I'll venture to say we shall not be robbed on the journey."

"Well, sir, the horses won't be here for an hour yet, and if you'll join me in a bit of supper I was going to have when you came in, it will help to pass the time till we are ready to start."

Daly assented, not the less readily that he had not eaten anything since morning, and Freney left the room to hasten the preparations for the meal.

"Come, Freney," said Daly, as the other entered the room a few moments after, "was it the strength of conscious rectitude that made you stand my fire as you did a while ago, or did you think me so bad a marksman at four paces?"

"Neither, sir," replied the robber, laughing; "I saw the pan of the lock half open as you drew it from your pocket, and I knew the priming must have fallen out; but for that—"

"You had probably fired, yourself?"

"Just so," rejoined he, with a short nod. "I could have shot you before you levelled at me. Now, sir, here's something far better than burning powder. I am sure you are too old a traveller not to be able to eat a rasher of bacon."

"And this I take to be as free of any allegiance to the king as yourself," said Daly, as he poured out a wineglass-ful of "poteen" from a short black bottle.

"You 're right, sir," said Freney, with a laugh. "We 're both duty free. Let me help you to an egg."

"I never ate better bacon in my life," said Daly, who seemed to relish his supper with considerable gusto.

"I'm glad you like it, sir. It is a notion of mine that Costy Moore of Kilcock cures a pig better than any man in this part of Ireland; and though his shop is next the police-barracks, I went in there myself to buy this."

Daly stared, with something of admiration in his look, at the man whose epicurism was indulged at the hazard of his neck; and he pledged the robber with a motion of the head that betokened a high sense of his daring. "I've heard you have had some close escapes, Freney."

"I was never taken but once, sir. A woman hid my shoes when I was asleep. I was at the foot of the Galtee mountains: the ground is hard and full of sharp shingle, and I could n't run. They brought me into Clonmel, and I was in the heaviest irons in the jail before two hours were over. That's the strong jail, Mr. Daly; they 've the best walls and the thickest doors there I have ever seen in any jail in Ireland. For," added he, with a sly laugh, "I went over them all, in a friendly sort of a way."

"A kind of professional tour, Freney?"

"Just so, sir; taking a bird's-eye view of the country from the drop, because, maybe, I would n't have time for it at another opportunity."

"You 're a hardened villain!" said Daly, looking at him with an expression the robber felt to be a finished compliment.

"That's no lie, Mr. Daly; and if I wasn't, could I go on for twenty years, hunted down like a wild beast, with fellows tracking me all day, and lying in watch for me all night? Where we are sitting now is the only spot in the whole island where I can say I 'm safe. This is my brother's cabin."

"Your brother is the same man that opened the door for me?"

Freney nodded, and went on: "He's a poor laboring man, with four acres of wet bog for a farm, and a young woman, in the ague, for a wife, and if it was n't for myself he 'd be starving; and would you believe it, now, he 'd not take to the road for one night—just one single night—to be as rich as the Duke of Leinster; and here am I"—and, as he spoke, his chest expanded, and his dark eyes flashed wildly—"here am I, that would rather be on my black mare's back, with my holsters at the saddle, watching the sounds of wheels on a lonely road, than I 'd be any gentleman in the land, barring your own self."

"And why me?" said Daly, in a voice whose melancholy cadence made it solemn as a death-bell.

"Just because you 're the only man I ever heard tell of that was fond of danger for the fun of it. Did n't I see the leap you took at the Black Lough, just to show the English Lord-Lieutenant how an Irish gentleman rides, with the rein in your mouth, and your hands behind your back? Isn't that true?"

Daly nodded, and muttered, "I have the old horse still."

"By the good day! I 'd spend a week in Newgate to see you on his back."

"Well, Freney," said Daly, who seemed not disposed to encourage a conversation so personal in its allusions, "where have you been lately?—in the South?"

"No, sir; I spent the last fortnight watching an old fox that doubled on me at last,—old Hickman, of Loughrea, that used to be."

"Old Hickman!—what of him?" cried Daly, whose interest became at once excited by the mention of the name.

"I found out, sir, that he was to be down here at Kildare to receive his rents,—for he owns a fine estate here,—and that, besides, Tom Gleeson, the great agent from Dublin, was to meet him, as some said, to pay him a large sum of money for the Knight of Gwynne,—some heavy debt, I believe, owing for many a year."

"Yes, go on. What then?"

"Well. I knew the reason Hickman wanted the money here: Lord Tyrawley was going to sell him a part of Gore's Wood, for hard cash—d 'ye mind, sir, hard cash—down on the nail, for my Lord likes high play at Daly's—"

"D——n Lord Tyrawley!" said Daly, impatiently. "What of Hickman?"

"Well, d——n him too! He's a shabby negur. I stopped 'him at Ball's Bridge once, and got but three guineas and some shillings for my pains. But to come back to old Hickman: I found he had arrived at the 'Black Dog,' and that Gleeson had come the same evening, and so I disguised myself like an old farmer the next morning, and pretended I wanted his advice about an asthma that I had, just to see the lie of the old premises, and whether he was alone, or had the two bailiffs with him, as usual. There they were, sir, sure enough, and well armed too, and fresh hasps on the door, to lock it inside, all secure as a bank. I saw these things while the old doctor was writing the prescription, for he tore a leaf out of his pocket-book to order me some stuff for the cough,—faith, 't is pills of another kind they 'd have given me if they found me out. That was all I got for my guinea in goold, not to speak of the danger;" and, so saying, he pulled a crumpled piece of paper from his pocket, and held it out towards Daly. "That's not it, sir; 't is the other side the writing is on."

But Daly's eyes were fixed upon the paper, which he held firmly between both hands.

"Ay, I see what you are looking at," said Freney; "that was a kind of memorandum the old fellow made of the money Gleeson paid him the day before."

Daly paid no attention to the remark, but muttered half aloud the contents of the document before him: "Check on Ball for eighteen thousand, payable at sight,—thirty-six thousand eight hundred and ten pounds in notes of the Bank of England,—gold, seventeen hundred guineas."

"There was a lob," cried Freney, as he rubbed his hands together. "I was set up for life if I got half of it! And now, Mr. Daly, just tell me one thing: isn't Mr. Darcy there as bad as myself, to take all this money for his vote?"

"How do you mean?" said Daly, sternly.

"I mean that a gentleman born and bred as he is, oughtn't to sell his country for goold; that if a blackguard like myself takes to the road, it's all natural and reasonable, and the world's little worse off when they hang half a dozen of my kind; but for a real born gentleman of the old stock of the land to go and take money for his vote in Parliament!"

"And who dares to say he did so?" cried Daly, indignantly.

"Faix, that's the story up in Dublin; they say he 'd no other way of clearing off the debts on his property. Bad cess to me if I 'd do it! Here I am, a robber and a highwayman, I don't deny it, but may I wear hemp for a handkerchief if I 'd sell my country. Bad luck to the Union, and all that votes for it," said he, as, filling a bumper of whiskey, he tossed it off to this laudable sentiment.

"If you had n't wronged my friend the Knight of Gwynne, I'm not certain that I wouldn't have pledged your toast myself."

"If he 's a friend of yours I say nothing against him; but sure when he —"

"Once for all," said Daly, sternly, "this story is false;" while he added, in a low muttering to himself, "corruption must needs have spread widely when such a calumny was even ventured on. — And so, Freney, Hickman escaped you?"

"He did, sir," said Freney, sighing; "he made a lodgment in Kildare next day, and more of the money he carried up to town, guarded all the way by the two fellows I told you. Ah! Mr. Daly, if all the world was as cunning as old Peter, I might give up the road as a bad job. There! do you hear that? Listen, sir."

"What is it?" said Daly, after a moment's silence.

"They're my nags, sir, coming up the road. I'd know their trot if I heard it among a troop of dragoons. 'T is clippers they are."

As he spoke he arose from the table, and, lighting a small lantern he always carried with him, hastened to the door, where already the two horses were standing, a bare-legged "gossoon" holding the bridles.

Jemmy surveying the outside Jarl.

"Well, Jemmy, what's the news to-night?" said Freney.

"Nothing, sir, at all. I passed the down mail at Seery's Mill, and when the coachman heard the step of the horses, he laid on the wheelers wid all his might, and sat down on the footboard, and the two outside passengers lay flat as a pancake on the top when I passed. I could n't help giving a screech out of me for fun, and the old guard let fly, and sent a ball through my 'caubeen;'" and as he said these words he exhibited his ragged felt hat, which, in addition to its other injuries, now displayed a round bullet-hole through either side.

"Serve you right," said Freney, harshly; "I wish he'd levelled three inches lower. That young rascal, sir, keeps the whole road in a state of alarm that stops all business on it." Then he added, in a whisper, "but he never failed me in his life. I 've only to say when and where I want the horses, and I 'd lay my neck on it he's there."

Daly, who had been for some minutes examining the two horses by the lantern with all the skill of an adept, now turned the light full upon the figure of the boy whose encomium was thus pronounced. The urchin, as if conscious that he was passing an inspection, set his tattered hat jauntily on one side, and with one arm a-kimbo, and a leg advanced, stood the very perfection of ragged, self-sufficient rascality. Though at most not above fourteen years of age, and short in size even for that, his features had the shrewd intelligence of manhood; a round, wide head, covered with dark red hair, projected over two eyes set wide apart, whose bad expression was ingeniously improved by a habit of squinting at pleasure,—a practice with which he now amused himself, as Mr. Daly continued to stare at him. His nose, which a wound had partly separated from the forehead, was short and wide, leaving an unnatural length to the lower part of the face, where an enormous mouth, garnished with large and regular teeth, was seen,—a feature that actually gave a look of ferocity even to a face so young.

"It's plain to see what destiny awaits that young scoundrel," said Daly, as he gazed almost sadly at the assemblage of bad passions so palpably displayed in his countenance.

"I 'd wager the young devil knows it himself, and can see the gallows even now before him."

A wild burst of frantic laughter broke from the urchin as, in the exuberance of his merriment, he capered round Daly with gambols the most strange and uncouth, and then, mimicking an air of self-admiration, he strutted past, while he broke into one of the slang ditties of the day:—

> "With beauty and manners to plaze,
> I 'll seek a rich wife, and I 'll find her,
> And live like a Lord all my days,
> And sing, Tally-high-ho the Grinder!"

Freney actually screamed with laughter as he watched the mingled astonishment and horror depicted in Daly's face.

"That fellow's fate will lie heavily on your heart yet," said Daly, in a voice whose solemn tones at once arrested Freney's merriment, while the "gossoon," with increased animation and in a wilder strain, burst forth,—

> "My Lord cheats at play like a rogue,
> And my Lady flings honor behind her;
> And why wold n't I be in vogue,
> And sing, Tally-high-ho the Grinder!"

"Come," said Daly, turning away, for, amid all his disgust, a sense of the ludicrous was stealing over him, and the temptation to laugh was struggling in him,—"come, let us be off; you have nothing to wait for, I suppose?"

"Nothing, sir; I'm ready this instant. Here, Jemmy, take this portmanteau, and meet us outside of Maynooth, under the old castle wall."

"Stay," cried Daly, whose misgivings about the safe arrival of his luggage would have made him prefer any other mode of transmission; "he 'll scarcely be in time."

"Not in time! I wish I'd a bet of fifty guineas on it that he would not visit every stable on the road, and know every traveller's name and business, and yet be a good half hour before us. Off with you! Away!"

Diving under the two horses, the "gossoon" appeared at the other side of the road, and then, with a wild spring in the air, and an unearthly shout of laughter, he cleared the fence before him and disappeared, while as he went the strain of his slang song still floated in the air, and the refrain, "Tally-high-ho the Grinder," could be heard through the stillness of the night.

"Take the dark horse, sir; you 're heavier than me," said Freney, as he held the stirrup.

"A clever hack, faith," said Daly, as he seated himself in the saddle, and gathered up the reins.

"And mounts you well," cried Freney, admiring both horse and rider once more by the light before he extinguished the lantern.

The storm had now considerably abated, and they rode on at a brisk pace, nor did they draw rein till the tall ruined castle of Maynooth could be seen, rearing its dark head against the murky sky.

"We part here," said Daly, who for some time had been lost in thought, "and I have nothing but thanks to offer you for this night's service, Freney; but if the time should come that I can do you a good turn—"

"I 'll never ask it, sir," said Freney, interrupting him.

"And why not? Are you too proud?"

"Not too proud to be under any obligation to you," said the robber, stopping him, "but too proud of the honor you did me this night by keeping my company, ever to hurt your fame by letting the world know it. No, Mr. Daly, I knew your courage well; but this was the bravest thing ever you did."

He sprang from his horse as he spoke, and gave a long, shrill whistle. A deep silence followed, and he repeated the signal, and, soon after, the tramp of naked feet was heard on the road, and Jemmy advanced towards them at his ordinary sling trot.

"Take the trunk up to the town."

"No, no," said Daly, "I'll do that myself;" and he relieved the urchin of his burden, taking the opportunity to slip some crown-pieces into his willing hand while he did so.

"Good-bye, sir," said Freney, taking off his hat with courteous deference.

"Good-bye, Freney," said Daly, as he seized the robber's hand and shook it warmly. "I'll soon be shaking hands with twenty fellows not a whit more honest," said Daly, as he looked after him through the gloom. "Hang me if I don't think he's better company, too!" and with this very flattering reflection on some parties unknown, he plodded along towards the town.

Here, again, new disappointment awaited him: a sudden summons had called the members of both political parties to the capital, and horses were not to be had at any price.

"'T is the Lord's marciful providence left him only the one arm," said a waiter, as he ushered Daly into a sitting-room, and cast a glance of most meaning terror at the retiring figure of Sandy.

"What do you mean?" asked Daly, hastily.

"It's what he smashed the best chaise in the yard, as if it was a taycup, this morning. Mr. Tisdal ordered it to be ready at seven o'clock, to take him up to town, and, when it came to the door, up comes that long fellow with his one arm, and says, 'This will do for my master,' says he, and cool and aisy he gets up into the chaise, and sits down, and when he was once there, by my conscience you might as well try to drain the canal with a cullender as get him out again! We had a fight that lasted nigh an hour, and signs on it, there's many a black eye in the stable-yard to show for it; but he beat them all off, and kept his ground. 'Never mind,' said Mr. Tisdal, and he whispered a word to the master; and what did they do, sir, but nailed him up fast in the chaise, and unharnessed the horses, put them to a jaunting-car, and started with Mr. Tisdal before you could turn round."

"And Sandy," cried Daly, "what did he do?"

"Sandy?—av it's that you call him,—a divil a doubt but he's sandy and stony too,—he made a drive at the front panel wid one leg, and away it went; and he smashed open the door with his fist; and put that short stump of an arm through the wood as if it was cheese. 'T is a holy show, the same chaise now! And when he got out, may I never spread a tablecloth if you'd see a crayture in the street: they run in every direction, as if it was the duke's bull was out of the paddock, and it's only a while ago he grew raysonable."

However little satisfactory the exploit was to the innkeeper and his household, it seemed to sharpen Daly's enjoyment of his breakfast, and compensate him for the delay to which he was condemned. The messenger sent to seek for horses returned at last without them, and there was now no alternative but to await, with such patience as he could muster, some chaise for town, and thus reach Dublin before nightfall.

A return chaise from Kilcock was at last secured, and Daly, with his servant on the box, proceeded towards Dublin.

It was dark when they reached the capital, and drove with all the speed they could accomplish to the Knight's house in Henrietta Street. Great was Daly's discomfort to learn that his friend Darcy had just driven from the door.

"Where to?" said he, as he held his watch in his hand, as if considering the chances of still overtaking him.

"To a dinner-party, sir, at Lord Castlereagh's," said the servant.

"At Lord Castlereagh's!" And nothing but the presence of the man repressed the passionate exclamation that quivered on his lip.

"Yes, sir, his Lordship and Mr. Heffernan called here—"

"Mr. Heffernan,—Mr. Con Heffernan do you mean?" interrupted he, quickly. "Ah! I have it now. And when was this visit?"

"On Monday last, sir."

"On Monday," said Daly to himself. "The very day the letter was written to me: there's something in it, after all. Drive to Kildare Place, and as fast as you can," said he, aloud, as he sprang into the chaise.

The steps were up, the door banged to, the horses lashed into a gallop, and the next moment saw the chaise at the end of the street.

Short as the distance was,—scarcely a mile to Heffer-nan's house,— Daly's impatient anxiety made him think it an eternity. His object was to reach the house before Heffernan started; for he judged rightly that not only was the Secretary's dinner planned by that astute gentleman, but that its whole conduct and machinery rested on his dexterity.

"I know the fellow well," muttered Daly,—"ay, and, by Heaven! he knows *me*. His mock candor and his counterfeit generosity have but a bad chance with such men as myself; but Darcy's open, unsuspecting temperament is the very metal he can weld and fashion to his liking."

It was in the midst of reflections like these, mingled with passionate bursts of impatience at the pace, which was, notwithstanding, a sharp gallop, that they dashed up to Heffer-nan's door. To make way for them, a chariot that stood there was obliged to move on.

"Whose carriage is this?" said Daly, as, without waiting for the steps to be lowered, he sprang to the ground.

"Mr. Heffernan's, sir."

"He is at home, then?"

"Yes, sir; but just about to leave for a dinner-party."

"Stand by that chariot, Sandy, and take care that no one enters it till I come back," whispered Daly in his servant's ear. And Sandy took up bis post at the door like a sentinel on duty. "Tell your master," said Daly to the servant, who stood at the open hall-door, "that a gentleman desires to speak with him."

"He's just going out, sir."

"Give my message," said Daly, sternly.

"With what name, sir?"

"Repeat the words as I have given them to you, and don't dictate to me how I am to announce myself," said he, harshly, as he opened the door and walked into the parlor.

Scarcely had he reached the fireplace when a bustle without proclaimed that Heffernan was passing downstairs, and the confused sound of voices was heard as he and his servant spoke together. "Ah! very well," said Heffernan, aloud; "you may tell the gentleman, John, that I can't see him at present. I 've no notion of keeping dinner waiting half an hour." And so saying, he passed out to enter the carriage.

"Na, na," said Sandy, as the footman offered his arm to assist his master to mount the steps; "ye maun wait a wee. I trow ye hae no seen my master yet."

"What means this insolence? Who is this fellow? — push him aside."

"That's na sae easy to do," replied Sandy, gravely; "and though I hae but one arm, ye 'll no be proud of yer-sel 'gin you try the game."

"Who are you? By what right do you stop me here?" said Heffernan, who, contrary to his wont, was already in a passion.

"I'm Bagenal Daly's man; and there's himsel in the parlor, and he'll tell you mair, maybe."

The mention of that name seemed to act like a spell upon Heffernan, and, without waiting for another word, he turned back hastily, and re-entered the house. He stopped as he laid his hand on the handle of the door, and his face, when the light fell on it, was pale as death; and although no other sign of agitation was perceptible, the expression of his features was very different from ordinary. The pause, brief as it was, seemed sufficient to rally him, for, opening the door with an appearance of haste, he advanced towards Daly, and, with an outstretched hand, exclaimed, —

"My dear Mr. Daly, I little knew who it was I declined to see. They gave me no name, and I was just stepping into my carriage when your servant told me you were here. I need not tell you that I would not deny myself to *you*."

"I believe not, sir," said Daly, with a strong emphasis on the words. "I have come a long journey to see and speak with you."

"May I ask it, as a great favor, that you will let our interview be for to-morrow morning? You may name your hour, or as many of them as you like—or will you dine with me?"

"We'll dine together to-day, sir," said Daly.

"That's impossible," said Heffernan, with a smile which all his tact could not make an easy one. "I have been engaged for four days to Lord Castlereagh,—a party which I had some share in assembling together,—and, indeed, already I am five-and-twenty minutes late."

"I regret deeply, sir," said Daly, as, crossing his hands behind his back, he slowly walked up and down the room,—"I regret deeply that I must deprive the noble Secretary's dinner-party of so very gifted a guest. I know something of Mr. Heffernan's entertaining powers, and I have heard even more of them; but for all that, I must be unrelenting, and—"

"The thing is really impossible."

"You will dine with me to-day," was the cool answer of Daly, as, fixing his eyes steadily on him, he uttered the words in a low, determined tone.

"Once for all, sir—" said Heffernan, as he moved towards the door.

"Once for all," repeated Daly, "I will have my way. This is no piece of caprice,—no sudden outbreak of that eccentricity which you and others affect to fasten on me. No, Mr. Heffernan; I have come a hundred and fifty miles with an object, and not all the wily dexterity of even you shall balk me. To be plain, sir, there are reports current in the clubs and society generally that you have been the means of securing the Knight of Gwynne to the side of Government. I know—ay, and you know—how many of these rumors originate on the shallow foundation of men being seen together in public, and cultivating an intimacy on purely social grounds. Now, Mr. Heffernan, Darcy's opinions, it is well known, are not those of the Ministry, and the only result of such calumnies will be that he, the head of a family, and a country gentleman of the highest rank, will be drawn into a dangerous altercation with some of those lounging puppies that circulate such slanders. I am his friend, and, as it happens, with no such ties to life and station as he possesses. I will, if possible, place myself in a similar position, and, to do so, I know no readier road than by keeping your company. I will give the gentlemen every pretext to talk of me as they have done of him; and if I hear a mutter, or if I see a signal that the most suspicious nature can torture into an affront, I will teach the parties that if they let their tongues run glibly, they at least shall keep their hair-triggers in order. Now, sir, you 'll not only dine with me to-day, but you 'll do so in the large room of the Club. I 've given you my reasons, and I tell you flatly that I will hear nothing in opposition to them; for I am quite ready to open the ball with Mr. Con Heffernan."

Heffernan's courage had been proved on more than one occasion; but, somehow, he had his own reasons, it would seem, for declining the gage of battle here. That they were valid ones would appear from the evident struggle compliance cost him, as, with a quivering lip and whisper, he said:

"There may be much force in what you say, Mr. Daly,—your motives, at least, are unquestionable. I will offer, therefore, no further opposition." So saying, he opened the door to permit Daly to pass out. "To the Club," said he to the footman, as they both seated themselves in the chariot.

"The Club, sir!" repeated the astonished servant.

"Yes, to Daly's Club," said Bagenal himself. And they drove off.

CHAPTER XVIII
LORD CASTLEREAGH'S DINNER-PARTY

The day of Lord Castlereagh's dinner-party had arrived, and the guests, all save Mr. Heffernan, were assembled in the drawing-room. The party was small and select, and his Lordship had gone through the usual routine of introducings, when Hamilton asked if he still expected any one.

"Yes; Mr. Heffernan promised to make one of our twelve; he is generally punctuality itself, and I cannot understand what detains him."

"He said he 'd call for me on his way," said Lord Beerhaven, "and I waited some time for him; but as I would not risk spoiling your Lordship's *entrées*, I came away at last."

This speech was made by one who felt no small uneasiness on his own part respecting the cookery, and took the occasion of suggesting his fears, as a hint to order dinner.

"Shall we vote him present, then?" said Lord Castle-reagh, who saw the look of dismay the further prospect of waiting threw over the party.

"By all means," said Lord Beerhaven; "Heffernan never eats soup."

"I don't think he cares much for fish, either," said Hamilton.

"I think our friend Con is fond of walnuts," said the Knight, dryly.

"Them 's the unwholesomest things he could eat," muttered old Hickman, who, although seated in a corner of the room, and partly masked by his son and grandson, could not be altogether secluded from earshot.

"Are they indeed?" said the bishop, turning sharply round; for the theme of health was one that engaged all his sympathies; and although his short apron covered a goodly rotundity of form, eating exacted to the full as many pains as it afforded pleasures to the Churchman.

"Yes, my Lord," said Hickman, highly gratified to obtain such exalted notice; "there's an essential oil in them that destroys the mucous membrane—"

"Destroys the mucous membrane!" said the bishop, interrupting him.

"Mine is pretty much in that way already," said Lord Beerhaven, querulously; "five-and-twenty minutes past six."

"No, no, my dear Darcy," said Lord Drogheda, who, having drawn the Knight aside, was speaking in an earnest but low tone, "I never was easier in my life, on the score of money; don't let the thing give you any trouble; consult Gleeson about it, he's a clever fellow, and take your own time for the payment."

"Gleeson is a clever fellow, my Lord, but there are straits that prove too much even for his ingenuity."

"Ah! I know what you mean," said Lord Drogheda, secretly, "you 've heard of that Spanish-American affair, — yes, he made a bad hit there; some say he'll lose fifty thousand by it."

Dinner was at this moment announced, and the Knight was unable to learn further on a subject the little he had heard of which gave him great sorrow. Unfortunately, too, his position at table was opposite, not next, to Lord Drogheda, and he was thus compelled to wait for another opportunity of interrogating him.

Lord Castlereagh has left behind him one reputation which no political or party animosity has ever availed to detract from, that of being the most perfect host that ever dispensed the honors of a table. Whatever seeming reserve or coldness he maintained at other times, here he was courteous to cordiality; his manner, the happy union of thorough good-breeding and friendly ease. Gifted with a most retentive memory, and well versed on almost every topic that could arise, he possessed that most difficult art, the power of developing the resources and information of others, without ever making any parade of his own acquirements; or, what is still harder, without betraying the effort which, in hands less adroit, becomes the most vulgar of all tricks, called "drawing out."

With all these advantages, and well suited as he was to meet every emergency of a social meeting, he felt on the present occasion far less at ease than was his wont. The party was one of Heffernan's contriving, — the elements were such as he himself would never have dreamed of collecting together, — and he relied upon his "ancient" to conduct the plan he had so skilfully laid down. It was, as he muttered to himself, "Heffernan's Bill," and he was not coming forward to explain its provisions or state its object.

Happily for the success of such meetings in general, the adjuncts contribute almost equally with the intellectual resources of the party; and here Heffernan, although absent, had left a trace of his skill. The dinner was admirable. Lord Castlereagh knew nothing of such matters; the most simple, nay, the most ill-dressed, meats would have met equal approval from him with the greatest triumphs of the art; and as to wine, he mixed up his madeira, his claret, and his burgundy together in a fashion which sadly deteriorated him in the estimation of many of his more cultivated acquaintances.

All the detail of the dinner was perfect, and Lord Beer-haven, his fears on that score allayed, emerged from the cloud of his own dreary anticipations, and became one of the pleasantest of the party. And thus the influence of good cheer and easy converse extended its happy sway until even Mr. Hickman O'Reilly began to suffer less anxiety respecting his father's presence, and felt relieved at the preoccupation the good things of the table exacted from the old doctor.

The party was of that magnitude which, while enabling the guests to form into the twos and threes of conversational intimacy, yet affords, from time to time, the opportunity of generalizing the subject discussed, and drawing, as it were, into a common centre the social abilities of each. And there Lord Castlereagh shone conspicuously, for at the same time that he called forth all the anecdotic stores of Lord Beerhaven, and the witty repartee for which Hamilton was noted, he shrouded the obtrusive old Hickman, or gave a character of quaint originality to remarks which, with less flattering introduction, had been deemed low-lived and vulgar.

The wine went freely round, and claret, whose flavor might have found acceptance with the most critical, began to work its influence upon the party, producing that pleasant amalgamation in which individual peculiarities are felt to be the attractive, and not the repelling, properties of social intercourse.

"What splendid action that horse you drive has, Mr. Beecham O'Reilly," said Lord Loughdooner, who had paid the most marked attention to him during dinner. "That's the style of moving they're so mad after in London, — high and fast at the same time."

"I gave three hundred and fifty for him," lisped out the youth, carelessly, "and think him cheap."

"Cheap at three hundred and fifty!" exclaimed old Hickman, who had heard the fact for the first time. "May I never stir from the spot, but you told me forty pounds."

"When you can pick up another at that price let me know, I beg you," said Lord Loughdooner, coming to the rescue, and with a smile that seemed to say, "How well you quizzed the old gentleman! I say, Hamilton, who bought your gray?"

"Ecclesmere bought him for his uncle."

"Why, he starts, or shies, or something of that sort, don't he?"

"No, my Lord, he 'comes down,' which is what the uncle does not; and as he stands between Ecclesmere and the Marquisate—"

"That's what I've always maintained," said the bishop to Lord Castlereagh. "The potato disposes to acidity. I know the poor people correct that by avoiding animal food,—a most invaluable fact."

"There are good grounds for your remark," said Lord Castlereagh to the Knight, while he smiled an easy assent to the bishop, without attending to him, "and the social relations of the country will demand the earliest care of the Government whenever measures of immediate importance permit this consideration. We have been unfortunate in not drawing closer to us men who, like yourself, are thoroughly acquainted with the condition of the people generally. It is not too late—"

"Too late for what?" interrupted Lord Drogheda. "Not too late for more claret, I trust; and the decanter has been standing opposite to me these ten minutes."

"A thousand pardons!—O'Reilly, will you touch that bell? Thanks."

The tone of easy familiarity with which he spoke covered Hickman with a flush of ecstatic pleasure.

"They ginger them up so, nowadays," said Lord Loughdooner to Beecham O'Reilly.

"Ginger!" chimed in Hickman,—"the devil a finer thing for the stomach. I ask your pardon, my Lord, for saying his name, but I 'll give you a receipt for the windy bile worth a guinea-note."

"Take a pinch of snuff, Dr. Hickman," said Lord Castle-reagh, who saw the mortification of the two generations at the old man's vulgarity.

"Thank you, my Lord. 'Tis blackguard I like best: them brown snuffs ruins the nose entirely.—I was saying about the mixture," said he, addressing the bishop. "Take a pint of infusion of gentian, and put a pinch of coriander seeds, and the peel of a Chaney orange—"

"I recommend a bumper of that claret, my Lord," said Lord Castlereagh, determined to cut short the prescription, which now was being listened to by the whole board; "and when I add the health of the primate, I 'm sure you 'll not refuse me." The toast was drunk with all suitable honors, and the Secretary resumed in a whisper: "He wants our best wishes on that score, poor fellow, if they could serve him. He's not long to be with us, I fear."

"Indeed, my Lord!" said the bishop, eagerly.

"Alas! too true," sighed Lord Castlereagh; "he 'll be a severe loss, too. I wanted to have some minutes' talk with you on the matter. These are times of no common emergency, and the men we promote are of great consequence at this moment. Say to-morrow, about one."

"I 'll be punctual," said the bishop, taking out his tablets to make a note of what his memory would retain to the end of his life.

Lord Castlereagh caught the Knight's eye at the instant, and they both smiled, without being able to control their emotion.

"And so," said Lord Castlereagh, hastening to conceal his laugh, "my young relation continues to enjoy the hospitalities of your house. I don't doubt in the least that he reckons that wound the luckiest incident of his life."

"My friend Darcy paid even more dearly for it," said Lord Drogheda, overhearing the remark; "but for Heffernan's tidings, I should certainly have lost my wager."

"I assure you, Knight," broke in Hickman O'Reilly, "it was through no fault of mine that the altercation ended so seriously. I visited Captain Forester in his room, and thought I obtained his pledge to take no further notice of the affair."

"And I, too, told him the style of fellow MacDonough was," said Beecham, affectedly.

"I have heard honorable mention of both facts, gentlemen," said Darcy, dryly; "that nothing could have less contributed to a breach of the peace than Mr. Beecham O'Reilly's conduct, my friend Daly is willing to vouch for."

"I wish his own had been equally prudent and pacific," said Hickman O'Reilly, reddening at the taunt conveyed in the Knight's speech.

"Daly is unquestionably the best friend on the ground—"

"On or off the ground, my Lord Loughdooner," interrupted the Knight, warmly; "he may be, now and then, somewhat hasty or rash; but rich as our country is in men of generous natures, Bagenal Daly is second to none."

"I protest, gentlemen," said the bishop, gravely; "I wish I could hear a better reason for the panegyric than his skill as a duellist."

"True for you, my Lord," muttered old Hickman, in a whisper; "he's readier with a pistol-bullet than with the interest on his bond."

"He 'd favor you with a discharge in full, sir, if he heard the observation," said Hamilton, laughing.

"A letter, my Lord," said a servant, presenting a sealed epistle to the Secretary.

"Heffernan's writing, gentlemen, so I shall, with your permission, read it." He broke the seal, and read aloud: "'My dear Lord,—An adventure, which would be laughable if it were not so provoking, prevents my coming to dinner, so I must leave the menagerie—'" Here he dropped his voice, and, crumpling up the letter, laughingly remarked, "Oh, we shall hear it all later on, I've no doubt."

"By the by, my Lord, there's a House to-night, is there not?"

"No, bishop; we moved an adjournment for to-morrow evening. You'll come down for the debate, won't you?"

The bishop nodded significantly, and sipped his wine. There was now a pause. This was the great topic of the day, and yet, up to this moment, not even a chance allusion to politics had been dropped, and all recoiled from adventuring, even by a word, on a theme which might lead to disagreement or discordance. Old Hickman, however, dated his origin in life too far back for such scruples, and, leaning across the table, said, with an accent to which wine imparted a tone of peculiar cunning, "I wish you well through it, my Lord; for, by all accounts, it is dirty work."

The roar of laughter that followed the speech actually shook the table, Lord Castlereagh giving way to it with as much zest as the guests themselves. Twice he essayed to speak, but each time a fresh burst of mirth interrupted him, while old Hickman, unable to divine the source of the merriment, stared at each person in turn, and at last muttered his consolatory "Ay," but with a voice that showed he was far from feeling satisfied.

"I wish you'd made that speech in the House, Mr. Hickman," said Lord Drogheda; "I do believe you'd have been the most popular man in Ireland."

"I confess," said Lord Castlereagh, wiping his eyes, "I cannot conceive a more dangerous opponent to the Bill."

"If he held your own bill, with a protest on it," whispered Hamilton, "your opinion would not be easily gainsaid."

"May I ask for a cup of coffee?" said the bishop, rising, for he saw that although as yet no untoward results had followed, at any moment something unpleasant might occur. The party rose with him, and adjourned to the drawing-room.

"Singular old man!" said Lord Castlereagh, in a whisper to the Knight. "Shrewd and cunning, no doubt, but scarcely calculated, as our friend Drogheda thinks, to distinguish himself in the House of Commons."

"Do you think the Upper House would suit him better, my Lord?" said Darcy, slyly.

"I see, Knight," said Lord Castlereagh, laughing, "you have caught up the popular joke of the day."

"I trust, my Lord, it may be no more than a joke."

"Can you doubt it?"

"At the present moment," said the Knight, gravely, "I see no reason for doubting anything merely on the score of its unlikelihood; your Lordship's colleagues have given us some sharp lessons on the subject of credulity, and we should be more unteachable than the savage if we had not learnt something by this time."

Lord Castlereagh was about to answer, when Lord Drogheda came forward to say "Good night." The others were going too, and in the bustle of leave-taking some moments were passed.

"Your carriage has not come yet, sir," replied a servant to the Knight.

"Shall we take you home, Darcy," said Lord Drogheda; "or are you going to the Club?"

"Let me say no to that offer, Knight," interposed Lord Castlereagh, "and give me the pleasure of your company till the carriage arrives."

Darcy acceded to a request, the courteous mode of making which had already secured its acceptance, and the Knight sat down at the fire *tête-à-tête* with the Secretary.

"I was most anxious for a moment like this," said Lord Castlereagh, with the air of one abandoning himself to the full liberty of sincerity. "It very seldom happens to men placed like myself to have even a few brief minutes' intercourse with any out of the rank of partisans or opponents.

"I will not disguise from you how highly I should value the alliance of yourself to our party; I place the greatest price upon such support, but there is something better and more valuable than even a vote in a strong division, and that is, the candid judgment of a man who has enjoyed your opportunities and your powers of forming an opinion. Tell me now, frankly,—for we are here in all freedom of intercourse,—what do you object to? What do you fear from this contemplated enactment?"

"Let me rather hear," said the Knight, smiling, "what do you hope from it,—how you propose it to become the remedy of our existing evils? Because I shall thereby see whether your Lordship and myself are like-minded on the score of the disease, before we begin to discuss the remedy."

"Be it so, then," said the Secretary, gayly; and at once, without hesitation, he commenced a short and most explicit statement of the Government intentions. Arguments that formed the staple of long Parliamentary harangues he condensed into a sentence or two; views that, dilated upon, sufficed to fill the columns of a newspaper, he displayed palpably and boldly, exhibiting powers of clear and rapid eloquence for which so few gave him credit in public life. Not an epithet nor an expression could have been retrenched from a detail which denoted faculties of admirable training, assisted by a memory almost miraculous. Stating in order the various objections to the measure, he answered each in turn; and wherever the reply was not sufficiently ample and conclusive, he adroitly took occasion to undervalue either the opinion or the source from which it originated, exhibiting, while restraining, considerable powers of sarcasm, and a thorough insight into the character of the public men of the period.

If the Knight was unconvinced by the arguments, he was no less astonished by the abilities of the Secretary. Up to that hour he had been a follower of the popular notion of the Opposition party, which agreed in decrying his talents, and making his displays as a speaker the touchstone of his capacity. Darcy was too clever himself to linger longer in this delusion. He saw the great and varied resources of the youthful statesman tested by a question of no common difficulty, and he could not control the temptation of telling him, as he concluded, —

"You have made me a convert to the union—"

"Have I, indeed?" cried the Secretary, in an ecstasy of pleasure.

"Hear me out, my Lord, — to the union of great political abilities with the most captivating powers of conversation. Yes, my Lord, I am old enough to make such a remark without the hazard of being deemed impertinent or a flatterer, — *your* success in life is certain."

"But the Bill!" cried Lord Castlereagh, while his handsome face was flushed between delight and eagerness, — "the Bill!"

"Is an admirable Bill for England, my Lord, and were there not two sides to a contract, would be perfect, — indeed, until I heard the lucid statement you have just made, I never saw one-tenth part of the advantages it must render to your country, nor, consequently, — for we move not in parallel lines, — the great danger with which it is fraught to mine. Let me now explain more fully."

With these words the Knight entered upon the question of the Union in all its relations to Ireland; and while never conceding, nor even extenuating, the difficulties attendant upon a double legislature, he proceeded to show the probable train of events that must result on the passing of the measure, strengthening his anticipations by facts derived from deep knowledge of the country.

Far be it from us to endeavor to recapitulate his arguments: some of them, now forgotten, were difficult enough to answer; others, treasured up, have been fashionable fallacies in our own day. Such as they were, they were the reasons why an Irish gentleman demurred to surrendering privileges that gave his own country rank, place, and preeminence, without the evidence of any certain or adequate compensation.

"Do not tell me, my Lord, that we shall hold our influence and our station in the Imperial Parliament. There are many reasons against such a belief. We shall be in the minority, a great minority; a minority branded with provincialism as our badge, and accused of prejudice and narrow-sightedness, from the very fact of our nationality. No, no; we shall occupy a very different position in your country: and who will take our places here? That's a point your Lordship has not touched upon, but I 'll tell you. The demagogue, the public disturber, the licensed hawker of small grievances, every briefless lawyer of bad fortune and worse language, every mendicant patriot that can minister to the passions of a people deserted by their natural protectors,—the day will come, my Lord, when these men will grow ambitious, their aspirings may become troublesome; if you coerce them, they are martyrs,—conciliate them, and they are privileged. What will happen then? You will be asked to repeal the Union, you will be charged with all the venality by which you carried your Bill, every injustice with which it is chargeable, and with a hundred other faults and crimes with which it is unconnected. You will be asked, I say, to repeal the Union, and make of this miserable rabble, these dregs and sweepings of party, a Parliament. You shake your head. No, no, it is by no means impossible,—nay, I don't think it even remote. I speak as an old man, and age, if it have many deficiencies as regards the past, has at least some prophetic foresight for the future. You will be asked to repeal the Union, to give a Parliament to a country which you have drained of its wealth, from which you have seduced the aristocracy; to restore a deliberative body to a land whose resources for self-legislation you have studiously and industriously ruined. Think, then, twice of a measure from which, if it fail, there is no retreat, and the opposition to which may come in a worse form than a vote in the House of Commons. I see you deem my anticipations have more gloom than truthfulness; I hope it may be so."

"The Knight of Gwynne's carriage," cried a servant, throwing wide the door.

"How opportune!" said Darcy, laughing; "it is so satisfactory to have the last shot at the enemy."

"Pray don't go yet,—a few moments more."

"Not a second, my Lord; I dare not. The fact is, I have strenuously avoided this subject; an old friend of mine, Bagenal Daly, has wearied me of it,—he is an Anti-Unionist, but on grounds I scarcely concur in. Your Lordship's defence of the measure I also demur to. I am like poor old Murray, the Chief Justice of the Common Pleas, who, when called on for his opinion in a case where Judge Wallace was in favor of a rule, and Judge Mayne against it, he said, 'I agree with my brother Mayne for the cogent reasons laid down by my brother Wallace.'"

"So," said the Secretary, laughing heartily, "I have convinced you against myself."

"Exactly, my Lord. I came here this evening intending not to vote on the Bill,—indeed, I accepted your Lordship's hospitality without a thought upon a party question; I am equally certain you will acquit me of being a spy in the camp. To-morrow I intend to vote against you."

"I wish I could have the same esteem for my friends that I now pledge for my—"

"Don't say 'enemy,' my Lord; we both aspire to the same end,—our country's good. If we take different roads, it is because each thinks his own path the shortest. Good night."

Lord Castlereagh accompanied the Knight to his carriage, and again shook his hand cordially as they parted.

CHAPTER XIX
A DAY OF EXCITEMENT

Great was the Knight's astonishment, and not less his satisfaction, as he entered the breakfast-room the morning after his dinner with the Secretary, to find Bagenal Daly there before him. They met with all the cordial warmth of men whose friendship had continued without interruption for nigh half a century; each well disposed to prize good faith and integrity at a time when so many lapsed from the path of honor and principle.

"Well, Darcy," cried Daly, the first greetings over, "there is little hope left us; that rascally newspaper already proclaims the triumph,—a majority of twenty-eight."

"They calculate on many more; you remember what old Hayes, of the Recruiting Staff, used to say: 'There was no getting fellows to enlist when the bounty was high; make it half-a-crown,' said he, 'and I 'll raise a battalion in a fortnight.'"

"Is Castlereagh adopting the policy?"

"Yes, and with infinite success! Some that held out for English Peerages are fain to take Irish Baronetcies, expectant Bishops put up with Deaneries, and an acquaintance of ours, that would take nothing below a separate command, is now satisfied to make his son a clerk in the War Office."

"I 'm sorry for it," said Daly, as he arose and paced the room backwards and forwards, "sincerely sorry. I had fostered the hope that if they succeeded in corrupting *our* gentry, they had polluted *their own* Peerage. I wish every fellow had been bought by an Earldom at least. I would like to think that this Judas Peerage might become a jest and a scoff among their order."

"Have no such expectation, Bagenal," said the Knight, reflectively; "their origin will be forgiven before the first generation dies out. To all purposes of worldly respect and esteem, they 'll be as high and mighty Lords as the best blood of all the Howards. The penalty will fall upon England in another form."

"How? Where?"

"In the Lower House, politics will become a trade to live by, and the Irish party, with such an admirable market for grievances, will be a strong and compact body in Parliament, too numerous to be bought by anything save great concessions. Englishmen will never understand the truth of the condition of the country from these men, nor how little personal importance they possess at home. They will be regarded as the exponents of Irish opinion; they will browbeat, denounce, threaten, fawn, and flatter by turns; and Ireland, instead of being easier to govern, will be rendered ten times more difficult, by all the obscuring influences of falsehood and misrepresentation. But let us quit the theme. How have you left all at the Abbey?"

"Well and happy; here are my despatches." And he laid on the table several letters, the first the Knight had received since his arrival, save a few hurried lines from Lady Eleanor. Darcy broke the envelopes, and skimmed the contents of each.

"How good!" cried he, handing Lord Netherby's letter across the table; "this is really amusing!"

"I have seen it," said Daly, dryly. "Lady Eleanor asked my opinion as to what answer she should make."

"Insolent old miser!" broke in Darcy, who, without attending to Daly's remark, had been reading Lady Eleanor's account of Dr. Hickman's proposal. "I say, Bagenal, you 'll not believe this. What social earthquakes are we to look for next? Read that." And with a trembling hand he presented the letter to Daly.

If the Knight's passion had been more openly displayed, Daly's indignation seemed to evoke deeper emotion, for his brows met, and his stern lips were clenched, as he perused the lines.

"Darcy," said he, at length, "O'Reilly must apologize for this; he must be made to disavow any share in the old man's impertinence—"

"No, no," interrupted Darcy, "never speak of it again; rest assured that Lady Eleanor received the offer suitably. The best thing we can do is to forget it. If," added he, after a pause, "the daring that prompted such a proposition has not a deeper foundation than mere presumption. You know these Hickmans have purchased up my bonds and other securities?"

"I heard as much."

"Well, Gleeson is making arrangements for the payment. One large sum, something like £20,000—"

"Was paid the day before yesterday," said Daly; "here is a memorandum of the moneys."

"How the deuce came you by the information? I have heard nothing of it yet."

"That entails somewhat of a story," said Daly; "but I 'll be brief with it." And in a few words he narrated his meeting with the robber Freney, and how he had availed himself of his hospitality and safe convoy as far as Maynooth.

"Ireland forever!" said the Knight, in a burst of happy laughter; "for every species of incongruity, where was ever its equal? An independent member of the Legislature sups with a highwayman, and takes a loan of his hackney!"

"Ay, faith," said Daly, joining in the laugh; "and had I not been one of the Opposition, I had been worth robbing, and consequently not so civilly treated. By Jove! Darcy, I felt an evening with Freney to be a devilish good preparation for the company I should be keeping up in town."

"I'll wager ten pounds you talked politics together."

"That we did, and he is as stout an Anti-Unionist as the best of us, though he told me he signed a petition in favor of the Bill when confined in Clonmel jail."

"Is that true, Bagenal? did they hawk a petition for signature among the prisoners of a jail?"

"He took his oath of it to me, and I intend to declare it in the House."

"What if asked for your authority?"

"I 'll give it," said Daly, determinedly. "Ay, faith, and if I catch a sneer or a scoff amongst them, I 'll tell them that a highwayman is about as respectable and somewhat more courageous than a bribed representative."

If the Knight enjoyed the absurdity of Daly's supper with the noted Freney, he laughed till the tears came at the account of his dining with Con Heffernan. Darcy could appreciate the dismay of Heffernan, and the cool, imperturbable tyranny of Daly's manner throughout, and would have given largely to have witnessed the *tête-à-tête*.

"I will do him the justice to say," said Daly, "that when he found escape impossible, he behaved as well as any man, his conversation was easy and unaffected, and his manner perfectly well-bred. Freney was more anecdotic, but Heffernan saw deeper into mankind."

"I hope you hinted the comparison?" said Darcy, slyly.

"Yes, I observed upon the superiority practical men possess in all the relations of social intercourse, and quoted Freney and himself as instances!"

"And he took it well?"

"Admirably. Once, and only once, did he show a little disposition to turn restive; it was when I remarked upon the discrepancy in point of destiny, the one being employed to empty, the other to fill, the pockets of his Majesty's lieges. He winced, but it was over in a second. His time was up at ten o'clock, but we sat chatting till near twelve, and we parted with what the French term a 'sense of the most distinguished consideration' on each side."

"By Jove! I envy the fellows who sat at the other tables and saw you."

"They were most discreet in their observations," remarked Daly, significantly. "One young fellow, it is true, coughed twice or thrice as a signal to a friend across the room, but I ordered the waiter to bring me a plate, and, taking three or four bullets out of my pocket, sent them over to him, with my respectful compliments, as 'admirable pills for a cough.' The cure was miraculous."

"Excellent! Men have taken out a patent for a poorer remedy. And now, Bagenal, for the reason of your journey. What, in the name of everything strange and eccentric, brought you up to town? Don't affect to tell me you came for the debate."

"And why not?" said Daly, who, unwilling to reveal the true cause, preferred to do battle on this pretence. "I admit as freely as ever I did, I'm no lover of Parliament. I have slight respect or esteem for deliberative assemblies split up into factions and parties. A Government, to my thinking, should represent unity as the chief element of strength; but such as it is,—bad enough and base enough, in all conscience,—yet it is the last remnant of national power left, the frail barrier between us and downright provincialism. But I had another reason for coming up,—half-a-dozen other reasons, for that matter,—one of them was, to see your invaluable business man, Gleeson, who, from some caprice or other about a higher rate of interest, has withdrawn my sister's fortune from the funds to invest it in some confounded mortgage. I suppose it's all right, and judicious to boot; but Maria, like every other Daly I ever heard of, has a will of her own, and has commissioned me to have the money restored to its former destination. I verily believe, Darcy, the most troublesome animal on the face of the globe is an old maid with a small funded capital. At one moment deploring the low rate of interest and dying for a more profitable use of the money; at another, decrying all deposit save the Bank, she inveighs against public theft and private credit, and takes off three-and-a-half per cent of her happiness in pure fretting."

"Is she quite well?" said the Knight, in an accent which a more shrewd observer than Daly might have perceived was marked by some agitation.

"I never knew her better; as fearless as we both remember her at sixteen; and, save those strange intervals of depression she has labored under all through her life, the same gay-hearted spirit she was when the flattered heiress and beauty long, long years ago."

The Knight heaved a sigh. It might have been for the years thus passed, the pleasant days of early youth and manhood so suddenly called up before him; it might have been that other and more tender memories were crowding on his mind; but he turned away, and leaned on the chimney-piece, lost in deep thought.

"Poor girl," said Daly, "there is no question of it, Darcy, but she must have formed some unfortunate attachment; she had pride enough always to rescue her from the dangers of an unsuitable marriage, but her heart, I feel convinced, was touched, and yet I never could find a clew to it. I suspected something of the kind when she refused Donington,—a handsome fellow, and an old title. I pressed her myself on the subject,—it was the only time I did so,—and I guessed at once, from a chance phrase she dropped, that there had been an old attachment somewhere. Well, well, what a lesson might be read from both our fortunes! The beauty—and you remember how handsome she was—the beauty with a splendid fortune, a reduced maiden lady; and myself"—he heaved a heavy sigh, and, with clasped hands, sat back in the chair, as he added—"the shattered wreck of every hope I once set out with."

The two old men's eyes met, and, although undesignedly, exchanged looks of deepest, most affectionate interest. Daly was the first to rally from his brief access of despondency, and he did so with the physical effort he would have used to shake a load from his shoulders.

"Well, Darcy, let us be up and stirring; there's a meeting at Barrington's at two: we must not fail to be there."

"I wish to see Gleeson in the mean while," said the Knight; "I am uneasy to learn what has been done with Hickman, and what day I can leave town."

"Send Sandy out with a note, and tell him to come to dinner here at six."

"Agreed; nothing could be better; we can talk over our business matters comfortably, and be down at the House by nine or ten."

The note was soon written, and Sandy despatched, with orders to wait for Gleeson's return, in case he should be absent when he arrived.

The day for the evening of which was fixed the second reading of the Bill of Union, was a busy one in Dublin. Accounts the most opposite and contradictory were everywhere in circulation: some asserting that the

Ministerial majority was certain; others, equally positive, alleging that many of their supposed supporters had lapsed in their allegiance, and that the most enormous offers had been made, without success, to parties hitherto believed amongst the ranks of the Government. The streets were crowded, not by persons engaged in the usual affairs of trade and traffic, but by groups and knots talking eagerly over the coming event, and discussing every rumor that chance or scandal suggested.

Various meetings were held in different parts of the town: at some, the Government party were canvassing the modes of reaching the House in safety, and how best they might escape the violence of the mob; at others, the Opposition deliberated on the prospects before them, and by what stratagems the debate might be prolonged till the period when, the Wicklow election over, Mr. Grattan might be expected to take his seat in the House, since, by a trick of "the Castle party," the writ had been delayed to that very morning.

Con Heffernan's carriage was seen everywhere, and some avowed that at five o'clock he was driving with the third pair of posters he had that day employed. Bagenal Daly was also a conspicuous character "on town;" on foot and alone, he was at once recognized by the mob, who cheered him as an old but long-lost-sight-of acquaintance. The densest crowd made way for him as he came, and every mark of respect was shown him by those who set a higher price on his eccentricity and daring than even upon his patriotism; and a murmuring commentary on his character followed him as he went.

"By my conscience! it 's well for them they have n't to fight for the Union, or they would n't like old Bagenal Daly agin them!"

"He looks as fresh and bould as ever he did," said another; "sorra a day oulder than he was twenty-eight years ago, when I seen him tried for his life at Newgate."

"Was you there, Mickey?" cried two or three in a breath.

"Faix was I, as near as I am to you. 'Twas a coal-heaver he kilt, a chap that was called Big Sam; and they say he was bribed by some of the gentlemen at Daly's Club House to come up to Bagenal Daly in the street and insult him about the beard he wears on his upper lip, and sure enough so he did,—it was Ash Wednesday mor by token,—and Sam had a smut on his face just to imitat(e) Mr. Daly's. 'We are a purty pair, ain't we?' says Sam, grinning at him, when they met on Essex Bridge. And wid that he slips his arm inside Mr. Daly's to hook wid his."

"To walk beside him, is't?"

"Just so, divil a less. 'Come round to the other side of me,' says Daly, 'for I want to step into Kertland's shop.' And in they went together, and Daly asks for a pound of strong white soap, and pays down one-and-eight-pence for it, and out they comes again quite friendly as before. 'Where to now?' says Sam, for he held a grip of him like a bailiff. 'Across the bridge,' says Daly; and so it was. When they reached the middle arch of the bridge, Daly made a spring and got himself free, and then, stooping down, caught Sam by the knees, and before you could say 'Jack Robinson,' hurled him over the battlements into the Liffey. 'You can wash your face now,' says he, and he threw the soap after him; divil a word more he said, but walked on, as cool as you saw him there."

"And Sam?" said several together.

"Sam was drowned; there came a fresh in the river, and they took him up beyond the North Wall—a corpse."

"Millia murther! what did Daly do?"

"He took his trial for it, and sorra excuse he gave one way or other, but that he 'did n't know the blackguard couldn't swim.'"

"And they let him off?"

"Let him off? Arrah, is it hang a gentleman?"

"True for you," chimed in the bystanders; "them that makes the laws knows better than that!"

Such was one of the narratives his reappearance in Dublin again brought up; and, singular enough, by the respect shown him by the mob, derived much of its source in that same feeling of awe and dread they manifested towards one they believed privileged to do whatever he pleased. Alas for human nature! the qualities which find favor with the multitude are never the finer and better traits of the heart, but rather the sterner features that emanate from a strong will and firm purpose.

If the voices of the closely compacted mass which filled the streets and avenues of Dublin on that day could have been taken, it would have been found that Bagenal Daly had an overwhelming majority; while, on a converse scrutiny, it would appear that not a gentleman in Ireland entertained for that mob sentiments of such thorough contempt as he did. Nor was the sentiment concealed by him. The crowd which, growing as it went, followed him from place to place throughout the city, would break forth at intervals into some spontaneous shout of admiration, and a cheer for Bagenal Daly, commanded by some deep throat, would be answered in a deafening roar of voices. Then would Daly turn, and, as the moving mass fell back, scowl upon their unwashed faces with such a look of scorn that even they half felt the insult. In such wise was his progress through the streets of Dublin, now moving slowly onward, now turning to confront the mob that in slavish adulation still tracked his steps.

It was at a moment like this, when, standing at bay, he scowled upon the dense throng, Heffernan's carriage drove slowly past, and Con, leaning from the window, called out in a dramatic tone, "Thy friends, Siccius Dentatus, thy friends!"

Daly started, and as his cheek reddened, answered, "Ay, and by my soul, for the turning of a straw, I 'd make them your enemies." And as if responsive to the threat, a groan for "the Castle hack, three groans for Con Heffernan," were shouted out in tones that shook the street. For a second or two Daly's face brightened, and his eyes sparkled with the fire of enterprise, and he gazed on the countless mass with a look of indecision; but, suddenly folding his arms, he dropped his head, and muttered, "No, no, it would n't do; robbery and pillage would be the whole of it;" and, without raising his eyes again, walked slowly homewards.

The hours wore on, and six o'clock came, but no sign of Gleeson, nor had Sandy returned with any answer.

"And yet I am positive he is not from home," said Darcy. "He pledged himself not to leave this until the whole business was completed. Honest Tom Gleeson is a man to keep to the strictest letter of his word."

"I 'd not think that less likely," said Daly, sententiously, "if the world had spared him the epithet. I hate the cant of calling a man by some title that should be common to all men, — at least, to all gentlemen."

"I cannot agree with you," said Darcy. "I deem it a proud thing for any one so to have impressed his reputation for honorable dealing on society that the very mention of his name suggests his character."

"Perhaps I am soured by what we have seen around us," said Daly; "but the mention of every virtue latterly has been generally followed by the announcement of the purchase of its possessor. I never hear of a good character that I don't think it is a puffing advertisement of 'a high-priced article to be had cheap for cash.'"

"You'll think better of the world after a glass or two of Madeira," said Darcy, laughing; "and rather than hear you inveigh against mankind, I'll let Gleeson eat his soup cold." And, so saying, he rang the bell and ordered dinner.

The two friends dined pleasantly, and although, from time to time, some stray thought of Gleeson's absence would obtrude, they chatted away agreeably till past nine o'clock.

"I begin to suspect that Sandy may have met some acquaintance, and lingered to pledge 'old times' with him," said Darcy, looking at his watch. "It is now nearly twenty minutes past nine."

"I'll stake my life on it, Sandy is true to his mission. He'd not turn from the duty intrusted to him to hobnob with a Prince of the Blood. Here he comes, however; there was a knock at the door."

But no; it was a few hurried lines in pencil from the House, begging of them to come up at once, as the Ministerial party was mustering in strength, and the Opposition benches filling but slowly. While deliberating on what course to take, a second summons came from one of the leading men of the party. It was brief, but significant: "Come up quickly. They are evidently pushed hard. Toler has sent a message to O'Donnell, and they are gone out, and Harvey says Castlereagh has six of his fellows ready to provoke us.—W. T."

"That looks like business, Darcy," cried Daly, in a transport of delight. "Let us lose no time; there's no knowing how soon so much good valor may ooze out."

"But Gleeson—"

"If he comes, let him follow us to the House. We can walk; there's no use waiting for the carriage." Then added, in a mutter to himself, "I'd give a hundred down to have a shot at the Attorney-General. There, that's Sandy's voice in the hall;" and at the same instant the trusty servant entered.

"Well, have you seen him?"

"Is he at home?"

"No, sirs, he's no at hame, that's clear. When I asked for him, they told me he was in bed, asleep, for that he was just arrived after a long journey;

and so I waited a bit, and gaed out for a walk into the shrubberies, where I could have a look at his chamber windows, and sure enough they were a' closed. I waited a while longer, but he was still sleeping, and they dared na wake him; and so it came to nigh five o'clock, and then I was fain to send up the bit letter by the flunkie, and ask for the answer; but none came."

"Did you say that the letter was from me?" said the Knight, hastily.

"Na, sir; but I tauld them what most people mind as well, that Mister Bagenal Daly sent me. It's a name few folk are fond to trifle wi'."

"Go on, Sandy," said Daly, "What then?"

"Weel, sir, I sat down on the stair at the foot of the big clock, and said to mysel, 'I 'll gie ye ten minutes mair, but not a second after.' And sure enough ye might hear every tick of her through the house, a' was so still and silent. Short as the time was, I thought it wad never gae past, for I did no tak my eyes aff o' her face. When the ten minutes was up, I stole gently up the stair, and opened the door. A was dark inside, so I opened the window, and there was the bed—empty; nobody had lain in it syne it was made. There was a bit ashes in the grate, and some burned paper on the hearth, but na other sign that onybody was there at a', sae I crept back again, and met the flunkie as he was coming up, for he had just missed me, and was in a real fright where I was gone to. I saw by his face that he was found out, and so I laid my hand on his shoulder, and said, 'Ye ha tauld me ane lee; ye maun tak care no to tell me anither. Where is yer maister?' Then came out the truth. Mr. Gleeson was gane awa to England. He sailed for Liverpool in the 'Shamrock.'"

"Impossible!" said Darcy. "He could not be away from Dublin at this moment."

"It's even sae," replied Sandy, gravely; "for when I heard a' that I could from the flunkie, I put him into the library, and locked the door on him, and then went round to the stable-yard, where the coachman was sitting in the harness-room, smoking. 'And so he's off to England,' said I to him, as if I kenned it a'.

"'Just sae,' said he, wi' the pipe in his mouth. "'And he's nae to be back for some time,' said I, speerin' at him.

"'On Friday,' said he; and he smoked away, and never a word mair could I get out o' him."

"Why, Sandy," said the Knight, laughing, "they'd make you a prefect of police if they had you in France."

"I dinna ken, sir," said Sandy, not exactly appreciating what the nature of the appointment might portend.

"I only hope Gleeson may not hear of the perquisition on his return," said the Knight, in a whisper to Daly. "Our friend Sandy pushes his spirit of inquiry somewhat far."

"I don't know that," said Daly, thoughtfully; "he's a shrewd fellow, and rarely makes a mistake of that kind. But come, let us lose no more time."

"I half suspect the reason of this mystery about Gleeson," said the Knight, who stood musing deeply on the event; "a few words Drogheda let fall yesterday, going in to dinner,—some unfortunate speculation in South America: this may require his keeping out of the way for a little time. But why not say so, manfully?—I'm sure I'm ready to assist him."

"Come along, Darcy, we must walk; they say no carriage can get through the mob." And, with these words, he took the Knight's arm and sallied forth, while Sandy followed, conveying a large cloth cloak over his arm, which only partially concealed an ominous-looking box of mahogany wood, strapped with brass.

A crowd awaited them as they reached the street, by which they were escorted through the denser mass that thronged the great thoroughfare, the mere mention of their names being sufficient to force a passage even where the mob stood thickest.

The space in front of the Parliament House and before the College was filled with soldiers; while patrols of cavalry traversed every avenue leading to it, for information had reached the Government that violence might be apprehended from a mob whose force and numbers were alluded to by members within the House in terms meant to intimidate, while the presence of the soldiery was retorted by the Opposition as a measure of tyranny and oppression of the Castle party. Brushing somewhat roughly through the armed line, Daly, with the Knight beside him, entered the space, and was passing onward, when a bustle and a confused uproar behind him arrested his steps. Believing that it might be to Sandy's progress some objection was offered, Daly wheeled round, when he saw two policemen in the act of dragging away a boy, whose loud cries for help from the mob were incessant, while he mingled the name of Mr. Daly through his entreaties.

"What is it?" said Daly. "Does the fellow want me?"

"Never mind him," said Darcy; "the boy has caught up your name, and that's all."

But the urchin struggled and kicked with all his might; and, although overpowered by superior strength, gave battle to the last, screaming at the top of his voice, "One word with Mr. Daly,—just one word!"

Bagenal Daly turned back, and, approaching the scene of contest, said, "Have you anything to say to me? I am Mr. Daly."

"If they 'd let me go my hands, I 've something to give you," said the boy, who, although sorely bruised and beaten, seemed to care less for his own troubles than for the object of his enterprise.

At a word from Daly, the policemen relinquished their hold, and stood guard on either side, while the boy, giving himself a shake, leered up in Daly's face with an expression he could not fail to recognize.

"There's a way to treat a young gentleman at home for the Christmas holidays!" said the imp, with a compassionate glance at his torn and tattered garments, while the words and the tone they were uttered in sent a shout of laughter through the mob.

"What, Jemmy!" said Daly, stooping down and accosting him in a whisper, for it was no other than that reputable youth himself, "you here?"

"Just so, sir. Ain't I in a nice way to appear at the Privy Council?"

The police were growing impatient at the continued insolence of the fellow, and were about to lay hold on him once more, when Daly interposed, and said, in a still lower voice, "Have you anything to tell me?"

"I 've a bit of paper for you somewhere, from one you know, if them blackguards the 'polis' has not made me lose it."

"Be quick, then," said Daly, "and see after it." For Darcy was chafed at a delay he could not see any reason for.

"Here it is," said the imp, taking a piece of dirty and crumpled paper from the lining of his hat; "there, you have it now safe and sure. Give my best respects to Alderman Darby," added he to the police; "say I was too hurried to call;" and with that he dived between the legs of one of them, dashed through the line of soldiers, and was speedily concealed among the dense crowd outside, where shouts of approving laughter welcomed him.

"A rendezvous or a challenge, Bagenal,—which?" said the Knight, laughing, as Daly stood endeavoring, by the light of a lamp in the corridor, to decipher the torn scrawl.

The other made no reply, but, holding the paper close to his eyes, stood silent and motionless. At last an expression of impatient anger burst from him: "That imp of h—ll has almost effaced the words,—I cannot make them out!" Then he added, in a low muttering, "I trust in Heaven I have not read them aright. Come here, Darcy." And, so saying, he grasped the Knight's hand, and led him along to one of the many small chambers used as offices of the House.

"Ah! they're looking anxiously out for you, sir," said a young man who stood with his back to the fire, reading a paper. "Mr. Ponsonby has just been here."

"Leave us together here for a few minutes," said Daly, "and let there be no interruption." And as he spoke, he motioned to the door with a gesture there was no mistaking. The clerk left the room, and they were alone.

"Maurice Darcy," said Daly, as he turned the key in the lock, "you have a stout heart and a courage I never saw fail, and you need both at this moment."

"What is it, Bagenal?" gasped the Knight, as a most deadly pallor covered his face. "Is my wife—are my children—"

"No, no; be calm, Darcy, they are all well."

"Go on, then," cried he, with a firmer voice; "I'll listen to you patiently."

"Read that," said Daly, as he held the paper near the candle; and the Knight read aloud: "'Honored Sir,—I saw the other night you were troubled when I spoke of Gleeson, and I take the occasion of—'" "'warning you,' I think the words are," broke in Daly.

"So it is:—'warning you honest Tom is away to America!'" The paper fell from Darcy's hand, and he staggered back into a seat.

"With they say above a hundred thousand pounds, Darcy," continued Daly, taking up the fragment. "If the news be true—"

"If so, I'm ruined; he received the whole loan on Saturday last,—he could not delay Hickman's payment beyond Wednesday without suspicion."

"Ah! I see it all, and the American packet does not sail till to-morrow morning from Liverpool."

"But it may all be false," said Darcy. "Who writes you this story?"

"It is signed 'F.,' and Freney is the man; I know the fellow that brought it."

"I 'll not believe a word of it, Bagenal," said the Knight, impetuously. "I 'll not credit the calumny of a highwayman against the honor of one I have known and respected for years. It is false, depend upon it."

"Yet how it tallies with Sandy's tidings; there is something in it. Hush! Darcy, don't speak; there is some one passing."

The sounds of feet and voices were heard at the same instant without, and among them the clear, distinctive accents of Hickman O'Reilly.

"Yes," said he, "if the news had come a little earlier, Lord Castlereagh, would have found some of our patriots less stern in virtue. Gleeson will have carried away half a province with him."

"There," whispered Daly, "you heard that,—the news is about already."

But Darcy was now totally overcome, and, with his head resting on the table, neither spoke nor stirred. "Bagenal," said he, at length, but in a voice faint as a whisper, "I am too ill to face the House; let us turn homewards."

"I 'll see for a carriage," said Daly, who issued forth to take the first he could find.

"I say, Hamilton," cried a member, as he alighted from his chariot, "there's the Knight of Gwynne and Bagenal Daly in Castlereagh's carriage."

"Daly said he could drive a coach-and-six through the Bill!" replied the other; "perhaps he's gone to practise with a pair first."

CHAPTER XX
THE ADJOURNED DEBATE

Although the debate had commenced at seven o'clock, none of the great speakers on either side arose before eleven. Some fierce skirmishes had, indeed, occurred; personalities and sarcasms the most cutting had been interchanged with a freedom that showed that if shame were in a great measure departed, personal daring and intrepidity were qualities still in repute. The Ministerial party, no longer timid or wavering, took no pains to conceal their sense of coming victory, and even Lord Castlereagh, usually so guarded on every outward observance, entered the House and took his seat with a smile of conscious triumph that did not escape observation from either friends or opponents.

The tactics of the Treasury benches, too, seemed changed: not waiting, as hitherto, to receive and repel the attack of the Opposition, they now became themselves the assailants, and evinced, by the readiness and frequency of their assaults, the perfect organization they had attained. The Opposition members, who opened the debate, were suffered to proceed without any attempt at reply, an ironical cheer, a well-put question, some home-thrust as to former opinions, alone breaking the thread of an argument which, even from its monotony, was becoming less effective.

Sir Henry Parnell, the late Chancellor of the Exchequer, and who had been dismissed from office for his opinions on the Union, was the first speaker; with a moderation, in part the result of his former position with regard to those who had been his colleagues, he limited himself to a strict examination of the measure in its bearings and consequences, and never, even for a moment, digressed into anything like reflection on the motives of its advocates. His speech was able and argumentative, but evidently unsatisfactory to his party, who seemed impatient and uneasy till he concluded, and hailed Ponsonby, who rose after him, with cheers that showed their expectations were now, at least, more likely to be realized.

Whether the occasion alone was the cause, or that catching the excitement of his supporters, Ponsonby deviated from the usually calm and temperate character he was accustomed to assume in the House, and became warm and impassioned. Disdaining to examine the relative merits or demerits of the proposed Bill, he boldly pronounced Parliament incompetent to decide it, and concluded by declaring that, if carried, the measure might endanger not only the ties of amity between the two nations, but dissolve those of allegiance also. A loud burst of mingled indignation and irony broke from the Treasury benches at this daring flight, when the speaker, at once collecting himself, turned the whole force of his attack on the Secretary. With slow and measured intonation, he depicted the various stages of his political career, recalling to memory the liberal pledges he had once contracted, and the various shades of defection by which he had at last reached the position in which he could "betray Ireland."

None were prepared for the degree of eloquent power Ponsonby displayed on this occasion; and the effect of such a speech from one habitually calm, even to coldness, was overwhelming. It was not Lord Castlereagh's intention to have spoken at this early hour of the debate; but, apologizing for occupying the time of the House by a personality, he arose, not self-possessed and at ease, but flushed and excited.

Without adverting for a second to the measure in debate, he launched forth into a most violent invective on his adversary. With a vehement passion that only his nearest friends knew him to possess, he exposed every act of his political life; taunted him with holding opinions liberal enough to be a patriot, but sufficiently plastic to be marketable; he accused his very calmness as being a hypocritical affectation of fairness, while in reality it was but the tacit admission of his readiness to be bought; and at length pushed his violent sarcasm so far that a loud cry of "Order!" burst forth from the Opposition, while cheers of defiance were heard along the densely crowded ranks of the Ministerial party.

From this moment the discussion assumed a most bitter character; assertions and denials, uttered in language the most insulting, were heard at every moment, and no speaker could proceed without some interruption which demanded several minutes to subdue. More than one member was seen to cross the floor and interchange a few words with an adversary, the import of which, as he returned to his place, no physiognomist need have doubted. It was not debate or discussion, it was the vehement outpouring of personal and political hatred, by men whose passions were no longer restrainable, and many of whom saw in this the last occasion of their ever being able to confront their enemies. Language that could not be uttered with impunity elsewhere, was heard at every moment; open declarations were made that, the Bill once carried, allegiance and loyalty were dissolved;

and Sir Neil O'Donnell went so far as to say that he regarded the measure as an act of treason, and would place himself at the head of his regiment to oppose and annul it.

It was in a momentary pause of this bitter conflict that rumor announced the arrival of the Knight of Gwynne and Bagenal Daly at the House. Never were reinforcements more gladly hailed by a weakened and disabled army; cheers of triumphant delight broke from the Opposition benches, answered by others, not less loud and taunting, from the Ministerial side, and every eye was turned eagerly towards the door by which they were expected to enter.

To such a pitch of violence had partisanship carried the members on both sides, expressions of open defiance and insult were exchanged in the midst of this scene of tumult, nor was the authority of the Speaker able to restore order for several minutes; when at last the doors were thrown open, and Hickman O'Reilly entered, and walked up the body of the House. Shouts of loud laughter now resounded from either side; such an apparition at the moment was the most ludicrous contrast to that expected, and a boisterous gayety succeeded to the late scene of acrimony and intemperance.

The individual himself seemed somewhat puzzled at these unlooked-for marks of public notice, and stared around him in astonishment, till his eyes rested on the spot where Lord Castlereagh sat whispering with Mr. Corry. Brief as was the glance, it seemed to have conveyed some momentous intelligence to the gazer, for he became at first scarlet, and then pale as death; he looked again, but the Secretary had turned his head away, and Corry was coolly unfolding the plaits of a white cambric handkerchief, and apparently only occupied with that object. At this moment Hickman was standing with one foot upon the steps which led towards the Treasury benches: he wheeled abruptly round, and walked over to the other side of the House, where he sat down between Egan and Ponsonby.

The cheers of the Opposition now burst forth anew, and with a deafening clamor, while from back and cross benches, and everywhere within reach, hands were eagerly stretched forth to grasp O'Reilly's. Never was support less expected, never an alliance less speculated on, and the cries of exultation were almost maddening. How long the scene of tumultuous excitement might have lasted, it is difficult to say, when Lord Castlereagh rose, with a calm dignity of manner that never in the most trying moments forsook him. "He begged to remind the gentlemen opposite that if these triumphant expressions were not indecorous, they were at least premature; that the momentous occasion on which they were met demanded all the temperate and calm consideration which they could bestow upon it; that the time for the adoption of any course would not be distant, and would sufficiently show to which side, with most propriety, the expression of triumph belonged."

The hint was significant; the foreshadowed victory was too plainly and too palpably predicted to admit of a doubt, and a chilling silence succeeded to the former uproar. The individual whose address this long scene of tumult had interrupted was now suffered to proceed. He was a law-serjeant, a man of inferior capacity and small professional repute, whose advocacy of the Government plan had raised him to an unbecoming and dangerous eminence at the Bar. Without the slightest pretensions as a speaker, or one quality that should adorn a statesman, he possessed other gifts scarcely less valuable at that day: he was a ready pistol; he came of a fighting family, not one of whom did not owe some advancement in life to a cool hand and a steady eye; and he occupied his place in the Ministerial van by virtue of this signal accomplishment. As incapable of feeling the keen sarcasm of his opponents as he was of using a similar weapon, he was yet irascible from temperament, and overbearing in manner, and was used by his party as men employ a fire-ship, — with a strong conviction that it may damage more than the enemy.

To cover the deficiencies of his oratory, as well as to add poignancy to his personalities, it was the invariable custom of his friends to cheer him vociferously at the end of every sentence which contained anything like attack on the Opposition; and to this species of backing he was indebted for the courage that made him assail men incomparably above him in every quality of intellect.

Mr. Plunkett was now the object of his invective, nor was the boldness of such a daring its least recommendation. Few of the Government side of the House would have adventured to cross weapons with this master of sarcasm and irony; none but the Serjeant Nickolls could have done so without a strong fear of consequences. He, however, was unconcerned for the result as it affected himself personally; and as for the withering storm that awaited him, the triple hide of his native dulness was an armor of proof that nothing could penetrate. From Plunkett he passed on to Bushe, from Bushe to Grattan; no game flew too high for his shafts, nor was any invective coarse enough to level at the great leaders of the Opposition. If the overbearing insolence of his harangue delighted his own party, it called down peals of laughter from his opponents, who cheered every figurative absurdity and every illogical conclusion with shouts of ironical admiration.

Lord Castlereagh saw the mischief, and would gladly have cut short the oration; but the speaker was revelling in an imaginary victory, and would listen to no suggestions whatever. Passing from the great names of the Irish party, he launched forth in terms of insult towards the county members, whom he openly accused of holding their opinions under a mistaken hope that they were a marketable commodity, and that as some stanch adherents of the Crown had reaped the honors due to "their loyalty," these quasi-patriots were only waiting for their price. The allusion was so palpable that every eye was turned to where Hickman O'Reilly sat, and whose confusion was now overwhelming.

"Ay," continued the speaker, now carried beyond all self-restraint by the evident sensation he had caused, "there are gentlemen opposite whose confessions would reveal much of this kind of independence. I have my eye on some of them,—men who will be Patriots if they cannot be Peers, ready to put on the cap of liberty for the Mob if they cannot get the coronet from the Crown. Many, too, are absent from this debate: they stand out, perhaps, for high terms; they have got Peerages for their wives, and now, like a hackney-coachman, not content with their fare, they want 'something for themselves.' I heard of two such a while ago; they even came as far as the lobby of this House, where they halted and hesitated: a mitre or a regiment, a blue ribbon or a red one, would have turned the scale, perhaps. Why are they not here now? I ask, what has become of them?"

"Name! name!" screamed the Opposition, in a torrent of mad excitement, while the Government party, outrageous at the blundering folly of the whole harangue, endeavored to pull the speaker back into his seat. Never was such a scene: one party lashed to madness by suspected treachery and open insult; the other indignant at the stupidity of a man who, in his attempts at attack, had raked up every calumny against his own friends. Already, more than one hand was laid on his arms to press him down into his seat, when he, with the obstinacy of thorough dullness, shook himself free, and called out, "I 'm ready to name."

Again the cries of "Name!" were shouted, mingled with no less vociferous cries of "No, no!" and the struggle now had every appearance of a personal one, when the Speaker, calling to order, asked if it was the sense of the House that the Serjeant should gives the names he alluded to.

"I 'll soon cut the matter short," called out the Serjeant, in a voice that resounded through every corridor of the House. "I mean the Knight of Gwynne and Bagenal Daly."

A cry of "Order! order!" now arose from all parts of the House, the direct mention of any member by name being a liberty unprecedented.

"I beg to correct myself," said the Serjeant. "I should have said the honorable members for Mayo and Old Castle. I ask again, why are they not here?"

"Better you had never put the question," said a deep, low voice from beneath the gallery; and at the same instant Bagenal Daly advanced along one of the passages, and took his place at the table directly in front of the Serjeant. A tremendous cheer now broke from the Opposition benches, which the Ministerial party in vain essayed to return.

"I perceive, sir," said the Serjeant, with an effort to resume his former ease,—"I perceive I have succeeded in conjuring up one at least of these truant spirits, and I cannot do better than leave him to make his explanations to the House."

With this lame, disjointed conclusion the learned Serjeant sat down; and although the greatest exertions were made by his friends to cover this palpable failure, the cries of derision drowned all other sounds, and before they were silenced, a shout of "Daly! Daly!—Bagenal Daly!" resounded through the building.

Daly arose slowly, and saluted the Speaker with a most deferential courtesy. It was several minutes before the tumult had sufficiently subsided to make his words audible; but when silence prevailed, he was heard to regret, in terms of unaffected ease, that any circumstance might occur which should occupy the time of the House by observations from one so rude and unlettered as himself, nor would he now venture on the trespass, were the occasion merely a personal one. From this he proceeded to state that great emergencies were always occurring, in which even the humblest opinions should be made known as evidencing the probable impressions upon others as lowly circumstanced as he who now addressed them.

"Such is the present one," said he, raising his voice, and looking around him with a glance of bold defiance. "You are about to take away the right of self-government from a nation, and every man in the land, not only such as sit here, sir, but every man to whose future ambition a seat in this House may form a goal, every man has a deep interest in your proceedings. It is a grave and weighty question, whose conditions impose the conviction that we are unfit to legislate for ourselves,—that we are too weak, or too venal, or too ignorant, or too dishonest. To that conclusion you must come, or no other. Absence from Ireland must suggest enlightenment on her interests; distance must lend knowledge as well as enchantment, or an English Parliament cannot be better than our own. I have listened attentively, but unconvinced, to all arguments on this head; I have heard over and over again the long catalogue of benefits to accrue to this country when the power of realizing them herself has been wrested from her, and I have thought of Lear and his daughters! It would seem to me, however, that the social welfare and the commercial prosperity of a people are themes too vulgar for the high consideration of our times. The real question at issue is not whether a Parliament should or should not continue to sit here, but what shall I, and others like me, benefit by voting it away forever?"

"Order! order!" called out several voices.

But Daly resumed: "I ask pardon. It is more parliamentary to put the case differently, and I shall, under correction, do so. Well, sir, we may benefit largely. I trust I am not disorderly in saying that peerages, bishoprics, regiments, frigates, commissionerships, and Heaven knows what more, will reward us when our utility to the State has met the approval of an Imperial Parliament. I can well credit every promise of such gratitude, and have only to ask in turn, Are these the arguments that should sway us now? Is it because we are bungling legislators that they wish for us in London?—is it because we are venal they seek our company, because we are inefficient they ask for our cooperation? Are they so supremely right-minded, honorable, and far-seeing that they need the alloy of our dulness to make them mortal? And suppose such the case, will it be gratifying to us to become the helots to this people? Will our national pride be flattered because our eloquence is sneered at, our law derided, our political knowledge a scoff, and our very accent a joke? Do not tell me such things are unlikely; we are far weaker on the point than we like to confess. For myself, I can imagine the sense of shame—of deep, heartfelt, abasing shame—I should feel at seeing some of those I see here rise in a British House of Commons to address that body, while the rumor should run, 'He is the member for Meath or for Wicklow.' I can picture to myself such a man: a man of low origin and mean capacity; a man who carves his path in life less from his own keen abilities than that others shrink from his contact, and leave him unopposed in every struggle; a pettifogger at the Bar; a place-hunter at the Parliament; half beggar, half bravo, with a petition for the Minister, and a pistol for the Opposition. Imagine a man like this, and reflect upon the feeling of every gentleman at hearing the rumor announce, 'Ay, that's a learned Serjeant, a leader at the Bar of Ireland.'"

The last words were delivered in a tone of direct personality, as, turning towards where Nickolls sat, Daly threw at him a look of defiance. The whole House arose as if one man, with cheers and counter-cheers, and loud yells of insult, mingled with cries of "Order!" Nor was it till after a long and desperate wordy altercation that the clamor was subdued, and decorum at length restored. Then it was remarked that Nickolls had left the House.

The Speaker immediately ordered the Serjeant of the House to place Daly under arrest,—a measure which, however dictated by propriety, seemed to call forth a burst of indignation from the Opposition benches.

"I hope, sir," said Daly, rising with an air of most admirably feigned humility,—"I hope, sir, you will not execute this threat,—the inconvenience to me will be very great: I was about to pair off with the honorable and learned member for Newry."

The mention of the town for which the Serjeant sat in Parliament renewed the laughter which now prevailed on both sides of the House.

"I cannot understand the mirth of the gentlemen opposite," said Daly, with affected simplicity, "without it be from their astonishment that the Government can spare so able and so eloquent an advocate as the honorable and learned gentleman; but let them reassure themselves and look around, and, believe me, they'll find the Treasury benches filled by gentlemen as like him as possible."

The Speaker reissued the order to the Serjeant-at-Arms, and Daly now came forward to the table and begged in all form to know the reason of such severity. "If, sir," said he, in conclusion,—"if I could believe it possible that you anticipate any personal collision between myself and any member of this House, I have only to say that I am bound over in the sum of two thousand pounds to keep the peace within the limits of this kingdom. I take out a license at two pounds fifteen to kill game, it is true; but I 'd not pay sixpence for the privilege to shoot a lawyer."

The fact of the heavy recognizances to which Daly alluded was at once confirmed by several members, and after a brief conversation with the Speaker the matter was dropped.

It was, as may be supposed, a considerable time before the debate could assume its due decorum and solemnity after an incident like this; for although hostile collisions were neither few nor unfrequent, an insult of so violent a character had never before been witnessed.

At length, however, order was restored, and another speaker addressed the House. All had assumed its wonted propriety, when a messenger delivered into Daly's hands a small sealed note; he glanced at the contents and rose immediately. Lord Castlereagh's quick eye caught the motion, and he at once called on the Speaker to interfere. "I have myself seen a letter conveyed to the honorable member's hands," said he; "it requires no peculiar gift of divination to guess the object."

"I will satisfy the noble lord at once," said Daly; "there is the letter I have received: I pledge my word of honor the subject is purely a private one, having no reference whatever to anything that has passed here." He held out the letter as he spoke, but Lord Castlereagh declined to peruse it, and expressed his regret at having made the remark. Daly bowed courteously to him, and left the House.

"Well, Sandy," said he, as soon as he reached the corridor, where his faithful follower stood waiting his coming, "what success?"

"No sae bad," said Sandy. "I 've got a wherry, ane of them Wicklow craft; she's only half-decked, but she's a stout-looking sea-boat, and broad in the beam."

"And the wind, how's that?"

"As it should be,—west, or west wi' a point north."

"Is there enough of it?"

"Enough! I trow there is," said Sanders, with a grin; "if there be no a blast too much. Hear till it now." And, as if waiting for the remark, a tremendous gust of wind shook the strong building, while the clanking sound of falling slates and chimney-pots resounded through the street.

"There's music for ye," said Sandy; "there came a clap like that when I had a'maist made the bargain, and the carles would no budge without ten guineas mair. I promised them fifty, and the handsel whatever your honor liked after."

"It's all right,—quite right," said Daly, wishing to stop details he never listened to with patience.

"It's a' right, I know weel enough," said Sandy, querulously; "but it wad no be a' right av ye went yersel'; they 'd have a gude penny, forbye what I say."

"And what say the fellows of this wind,—is it like to last?"

"It will blow hard from the west for three or four days mair, and then draw round to the north."

"But we shall get to Liverpool before noon to-morrow."

"Maybe," said Sandy, with a low, dry laugh.

"Well, I mean if we do get there. You told them I 'd double the pay if we catch the American ship in the Mersey. I'd triple it; let them know that."

"They canna do mair than they can do: ten pounds is as good as ten hundred."

While this conversation was going forward, they had walked on together, and were now at the entrance door of the House, where a group of four persons stood under the shadow of the portico.

"Mr. Daly, I presume," said one, advancing, and touching his hat in salutation. "We have waited somewhat impatiently for your coming."

"I should regret it, sir, if I was aware you did me the honor to expect me."

"I am the friend of Serjeant Nickolls, sir," said the other, in a voice meant to be eloquently meaning.

"For your sake, the fact is to be deplored," answered Daly, calmly. "But proceed."

With a great effort to subdue his passion, the other resumed: "It does not require your experience in such matters to know that the insult you have passed upon a high-minded and honorable gentleman—the gross and outrageous insult—should be atoned for by a meeting. We are here for this purpose, ready to accompany you, as soon as you have provided yourself with a friend, to wherever you appoint."

"Are you aware," said Daly, in a whisper, "that I am bound over in heavy recognizances—"

"Ah, indeed!" interrupted the other; "that, perhaps, may explain—"

"Explain what, sir?" said Daly, as he grasped the formidable weapon which, more club than walking-stick, he invariably carried.

"I meant nothing; I would only observe—"

"Never observe, sir, when there's nothing to be remarked. I was informing you that I am bound over to keep the peace in this same kingdom of Ireland; circumstances compel me to be in England to-morrow morning,—circumstances of such moment that I have myself hired a vessel to convey me thither,—and although the object of my journey is far from agreeable, I shall deem it one of the happiest coincidences of my life if it can accommodate your friend's wishes. Nothing prevents my giving him the satisfaction he desires on English ground. I have sincere pleasure in offering him, and every gentleman of his party, a passage over—the tide serves in half an hour. Eh, Sandy?"

"At a quarter to twelve, sir."

"The wind is fair."

"It is a hurricane," replied the other, almost shuddering.

"It blows fresh," was Daly's cool remark.

For a moment or two the stranger returned to his party, with whom he talked eagerly, and the voices of the others were also heard, speaking in evident excitement.

"You have the pistols safe, Sandy?" whispered Daly.

"They 're a' safe, and in the wherry; but you 'll no want them this time, I trow," said Sandy, with a shrug of his shoulders; "yon folk would rather bide where they are the night, than tak' a bit o' pleasure in the Channel."

Daly smiled, and turned away to hide it, when the stranger again came forward. "I have consulted with my friends, Mr. Daly, who are also the friends of Serjeant Nickolls; they are of opinion that, under the circumstances of your being bound over, this affair cannot with propriety go further, although it might not, perhaps, be unreasonable to expect that you, feeling the peculiar situation in which you stand, might express some portion of regret at the utterance of this most severe attack."

"You are really misinformed on the whole of the business," said Daly. "In the few words I offered to the House, I was but responding to the question of your friend, who asked, I think somewhat needlessly, 'Where was Bagenal Daly?' I have no regrets to express for any terms I applied to him, though I may feel sorry that the forms of the House prevented my saying more. I am ready to meet him now; or, as he seems to dislike a breeze, when the weather is calmer. Tell him so; but tell him besides, that if he utters one syllable in my absence that the most malevolent gossip of a club-room can construe into an imputation on me, by G—d I'll break every bone in his cowardly carcass! Come, Sandy, lead on. Good evening, sir. I wish you a bolder friend, or better weather." So saying, he moved forward, and was soon hastening towards the North Wall, where the wherry was moored.

"It's unco like the night we were wrecked in the Gulf," said Sandy. "I mind the moon had that same blue color, and the clouds were a' below, and none above her."

"So it is, Sandy,—there 's a heavy sea outside, I 'm sure. How many men have we?"

"Four, and a bit o' a lad that's as gude as anither. Lord save us! there was a flash! I wish it wud come to rain, and beat down the sea; we 'd have aye wind enough after."

"Where does she lie?"

"Yonder, sir, where you see the light bobbing. By my certie, but the chiels were no far wrang. A bit fighting 's hard bought by a trip to sea on such a night as this."

CHAPTER XXI
TWO OF A TRADE

When the newspapers announced the division on the adjourned debate, they also proclaimed the flight of the defaulter; and, wide as was the disparity between the two events in point of importance, it would be difficult to say which more engaged the attention of the Dublin public on that morning, the majority for the Minister, or the published perfidy of "Honest Tom Gleeson."

Such is, however, the all-engrossing interest of a local topic, aided, as in the present case, by almost incredulous amazement, the agent's flight was talked of and discussed in circles where the great political event was heard as a matter of course. Where had he fled to? What sum had he carried away with him? Who would be the principal losers? were all the questions eagerly discussed, but none of which excited so much diversity of opinion as the single one: What was the cause of his defalcation? His agencies were numerous and profitable, his mode of life neither extravagant nor ostentatious; how could a man with so few habits of expense have contracted debts of any considerable amount, or what circumstances could induce him to relinquish a station of respectability and competence for a life-long of dishonorable exile?

Such has been our progress of late years in the art of revealing to the world at large the hidden springs of every action and event around us that a secret is in reality the only thing now impossible. Forty-five years ago, this wonderful exercise of knowledge was in a great measure unknown; the guessers were then a large and respectable class in society, and men were content with what mathematicians call approximation. In our own more accurate days, what between the newspaper, the club-room, and "'Change," such mystery is no longer practicable. One day, or two at furthest, would now proclaim every item in a man's schedule, and afford that most sympathetic of all bodies, the world, the fruitful theme of expatiating on his folly or his criminality. In the times we refer to, however, it was only the "Con Heffermans" of society that ventured even to speculate on the secret causes of these events.

Although the debate had lasted from eight o'clock in the evening to past eleven on the following morning, before twelve Mr. Heffernan's carriage was at the door, and the owner, without any trace of fatigue, set off to ascertain so much as might be learned of this strange and unexpected catastrophe. It was no mere passion to know the current gossip of the day, no prying taste for the last piece of scandal in circulation,—Con Heffernan was above such weaknesses; but he had a habit—one which some men practise even yet with success—of whenever the game was safe, taking credit to himself for casualties in which he had no possible connection, and attributing events in which he had no share to his own direct influence. After all, he was in this only imitating the great navigators of the globe, who have established the rule that discovery gives a right only second to actual creation.

This was, however, a really provoking case; no one knew anything of Gleeson's embarrassments. Several of those for whom he acted as agent were in Dublin, but they were more amazed than all others at his flight; most of them had settled accounts with him very lately, some men owed him small sums. "Darcy perhaps knows something about him," was a speech Heffernan heard more than once repeated; but Darcy's house was shut up, and the servant announced "he had left town that morning." Hickman O'Reilly was the next chance; not that he had any direct intercourse with Gleeson, but his general acquaintanceship with moneyed men and matters made him a likely source of information; while a small sealed note addressed to Dr. Hickman was in possession of a banker with whom Gleeson had transacted business the day before his departure. But O'Reilly had left town with his son. "The doctor, sir, is here still; he does not go before to-morrow," said the servant, who, knowing that Heffernan was a person of some consequence in the Dublin world, thought proper to give this piece of unasked news.

"Will you give Mr. Con Heffernan's compliments, and say he would be glad to have the opportunity of a few minutes' conversation?" The servant returned immediately, and showed him upstairs into a back drawing-room, where, before a table covered with law papers and parchments, sat the venerable doctor. He had not as yet performed the usual offices of a toilet, and, with unshaven chin and uncombed hair, looked the most melancholy contrast of age, neglect, and misery, with the gorgeous furniture of a most splendid apartment.

He lifted his head as the door opened, and stared fixedly at the new-comer, with an expression at once fierce and anxious, so that Heffernan, when speaking of him afterwards, said that, "Dressed as he was, in an old flannel morning-gown, dotted with black tufts, he looked for all the world like a sick tiger making his will."

"Your humble servant, sir," said he, coldly, as Heffernan advanced with an air of cordiality; nor were the words and the accents they were uttered in lost upon the man they were addressed to. He saw how the land lay, in a second, and said eagerly, "He has not left town, I trust, sir; I sincerely hope your son has not gone."

"Yes, sir, he's off; I'm sure I don't know what he'd wait for."

"Too precipitate,—too rash by far, Mr. Hickman," said Heffernan, seating himself, and wiping his forehead with an air of well-assumed chagrin.

"Maybe so," repeated the old man two or three times over, while he lowered his spectacles to his nose, and began hunting among his papers, as though he had other occupation in hand of more moment than the present topic.

"Are you aware, sir," said Heffernan, drawing his chair close up, and speaking in a most confidential whisper,—"are you aware, sir, that your son mistook the signal,—that when Mr. Corry took out his handkerchief and opened it on his knee, that it was in token of Lord Castlereagh's acquiescence of Mr. O'Reilly's demand,—that, in short, the peerage was at that moment his own if he wished it?"

The look of dogged incredulity in the old man's face would have silenced a more sensitive advocate than Heffer-nan; but he went on: "If any one should feel angry at what has occurred, I am the person; I was the guarantee for your son's vote, and I have now to meet Lord Castle-reagh without one word of possible explanation."

"Hickman told me," said the old man, with a voice steady and composed, "that if Mr. Corry did not raise the handkerchief to his mouth, the terms were not agreed upon; that opening it before him only meant the bargain was not quite off: more delay, more talk, Mr. Heffernan; and I think there was enough of that already."

"A complete mistake, sir,—a total misconception on his part."

"Just like Beecham being blackballed at the club," said the doctor, with a sarcastic bitterness all his own.

"With that, of course, we cannot be charged," said Heffernan. "Why was he put up without our being apprised of it? The blackballing was Bagenal Daly's doing—"

"So I heard," interrupted the other; "they told me that; and here, look here, here's Daly's bond for four thousand six hundred. Maybe he won't be so ready with his bank-notes as he was with his black ball—ay!"

"But, to go back to the affair of the House—"

"We won't go back to it, sir, if it's the same to you. I'm glad, with all my heart, the folly is over,—sorra use I could see in it, except the expense, and there's plenty of that. The old families, as they call them, can't last forever, no more than old houses and old castles; there's an end of everything in time, and if Hickman waits, maybe his turn will come as others' did before him. Where's the Darcys now, I'd like to know?—" Here he paused and stammered, and at last stopped dead short, an expression of as much confusion as age and wrinkles would permit covering his hard, contracted features.

"You say truly," said Heffernan, finishing what he guessed to be the sentiment,—"you say truly, the Darcys have run their race; when men's incumbrances have reached the point that his have, family influence soon decays. Now, this business of Gleeson's—" Had he fired a shot close to the old man's ear he could not have startled him more effectually than by the mention of this name.

"What of Gleeson?" said he, drawing in his breath, and holding on the chair with both hands.

"You know that he is gone,—fled away no one knows where?"

"Gleeson! Honest Tom Gleeson ran away!" exclaimed Hickman; "no, no, that's impossible,—I'd never believe that."

"Strange enough, sir, that the paragraphs here have not convinced you," said Heffernan, taking up the newspaper which lay on the table, and where the mark of snuffy fingers denoted the very passage in question.

"Ay! I did n't notice it before," muttered the doctor, as he took up the paper, affecting to read, but in reality to conceal his own confusion.

"They say the news nearly killed Ðarcy; he only heard it when going into the House last night, and was seized with an apoplectic fit, and carried home insensible." This latter was, it is perhaps needless to say, pure invention of Heffernan, who found it necessary to continue talking as a means of detecting old Hickman's game. "Total ruin to that family of course results. Gleeson had raised immense sums to pay off the debts, and carried all away with him."

"Ay!" muttered the doctor, as he seemed greatly occupied in arranging his papers on the table.

"You'll be a loser too, sir, by all accounts," added Heffernan.

"Not much,—a mere trifle," said the doctor, without looking up from the papers. "But maybe he's not gone, after all; I won't believe it yet."

"There seems little doubt on that head," said Heffernan; "he changed three thousand pounds in notes for gold at Ball's after the bank was closed on Tuesday, and then went over to Finlay's, where he said he had a lodgment to make. He left his great-coat behind him, and never came back for it. I found that paper—it was the only one—in the breast pocket."

"What is it? what is it?" repeated the old man, clutching eagerly at it.

"Nothing of any consequence," said Heffernan, smiling; and he handed him a printed notice, setting forth that the United States barque, the "Congress," of five hundred tons burden, would sail for New York on Wednesday, the 16th instant, at an hour before high water. "That looked suspicious, didn't it?" said Heffernan; "and on inquiry I found he had drawn largely out of, not only the banks in town, but from the provincial ones also. Now, that note addressed to yourself, for instance—"

"What note?" said Hickman, starting round as his face became pale as ashes; "give it to me—give it at once!"

But Heffernan held it firmly between his fingers, and merely shook his head, while, with a gentle smile, he said, "The banker who intrusted this letter to my hands was well aware of what importance it might prove in a court of justice, should this disastrous event demand a legal investigation."

The old doctor listened with breathless interest to every word of this speech, and merely muttered at the close the words, "The note, the note!"

"I have promised to restore the paper to the banker," said Heffernan.

"So you shall,—let me read it," cried Hickman, eagerly; and he clutched from Heffernan's fingers the document, before the other had seemingly determined whether he would yield to his demand.

"There it is for you, sir," said the doctor; "make what you can of it;" and he threw the paper across the table.

The note contained merely the words, "Ten thousand pounds." There was no signature or any date, but the handwriting was Gleeson's.

"Ten thousand pounds," repeated Heffernan, slowly; "a large sum!"

"So it is," chimed in Hickman, with a grin of self-satisfaction, while a consciousness that the mystery, whatever it might be, was beyond the reach of Heffernan's skill, gave him a look of excessive cunning, which sat strangely on features so old and time-worn.

"Well, Mr. Hickman," said Heffernan, as he arose to take leave, "I have neither the right nor the inclination to pry into any man's secrets. This affair of Gleeson's will be sifted to the bottom one day or other, and that small transaction of the ten thousand pounds as well as the rest. It was not to discuss him or his fortunes I came here. I hoped to have seen Mr. O'Reilly, and explained away a very serious misconception. Lord Castlereagh regrets it, not for the sake of the loss of Mr. O'Reilly's support, valuable as that unquestionably is, but because a wrong interpretation would seem to infer that the conduct of the Treasury bench was disingenuous. You will, I trust, make this explanation for me, and in the name of his Lordship."

"Faith, I won't promise it," said old Hickman, looking up from a long column of figures which he was for some minutes poring over; "I don't understand them things at all; if Bob wanted to be a lord, 't is more than ever I did,—I don't see much pleasure there is in being a gentleman. I know, for my part, I 'd rather sit in the back parlor of my little shop in Loughrea, where I could have a chat over a tumbler of punch with a neighbor, than all the grandeur in life."

"These simple, unostentatious tastes do you credit before the world, sir," said Heffernan, with a well put-on look of admiration.

"I don't know whether they do or not," said Hickman, "but I know they help to make a good credit with the bank, and that's better—ay!"

Heffernan affected to relish the joke, and descended the stairs, laughing as he went; but scarcely had he reached his carriage, however, than he muttered a heavy malediction on the sordid old miser whose iniquities were not less glaring because Con had utterly failed to unravel anything of his mystery.

"To Lord Castlereagh's," said he to the footman, and then lay back to ponder over his late interview.

The noble Secretary was not up when Con arrived, but had left orders that Mr. Heffernan should be shown up to his room whenever he came. It was now about five o'clock in the afternoon, and Lord Castlereagh, wrapped up in a loose morning-gown, lay on the bed where he had thrown himself, without undressing, on reaching home. A debate of more than fifteen hours, with all its strong and exciting passages, had completely exhausted his strength, while the short and disturbed sleep had wearied rather than refreshed him. The bed and the table beside it were covered with the morning papers and open letters and despatches, for, tired as he was, he could not refrain from learning the news of the day.

"Well, my Lord," said Heffernan, with his habitual smile, as he stepped noiselessly across the floor, "I believe I may wish you joy at last,—the battle is gained now."

"Heigho!" was the reply of the Secretary, while he extended two fingers of his hand in salutation. "What hour is it, Heffernan?"

"It is near five; but really there 's not a creature to be seen in the streets, and, except old Killgobbin airing his pocket-handkerchief at the fire, not a soul at the Club. Last night's struggle has nearly killed every one."

"Who is this Mr. Gleeson that has run off with so much money,—did you know him?"

"Oh, yes, we all knew 'honest Tom Gleeson.'"

"Ah! that was his sobriquet, was it?" said the Secretary, smiling.

"Yes, my Lord, such was he,—or such, at least, was he believed to be, till yesterday evening. You know it's the last glass of wine always makes a man tipsy."

"And who is ruined, Heffernan,—any of our friends?"

"As yet there's no saying. Drogheda will lose something considerable, I believe; but at the banks the opinion is that Darcy will be the heaviest loser of any."

"The Knight?"

"Yes, the Knight of Gwynne."

"I am sincerely sorry to hear it," said Lord Castlereagh, with an energy of tone he had not displayed before; "if I had met half-a-dozen such men as he is, I should have had some scruples—" He paused, and at the instant caught sight of a very peculiar smile on Heffernan's features; then, suddenly changing the topic, he said, "What of Nickolls,—is he shot?"

"No, my Lord, there was no meeting. Bagenal Daly, so goes the story, proposed going over to the Isle of Man in a row-boat."

"What, last night!" said the Secretary, laughing.

"Yes, when it was blowing the roof off the Custom House; he offered him his choice of weapons, from a blunderbuss to a harpoon, and his own distance, over a handkerchief, or fifty yards with a rifle."

"And was Nickolls deaf to all such seductions?"

"Quite so, my Lord; even when Daly said to him, 'I think it a public duty to shoot a fellow like you, for, if you are suffered to live, the Government will make a judge of you one of these days.'"

"What profound solicitude for the purity of the judgment seat!"

"Daly has reason to think of these things; he has been in the dock already, and perhaps suspects he may be again."

"Poor Darcy!" said Lord Castlereagh to himself, in a half whisper, "I wish I knew you were not a sufferer by this fellow's flight. By the bye, Heffernan, sit down and write a few lines to Forester; say that Lord Cornwallis is greatly displeased at his protracted absence. I am tired of making excuses for him, and as I dine there to-day, I shall be tormented all the evening."

"Darcy's daughter is very good-looking, I hear," said Heffernan, smiling slyly, "and should have a large fortune if matters go right."

"Very possibly; but old Lady Wallincourt is the proudest dowager in England, and looks to the blood-royal for alliances. Forester is entirely dependent on her; and that reminds me of a most solemn pledge I made her to look after her 'dear Dick,' and prevent any entanglement in this barbarous land,—as if I had nothing else to think of! Write at once, Heffernan, and order him up; say he 'll lose his appointment by any further delay, and that I am much annoyed at his absence."

While Heffernan descended to the library to write, Lord Castlereagh turned once more to sleep until it was time to dress for the Viceroy's dinner.

CHAPTER XXII
"A WARNING" AND "A PARTING"

If we wanted any evidence of how little avail all worldly wisdom is, we might take it from the fact that our severest calamities are often impending us at the moments we deem ourselves most secure from misfortune. Thus was it that while the events were happening whose influence was to shadow over all the sunshine of her life, Lady Eleanor Darcy never felt more at ease. That same morning the post had brought her a letter from the Knight,—only a few lines, hastily written, but enough to allay all her anxiety. He spoke of law arrangements, then almost completed, by which any immediate pressure regarding money might be at once obviated, and promised, for the very first time in his life, to submit to any plan of retrenchment she desired to adopt. Had it been in her power, she could not have dictated lines more full of pleasant anticipation. The only drawback on the happiness of her lot in life was the wasteful extravagance of a mode of living which savored far more of feudal barbarism than of modern luxury.

Partly from long habit and association, partly from indolence of character, but more than either from a compassionate consideration of those whose livelihood might be impaired by any change in his establishment, the Knight had resisted all suggestion of alteration. He viewed the very peculations around him as vested rights, and the most he could pledge himself to was, that when the present race died out he would not appoint any successors.

The same post that brought this pleasant letter, conveyed one of far less grateful import to Forester. It was a long epistle from his mother, carefully worded, and so characteristic withal, that if it were any part of our object to introduce that lady to our readers, we could not more easily do so than through her own letter. Such is not, however, our intention; enough if we say that it was a species of domestic homily, where moral principles and worldly wisdom found themselves so inextricably interwoven, no mean skill could have disentangled them. She had learned, as careful mothers somehow always contrive to learn, that her son was domesticated in the house with a very charming and beautiful girl, and the occasion seemed suitable to enforce some of those excellent precepts which hitherto had been deficient in force for want of a practical example.

Had Lady Wallincourt limited herself to cautious counsels about falling in love with some rustic beauty in a remote region, Forester might have treated the advice as one of those matter-of-course events which cause no more surprise than the receipt of a printed circular; but she went further. She deemed this a fitting occasion to instruct her son into the mystery of that craft, which, in her own experience of life, she had seen make more than one man's fortune, and by being adepts in which many of her own family had attained to high and lasting honors. This science was neither more nor less than success in female society. "I will not insult either your good taste or your understanding," wrote she, "by any warning against falling in love in Ireland. Beauty is—France excepted—pretty equally distributed through the world; neither is there any nationality in good looks, for, nowadays, admixture of race has obliterated every peculiarity of origin. In all, then, that concerns manner, tone, and breeding, your own country possesses the true standard: every deviation from this is a fault. What is conventional must be right, because it is the exponent of general opinion on those topics for which each feels interested. Now, the Irish, my dear boy, the Irish are never conventional; they are clannish, provincial, peculiar, but never conventional. Their pride would seem to be rather to ruffle than fall in with the general sympathies of society. They forget that the social world is a great compact, and they are always striving for individual successes by personal distinction: this is the very acme of vulgarity.

"If they, however, are very indifferent models for imitation, they afford an excellent school for your own training; they are a shrewd, quick-sighted race, with a strong sense of the ludicrous, and are what the French call *malin* to a degree. To win favor among them without any subservient imitation of their own habits, which would be contemptible, is not over easy.

"If I am rightly informed, you are at present well circumstanced to profit by my counsels. I am told of a very agreeable and very pretty girl with whom you ride and walk out constantly, and, far from feeling any maternal uneasiness,—for I trust I know my son,—I am rejoiced at the circumstance. Make the most of such an advantage by exercising your own abilities and powers of pleasing, give yourself the habit of talking your very best on every topic, without pedantry or any sign of premeditation. Practise that blending of courteous deference to a woman's opinions with a subdued consciousness of your own powers, which I have spoken to you of in your dear father's character. Seldom venture on an axiom, never tell an anecdote; be most guarded in any indulgence of humor: a laugh is the most dangerous of all triumphs. It is the habit to reproach us with our frigidity,—I believe not without reason; cultivate, then, a certain amount of warmth which may suggest the idea of earnestness, apart from all suspicion of enthusiasm, which I have often told you is low-lived. Watch carefully by what qualities your success is more advanced; examine yourself as to what defects you experience in your own character; make yourself esteemed as a means of being estimable; win regard, and the habit of pleasing will give a charm to your manner, even when you are not desirous to secure affection. Your poor dear father often confessed the inestimable advantages of his first affairs of the heart, and used to say, whenever by any adroit exercise of his captivation he had gained over an adverse Maid of Honor, I owe that to Louisa, for such was the name of the young lady,—I forget now who she was. The mechanism of the heart is alike in all lands; the means of success in Ireland will win victory where the prize is higher. In all this, remember, I by no means advise you to sport with any young lady's feelings, nor to win more of her affection than may assure you that the entire could also become yours: a polite chess-player will rest satisfied to say, 'check,' without pushing the adversary to 'mate.'

"It will soon be time you should leave the army, and I hope to find you have acquired some other education by the pursuit than mere knowledge of dress."

This is a short specimen of the maternal Machiavelism by which "the most fascinating woman of her set" hoped to instruct her son, and teach him the road to fortune.

Such is the fatal depravity of every human heart that any subtle appeal to selfishness, if it fail to flex the victim to the will, at least shakes the strong sense of conscious rectitude, and makes our very worthiness seem weakness.

Forester's first impression was almost anger as he read these lines, the second time he perused them he was far less shocked, and at last was puzzled whether more to wonder at the keen worldly knowledge they betrayed, or the solicitude of that affection which consented to unveil so much of life for his guidance. The result of all these conflicting emotions was depression of spirits, and a discontent with himself and all the world; nor could the fascinations of that little circle in which he lived so intimately, subdue the feeling.

Lady Eleanor saw this, and exerted herself with all her wonted powers to amuse and interest him; Helen, too, delighted at the favorable change in her mother's spirits, contributed to sustain the tone of light-hearted pleasantry, while she could not restrain a jest upon Forester's unusual gloominess.

The manner whose fascinations had hitherto so many charms, now almost irritated him; the poison of suspicion had been imbibed, and he continually asked himself, what if the very subtlety his mother's letter spoke of was now practised by her? If all the varied hues of captivation her changing humor wore were but the deep practised lures of coquetry? His self-love was piqued by the thought, as well as his perceptive shrewdness, and he set himself, as he believed, to decipher her real nature; but, such is the blindness of mere egotism, in reality to misunderstand and mistake her.

How often it happens in life that the moment a doubt prevails as to some trait or feature of our character, we should exactly seize upon that very instant to indulge in some weakness or passing levity that may strengthen a mere suspicion, or make it a certainty.

Helen never seemed gayer than on this evening, scarcely noticing Forester, save when to jest upon his morose and silent mood; she talked, and laughed, and sang in all the free joyousness of a happy heart, unconsciously displaying powers of mind and feeling which, in calmer moments, lay dormant and concealed.

The evening wore on, and Helen had just risen from her harp,—where she was playing one of those wild, half-sad, half-playful melodies of her country,—when a gentle tap came to the door, and, without waiting for leave to enter, old Tate appeared.

The old man was pale, and his features wore an expression of extreme terror; but he was doing his very utmost, as it seemed, to struggle against some inward fear, as, with a smile of far more melancholy than mirth, he said, "Did ye hear it, my Lady? I 'm sure ye heerd it."

"Heard what, Tate?" said Lady Eleanor.

"The—but I see Miss Helen's laughing at me. Ah! don't then, Miss, darlin',—don't laugh."

"What was it, Tate? Tell us what you heard."

"The Banshee, my Lady! Ay, there 's the way,—I knew how 't would be; you 'd only laugh when I tould you."

"Where was it you heard it?" said Lady Eleanor, affecting seriousness to gratify the old man's superstition.

"Under the east window, my Lady; then it moved across the flower-garden, and down to the shore beneath the big rocks."

"What was it like, Tate?"

"'T was like a funeral 'coyne' first, Miss, when ye heerd it far away in the mountain; and then it rose, and swelled fuller and stronger, till it swam all round me, and at last died away to the light, soft cry of an infant."

"Exactly, Tate; it was Captain Forester sighing. I never heard a better description in my life."

"Ah! don't laugh, my Lady,—don't now, Miss Helen, dear. I never knew luck nor grace come of laughing when the warnin' was come. 'T is the Captain, there, looks sad and thoughtful,—the Heavens bless him for it! He knows 'tis no time for laughing."

Forester might have accepted the eulogy in better part, perhaps, had he understood it; but as it was, he turned abruptly about, and asked Lady Eleanor for an explanation of the whole mystery.

"Tate thinks he has heard—"

"Thinks!" interrupted the old man, with a sorrowful gesture of both hands. "Musha! I'd take the Gospel on it; I heard it as plain as I hear your Ladyship now."

Lady Eleanor smiled, and went on—"the cry of the Banshee, that dreadful warning which, in the superstition of the country, always betokens death, or at least some great calamity, to the house it is heard to wail over."

"A polite attention, to say the least," said Forester, smiling sarcastically, "of the witch or fairy or whatever it is, to announce to people an approaching misfortune. And has every cabin got its own Ban—what do you call it?"

"The cabins has none," said Tate, with a loot of severe reproach, the most remote possible from his habitual air of deference; "'tis only the ouldest and most ancient families, like his honor the Knight's, has a Banshee. But it's no use talking; I see nobody believes me."

"Yes, Tate, I do," cried Helen, with an earnestness of manner, either really felt, or assumed to gratify the poor old man's superstitious veneration; "just tell me how you heard it first."

"Like that!" whispered Tate, as he held up his hand to enforce silence; and at the same instant a low, plaintive cry was heard, as if beneath the very window. The accent was not of pain or suffering, but of melancholy so soft, so touching, and yet so intense, that it stilled every voice within the room, where now each long-drawn breath was audible.

There is a lurking trait of superstition in every human heart, which will resist, at some one moment or other, every effort of reason and every scoff of irony. An instant before, and Forester was ready to jest with the old man's terrors, and now his own spirit was not all devoid of them. The feeling was, however, but of a moment's duration; suspicion again assumed its sway, and, seizing his hat, he rushed from the room, to search the flower-garden and examine every spot where any one might lie concealed.

"There he goes now, as if he could see *her*; and maybe 't would be as well for him he did n't," said Tate, as, in contempt of the English incredulity, he gazed after the eager youth. "Is his honor well, my Lady?—when did you hear from him?"

"We heard this very day, Tate; he is perfectly well."

"And Master Lionel—the captain, I mane—but I only think he's a child still."

"Quite well, too," said Helen. "Don't alarm yourself, Tate; you know how sadly the wind can sigh through these old walls at times, and under the yew-trees, too, it sounds drearily; I 've shuddered to myself often, as I 've heard it."

"God grant it!" said old Tate, piously; but the shake of his head and the muttering sounds between his teeth attested that he laid no such flattering unction to his heart as mere disbelief might offer. "'T is n't a death-cry, anyhow, Miss Helen," whispered he to Miss Darcy, as he moved towards the door; "for I went down to the back of the abbey, where Sir Everard was buried, and all was still there."

"Well, go to bed now, Tate, and don't think more about it; if the wind—"

"Ah! the wind! the wind!" said he, querulously; "that's the way it always is,—as if God Almighty had no other way of talking to our hearts than the cry of the night-wind."

"Well, Captain Forester, what success? Have you confronted the spectre?" said Lady Eleanor, as he re-entered the apartment.

"Except having fallen into a holly-bush, where I rivalled the complaining accents of the old witch, I have no adventure to recount; all is perfectly still and tranquil without."

"You have got your cheek scratched for following the siren," said Lady Eleanor, laughing; "pray put another log on the fire, it is fearfully chilly here."

Old Tate withdrew slowly and unwillingly; he saw that his intelligence had failed to produce a proper sense of terror on their minds; and his own load of anxiety was heavier, from want of participation.

The conversation, by that strange instinct which influences the least as well as the most credulous people, now turned on the superstitions of the peasantry, and many a legend and story were remembered by Lady Eleanor and her daughter, in which these popular beliefs formed a chief feature.

"It is unfair and unwise," said Lady Eleanor, at the conclusion of one of these stories, "to undervalue such influences; the sailor, who passes his life in dangers, watches the elements with an eye and an air that training have rendered almost preternaturally observant, and he sees the sign of storm where others would but mark the glow of a red sunset; so among a primitive people communing much with their own hearts in solitary, unfrequented places, imagination becomes developed in undue proportion, and the mind seeks relief in creative efforts from the wearying sense of loneliness; but even these are less idle fancies than conclusions come to from long and deep thought. Some strange process of analogy would seem the parent of superstitions which we know to be common to all lands."

"Which means, that you half believe in a Banshee!" said Forester, smiling.

"Not so; but that I cannot consent to despise the frame of mind which suggests these beliefs, although I have no faith in the apparitions. Poor Tate, there, had never dreamed of hearing the Banshee cry if some painful thought of impending misfortune had not suggested her presence; his fears may not be unfounded, although the form they take be preternatural."

"I protest against all such plausibilities," said Helen. "I 'm for the Banshee, as the Republicans say in France, 'one and indivisible.' I 'll not accept of natural explanations. Mr. Bagenal Daly says, we may well believe in spirits, when we put faith in the mere ghost of a Parliament."

"Helen is throwing out a bait for a political discussion," said Lady Eleanor, laughing, "and so I 'll even say good night, Captain Forester, and pleasant dreams of the Banshee."

Forester rose and took his leave, which, somehow, was colder than usual. His mother's counsels had got possession of his mind, and distrust perverted every former source of pleasure.

"Her manner is all coquetry," said he, angrily, to himself, as he walked towards his room.

Poor fellow! and what if it were? Coquetry is but a gilding, to be sure; but it can never be well laid on if the substance beneath is not a precious metal.

There was, at the place where the river opened into the sea, a small inlet of the bay guarded by two bold and rocky headlands, between which the tide swept with uncommon violence, accumulating in time a kind of bar, over which, even in calm weather, the waves were lashed into breakers, while the waters within were still as a mountain lake. The ancient ruin we have already alluded to passingly, stood on a little eminence fronting this small creek, and although unmarked by any architectural beauty, or any pretensions, save the humble possession of four rude walls pierced by narrow windows, and a low doorway formed of three large stones, was yet, in the eyes of the country people, endowed with some superior holiness,— so it is certain the little churchyard around bespoke. It was crowded with graves, whose humble monuments consisted in wooden crosses, decorated in recent cases with little garlands of paper or wild flowers, as piety or affection suggested. The fragments of ship-timber around showed that they who slept beneath had been mostly fishermen, for the chapel was peculiarly esteemed by them; and at the opening of the fishing season a mass was invariably offered here for the success of the herring-fishery, by a priest from a neighboring parish, whose expenses were willingly and liberally rewarded by the fishermen.

In exact proportion with the reverence in which this spot was regarded by day was the fear and dread entertained of it by night. Stories of ghosts and evil spirits were rife far and near of that lonely ruin, and the hardiest seamen, who would brave the wild waves of the Atlantic, would not venture alone within these deserted walls after dark. Helen remembered, as a child, having been once there after sunset, induced by an intense curiosity to hear or see something of those sounds and shapes her nurse had told of, and what alarm her absence created among the household increased when it was discovered where she had been.

The same strange desire to hear if it might be that sad and wailing voice which all had so distinctly heard in the drawing-room, led her, when she had wished her mother good-night, to leave her chamber, and, crossing the flower-garden, to descend to the beach by a small door which opened to a little pathway down to the sea. When the superstitions whose terrors have affrighted childhood are either conquered by reason or uprooted by worldly influence, they still leave behind them a strange passion for the marvellous, which in imaginative temperaments is frequently greatly developed, and becomes a great source of enjoyment or suffering to its possessor. Helen Darcy's nature was of this kind, and she would gladly have accepted all the tremors and terrors of her nursery days to feel once again that intense awe, that anxious heart-beating expectancy, a ghost story used to create within her.

The night was calm and starlit, the sea was tranquil and unruffled, except where the bar broke the flow of the tide, and marked by a long line of foam the struggling breakers, whose hoarse plash was heard above the rippling on the strand. Even in the rocky caves all was still, not an echo resounded within those dreary caverns where at times the thunder's self was not louder. Helen reached the little churchyard; she knew every path and foot-track through it, and at last, strolling leisurely onward, entered the ruin and sat down within the deep window that looked over the sea.

For some time her attention was directed seaward, watching the waves as they reflected back the spangled heaven, or sank again in dark shadow, when suddenly she perceived the figure of a man, who appeared slowly pacing the beach immediately beneath where she sat.

What could have brought any one there at such an hour she could not imagine; and however few her terrors of the world of spirits, she would gladly at this moment have been safe within the abbey. While she debated with herself how to act—whether to remain in her present concealment, or venture on a sudden flight—the figure halted exactly under the window. Her doubts and fears were now speedily resolved, for she perceived it was Forester, who, induced by the beauty of the night, had thus strolled out upon the shore. "What if I should put his courageous incredulity to the test?" thought Helen; "the moment is propitious now. I could easily imitate the cry of the Banshee!" The temptation was too strong to be resisted, and without further thought she uttered a low, thrilling wail, in an accent of most touching sorrow. Forester started and looked up, but the dark walls were in deep shadow; whatever his real feelings at the moment, he lost no time in clambering up the bank on which the ruin stood, and from which he rightly judged the sound proceeded. Helen was yet uncertain whether to attribute this step to terror or the opposite, when she heard his foot as he traversed the thickly-studded graveyard,—a moment more, and he would be in the church itself, where he could not fail to discover her by her white dress. But one chance offered of escape, which was to leap from the window down upon the strand: it was deeper than she fancied, nearly twice her own height; but then detection, for more than one good reason, was not to be thought of.

Helen was not one of those who long hesitate when their minds are to be made up; she slipped noiselessly between the stone mullion and the side of the window, and sprang out; unfortunately one foot turned on a small stone, and she fell on the sand, while a slight accent of pain unconsciously broke from her. Before she could rise, Forester was beside her; with one arm round her waist, he half pressed, as he assisted her to recover her feet.

"So, fair spirit," said he, jocularly, "I have tracked you, it would seem;" then, for the first time discovering it was Helen, he muttered in a different tone, "I ask pardon, Miss Darcy; I really did not know—"

"I am sure of that, Captain Forester," said she, disengaging herself from his aid. "I certainly deserve a lesson for my silly attempt to frighten you, and I believe I have sprained my ankle. Will you kindly send Florence to me?"

"I cannot leave you here alone, Miss Darcy; pray take my arm, and let me assist you back to the abbey."

The tone of deference he now spoke in, and the increasing pain, concurred to persuade her, and she accepted the proffered assistance.

"The absurdity of this adventure is not repaid by the pleasure of having frightened you," said she, laughing; "if I could only say how terrified you were—"

"You might indeed have said so," interrupted Forester, "had I guessed the figure I saw leap out was yours."

"It was even higher than I thought," said she, avoiding to remark the fervent accents in which these words were spoken.

Forester was silent; his heart was full to bursting; the passion so lately dashed by doubts and suspicions returned with tenfold force now that he felt her arm within his own as step by step they moved along.

"You are in great pain, I fear," said he, tremulously.

"No, not now. I am so much more ashamed of my folly than a sufferer from it that I could forgive the sprain if I could the silly notion that caused it. 'Twas an unlucky fancy, to say the least of it."

Again there was a pause, and although they walked but slowly, they were fast approaching the little gate that opened into the flower-garden. Forester was silent. "Was it from this cause, or by some secret freemasonry of the female heart that she suspected what was passing in his mind, and exerted herself to move on more rapidly?

"Take time, Miss Darcy; not so fast; if not for your sake, for mine at least."

The last few words were scarcely above a whisper, but every one of them reached her to whom they were addressed; whether affecting not to hear them, or preferring to mistake their meaning, Helen made no answer.

"I said for *my* sake," resumed he, with a courage that demanded all his energy, "because on these few moments the whole fortune of my future life is placed. I love you."

"Nay, Captain Forester," said she, smiling, "this is not quite fair; I failed in my attempt to terrify you, and have paid the penalty: let there not be a further one of my listening to what I should not hear."

"And why not hear it, Helen? Is the devotion of one even humble as I am, a thing to offend? Is it the less sincere that I feel how much you are above me in every way? Will not my very presumption prove how fervent is the passion that has made me forget all save itself,—all save you?"

Truth has its own accents, however weak the words it syllables. Helen laughed not now, but walked on with quicker steps; while the youth, the barrier once passed, poured forth with heartfelt eloquence his tale of love, recalling to her mind by many a slight, unnoticed trait, his long-pledged devotion; how he had watched and worshipped her, seeking to win favor in her eyes, and seem not all unworthy of her heart.

"It is true," said he, "I cannot, dare not, ask in return for an affection which should repay my own; but let me hope that what I now speak, the devotion I pledge, is no rejected offering; that although you care not for me, you will not crush forever one who lives but in your smile, that you will give me time to show myself more worthy of the prize I strive for. There is no trial I would not dare—"

"I must interrupt you, Captain Forester," said Helen, with a voice that all her efforts had not rendered quite steady; "it would be an ungenerous requital for the sentiments you say you feel—"

"Say!—nay, Helen, I swear it, by every hope that now thrills within me—"

"It would be," resumed she, tremulously, "an ungenerous requital for this, were I to practise any deception on you. I am sincerely, deeply sorry to hear you speak as you have done. I had long since learned to regard you as the friend of Lionel, almost like a brother. The pleasure your society afforded one I am most attached to increased the feeling; and as intimacy increased between us, I thought how happy were it if the ambitions of life did not withdraw from home the sons whose kindness can be as thoughtful and as tender as that of the daughters of the house. Shall I confess it? I almost wished my brother like you; but yet all this was not love,—nay, for I will be frank, at whatever cost,—I had never felt this towards you, if I suspected your sentiments towards me—"

"But, dearest Helen—"

"Hear me out. There is but one way in which the impropriety of such a meeting as this can be obviated, chance though it be, and that is, by perfect candor. I have told you the simple truth, not with any undervaluing sense of the affection you proffer, still less with any coquetry of reserve. I should be unworthy of the heart you offer me, since I could not give my own in exchange."

"Do you deny me all hope?" said he, in an accent almost bursting with grief.

"I am not arrogant enough to say I shall never change; but I am honest enough to tell you that I do not expect it."

"Farewell, then, Helen! I do not love you less that you have taught me to think more humbly of myself. Good-by—forever!"

"It is better it should come to this," said Helen, faintly; and she held out her hand towards him. "Good-by, Forester!"

He pressed one long and burning kiss upon her hand, and turned away, while she, pushing open the door, entered the little garden. Scarcely, however, was the door closed behind her, when the calm courage in which she spoke forsook her, and she burst into tears.

So is it, the heart can be moved, even its most tender chords, when the touch that stirs it is less of love than sorrow.

CHAPTER XXIII
SOME SAD REVELATIONS

It was on the fourth day after the memorable debate we have briefly alluded to, that the Knight of Gwynne was sitting alone in one of the large rooms of his Dublin mansion. Although his servants had strict orders to say he had left town, he had not quitted the capital, but passed each day, from sunrise till late at night, in examining his various accounts, and endeavoring with what slight business knowledge he possessed, to ascertain the situation in which he stood, and how far Gleeson's flight had compromised him. There is no such chaotic confusion to the unaccustomed mind as the entangled web of long-standing moneyed embarrassments, and so Darcy found it. Bills for large sums had been passed, to provide for which, renewals had been granted, and this for a succession of years, until the debt accumulating had been met by a mortgage or a bond: many of these bills were missing—where were they? was the question, and what liability might yet attach to them?

Again, loans had been raised more than once to pay off these encumbrances, the interest on which was duly charged in his account, and yet there was no evidence of these payments having been made; nor among the very last sent papers from Gleeson was there any trace of that bond, to release which the enormous sum of seventy thousand pounds had been raised. That the money was handed to Hickman, Bagenal Daly was convinced; the memorandum given him by Freney was a corroboration of the probability at least, but still there was no evidence of the transaction here. Even this was not the worst, for the Knight now discovered that the rental charged in his accounts was more than double the reality, Gleeson having for many years back practised the fraud of granting leases at a low, sometimes a merely nominal, rent, while he accepted renewal fines from the tenants, which he applied to his own purposes. In fact, it at length became manifest to Darcy's reluctant belief that his trusted agent had for years long pursued a systematic course of perfidy, merely providing money sufficient for the exigencies of the time, while he was, in reality, selling every acre of his estate.

The Knight's last hope was in the entail. "I am ruined—I am a beggar, it is true!" muttered he, as each new discovery broke upon him, "but my boy, my dear Lionel, at my death will have his own again." This cherished dream was not of long duration, for to his horror he discovered a sale of a considerable part of the estate in which Lionel's name was signed as a concurring party. This was the crowning point of his affliction; the ruin was now utter, without one gleam of hope remaining.

The property thus sold was that in the possession of the O'Reillys, and the sale was dated the very day Lionel came of age. Darcy remembered well having signed his name to several papers on that morning. Gleeson had followed him from place to place, through the crowds of happy and rejoicing people assembled by the event, and at last, half vexed at the importunity, he actually put his name to several papers as he sat on horseback on the lawn: this very identical deed was thus signed; the writing was straggling and irregular as the motion of the horse shook his hand. So much for his own inconsiderate rashness, but how, or by what artifice was Lionel's signature obtained?

Never had Lionel Darcy practised the slightest deception on his father; never concealed from him any difficulty or any embarrassment, but frankly confided to him his cares, as he would to one of his own age. How, then, had he been drawn into a step of this magnitude without apprising him? There was one explanation, and this was, that Glee-son persuaded the young man, that by thus sacrificing his own future rights he would be assisting his father, who, from motives of delicacy, could not admit of any negotiation in the matter, and that by ceding so much of his own property, he should relieve his father from present embarrassment.

Through all the revelation of the agent's guilt now opening before him, not one word of anger, one expression of passion, escaped the Knight till his eyes fell upon this paper; but then, grasping it in both hands, he shook in every limb with indignant rage, and in accents of bitterest hate invoked a curse upon his betrayer. The very sound of his own voice in that sileut chamber startled him, while a sick tremor crept through his frame at the unhallowed wish he uttered. "No, no," said he, with clasped hands, "it is not for one like me, whose sensual carelessness has brought my own to ruin, to speak thus of another; may Heaven assist me, and pardon him that injured me!"

The stunning effects of heavy calamity are destined in all likelihood to give time to rally against the blow—to permit exhausted Nature to fortify herself by even a brief repose against the harassing influences of deep sorrow. One who saw far into the human heart tells us that it is not the strongest natures are the first to recover from the shock of great misfortunes, but that "light and frivolous spirits regain their elasticity sooner than those of loftier character."

The whole extent of his ruin unfolded itself gradually before Darcy's eyes, until at length the accumulated load became too great to bear, and he sat in almost total unconsciousness gazing at the mass of law papers and accounts before him, only remembering at intervals, and then faintly, the nature of the investigation he was engaged in, and by an effort recalling himself again to the task: in this way passed the entire day we speak of. Brief struggles to exert himself in examining the various papers and letters on the table were succeeded by long pauses of apparent apathy, until, as evening drew near, these intervals of indifference grew longer, and he sat for hours in this scarce-waking condition.

It was long past midnight as a loud knocking was heard at the street door, and ere Darcy could sufficiently recall his wandering faculties from their revery, he felt a hand grasp his own—he looked up, and saw Bagenal Daly.

"Well, Darcy," said he, in a low whisper, "how stand matters here?"

"Ruined!" said he, in an accent hardly audible, but with a look that thrilled through the stern heart of Daly.

"Come, come, there must be a long space between *your* fortune and ruin yet. Have you seen any legal adviser?"

"What of Gleeson, Bagenal, has he been heard of?" said the Knight, not attending to Daly's question.

"He has had the fitting end of a scoundrel. He leaped overboard in the Channel—"

"Poor fellow!" said Darcy, while he passed his hand across his eyes; "his spirit was not all corrupted, Bagenal; he dared not to face the world."

"Face the world! the villain, it was the gallows he had not courage to face. Don't speak one word of compassion about a wretch like him, or you 'll drive me mad. There's no iniquity in the greatest crimes to compare with the slow, dastardly scoundrelism of your fair-faced swindler. It seems so, at least. The sailors told us that he went below immediately on their leaving the river, and, having locked the cabin door, spent his time in writing till they were in sight of the Holyhead light, when a sudden splash was heard, and a cry of 'A man overboard!' called every one to the deck; then it was discovered that the fellow had opened one of the stern-windows and thrown himself into the sea. They brought me this open letter, the last, it is said, he ever wrote, and, though unaddressed, evidently meant for you. You need not read it; it contains nothing but the whining excuses of a scoundrel who bases his virtue on the fact that he was more coward than cheat. Strangest thing of all, he had no property with him beyond some few clothes, a watch, and about three hundred guineas in a purse. This was deposited by the skipper with the authorities in Liverpool; not a paper, not a document of any kind. Don't read that puling scrawl, Darcy; I have no patience with your pity!"

"I wish he had escaped with life, Bagenal," said Darcy, feelingly; "it is a sad aggravation of all my sorrow to think of this man's suicide."

"And so he might, had he had the courage to take his chance. The 'Congress' passed us as we went up the river; she had her studding-sails set, and, with the strong tide in her favor, was cutting through the water as fast as ever a runaway scoundrel could wish or ask for. Gleeson's servant contrived to reach her in time, and got away safe, not improbably with a heavy booty, if the truth were known."

Daly continued to dwell on the theme, repeating circumstantially the whole of the examination before the Liverpool Justices, where the depositions of the case were taken, and the investigation conducted with strict accuracy; but Darcy paid little attention. The sad end of one for whom through years long he had entertained feelings of respect and friendship, seemed to obliterate all memory of his crime, and he had no other feelings in his heart than those of sincere grief for the suicide.

"There is but one circumstance in the whole I cannot understand," said Daly, "and that is why Gleeson paid off Hickman's bond last week, when he had evidently made up his mind to fly,—seventy thousand was such a sum to carry away with him, all safe and sound as he had it."

"But where's the evidence of such a payment?" said Darcy, sorrowfully; "the bond is not to be found, nor is it among the papers discovered at Gleeson's house."

"It may be found yet," said Daly, confidently. "That the money was paid I have not a particle of doubt on my mind; Freney's information, and the memorandum I showed you, are strong in corroborating the fact; old Hickman dared not deny it, if the bond never were to turn up."

"Heaven grant it!" said Darcy, fervently; "that will at least save the abbey, and rescue our old house from the pollution I dreaded."

"All that, however, does not explain the difficulty," said Daly, thoughtfully; "I wish some shrewder head than mine had the matter before him. But now that I have told you so much, let me have some supper, Darcy, for we forgot to victual our sloop, and had no sea-store but whiskey on either voyage."

Though this was perfectly true, Daly's proposition was made rather to induce the Knight to take some refreshment, which it was so evident he needed, than from any personal motive.

"They carried the second reading by a large majority; I read it in Liverpool," said Daly, as the servant laid the table for supper.

The Knight nodded an assent, and Daly resumed: "I saw also that an address was voted by the patriotic members of Daly's to Hickman O'Reilly, Esquire, M.P., for his manly and independent conduct in the debate, when he taunted the Government with their ineffectual attempts at corruption, and spurned indignantly every offer of their patronage."

"Is that the case?" said the Knight, smiling faintly.

"'All fact; while the mob drew his carriage home, and nearly smoked the entire of Merrion Square into blackness with burning tar-barrels."

"He has improved on Johnson's definition, Bagenal, and made patriotism the first as well as the last refuge of a scoundrel."

"I looked out in the House that evening, but could not see him, for I wanted him to second a motion for me."

"Indeed! of what nature?"

"A most patriotic one, to this effect: that all bribes to members of either House should be in money, that we might have at least the benefit of introducing so much capital into Ireland."

"You forget, Bagenal, how it would spoil old Hickman's market: loans would then be had for less than ten per cent."

"So it would, by Jove! That shows the difficulty of legislating for conflicting interests."

This conversation was destined only to occupy the time the servant was engaged about the table, but when he had withdrawn, the Knight and his friend at once returned to the eventful theme that engaged all their anxieties, and where the altered tones of their voices and eager looks betokened the deepest interest.

It would have been difficult to find two men more generally well informed, and less capable of comprehending or unravelling the complicated tissue of a business matter. At the same time, by dint of much mutual inquiry and discussion, they attained to that first and greatest of discoveries, namely, their own insufficiency to conduct the investigation, and the urgent necessity of employing some able man of law to go through all Gleeson's accounts, and ascertain the real condition of Darcy's fortune. With this prudent resolve, they parted: Darcy to his room, where he sat with unclosed eyes till morning; while Daly, who had disciplined his temperament more rigidly, soon fell fast asleep, and never awoke till roused by the voice of his servant Sandy.

"You must find out the fellow that brought the note from Freney," said Daly, the moment he opened his eyes.

"I was thinking so," said Sandy, sententiously.

"You'd know him again?"

"I'd ken his twa eyes amang a thousand."

"Very well, then, set off after breakfast and search for him; you used to know where devils of this kind were to be found."

"Maybe I havna quite forgot it yet," replied he, dryly; "but it winna do to gae there before nightfall."

"Lose no more time than you can help about it," said Daly; "bring him here if you can find him."

We have not the necessity, and more certainly it is far from our inclination, to dwell upon the accumulated calamities of the Knight, nor recount more particularly the sad disclosures which the few succeeding days made regarding his fortunes. His own words were correct; he was utterly ruined. Every species of iniquity which perfidy could practise upon unbounded confidence had been effected. His property subdivided and leased at nominal rents, debts long supposed to have been paid yet outstanding; mortgages alleged to have been redeemed still impending; while of the large sums raised to meet these encumbrances not one shilling had been paid by Gleeson, save perhaps the bond for seventy thousand; but even of this there was no evidence, except the vague assertion of one whose testimony the law would reject.

Such, in brief, were the sad results of that investigation to which the Knight's affairs were submitted, nor could all the practised subtlety of the lawyer suggest one reasonable chance of extrication from the difficulty.

"Your friend is a ruined man, sir," said he to Daly, as they both arose after a seven hours' examination of the various documents; "there is a strong presumption that many of these signatures are forged, and that the Knight of Gwynne never even saw the papers; but he appears to have written his name so carelessly, and in so many ways, as to have no clear recollection of what he did sign, and what he did not. It would be very difficult to submit a good case for a jury."

That the payment of the seventy thousand had been made he regarded as more than doubtful, coupling the fact of Gleeson's immediate flight with the temptation of so large a sum, while nothing could be less accurate than the robber's testimony. "We must watch the enemy closely on this point," said he; "we must exhibit not the slightest apparent doubt upon it. They must not be led to suspect that we have not the bond in our possession. This question will admit of a long contest, and does not press like the others. As to young Darcy's concurrence in the sale—"

"Ay, that is the great matter in my friend's eyes."

"He must be written to at once,—let him come over here without loss of time, and if it can be shown that this signature is a forgery, we might make it the ground of a compromise with the O'Reillys, who, to obtain a good title, would be glad to admit us to liberal terms."

"Darcy will never listen to that, depend upon it," said Daly; "his greatest affliction is for his son's ruin."

"We 'll see, we 'll see—the game shall open its own combinations as we go on; for the present, all the task of your friend the Knight is to carry a bold face to the world, let no rumor get abroad that matters are in their real condition. Our chance of extrication lies in the front we can show to the enemy."

"You are making a heavier demand than you are aware of,—Darcy detests anything like concealment. I don't believe he would practise the slightest mystery that would involve insincerity for twelve hours to free the whole estate."

"Very honorable indeed; but at this moment we must waive a punctilio."

"Don't give it that name to him,—that's all," said Daly, sternly. "I am as little for subterfuge as any man, and yet I did my best to prevent him resigning his seat in the House; this morning he would send a request to Lord Castlereagh, begging he might be permitted to accept an escheatorship; I need not say how willingly the proposal was accepted, and his name will appear in the 'Gazette' to-morrow morning."

"This conduct, if persisted in, will ruin our case," said the lawyer, despondingly. "I cannot comprehend his reasons for it."

"They are simple enough: his own words were, 'I can never continue to be a member of the legislature when the only privilege it would confer is freedom from arrest.'"

"A very valuable one at this crisis, if he knew but all," muttered the other. "You will write to young Darcy at once."

"That he has done already, and to Lady Eleanor also; and as he expects me at seven, I 'll take my leave of you till to-morrow."

"Well, Daly," said the Knight, as his friend entered the drawing-room before dinner, "how do you like the lawyer?"

"He's a shrewd fellow, and I suppose, for his calling, an honest one; but the habit of making the wrong seem right leads to a very great inclination to reverse the theorem, and make the right seem wrong."

"He thinks badly of our case, is n't that so?"

"He 'd think much better of it, and of us too, I believe, if both were worse."

"I am just as well pleased that it is not so," said Darcy, smiling; "a bad case is far more endurable than a bad conscience. But here comes dinner, and I have got my appetite back again."

CHAPTER XXIV
A GLANCE AT "THE FULL MOON"

To rescue our friend Bagenal Daly from any imputation the circumstance might suggest, it is as well to observe here, that when he issued the order to his servant to seek out the boy who brought the intelligence of Gleeson's flight, he was merely relying on that knowledge of the obscure recesses of Old Dublin which Sandy possessed, and not by any means upon a distinct acquaintance with gentlemen of the same rank and station as Jemmy.

When Daly first took up his residence in the capital, many, many years before, he was an object of mob worship. He had every quality necessary for such. He was immensely rich, profusely spendthrift, and eccentric to an extent that some characterized as insanity. His dress, his equipage, his liveries, his whole retinue and style of living were strange and unlike other men's, while his habits of life bid utter defiance to every ordinance of society.

In the course of several years' foreign travel he had made acquaintances the most extraordinary and dissimilar, and many of these were led to visit him in his own country. Dublin being less resorted to by strangers than most cities, the surprise of its inhabitants was proportionably great as they beheld, not only Hungarians and Russian nobles, with gorgeous equipages and splendid retinues, driving through the streets, but Turks, Armenians, and Greeks, in full costume; and, on one occasion, Daly's companion on a public promenade was no less remarkable a person than a North American chief, in all the barbaric magnificence of his native dress. To obviate the inconvenience of that mob accompaniment such spectacles would naturally attract, Daly entered into a compact with the leaders of the varions sets or parties of low Dublin, by which, on payment of a certain sum, he was guaranteed in the enjoyment of appearing in public without a following of several hundred ragged wretches in full cry after him. Nothing could be more honorable and fair than the conduct of both parties in this singular treaty; the subsidy was regularly paid through the hands of Sandy M'Grane, while the subsidized literally observed every article of the contract, and not only avoided any molestation on their own parts, but were a formidable protective force in the event of any annoyance from others of a superior rank in society.

The hawkers of the various newspapers were the deputies with whom Sandy negotiated this treaty, they being recognized as the legitimate interpreters of mob opinion through the capital; men who combined an insight into local grievances with a corresponding knowledge of general politics; and certain it is, their sway must have been both respected and well protected, for a single transgression of the compact with Daly never occurred.

Bagenal Daly troubled his head very little in the matter, it is true; for his own sake he would never have thought of such a bargain, but he detested the thought of foreigners carrying away with them from Ireland any unpleasant memories of mob outrage or insult; and desired that the only remembrance they should preserve of his native country should be of its cordial and hospitable reception. A great many years had now elapsed since these pleasant times, and Daly's name was scarcely more than a tradition among those who now lounged in rags and idleness through the capital,—a fact of which he could have had little doubt himself, if he had reflected on that crowd which followed his own steps but a few days before. Of this circumstance, however, he took little or no notice, and gave his orders to Sandy with the same conscious power he had wielded nearly fifty years back.

A small public-house, called the Moon, in Duck Alley, a narrow lane off the Cross Poddle, was the resort of this Rump Parliament, and thither Sandy betook himself on a Saturday evening, the usual night of meeting, as, there being no issue of newspapers the next morning, nothing interfered with a prolonged conviviality. Often and often had he taken the same journey at the same hour; but now, such is the effect of a long interval of years, the way seemed narrower and more crooked than ever, while as he went not one familiar face welcomed him as he passed; nor could he recognize, as of yore, his acquaintances amid the various disguises of black eyes and smashed noses, which were frequent on every side. It was the hour when crime and guilt, drunken rage and grief, mingled together their fearful agencies; and every street and alley was crowded by half-naked wretches quarrelling and singing: some screaming in accents of heartbroken anguish; others shouting their blasphemies with voices hoarse from passion; age and infancy, manhood in its prime, the mother and the young girl, were all there, reeling from drunkenness, or faint from famine; some struggling in deadly conflict, others bathing the lips and temples of ebbing life.

Through this human hell Sandy wended his way, occasionally followed by the taunting ribaldry of such as remarked him: such testimonies were very unlike his former welcomes in these regions; but for this honest Sandy cared little; his real regret was to see so much more evidence of depravity and misery than before. Drunkenness and its attendant vices were no new evils, it is true; but he thought all these were fearfully aggravated by what he now witnessed: loud and violent denunciations against every rank above their own, imprecations on the Parliament and the gentry that "sowld Ireland:" as if any political perfidy could be the origin of their own degraded and revolting condition! Such is, however, the very essence of that spirit that germinates amid destitution and crime, and it is a dangerous social crisis when the masses begin to attribute their own demoralization to the vices of their betters. It well behooves those in high places to make their actions and opinions conform to their great destinies.

Sandy's Northern blood revolted at these brutal excesses, and the savage menaces he heard on every side; but perhaps his susceptibilities were more outraged by one trail of popular injustice than all the rest, and that was to hear Hickman O'Reilly extolled by the mob for his patriotic rejection of bribery, while the Knight of Gwynne was held up to execration by every epithet of infamy; ribald jests and low ballads conveying the theme of attack upon his spotless character.

The street lyrics of the day were divided in interest between the late rebellion and the act of Union; the former being, however, the favorite theme, from a species of irony peculiar to this class of poetry, in which certain living characters were held up to derision or execration. The chief chorist appeared to be a fiend-like old woman, with one eye, and a voice like a cracked bassoon: she was dressed in a cast-off soldier's coat and a man's hat, and neither from face nor costume had few feminine traits. This fair personage, known by the name of Rhoudlum, was, on her appearing, closely followed by a mob of admiring amateurs, who seemed to form both her body-guard and her chorus. When Sandy found himself fast wedged up in this procession, the enthusiasm was at its height, in honor of an elegant new ballad called "The Two Majors." The air, should our reader be musically given, was the well-known one, "There was a Miller had Three Sons:" —

> "Says Major Sirr to Major Swan,
> You have two rebels, give me one;
> They pay the same for one as two,
> I 'll get five pounds, and I 'll share with you.
> Toi! loi! loi! lay."

"That's the way the blackguards sowld yer blood, boys!" said the hag, in recitative; "pitch caps, the ridin' house, and the gallows was iligant tratement for wearin' the green."

"Go on, Rhoudlum, go on wid the song," chimed in her followers, who cared more for the original text than prose vulgate.

"Arn't I goin' on wid it?" said the hag, as fire flashed in her eye; "is it the likes of you is to tache me how to modulate a strain?" And she resumed: —

> *"Says Major Swan to Major Sirr,*
> *One man's a woman! ye may take her.*
> *'T is little we gets for them at all —*
> *Oh! the curse of Cromwell be an ye all!*
> *Toi! loi! loll lay."*

The grand Demosthenic abruptness of the last line was the signal for an applauding burst of voices, whose sincerity it would be unfair to question.

"Where are you pushin' to! bad scran to ye! ye ugly varmint!" said the lady, as Sandy endeavored to force his passage through the crowd.

"Hurroo! by the mortial, it's Daly's man!" screamed she, in transport, as the accidental light of a window showed Sandy's features.

Few, if any, of those around had ever seen him; but his name and his master's were among the favored traditions of the place, and however unwilling to acknowledge the acquaintance, Sandy had no help for it but to exchange greetings and ask the way to "the Moon," which he found he had forgotten.

"There it is fornint ye, Mr. M'Granes," said the lady, in the most dulcet tones; "and if it's thinking of trating me ye are, 't is a 'crapper' in a pint of porter I 'd take; nothing stronger would sit on my heart now."

"Ye shall hae it," said Sandy; "but come into the house."

"I darn't do it, sir; the committee is sittin'—don't ye see, besides, the moon lookin' at you?" And she pointed to a rude representation of a crescent moon, formed by a kind of transparency in the middle of a large window, a signal which Sandy well knew portended that the council were assembled within.

"Wha's the man, noo?" said Sandy, with one foot on the threshold.

"The ould stock still, darlint," said Rhoudlum,—"don't ye know his voice?"

"That's Paul Donellan,—I ken him noo."

"Be my conscience! there's no mistake. Ye can hear his screech from the Poddle to the Pigeon House when the wind's fair."

Sandy put a shilling into the hag's hand, and, without waiting for further parley, entered the little dark hall, and turning a corner he well remembered, pressed a button and opened the door into the room where the party were assembled.

"Who the blazes are you? What brings you here?" burst from a score of rude voices together, while every hand grasped some projectile to hurl at the devoted intruder.

"Ask Paul Donellan who I am, and he'll tell ye," said Sandy, sternly, while, with a bold contempt for the hostile demonstrations, he walked straight up to the head of the room.

The recognition on which he reckoned so confidently was not forthcoming, for the old decrepit creature who, cowering beneath the wig of some defunct chancellor, presided, stared at him with eyes bleared with age and intemperance, but seemed unable to detect him as an acquaintance.

"Holy Paul does n't know him!" said half-a-dozen together, as, in passionate indignation, they arose to resent the intrusion.

"He may remember this better," said Sandy, as, seizing a full bumper of whiskey from the board, he threw it into the lamp beneath the transparency, and in a moment the moon flashed forth, and displayed its face at the full. The spell was magical, and a burst of savage welcome broke from every mouth, while Donellan, as if recalled to consciousness, put his hand trumpet-fashion to his lips, and gave a shout that made the very glasses ring upon the board. Place was now made for Sandy at the table, and a wooden vessel called "a noggin" set before him, whose contents he speedily tested by a long draught.

"I may as weel tell you," said Sandy, "that I am Bagenal Daly's man. I mind the time it wad na hae been needful to say so much,—my master's picture used to hang upon that wall."

Had Sandy proclaimed himself the Prince of Wales the announcement could not have met with more honor, and many a coarse and rugged grasp of the hand attested the pleasure his presence there afforded.

"We have the picture still," said a young fellow, whose frank, good-humored face contrasted strongly with many of those around him; "but that old divil, Paul, always told us it was a likeness of himself when he was young."

"Confound the scoundrel!" said Sandy, indignantly; "he was no mair like my maister than a Dutch skipper is like a chief of the Delawares. Has the creature lost his senses a'togither?"

"By no manner of manes. He wakes up every now and then wid a speech, or a bit of poethry, or a sentiment."

"Ay," said another, "or if a couple came in to be married, see how the old chap's eyes would brighten, and how he would turn the other side of his wig round before you could say 'Jack Robinson.'"

This was literally correct, and was the simple manouvre by which Holy Paul converted himself into a clerical character, the back of his wig being cut in horse-shoe fashion, in rude imitation of that worn by several of the bishops.

"Watch him now—watch him now!" said one in Sandy's ears; and the old fellow passed his hand across his eyes as if to dispel some painful thought, while his careworn features were lit up with a momentary flash of sardonic drollery.

"Your health, sir," said he to Sandy; "or, as Terence has it, 'Hic tibi, Dave'—here 's to you, Davy."

"A toast, Paul! a toast! Something agin the Union,—something agin old Darcy."

"Fill up, gentlemen," said Paul, in a clear and distinct voice. "I beg to propose a sentiment which you will drink with a bumper. Are you ready?"

"Ready!" screamed all together.

"Here, then,—repeat after me:—

"Whether he's out, or whether he's in,
It does n't signify one pin;
Here's every curse of every sin
On Maurice Darcy, Knight of Gwynne."

"Hold!" shouted Sandy, as he drew a double-barrelled pistol from his bosom. "By the saul o' my body the man that drinks that toast shall hae mair in his waim than hot water and whiskey. Maurice Darcy is my maister's friend, and a better gentleman never stepped in leather: who dar say no?"

"Are we to drink it, Paul?"

"As I live by drink," cried Paul, stretching out both hands, "this is my *alter ego*, my duplicate self, Sanders M'Grane's, 'revisiting the glimpses of the moon,' *post totidem annos!*" And a cordial embrace now followed, which at once dispelled the threatened storm.

"Mr. M'Grane's health in three times three, gentlemen;" and, rising, Paul gave the signal for each cheer as he alone could give it.

Sandy had now time to throw a glance around the table, where, however, not one familiar face met his own; that they were of the same calling and order as his quondam associates in the same place he could have little doubt, even had that fact not been proclaimed by the names of various popular journals affixed to their hats, and by whose titles they were themselves addressed. The conversation, too, had the same sprinkling of politics, town gossip, and late calamities he well remembered of yore, interspersed with lively commentaries on public men which, if printed, would have been suggestive of libel.

The new guest soon made himself free of the guild by a proposal to treat the company, on the condition that he might be permitted to have five minutes' conversation with their president in an adjoining room. He might have asked much more in requital for his liberality, and without a moment's delay, or even apprising Paul of what was intended, the "Dublin Journal" and the "Free Press" took him boldly between them and carried him into a closet off the room where the carouse was held.

"I know what you are at," said Paul, as soon as the door closed. "Daly wants a rising of the Liberty boys for the next debate,—don't deny it, it's no use. Well, now, listen, and don't interrupt me. Tom Conolly came down from the Castle yesterday and offered me five pounds for a good mob to rack a house, and two-ten if they'd draw Lord Clare home; but I refused,—I did, on the virtue of my oath. There's patriotism for ye!—yer soul, where 's the man wid only one shirt and a supplement to his back would do the same?"

"You 're wrang,—we dinna want them devils at a'; it 's a sma' matter of inquiry I cam about. Ye ken Freney?"

"Is it the Captain? Whew!" said Paul, with a long whistle.

"It's no him," resumed Sandy, "but a wee bit of a callant they ca' Jamie."

"Jemmy the diver,—the divil's own grandson, that he is."

"Where can I find him?" said Sandy, impatiently.

"Wait a bit, and you'll be sure to see him at home in his lodgings in Newgate."

"I must find him out at once; put me on his track, and I 'll gie a goold guinea in yer hand, mon. I mean the young rascal no harm; it's a question I want him to answer me, that's all."

"Well, I'll do my best to find him for you, but I must send down to the country. I'll have to get a man to go beyond Kilcullen."

"We 'll pay any expense."

"Sure I know that." And here Paul began a calculation to himself of distances and charges only audible to Sandy's ears at intervals: "Two and four, and six, with a glass of punch at Naas—half an hour at Tims'—the coach at Athy—ay, that will do it. Have ye the likes of a pair of ould boots or shoes? I 've nothing but them, and the soles is made out of two pamphlets of Roger Connor's, and them's the driest things I could get."

"I'll gie ye a new pair."

"You 're the son of Fingal of the Hills, divil a less. And now if ye had a cast-off waistcoat—I don't care for the color—orange or green, blue or yellow, *Tros Tyriusve mihiy* as we said in Trinity."

"Ye shall hae a coat to cover your old bones. But let us hae nae mair o' this—when may I expect to see the boy?"

"The evening after next, at eight o'clock, at the corner of Essex Bridge, Capel Street—'on the Rialto'—eh? that's the cue. And now let us join the revellers—*per Jove*, but I'm dry." And so saying, the miserable old creature broke from Sandy, and, assisted by the wall, tottered back to the room to his drunken companions, where his voice was soon heard high above the discord and din around him.

And yet this man, so debased and degraded, had been once a scholar of the University, and carried off its prizes from men whose names stood high among the great and valued of the land.

CHAPTER XXV
BAGENAL DALY'S COUNSELS

Every hour seemed to complicate the Knight of Gwynne's difficulties, and to increase that intricacy by which he already was so much embarrassed. The forms of law, never grateful to him, became now perfectly odious, obscuring instead of explaining the questions on which he desired information. He hated, besides, the small and narrow expedients so constantly suggested in cases where his own sense of right convinced him of the justice of his cause, nor could he listen with common patience to the detail of all those legal subtleties by which an adverse claim might be, if not resisted, at least protracted indefinitely.

His presence, far from affording any assistance, was, therefore, only an embarrassment both to Daly and the lawyer, and they heard with unmixed satisfaction of his determination to hasten down to the West, and communicate more freely with his family, for as yet his letter to Lady Eleanor, far from disclosing the impending ruin, merely mentioned Gleeson's flight as a disastrous event in the life of a man esteemed and respected, and adverting but slightly to his own difficulties in consequence.

"We must leave the abbey, Bagenal, I foresee that," said Darcy, as he took his friend aside a few minutes before starting.

Daly made no reply, for already his own convictions pointed the same way.

"I could not live there with crippled means and broken fortune; 'twould kill me in a month, by Jove, to see the poor fellows wandering about idle and unemployed, the stables nailed up, the avenue grass-grown, and not hear the cry of a hound when I crossed the courtyard. But what is to be done? Humbled as I am, I cannot think of letting it to some Hickman O'Reilly or other, some vulgar upstart, feasting his low companions in those old halls, or plotting our utter ruin at our own hearthstone; could we not make some other arrangement?"

"I have thought of one," said Daly, calmly; "my only fear is how to ask Lady Eleanor's concurrence to a plan which must necessarily press most heavily on her."

"What is it?" said Darcy, hastily.

"Of course, your inclination would be, for a time at least, perfect seclusion."

"That, above all and everything."

"Well, then, what say you to taking up your abode in a little cottage of mine on the Antrim coast? It is a wild and lonely spot, it's true, but you may live there without attracting notice or observation. I see you are surprised at my having such a possession. I believe I never told you, Darcy, that I bought Sandy's cabin from him the day he entered my service, and fitted it up, and intended it as an asylum for the poor fellow if he should grow weary of my fortunes, or happily survive me. By degrees, I have added a room here and a closet there, till it has grown into a dwelling that any one, as fond of salmon-fishing as you and I were, would not despise; come, will you have it?" Darcy grasped his friend's hand without speaking, and Daly went on: "That's right; I'll give orders to have everything in readiness at once; I'll go down, too, and induct you. Ay, Darcy, and if the fellows could take a peep at us over our lobster and a glass of Isla whiskey, they 'd stare to think those two jovial old fellows, so merry and contented, started, the day they came of age, with the two best estates in Ireland."

"If I had not brought ruin on others, Bagenal—"

"No more of that, Darcy; the most scandal-loving gossip of the Club will never impute, for he dare not, more than carelessness to your conduct, and I promise you, if you 'll only fall back on a good conscience, you 'll not be unhappy under the thatched roof of my poor shieling. My sincerest regards to Lady Eleanor and Helen. I see there is a crowd collecting at the sight of the four posters, so don't delay."

Darcy could do no more than squeeze the cordial hand that held his own, and, passing hastily out, he stepped into the travelling-carriage at the door, not unobserved, indeed, for about a hundred ragged creatures had now assembled, who saluted his appearance with groans and hisses, accompanied with ruffianly taunts about bribery and corruption; while one, more daring than the rest, mounted on the step, and with his face to the window, cried out: "My Lord, my Lord, won't you give us a trifle to drown your new coronet?"

The words were scarcely out, when, seizing him by the neck with one hand, and taking a leg in the other, Daly hurled the fellow into the middle of the mob, who, such is their consistency, laughed loud and heartily at the fellow's misfortunes; meanwhile, the postilions plied whip and spur, and ere the laughter had subsided, the carriage was out of sight.

"There is a gentleman in the drawing-room wishes to speak to you, sir," said a servant to Daly, who had just sat down to a conference with the lawyer.

"Present my respectful compliments, and say that I am engaged on most important and pressing business."

"Had you not better ask his name?" said the lawyer.

"No, no, there is nothing but interruptions here; at one moment it is Heffernan, with a polite message from Lord Castlereagh; then some one from the Club, to know if I have any objection to waive a standing order, and have that young O'Reilly balloted for once more; and here was George Falkner himself a while ago, asking if the Knight had really taken office, with a seat in the Cabinet. I said it was perfectly correct, and that he was at liberty to state it in his paper."

"You did!"

"Yes; and that he might add that I myself had refused the see of Llandaff, preferring the command of the West India Squadron. But, what's this? What do you want now, Richard?"

"The gentleman upstairs, sir, insists on my presenting his card."

"Oh, indeed!—Captain Forester!—I'll see him at once." And, so saying, Daly hastened upstairs to the drawing-room, where the young officer awaited him.

Daly was not in a mood to scrutinize very closely the appearance of his visitor, but he could not fail to feel struck at the alteration in his looks since last they met; his features were paler and marked by sorrow, so much so that Daly's first question was, "Have you been ill?" and as Forester answered in the negative, the old man fixed his eyes steadily on him, and said, "You have heard of our misfortune, then?"

"Misfortune! no. What do you mean?"

Daly hesitated, uncertain how to reply, whether to leave to time and some other channel to announce the Knight's ruin, or at once communicate it with his own lips.

"Yes, it is the better way," said he, half aloud, while, taking Forester's hand, he led him over to a sofa, and pressed him down beside him. "I seldom have made an error in guessing a man's character, throughout a long and somewhat remarkable life. I think I am safe in saying that you feel a warm interest in my friend Darcy's family?"

"You do me but justice; gratitude alone, if I had no stronger motive, secures them every good wish of mine."

"But you have stronger motives, young man," said Daly, looking at him with a piercing glance; "if you had not, I'd think but meanly of you, nor did I want that blush to tell me so."

Forester looked down in confusion. The abruptness of the address so completely unmanned him that he could make no answer. While Daly went on: "I force no confidences, young man, nor have I any right to ask them; enough for my present purpose that I know you care deeply for this family; now, sir, but a week back the ambition to be allied with them had satisfied the proudest wish of the proudest house—to-day they are ruined."

Overwhelmed with surprise and sorrow, Forester sat silently, while Daly rapidly, but circumstantially, narrated the story of the Knight's calamity, and the total wreck of his once princely fortune.

"Yes," said Daly, as with flashing eyes he arose and uttered aloud,— "yes, the broad acres won by many a valiant deed, the lands which his ancestors watered with their blood, lost forever; not by great crimes, not forfeited by any bold but luckless venture, for there is something glorious in that,—but stolen, filched away by theft. By Heaven! our laws and liberties do but hedge round crime with so many defences that honesty has nothing left but to stand shivering outside. Better were the days when the strong hand avenged the deep wrong, or, if the courage were weak, there was the Throne to appeal to against oppression. Forester, I see how this news afflicts you; I judged you too well to think that your own dashed hopes entered into your sorrow. No, no, I know you better. But come, we have other duties than to mourn over the past. Has Lord Castlereagh received Darcy's note, resigning his seat in Parliament?"

"He has; a new writ is preparing for Mayo." "Sharp practice; I think I can detect the fair round hand of Mr. Heffernan there,—no matter, a few days more and the world will know all; ay, the world, so full of honorable sentiments and noble aspirations, will smile and jest on Darcy's ruin, that they may with better grace taunt the vulgar assumption of Hickman O'Reilly. I know it well,—some would say I bought the knowledge dearly. When I set out in life, my fortune was nearly equal to the Knight's, my ideas of living and expenditure based on the same views as his own,—that same barbaric taste for profusion which has been transmitted to us from father to son. Ay, we retained everything of feudalism save its chivalry! Well, I never knew a day nor an hour of independence till the last acre of that great estate was sold, and gone from me forever. Fawning flattery, intrigue, and trickery beset me wherever I went; ruined gamblers, match-making mothers, bankrupt speculators, plotting political adventurers, dogged me at every step; nor could I break through the trammels by which they fettered me, except at the price of my ruin; when there was no longer a stake to play for, they left the table. Poor Darcy, however, is not a lonely stem, like me, riven and lightning-struck; he has a wife and children; but for that, I would not fear to grasp his stout hand and say, 'Come on to fortune.' Poor Maurice, whose heart could never stand the slightest wrong done the humblest cottier on his land, how will he bear up now? Forester, you can do me a great service. Could you obtain leave for a day or two?"

"Command me how and in what way you please," said the youth, eagerly.

"I understand that proffer, and accept it as freely as it is given."

"Nay, you are mistaken," said Forester, faltering. "I will be candid with you; you have a right to all my confidence, for you have trusted in me. Your suspicions are only correct in part; my affection is indeed engaged, but I have received none in return: Miss Darcy has rejected me."

"But not without hope?"

"Without the slightest hope."

"By Heaven, it is the only gleam of light in all the gloomy business," said Daly, energetically; "had Helen's love been yours, this calamity had been ten thousand times worse. Nay, nay, this is not the sentiment of cold and selfish old age; you wrong me, Forester, but the hour is come when every feeling within that noble girl's heart is due to those who have loved and cherished her from childhood. Now is the time to repay the watchful care of infancy, and recompense the anxious fears that spring from parental affection; not a sentiment, not a thought, should be turned from that channel now. It would be treason to win one smile, one passing look of kind meaning from those eyes, every beam of which is claimed by 'Home.' Helen is equal to her destiny,—that I know well; and you, if you would strive to be worthy of her, do not endeavor to make her falter in her duty. Trust me, there is but one road to a heart like hers,—the path of high and honorable ambition."

"You are right," said Forester, in a sad and humble voice,—"you are right; I offered her a heart before it was worthy of her acceptance."

"That avowal is the first step towards rendering it such one day," said Daly, grasping his hand in both his own. "Now to my request: you can obtain this leave, can you?"

"Yes, yes; how can I make it of any service to you?"

"Simply thus: I have offered, and Darcy has accepted, a humble cottage on the northern coast, as a present asylum for the family. The remote and secluded nature of the place will at least withdraw them from the impertinence of curiosity, or the greater impertinence of vulgar sympathy. A maiden sister of mine is the present occupant, and I wish to communicate the intelligence to her, that she may make any preparations which may be necessary for their coming, and also provide herself with some other shelter. Maria is as great a Bedouin as myself, and with as strong a taste for vagabondage; she 'll have no difficulty in housing herself, that's certain. The only puzzle is how to apprise her of the intended change: there is not a post-office within eight or ten miles of the place, nor, if there were, would she think of sending to look for a letter; there 's nothing for it but a special envoy: will you be the man?"

"Most willingly; only give me the route, and my instructions."

"You shall have both. Come and dine with me here at five—order horses to your carriage for eight o'clock, and I'll take care of the rest."

"Agreed," said Forester; "I'll lose no time in getting ready for the road—the first thing is my leave."

"Is there a difficulty there?"

"There shall be none," said Forester, hurriedly, as he seized his hat, and, bidding Daly good-bye, hastened downstairs and into the street. "They 'll refuse me, I know that," muttered he, as he went along; "and if they do, I'll pitch up the appointment on the spot; this slight service over, I'm ready to join my regiment." And so saying, he turned his steps towards the Castle, resolved on the course to follow.

Meanwhile Daly, after a brief consultation with the lawyer, sat down to write to his sister. Simple and easy as the act is to many—far too much so, as most men's correspondence would testify—letter-writing, to some people, is an affair of no common difficulty. Perhaps every one in this world has some stumbling-block of this kind ever before him: some men cannot learn chess, some never can be taught to ride, others, if they were to get the world for it, could not carve a hare. It would be unfair to quote newly introduced difficulties, such as how to bray in the House of Commons, the back step in the polka, and so on; the original evils are enough for our illustration.

Bagenal Daly's literary difficulties were manifold; he was a discursive thinker, passionate and vehement whenever the occasion prompted, and as unable to control such influences when writing as speaking; and, with very liberal ideas on the score of spelling, he wrote a hand which, if only examined upside down, might have passed for Hebrew, with an undue proportion of points; besides these defects, he entertained a thorough contempt for all writing as an exponent of men's sentiments. His opinion was, that speech was the great prerogative of living men, all other modes of expression being feeble and miserable expedients; and, to do him justice, he conformed, as far as in him lay, to his own theory, and made his writing as like his speaking as could be. Brevity was the great quality he studied, and for this reason we venture to present the epistle to our readers: —

Dear Molly, —

The bill is carried—or, what comes to the same, the third reading comes on next Tuesday, and they 'll have a majority—d——n their majority, I forget the number. I was told that bribes were plenty as blackberries. I wish they 'd leave as many stains after them. They offered me nothing—they were right there. There is a kind of bottle-nosed whale the Indians never harpoon; they call him "Hik-na-critchka,"—more bone than blubber. Darcy might have been an Earl, or a Marquis, or a Duke, perhaps; they wanted one gentleman so much, they 'd have bid high for him. Poor fellow, he is ruined now! that scoundrel Gleeson has run away with everything, forged, falsified, and thieved to any extent. Your unlucky four thousand, of course, is gone to the devil with the rest. I 'm sick of cant. People talk of badgers and such like, and yet no one says a word about exterminating attorneys! The rascal jumped over in the Channel, and was drowned—the shark got a bitter pill that swallowed him. I have told Darcy he might have "the Corvy;" you can easily find a wigwam down the coast. Forester, who brings this, knows all. We must all economize, I suppose. I 've given up Maccabaw already, and taken to Blackguard, in compliment to the Secretary. I must sell or shoot old Drummer at last, he can't draw his breath, and won't draw the gig. I only remain here till the House is up, when I must be up too and stirring—there is a confounded bond—no matter, more at another time.

Yours ever,

Bagenal Daly.

St. George is to be the Chief Baron—an improvement of the allegory, "Justice will be deaf as well as blind." Devil take them all!

The chorus of a Greek play, so seemingly abstruse and incoherent to our present thinking, was, we are told, made easily comprehensible by the aid of gesture and pantomime; and in the same way, by supplying the fancied accompaniment of her brother's voice and action, Miss Daly was enabled to read and understand this strange epistle. Bagenal gave himself little trouble in examining how far it conveyed his meaning; but, like a careless traveller who huddles his clothes into his portmanteau, and is only anxious to make the lock meet, his greatest care was to fold up the document and inclose it within an envelope; that done, he hoped it was all right,—in any case, his functions were concluded regarding it, for, as he muttered to himself, he only contracted to write, not to read, his own letter.

Forester was punctual to the hour appointed; and if not really less depressed than before, the stimulating sense of having a service to perform made him seem less so. His self-esteem was flattered, too, by his own bold line of acting, for he had just resigned his appointment on the Staff, his application for leave having been unsuccessful. The fact that his rash conduct might involve him in trouble or difficulty was not without its own sense of pleasure, for, so is it in all rebellion, the great prompter is personal pride. He would gladly have told Daly what had happened; but a delicate fear of increasing the apparent load of obligation prevented him, and he consequently confined his remarks on the matter to bis being free, and at liberty to go wherever his friend pleased.

"Here, then," said Daly, leading him across the room to a table, on which a large map of Ireland lay open, "I have marked your route the entire way. Follow that dark line with your eye northwards to Coleraine,—so far you can travel with your carriage and post-horses; how to cross this bit of desert here I must leave to yourself: there may be a road for a wheeled carriage or not, in my day there was none; that is, however, a good many years back; the point to strive for should be somewhere hereabouts. This is Dunluce Castle—well, if I remember aright, the spot is here: you must ask for 'the Corvy,'—the fishermen all know the cabin by that name; it was originally built out of the wreck of a French vessel that was lost there, and the word Corvy is a Northern version of Corvette. Once there,—and I know you 'll not find any difficulty in reaching it,—my sister will be glad to receive you; I need not say the accommodation does not rival Gwynne Abbey, no more than poor Molly does Helen Darcy; you will be right welcome, however,—so much I can pledge myself, not the less so that your journey was undertaken from a motive of true kindness. I don't well know how much or how little I have said in that letter; you can explain all I may have omitted,—the chief thing is to get the cabin ready for the Darcys as soon as may be. Give her this pocket-book,—I was too much hurried to-day to transact business at the bank; but the north road is a safe one, and you 'll not incur any risk. And now one glass to the success of the enterprise, and I 'll not detain you longer; I 'll give you old Martin's toast:—

"*May better days soon be our lot,*
Or better courage, if we have them not."

Forester pledged the sentiment in a bumper, and they parted.

"Good stuff in that young fellow," muttered Daly, as he looked after him; "I wish he had some Irish blood, though; these Saxons require a deal of the hammer to warm them, and never come to a white heat after all."

CHAPTER XXVI
"THE CORVY"

If the painter's license enables him to arrange the elements of scenery into new combinations, disposing and grouping anew, as taste or fancy may dictate, the novelist enjoys the lesser privilege of conveying his reader at will from place to place, and thus, by varying the point of view, procuring new aspects to his picture; less in virtue of this privilege than from sheer necessity, we will now ask our readers to accompany us on our journey northward.

Whether it be the necessary condition of that profusion of nature's gifts, so evident in certain places, or a mere accident, certain it is there is scarcely any one spot remarkable for great picturesque beauty to arrive at which some bleak and uninteresting tract must not be traversed. To this rule, if it be such, the northern coast of Ireland offers no exception.

The country, as you approach "the Causeway," has an aspect of dreary desolation that only needs the leaden sky and the drifting storm of winter to make it the most melancholy of all landscapes. A slightly undulating surface extends for miles on every side, scarcely a house to be seen, and save where the dip of the ground affords shelter, not a tree of any kind. A small isolated spot of oats, green even in the late autumn, is here and there to be descried, or a flock of black sheep wandering half wild o'er these savage wastes; vast masses of cloud, dark and lowering as rain and thunder can make them, hang gloomily overhead, for the tableland is still a lofty one, and the horizon is formed by the edge of those giant cliffs that stand the barriers of the western ocean, and against whose rocky sides the waves beat with the booming of distant artillery.

It was in one of those natural hollows of the soil, whose frequency seems to acknowledge a diluvian origin, that the little cottage which Sandy once owned stood. Sheltered on the south and east by rising banks, it was open on the other sides, and afforded a view seaward which extended from the rocky promontory of Port Rush to the great bluff of Fairhead, whose summit is nigh one thousand seven hundred feet above the sea.

Perhaps in all the sea-board of the empire, nothing of the same extent can vie in awful sublimity with this iron-bound coast. Gigantic cliffs of four and five hundred feet, straight as a wall, are seen perforated beneath by lofty tunnels, through which the wild waters plunge madly. Fragments of basalt, large enough to be called islands, are studded along the shore, the outlines fanciful and strange as beating waves and winds can make them, while, here and there, in some deep-creviced bay, the water flows in with long and measured sweep, and, at each moment retiring, leaves a trace upon the strand, fleeting as the blush upon the cheek of beauty; and here a little group of fisher children may be seen at play, while the nets are drying on the beach, the only sight or sound of human life, save that dark moving speck, alternately seen as the great waves roll on, be such, and, while tossing to and fro, seems by some charmed influence fettered to the spot. Yes, it is a fishing-boat that has ventured out at the half ebb, with the wind off shore, — hazardous exploit, that only poverty suggests the courage to encounter!

In front of one of these little natural bays stood "the Corvy;" and the situation might have been chosen by a painter, for, while combining every grand feature of the nearer landscape, the Scottish coast and even Staffa might be seen of a clear evening; while westward, the rich sunsets were descried in all their golden glory, tipping the rolling waves with freckled lustre, and throwing a haze of violet-colored light over the white rocks. And who is to say that, while the great gifts of the artist are not his who dwells in some rude cot like this, yet the heart is not sensitively alive to all the influences of such a scene, — its lonely grandeur, its tranquil beauty, or its fearful sublimity, — and that the peasant, whose associations from infancy to age are linked with every barren rock and fissured crag around, has not created for himself his own store of fancied images, whose power is not less deeply felt that it has asked for no voice to tell its workings.

"The Corvy" was a strange specimen of architecture, and scarcely capable of being classified in any of the existing orders. Originally, the hut was formed of the stern of the corvette, which, built of timbers of great size and strength, alone of all the vessel resisted the waves. This, being placed keel uppermost, as most consisting with terrestrial notions of building, and accommodated with a door and two windows, the latter being filled with two ship-lenses, comprised the entire edifice. Rude and uncouth as it unquestionably was, it was regarded with mingled feelings of envy and admiration by all the fishermen for miles round, for while they had contributed their tackle and their personal aid to place the mass where it stood, they never contemplated its becoming the comfortable dwelling they soon beheld, nor were these jealous murmurings allayed by the assumption of a lofty flagstaff, which, in the pride of conquest, old M'Grane displayed above his castle, little wotting that the banner that floated overhead waved with the lilies of France, and not the Union Jack of England.

Sandy's father, however, possessed those traits of character which confer ascendency, whether a man's lot be cast among the great or the humble; and he soon not only subdued those ungenerous sentiments, but even induced his neighbors to assist him in placing a small brass carronade on the keel, or, as he now termed it, the ridge of his dwelling, where, however little serviceable for warlike purposes, it made a very specious and imposing ornament.

Such was the inheritance to which Sandy succeeded, and such the possession he ceded for a consideration to Bagenal Daly, on that eventful morning their acquaintance began. In course of time, however, it fell to ruin, and lay untenanted and uncared for, when Miss Daly, in one of her rambling excursions, chanced to hear of it, and, being struck by the beauty of the situation, resolved to refit it as a summer residence. Her first intentions on this head were humble enough; two small chambers at either side of the original edifice—now converted into a species of hall and a kitchen—comprised the whole, and thither she betook herself, with that strange secret pleasure a life of perfect solitude possesses for certain minds. For a year she endured the inconveniences of her narrow dwelling tolerably well; but as she grew more attached to the spot, she determined on making it more comfortable; and, communicating the resolve to her brother, he not only concurred in the notion, but half anticipated his assent by despatching an architect to the spot, under whose direction a cottage containing several comfortable rooms was added, and with such attention to the circumstances of the ground, and such regard for the ancient character of the building, that the traces of its origin could still be discovered, and its old name of "the Corvy," be, even yet, not altogether inapplicable. The rude hulk was now, however, the centre of a long cottage, the timbers, partly covered by the small-leaved ivy, partly concealed by a rustic porch, displaying overhead the great keel and the flagstaff,—an ornament which no remonstrance of the unhappy architect could succeed in removing. As a sort of compromise, indeed, the carronade was dismounted, and placed beside the hall-door. This was the extreme stretch of compliance to which Daly assented.

The hall, which was spacious and lofty in proportion with other parts of the building, was fitted with weapons of war and the chase, brought from many a far-off land, and assembled with an incongruity that was no mean type of the owner. Turkish scimitars and lances, yataghans, and Malay creeses were grouped with Indian bows, tomahawks, and whale harpoons, while richly embroidered pelisses hung beside coats of Esquimaux seal, of boots made from the dried skin of the sun-fish. A long Swiss rifle was suspended by a blue silk scarf from one wall, and, over it, a damp, discolored parchment bore testimony, to its being won as a prize in the great shooting match of the Oberland, nearly forty years before. Beneath these, and stretching away into a nook contrived for the purpose, was the bark canoe in which Daly and Sandy made their escape from the tribe of the Sioux, by whom they were held in captivity for six years. Two very unprepossessing figures, costumed as savages, sat in this frail bark, paddle in hand, and to all seeming resolutely intent on their purpose of evasion. It would have been pardonable, however, for the observer not to have identified in these tattooed and wild-looking personages a member of Parliament and his valet, even though assisted to the discovery by their Indian names, which, with a laudable care for public convenience, had been written on a card, and suspended round the neck of each. Opposite to them, and in the corner of the hall, stood a large black bear, with fiery eyeballs and snow-white teeth, so admirably counterfeiting life as almost to startle the beholder; while over his head was a fearful, misshapen figure, whose malignant look and distorted proportions at once proclaimed it an Indian idol. But why enumerate the strange and curious objects which, notwithstanding their seeming incongruity, were yet all connected with Daly's history, and formed, in fact, a kind of pictorial narrative of his life? Here stood the cup, — a splendid specimen of Benvenuto's chisel, given him by the Doge of Venice, — and there was the embossed dagger presented by a King of Spain, with a patent of Grandee of the first class; while in a small glass case, covered with dust, and scarce noticeable, was a small and beautifully shaped satin slipper, with a rosette of now faded silver. But of this only one knew the story, and *he* never revealed it.

If we have taken an unwarrantable liberty with our reader by this too prolix description, our excuse is, that we might have been far more tiresome had we been so disposed, leaving, as we have, the greater part of this singular chamber unnoticed; while our *amende* is ready, and we will spare any further detail of the rest of the cottage, merely observing that it was both commodious and well arranged, and furnished not only with taste, but even elegance. And now to resume our long-neglected story.

It was about eight o'clock of a cold, raw February night, with occasional showers of sleet and sudden gusts of fitful wind, — that happy combination which makes up the climate of the north of Ireland, and, with a trifling abatement of severity, constitutes its summer as well as its winter, — that Miss Daly sat reading in that strange apartment we have just mentioned, and which, from motives of economy, she occupied frequently during the rainy season, as the necessity of keeping it aired required constant fires, not so necessary in the other chambers.

A large hearth displayed the cheerful blaze of burning bog-deal, and an old Roman lamp, an ancient patern, threw its lustre on the many curious and uncouth objects on every side. If the flashing jets of light that broke from the dry wood gave at times a false air of vitality to the stuffed figures around, in compensation it made the only living thing there seem as unreal as the rest.

Wrapped up in the great folds of a wide Greek capote she had taken from the wall, and the hood of which she had drawn over her head, Miss Daly bent over the yellow pages of an old quarto volume. Of her figure no trace could be marked, nor any guess concerning it, save that she was extremely tall. Her features were bold and commanding, and in youth must have been eminently handsome. The eyebrows were large and arched, the eyes dark and piercing, and the whole contour of the face had that character of thoughtful beauty so often seen in the Jewish race. Age and solitude, perhaps, had deepened the lines around the angles of the mouth and brought down the brows, so as to give a look of severity to features which, from this cause, became strikingly resembling her brother's. If time had made its sad inroad on those lineaments once so lovely, it seemed to spare even the slightest touch to that small white hand, which, escaping from the folds of her mantle, was laid upon the volume before her. The taper fingers were covered with rings, and more than one bracelet of great price glittered upon her wrist; nor did this taste seem limited to these displays, for in the gold combs that fastened, on either temple, her masses of gray hair, rich gems were set profusely, forming the strangest contrast to the coarse folds of that red-brown cloak in which she was enveloped.

However disposed to profit by her studies, Miss Daly was occasionally broken in upon by the sound of voices from the kitchen, which, by an unlucky arrangement of the architect, was merely separated from the hall by a narrow corridor. Sometimes the sound was of laughter and merriment; far oftener, however, the noises betokened strife; for so it is, in the very smallest household—there were but two in the present case—unanimity will not always prevail. The contention was no less a one than that great national dispute which has separated the island into two wide and opposing parties; Miss Daly's butler, or man of all work, being a stout representative of southern Ireland; her cook an equally rigid upholder of the northern province. If little Dan Nelligan had the broader cause, he was the smaller advocate, being scarcely four feet in height; while Mrs. M'Kerrigan was fifteen stone of honest weight, and with a *torso* to rival the Farnese Hercules. Their altercations were daily, almost hourly; for, living in a remote, unvisited spot, they seemed to console themselves for want of collision with the world by mutual disputes and disagreements.

To these family jars, habit had so reconciled Miss Daly that she seldom noticed them; indeed, the probability is that, like the miller who wakes up when the mill ceases its clamors, she might have felt a kind of shock had matters taken a quieter course. People who employ precisely the same weapons cannot long continue a warfare without the superiority of one or the other being sure to evince itself. The diversity of the forces, on the contrary, suggests new combinations, and with dissimilar armor the combat may be prolonged to any extent. Thus was it here; Dan's forte was aggravation,—that peculiarly Irish talent which makes much out of little, and, when cultivated with the advantages of natural gifts, enables a man to assume the proud political position of an Agitator, and in time a Liberator.

Mrs. M'Kerrigan, slow of thought, and slower of speech, was ill-suited to repel the assaults of so wily and constant a foe; she consequently fell back on the prerogatives of her office in the household, and repaid all Dan's declamation by changes in his diet,—a species of retribution the heaviest she could have hit upon.

Such was the present cause of disturbance, and such the reason for Dan's loud denunciations on the "black north," uttered with a volubility and vehemence that pertain to a very different portion of the empire. Twice had Miss Daly rung the little hand-bell that stood beside her to enforce order, but it was unnoticed in the clamor of the fray, while louder and louder grew the angry voice of Dan Nelligan, which at length was plainly audible in the hall.

"Look now, see then, may the divil howld a looking-glass to your sins, but I 'll show it to the mistress! I may, may I? That 's what you 're grumbling, ye ould black-mouthed Prasbytarien! 'T is the fine supper to put before a crayture wet to the skin!"

"Dinna ye hear the bell, Nelly?" This was an epithet of insult the little man could not endure. "Ye 'd ken the tinkle o' that, av ye heard it at the mass."

"Oh, listen to the ould heretic! Oh, holy Joseph! there 's the way to talk of the blessed ould ancient religion! Give me the dish; I 'll bring it into the parlor this minit, I will. I 'll lave the place,—my time 's up in March. I would n't live in the house wid you for a mine of goold!"

"Are ye no goin' to show the fish to the leddy?" growled out the cook, in her quiet barytone.

At this moment Miss Daly's bell announced that endurance had reached its limit, and Dan, without waiting to return the fire, hastened to the hall, muttering as he went, loud enough to be heard, "There, now, that's the mistress ringing, I 'm sure; but sorra bit one can hear wid your noise and ballyragging!"

"What is the meaning of this uproar?" said Miss Daly, as the little man entered, with a very different aspect from what he wore in the kitchen.

"'Tis Mrs. M'Kerrigan, my Lady; she was abusin' the ould families in the county Mayo, and I could n't bear it; and because I would n't hear the master trated that way, she gives me nothing but fish the day after a black fast, though she does be ating beef under my nose when I darn't touch meat, and it's what, she put an ould baste of a cod before me this evening for my supper, and here 's Lent will be on us in a few days more."

"How often have I told you," said Miss Daly, sternly, "that I 'll not suffer these petty, miserable squabbles to reach me? Go back to the kitchen; and, mark me, if I hear a whisper, or muttering ever so low in your voice, I 'll put you to spend the night upon the rocks."

Dan skulked from the room like a culprit remanded to jail; but no sooner had he reached the kitchen than, assuming a martial air and bearing, he strutted up to the fire and turned his back to it.

"Ay," said he, in a stage soliloquy, "it was what it must come to sooner or later; and now she may go on her knees, and divil a foot I 'll stay! It's not like the last time, sorra bit! I know what she 's at—' 'T is my way, Danny, you must have a pound at Avster '—bother! I 'm used to that now."

"There's the bell again, ye auld blethering deevil."

But Mrs. M'Kerrigan ran no risk of a reply now, for at the first tinkle Dan was back in the hall.

"There is some one knocking at the wicket without; see who it may be at this late hour of the night," said Miss Daly, without raising her head from the book, for, strange as were such sounds in that solitary place, her attention was too deeply fixed on the page before her to admit of even a momentary distraction of thought. Dan left the room with becoming alacrity, but in reality bent on anything rather than the performance of his errand. Of all the traits of his southern origin, none had the same predominance in his nature as a superstitious fear of spirits and goblins,—a circumstance not likely to be mitigated by his present lonely abode, independently of the fact that more than one popular belief attributed certain unearthly sights and sounds to the old timbers of "the Corvy," whose wreck was associated with tales of horror sufficient to shake stouter nerves than "Danny's."

When he received this order from his mistress, he heard it pretty much as a command to lead a forlorn hope, and sat himself down at the outside of the door to consider what course to take. While he was thus meditating, the sounds became plainly audible, a loud and distinct knocking was heard high above the whistling wind and drifting rain, accompanied from time to time by a kind of shout, or, as it seemed to Dan's ears, a scream like the cry of a drowning man.

"Dinna ye hear that, ye auld daft body?" said Nancy, as, pale with fear, and trembling in every limb, Dan entered the kitchen.

"I do indeed, Mrs. Mac,"—this was the peace appellation he always conferred on Nancy,—"I hear it, and my heart's beatin' for every stroke I listen to; 'tisn't afeard I am, but a kind of a notion I have, like a dhrame, you know "—(here he gave a sort of hysterical giggle)—"as if the ould French Captain was coming to look after his hand, that was chopped off with the hatchet when he grasped hold of the rock."

"He canna hae muckle use for it noo," responded Nancy, dryly, as she smoked away as unconcerned as possible.

"Or the mate!" said Dan, giving full vent to his store of horrors; "they say, when he got hold of the rope, that they gave it out so fast as he hauled on it, till he grew faint, and sank under the waves."

"He's no likely to want a piece of spunyarn at this time o' day," rejoined Nancy again. "He's knocking brawly, whoever he be; had ye no better do the leddy's bidding, and see who's there?"

"Would it be plazing to you, Mrs. Mac," said Dan, in his most melting accents, "to come as far as the little grass-plot, just out of curiosity, ye know, to say ye seen it?"

"Na, na, my bra' wee mon, ye maun ee'n gae by your-sel'; I dinna ken mickle about sperits and ghaists, but I hae a gude knowledge of the rheumatiz without seekin' it on a night like this. There's the leddy's bell again, she's no pleased wi' yer delay."

"Say I was puttin' on my shoes, Nancy," said Dan, as his teeth chattered with fear, while he took down an old blunderbuss from its place above the fire, and which had never been stirred for years past.

"Lay her back agen where ye found her," said Nancy, dryly; "is na every fule kens the like o' them! Take your mass-book, and the gimcracks ye hae ower your bed, but dinna try mortal weapons with them creatures."

Ironical as the tone of this counsel unquestionably was, Dan was in no mood to reject it altogether, and he slipped from its place within his breast to a more ostensible position a small blessed token, or "gospel," as it is called, which he always wore round his neck. By this time the clank of the bell kept pace with the knocking sounds without, and poor Dan was fairly at his wits' end which enemy to face. Some vague philosophy about the "devil you know, and the devil you don't," seemed to decide his course, for he rushed from the kitchen in a state of frenzied desperation, and, with the blunderbuss at full cock, took the way towards the gate.

The wicket, as it was termed, was in reality a strong oak gate, garnished at top with a row of very formidable iron spikes, and as it was hung between two jagged and abrupt masses of rock, formed a very sufficient outwork, though a very needless one, since the slightest turn to either side would have led to the cottage without any intervening barrier to pass. This fact it was which now increased Dan Nelligan's terrors, as he reasoned that nobody but a ghost or evil spirit would be bothering himself at the wicket, when there was a neat footpath close by.

"Who's there?" cried Dan, with a voice that all his efforts could not render steady.

"Come out and open the gate," shouted a deep voice in return.

"Not till you tell me where you come from, and who you are, if you are 'lucky.'"

"That I 'm not," cried the other, with something very like a deep groan; "if I were, I 'd scarce be here now."

"That's honest? anyhow," muttered Dan, who interpreted the phrase in its popular acceptation among the southern peasantry. "And what are you come back for, alanah?" continued he, in a most conciliating tone.

"Open the gate, and don't keep me here answering your stupid questions."

Though these words were uttered with a round, strong intonation that sounded very like the present world, Dan made no other reply than an endeavor to repeat a Latin prayer against evil spirits, when suddenly, and with a loud malediction on his obstinacy, Dan saw "the thing," as he afterwards described it, take a flying leap over the gate, at least ten feet high, and come with a bang on the grass, not far from where he stood. To fire off his blunderbuss straight at the drifting clouds over his head, and to take to flight was Dan's only impulse, screaming out, "the Captain 's come! he's come!" at the very top of his lungs. The little strength he possessed only carried him to the kitchen door, where, completely overcome with terror, he dropped senseless on the ground.

Forester's warm reception at the Corry.

While this was occurring, Miss Daly, alarmed by the report of fire-arms, but without any personal fears of danger, threw open the hall door and called out, "Who is there?" and as the dark shadow of a figure came nearer, "Who are you, sir?"

"My name is Forester, madam, — a friend of your brother's; for I perceive I have the honor to address Miss Daly."

By this time the stranger had advanced into the full light of the lamp within, where his appearance, tired and travel-stained as he was, corroborated his words.

"You have had a very uncourteous welcome, sir," said Miss Daly, extending her hand and leading him within the cottage.

"The reception was near being a warm one, I fear," said Forester, smiling; "for as I unfortunately, growing rather impatient, threw my carpet bag over the gate, intending to climb it afterwards, some one fired at me, — not with a good aim, however; for I heard the slugs rattling on a high cliff behind me."

"Old Dan, I am certain, mistook you for a ghost or a goblin," said Miss Daly, laughing, as if the affair were an excellent joke devoid of all hazard; "we have few visitors down here from either world."

"Really, madam, I will confess it, if the roads are only as impassable for ghosts as for men of mortal mould, I 'm not surprised at it. I left Coleraine at three o'clock to-day, where I was obliged to exchange my travelling carriage for a car, and I have been travelling ever since, sometimes on what seemed a highway, far oftener, however, across fields with now and then an intervening wall to throw down, — which we did, I own, unceremoniously; while lifting the horse twice out of deep holes, mending a shaft, and splicing the traces, lost some time. The driver, too, was once missing, — a fact I only discovered after leaving him half a mile behind. In fact, the whole journey was full of small adventures up to the moment when we came to a dead stand at the foot of a high cliff, where the driver told me the road stopped, and that the rest of my way must be accomplished on foot; and on my asking what direction to take, he brought me some distance off to the top of a rock, whence I could perceive the twinkling of a light, and said, 'That's the Corvy.' I did my best to secure his services as a guide, but no offer of money nor persuasions could induce him to leave his horse and come any further; and now, perhaps, I can guess the reason, — there is some superstition about the place at nightfall.''

"No, no, you 're mistaken there, sir; few of these people, however they may credit such tales, are terrified by them. It was the northern spirit dictated the refusal: his contract was to go so far, it would have 'put him out of his way' to go further, and his calculation was that all the profit he could fairly derive — and he never speculated on anything unfair — would not repay him. Such are the people of this province.''

"The trait is honest, I 've no doubt, but it can scarcely be the source of many amiable ones,'' said Forester, smarting under the recent inconvenience.

"We 'll talk of that after supper,'' said Miss Daly, rising, "and I leave you to make a good fire while I go to give some orders.''

"May I not have the honor to present my credentials first?'' said Forester, handing Bagenal Daly's letter to her.

"My brother is quite well, is he not?''

"In excellent health; I left him but two days since.''

"The despatch will keep, then,'' said she, thrusting it into a letter-rack over the chimney-piece, while she left the room to make the arrangement she spoke of.

Miss Daly's absence was not of long duration, but, brief as it was, it afforded Forester time enough to look around at the many strange and incongruous decorations of the apartment, nor had he ceased his wonderment when Dan, pale and trembling in every limb, entered, tray in hand, to lay the supper-table.

With many a sidelong, stealthy look, Dan performed his duties, as it was easy to see that however disposed to regard the individual before him as of this world's company, "the thing that jumped out of the sky," as he called it, was yet an unexplained phenomenon.

"I see you are surprised by the motley companionship that surrounds me," said Miss Daly; "but, as a friend of Bagenal's, and acquainted, doubtless, with his eccentric habits, they will astonish you less. Come, let me hear about him,—is he going to pay me a visit down here?"

"I fear not, at this moment," said Forester, with an accent of melancholy; "his friendship is heavily taxed at the present juncture. You have heard, perhaps, of the unhappy event which has spread such dismay in Dublin?"

"No! what is it? I hear of nothing, and see nobody here."

"A certain Mr. Gleeson, the trusted agent of many country gentlemen, has suddenly fled—"

Before Forester could continue, Miss Daly arose, and tore open her brother's letter. For a few seconds Forester was struck with the wonderful resemblance to her brother, as, with indrawn breath and compressed lips, she read; but gradually her color faded away, her hands trembled, and the paper fell from them, while, with a voice scarcely audible, she whispered: "And it has come to this!" Covering her face with the folds of her cloak, she sat for some minutes buried in deep sorrow; and when she again looked up, years seemed to have passed over, and left their trace upon her countenance: it was pale and haggard, and a braid of gray hair, escaping beneath her cap, had fallen across her cheek, and increased the sad expression.

"So is it," said she, aloud, but speaking as though to herself,—"so is it: the heavy hand is laid on all in turn; happier they who meet misfortune early in life, when the courage is high and the heart unshrinking: if the struggle be life-long, the victory is certain; but after years of all the world can give of enjoyment—You know Maurice?—you know the Knight, sir?"

"Yes, madam, slightly; but with Lady Eleanor and her daughter I have the honor of intimate acquaintance."

"I will not ask how he bears up against a blow like this. If his own fate only hung in the balance, I could tell that myself; but for his wife, to whom they say he is so devotedly attached—you know it was a love-match, so they called it in England, because the daughter of an Earl married the first Commoner in Ireland. And Bagenal advises their coming here! Well, perhaps he is right; they will at least escape the insolence of pity in this lonely spot. Oh! sir, believe me, there is a weighty load of responsibility on those who rule us; these things are less the faults of individuals than of a system. You began here by confiscation, you would finish by corruption. Stimulating to excesses of every kind a people ten times more excitable than your own,—now flattering, now goading,—teaching them to vie with you in display while you mocked the recklessness of their living, you chafed them into excesses of alternate loyalty or rebellion."

However satisfied of its injustice, Forester made no reply to this burst of passion, but sat without speaking as she resumed:—

"You will say there are knaves in every country, and that this Gleeson was of our rearing; but I deny it, sir. I tell you he was a base counterfeit we have borrowed from yourselves. That meek, submissive manner, that patient drudgery of office, that painstaking, petty rectitude, make up 'your respectable men;' and in this garb of character the business of life goes on with you. And why? Because you take it at its worth. But here, in Ireland, we go faster; trust means full confidence,—confidence without limit or bound; and then, too often, ruin without redemption. Forgive me, sir; age and sorrow both have privileges, and I perhaps have more cause than most others to speak warmly on this theme. Now, let me escape my egotism by asking you to eat, for I see we have forgotten our supper all this time."

From that moment Miss Daly never adverted further to the burden of her brother's letter, but led Forester to converse about his journey and the people whom, even in his brief experience, he perceived to be so unlike the peasantry of the West.

"Yes," said she, in reply to an observation of his, "these diversities of character observable in different places are doubtless intended, like the interminable varieties of natural productions, to increase our interest in life, and, while extending the sphere of speculation, to contribute to our own advancement. Few people, perhaps not any, are to be found without some traits of amiability; here there is much to be respected, and, when habit has dulled the susceptibility of first impressions, much also to be liked. But shall I not have the pleasure of showing you my neighbors and my neighborhood?"

"My visit must be of the shortest; I rather took than obtained my leave of absence."

"Well, even a brief visit will do something; for my neighbors all dwell in cottages, and my neighborhood comprises the narrow strip of coast between this hut and the sea, whose plash you hear this minute. To-morrow you will be rested from your journey, and if the day permits we 'll try the Causeway."

Forester accepted the invitation so frankly proffered, and went to his room not sorry to lay his head upon a pillow after two weary nights upon the road.

Forester was almost shocked as he entered the breakfast-room on the following morning to see the alteration in Miss Daly's appearance. She had evidently passed a night of great sorrow, and seemed with difficulty to bear up against the calamitous tidings of which he was the bearer. She endeavored, it is true, to converse on matters of indifference, — the road he had travelled, the objects he had seen, and so on; but the effort was ever interrupted by broken snatches of reflection that would vent themselves in words, and all of which bore on the Knight and his fortunes.

To Forester's account of her brother Bagenal's devotion to his friend she listened with eager interest, asking again and again what part he had taken, whether his counsels were deemed wise ones, and if he still enjoyed to the fullest extent the confidence of his old friend.

"It is no friendship of yesterday, sir," said she, with a heightened color and a flashing eye; "they knew each other as boys, they walked the mountains together as young men, speculated on the future paths fate might open before them, and the various ambitions which, even then, stirred within them. Bagenal was ever rash, headstrong, and impetuous, rarely firm in purpose till some obstacle seemed to defy its accomplishment. Maurice — the Knight, I mean — was not less resolute when roused, but more often so much disposed to concede to others that he would postpone his wishes to their own; and once believing himself in any way pledged to a course, would forget all, save the fulfilment of the implied promise. Such were the two dispositions, which, acting and reacting on each other, effected the ruin of both: the one wasted in eccentricity what the other squandered in listless indifference; and with abilities enough to have won distinction for humble men, they have earned no other reputation than that of singularity or convivialism.

"As for Bagenal," she said, after a pause, "wealth was never but an incumbrance to him; he was one of those persons who never saw any use for money, save in the indulgence of mere caprice; he treated his great fortune as a spoiled child will do a toy, and never rested till he had pulled it to pieces, and perhaps derived the same moral lesson too, — astonishment at the mere trifle which once amused him. But Maurice Darcy, — whose tastes were ever costly and cultivated, who regarded splendor not as the means of vulgar display, but as the fitting accompaniment of a house illustrious by descent and deeds, and deemed that all about and around him should bear the impress of himself, generous and liberal as he was, — how is he to bear this reverse? Tell me of Lady Eleanor; and Miss Darcy, is she like the Knight, or has her English blood given the character to her beauty?"

"She is very like her father," said Forester, "but more so even in disposition than in features."

"How happy I am to hear it," said Miss Daly, hastily; "and she is, then, high-spirited and buoyant? What gifts in an hour like this!"

"You say truly, madam, she will not sink beneath the stroke, believe me."

"Well, this news has reconciled me to much of your gloomier tidings," said Miss Daly; "and now let us wander out upon the hills; I feel as if we could talk more freely as we stroll along the beach."

Miss Daly arose as she spoke, and led the way through the little garden wicket, which opened on a steep pathway down to the shore.

"This will be a favorite walk with Helen, I'm certain," said she. "The caves are all accessible at low water, and the view of Fairhead finer than from any other point. I must instruct you to be a good and a safe guide. I must teach you all the art and mystery of the science, make you learned in the chronicles of Dunluce, and rake up for you legends of ghostcraft and shipwreck enough to make the fortunes of a romancer."

"I thank you heartily," said Forester; "but I cannot remain here to meet my friends."

"Oh, I understand you," said Miss Daly, who in reality put a wrong interpretation on his words; "but you shall be my guest. There is a little village about four miles from this, where I intend to take up my abode. I hope you will not decline hospitality which, if humble, is at least freely proffered."

"I regret deeply," said Forester, and he spoke in a tone of sorrow, "that I cannot accept your kindness. I stand in a position of no common difficulty at this moment." He hesitated, as if doubting whether to proceed or not, and then, in a more hurried voice, resumed: "There is no reason why I should obtrude my own petty cares and trials where greater misfortunes are impending; but I cannot help telling you that I have been rash enough, in a moment of impatience, to throw up an appointment I held on the Viceroy's Staff, and I know not how far the step may yet involve me with my relatives."

"Tell me how came you first acquainted with the Darcys?" said Miss Daly, as if following out in her own mind a train of thought.

"I will be frank with you," said Forester, "for I cannot help being so; there are cases where confidence is not a virtue, but a necessity. Every word you speak, every tone of your voice, is so much your brother's that I feel as if I were confiding to him in another form. I learned to know the Knight of Gwynne in a manner which you may deem, perhaps, little creditable to myself, though I trust you will see that I neither abused the knowledge nor perverted the honor of the acquaintanceship. It was in this wise."

Briefly, but without reserve, Forester narrated the origin of his first journey to the West, and, without implicating the honor of his relative, Lord Castlereagh, explained the nature of his mission, to ascertain the sentiments of the Knight, and the possibility of winning him to the side of the Government. His own personal adventures could not, of course, be omitted, in such a narrative; but he touched on the theme as slightly as he could, and only dwelt on the kindness he had experienced in his long and dangerous illness, and the long debt of gratitude which bound him to the family.

Of the intimacy that succeeded he could not help speaking, and, whether from his studied avoidance of her name, or that, when replying to any question of Miss Daly's concerning Helen Darcy, his manner betrayed agitation, certain it is that when he concluded, Miss Daly's eyes were turned towards him with an expression of deep significance that called the color to his cheek.

"And so, sir," said she, in a slow and measured voice, "you went down to play the tempter, and were captured yourself. Come, come, I know your secret; you have told it by signs less treacherous than words; and Helen,— for I tell you freely my interest is stronger for her,—how is she disposed towards you?"

Forester never spoke, but hung his head abashed and dejected.

"Yes, yes, I see it all," said Miss Daly, hurriedly; "you would win the affection of a generous and high-souled girl by the arts which find favor in your more polished world, and you have found that the fascinations of manner and the glittering *éclat* of an aide-de-camp have failed. Now, take my counsel. But first let me ask, is this affection the mere prompting of an idle or capricious moment, or do you love her with a passion round which the other objects of your life are to revolve and depend? I understand that pressure of the hand; it is enough. My advice is simple. You belong to a profession second to none in its high and great rewards: do not waste its glorious opportunities by the life of a courtier; be a soldier in feeling as well as in garb; let her whose heart you would win, feel that in loving you she is paying the tribute to qualities that make men esteem and respect you; that she is not bestowing her hand upon the mere favorite of a Court, but on one whose ambitions are high, and whose darings are generous. Oh! leave nothing, or as little as you may, to mere influence; let your boast be, and it will be a proud one, that with high blood and a noble name you have started fairly in the race, and distanced your competitors. This is my counsel. What think you of it?"

"I will follow it," said Forester, firmly; "I will follow it, though, I own it to you, it suggests no hope, where hope would be happiness."

"Well, then," said Miss Daly, "you shall spend this day with me, and I will not keep you another; you have made me your friend by this confidence, and I will use the trust with delicacy and with fidelity."

"May I write to you?" said Forester, "and will you let me hear from you again?"

"With pleasure; I should have asked it myself had you not done so. Now, let us talk of the first steps to be taken in this affair; and here is a bench where we can rest ourselves while we chat."

Forester sat down beside her, and, in the freedom of one to whom fortune had so unexpectedly presented a confidante, opened all the secret store of his cares and hopes and fears. It was late when they turned again towards "the Corvy," but the youth's step was lighter, and his brow more open, while his heart was higher than many a previous day had found him.

CHAPTER XXVII
THE KNIGHT'S RETURN

We must now for a brief space, return to the Knight, as with a heavy heart he journeyed homeward. Never did the long miles seem so wearisome before, often and often as he had travelled them. The little accidental delays, which once he had met with a ready jest, and in a spirit of kindly indulgence, he now resented as so many intentional insults upon his changed and ruined fortune. The gossiping landlords, to whom he had ever extended so much of freedom, he either acknowledged coldly, or repelled with distance; their liberties were now construed into want of deference and respect; the very jestings of the postboys to each other seemed so many covert impertinences, and equivocal allusions to himself; for even so much will the stroke of sudden misfortune change the nature, and convert the contented and happy spirit into a temperament of gloomy sorrow and suspicion.

Unconscious of his own altered feelings, and looking at every object through the dim light of his own calamity, he hurried along, not, as of old, recognizing each well-known face, saluting this one, inquiring after that; he sat back in his carriage, and, with his hat drawn almost over his eyes, neither noticed the way nor the wayfarers.

In this mood it was he entered Castlebar. The sight of his well-remembered carriage drew crowds of beggars to the door of the inn, every one of whom had some special prayer for aid, or some narrative of sickness for his hearing. By the time the horses drew up, the crowd numbered some hundreds of every variety, not only in age, but in raggedness, all eagerly calling on him by name, and imploring his protection on grounds the most strange and dissimilar.

"I knew the sound of the wheels; ax Biddy if I did n't say it was his honor was coming!" cried one, in a sort of aside intended for the Knight himself.

"Ye 're welcome home, sir; long may you reign over us," said an old fellow with a beard like a pilgrim. "I dreamed I seen you last night standing at the door there, wid a half-crown in your fingers. 'Ouid Luke,' says you, 'come here! — —'"

A burst of rude laughter drowned this sage parable, while a good-looking young woman, with an expression of softness in features degraded by poverty and its consequences, courtesied low, and tried to attract his notice, as she held up a miserable-looking infant to the carriage window. "Clap them, acushla! 't is proud he is to see you back again, sir; he never forgets the goold guinea ye gave him on New Year's Day! Don't be pushin' that way, you rude cray-tures; you want to hurt the child, and it's the image of his honor."

"Many returns of the blessed sason to you," growled out a creature in a bonnet, but in face and figure far more like a man than a woman; "throw us out a fippenny to buy two ounces of tay. Asy, asy; don't be drivin' me under the wheels—ugh! it's no place for a faymale, among such rapscallions."

"What did they give you, Maurice? how much did you get, honey?" cried a tall and almost naked fellow, that leaned over the heads of several others, and put his face close to the glass of the carriage, which, for safety's sake, the Knight now let down, while he called aloud to the postboys to make haste and bring out the horses.

"Tell us all about it, Maurice, my boy,—are you a lord, or a bishop?" cried the tall fellow, with an eagerness of face that told his own sad bereavement, for he was deranged in intellect from a fall from one of the cliffs on the coast. "By my conscience, I think I must change my politics myself soon; my best pantaloons is like Nat Fitzgibbon,—it has resigned its sate! Out with a bit of silver here!—quick, I didn't kiss the King's face this ten days."

To all these entreaties Darcy seemed perfectly deaf; if his eyes wandered over the crowd, they noticed nothing there, nor did he appear to listen to a word around him, while he again asked why the horses were not coming.

"We're doing our best, your honor," cried a postboy, "but it's mighty hard to get through these divils; they won't stir till the beasts is trampling them down."

"Drive on, then, and let them take care of themselves," said the Knight, sternly.

"O blessed Father! there's a way to talk of the poor! O heavenly Vargin! but you are come back cruel to us, after all!"

"Drive on!" shouted out Darcy, in a voice of angry impatience.

The postboys sprang into their saddles, cracked their whips, and dashed forward, while the mob, rent in a hundred channels, fled on every side, with cries of terror and shouts of laughter, according as the distance suggested danger or security. All escaped safely, except the poor idiot, Flury, who, having one foot on the step when the carriage started, was thrown backward, when, to save himself, he grasped the spring, and was thus half dragged, half carried along to the end of the street, and there, failing strength and fear combining, he relinquished his hold and fell senseless to the ground, where the wheel grazed but did not injure him as he lay.

With a cry of terror, the Knight called out "Stop!" and, flinging wide the door, sprang out. To lift the poor fellow up to a sitting posture was the work of a second, while he asked, in accents the very kindest, if he were hurt.

"Sorra bit, Maurice," said the fellow, whose faculties sooner rallied than if they were habitually under better control. "I was on the wrong side of the coach, that's all; 't is safer to be within. The clothes is not the better of it," said he, looking at his sleeve, now hanging in stripes.

"Never mind that, Flury; we'll soon repair that misfortune; it does not signify much."

"Does n't it, faith?" said the other, shaking his head dubiously; "'tis asy talking, but I can't turn my coat without showing the hole in it. 'T is only the rich can do that."

The Knight bit his lip; for even from the fool's sarcasm he could gather the imputations already rife upon his conduct. Another and a very different thought succeeded to this, and he blushed with shame to think how far his sense of his own misfortune had rendered him indifferent, not only to the kindly feelings, but the actual misery, of others. The right impulses of high-minded men are generally rapid in their action, like the spring of the bent bow when the cord is cut asunder. It did not cost Darcy many minutes to be again the warm-hearted, generous soul nature had made him.

"Come, Flury," said he to the poor fellow, as he stood ruefully surveying his damaged drapery, "give that among the people there in the town, and keep this for yourself."

"This is goold, Maurice,—yellow goold!"

"So it is; but you're not the less welcome to it; tell them, too, that I have had troubles of my own lately; and that's the reason I hurried on without exchanging a word with them."

"How do you know, Maurice, but I'll keep it all to myself?".

"I'd trust you with a heavier sum," said the Knight, smiling.

"I know why,—I know why, well enough,—because I'm a fool. Never mind, there's greater fools nor me going. What did they give you up there for your vote, Maurice,—tell me, how much was it?"

The Knight shook his head, and Flury resumed: "Didn't I say it? Wasn't I right? By my ould hat! there's two fools in the country now;—Maurice Darcy and Red Flury; and Maurice the biggest of the two! Whoop, the more the merrier; there 's room for us all!" And with this wise reflection, Flury gave a very wild caper and a wilder shout, and set off at the speed of a hare towards Castlebar.

The Knight resumed his journey, and in a more contented mood. The little incident had called on him for an exertion, and his faculties only needed the demand to respond to the call. He summoned to his aid, besides, every comforting reflection in his power; he persuaded himself that there were some hopes remaining still, and tried to believe the evil not beyond remedy. "After all," thought he, "we are together; it is not death has been dealing with us, nor is there any stain upon our fair fame; and, save these, all ills are light, and can be borne."

From thoughts like these he was aroused by the heavy clank of the iron gate, as it fell back to admit the carriage within the park, while a thousand welcomes saluted him.

"Thank you, Darby!—thank you, Mary! All well up at the abbey?"

But the carriage dashed past at full speed, and the answer was drowned in the tumult. The postboys, true to the etiquette of their calling, had reserved their best pace for the finish, and it was at the stride of a hunting gallop they now tore along.

It was a calm night, with a young faint moon and a starry sky, which, without displaying in bright light the details of the scenery, yet exhibited them in strong, bold masses, making all seem even more imposing and grander than in reality; the lofty mountain appeared higher, the dark woods vaster, and the wide-spreading lawn seemed to stretch away into immense plains. Darcy's heart swelled with pride as he looked, while a pang shot through him as he thought, if even at that hour he could call them his own.

They had now reached a little glen, where the postboys were obliged to walk their blown cattle; emerging from this, they passed a thick grove of beech, and at once came in sight of the abbey. Darcy leaned anxiously from the window to catch the first sight of home, when what was his amazement to perceive that the whole was lighted up from end to end. The great suite of state rooms were a blaze of lustres, which even at that distance glittered in their starry brilliancy, and showed the shadows of figures moving within. He well knew that Lady Eleanor never saw company in his absence, — what could this mean? Tortured with doubts that in his then state of mind took every painful form, he ordered the postilions to get on faster, and at the very top of their speed they tore along, over the wide lawn, across the terrace drive, up the steep ascent to the gate tower into the courtyard.

This was also brilliantly lighted by lamps from the walls, and also by the lights of numerous carriage lamps which crowded the ample space.

"What is this? Can no one tell me?" muttered the Knight, as he leaped from the carriage, and, seizing a livery servant who was passing, said, "What is going on here? What company has the abbey?"

"Full of company," said the man, in an English accent; "there 's my Lord —"

"Who do you mean?"

"The Earl of Netherby, sir, and Sir Harry Beauclerk, and Colonel Crofton, and —"

"When did they arrive?" said the Knight, interrupting a catalogue, every name of which, although unknown, sent a feeling like a stab through his heart.

"They came the evening before last, sir; Mr. Lionel Darcy, who arrived the same morning —"

"Is he here?" cried the Knight; and, without waiting for more, hastened forward.

The servants, of whom there seemed a great number about, were in strange liveries, and unknown to the Knight; nor was it without undergoing a very cool scrutiny from them that Darcy succeeded in gaining admittance to his own house. At last he reached the foot of the great stair, whence the sounds of music and the din of voices filled the air; servants hurried along with refreshments, or carried orders to others in waiting; all was bustle and excitement, in the midst of which Darcy stood only half conscious of the reality of what he saw, and endeavoring to reason himself into a conviction of what he heard. It was at this moment that several officers of a newly quartered regiment passed up, admiring, as they went, the splendor of the house, and the magnificent preparations they witnessed on every side.

"I say, Dallas," cried one, "you're always talking of your uncle Beverley: does he do the thing in this style, eh?"

"By Jove!" interposed a short, thick-set major, with a bushy beard and eyebrows, "this is what I call going the pace: do they give dinners here?"

"Yes, that they do," said a white-faced, ghostly looking ensign; "I heard all about this place from Giles of the 40th; he was quartered six months in this county, and used to grub here half the week. The old fellow is n't at home now, but they say he's a trump."

"Let's drink his health, Watkins," cried the first speaker, "here's champagne going up;" and so saying, the party gathered around two servants, one of whom carried an ice-pail with some bottles, and the other a tray of glasses.

"Does any one know his name, though?" said the major, as he held his glass to be filled.

"Yes, it's something like—Oh, you know that fellow that joined us at Coventry?"

"Brereton, is it?"

"No, hang it! I mean the fellow that had the crop-eared cob with the white legs. Never mind, here he goes, anyhow."

"Oh, I know who you mean,—it was Jack Quin."

"That's the name; and your friend here is called 'Gwynne,' I think. Here, gentlemen, I give you Gwynne's health, and all the honors; may he live a few centuries more—"

"With a warm heart and a cool cellar," added one.

"Pink champagne, and red-coats to drink it," chimed in the ensign.

"May I join you in that pleasant sentiment, gentlemen?" said the Knight, bowing courteously, as he took a glass from the tray and held it towards the servant.

"Make no apology, sir," said the major, eying him rather superciliously, for the travelling dress concealed the Knight's appearance, and distinguished him but slightly from many of those lounging around the doors.

"Capital ginger-beer that! eh?" said the ensign, as, winking at his companions, he proceeded to quiz the stranger.

"I have certainly drunk worse," said the Knight, gravely,—"at an infantry mess."

There was a pause before he uttered the last three words, which gave them a more direct application; a stare, half stupid, half impertinent, was, however, all they elicited, and the group moved on, while the Knight, disencumbering himself of his travelling gear, slowly followed them.

"Grim old gentlemen these, ain't they?" said the major, gazing at the long line of family portraits that covered the walls; "that fellow with the truncheon does not seem to like the look of us."

"Here's a bishop, I take it, with the great wig."

"That's a chancellor, man; don't you see the mace? But he's not a whit more civil-looking than the other; commend me to the shepherdess yonder, in blue satin. But come on, we 're losing time; I hear the flourish of a new dance. I say," said he, in a whisper, "do you see who we've got behind us?" And they turned and saw the Knight as he mounted the stairs behind them.

"A friend of the family, sir?" asked the major, in a voice that might bear the equivocal meaning of either impertinence or mere inquiry.

The Knight seemed to prefer taking it in the latter acceptation, as he answered mildly, "I have that honor."

"Ah! indeed; well, we 've the misfortune to be strangers in these parts; only arrived in the neighborhood last week, and were invited here through our colonel. Would you have any objection to present us?—Major Hopecot of the 5th, Captain Mills, Mr. Dallas, Mr. Fothergill, Mr. Watkins."

"How the major *is* going it!" lisped the ensign, while his goggle eyes rolled fearfully, and the others seemed struggling to control their enjoyment of such drollery.

"It will afford me much pleasure, sir, to do your bidding," said the Knight, calmly.

"Take the head of the column, then," resumed the major, making way for him to pass; and the Knight entered, with the others after him.

"My father—my dearest father!" cried a voice at the moment, and, escaping from her partner, Helen was in a moment in bis arms. The next instant Lionel was also at his side.

"My dear children!—my sweet Helen!—and Lionel, how well you 're looking, boy! Ah! Eleanor, what a pleasant surprise you have managed for me."

"Then perhaps you never got our letter," said Lady Eleanor, as she took his arm and walked forward. "I wrote the moment I heard from Lionel."

"And I, too, wrote you a long letter from London," said Lionel.

"Neither reached me; but the last few days I have been so busy, and so much occupied.—How are you, Conolly? Delighted to see you, Martin.—And Lady Julia, is she here? I must take a tour and see all my friends. First of all, I have a duty to perform; let me introduce these gentlemen. But where are they? Oh, I see them yonder." And, as he spoke, he led Lady Eleanor across the room to the group of officers, who, overwhelmed with shame at their discovery, stood uncertain whether they should remain or retire.

"Let me introduce Major Hopecot and the officers of the 5th," said he, bowing courteously. "These gentlemen are strangers, Lady Eleanor; will you take care that they find partners."

While the abashed subalterns left their major to make his speeches to Lady Eleanor, the Knight moved round the room with Helen still leaning on his arm. By this time Darcy's arrival was generally known, and all his old friends came pressing forward to see and speak to him.

"Lord Netherby," whispered Helen in the Knight's ear, as a tall and very thin old man, with an excessive affectation of youthfulness, tripped forward to meet him.

"My dear Lord," exclaimed Darcy, "what a pleasure, and what an honor to see you here!"

"You would not come to me, Knight, so there was nothing else for it," replied the other, laughing, as he shook hands with a great display of cordiality. "And you were quite right," continued he; "I could not have received you like this. There 's not so splendid a place in England, nor has it ever been my fortune to witness so much beauty." A half bow accompanied the last words, as he turned towards Helen.

"Take care, my Lord," said the Knight, smiling; "the flatteries of a courtier are very dangerous things when heard out of the atmosphere that makes them commonplace. We may take you literally, and have our heads turned by them."

At this moment Lionel joined them, to introduce several of his friends and brother officers who accompanied him from England, all of whom were received by the Knight with that winning courtesy of manner of which he was a perfect master; for, not affecting either the vices or frivolities of youth as a claim to the consideration of younger men, the Knight possessed the happy temper that can concede indulgence without asking to partake of it, and, while losing nothing of the relish for wit and humor, chasten both by the fruits of a life's experience.

"Now, Helen, you must go back to your partner; that young guardsman looks very sulkily at me for having taken you off—yes, I insist on it. Lionel, look to your friends, and I 'll join Lord Netherby's whist-table, and talk whenever permitted. Where 's poor Tate?" whispered he in Lady Eleanor's ear, as she just came up.

"Poor fellow! he has been ill for some days back; you know what a superstitious creature he is; and about a week since he got a fright,—some warning of a Banshee, I think; but it shook his nerves greatly, and he has kept his bed almost ever since. Lionel brought over some of these servants with him; but Lord Netherby's people are Legion, and the servants' hall now numbers something like seventy, I hear."

The Knight heaved a sigh; but, catching himself, tried to conceal it by a cough. Lady Eleanor had heard it, however, and stole a quick glance towards him, to evade which he turned abruptly round and spoke to some one near.

"Seventy, my dear Eleanor!" said he, after a pause, and as if he had been reflecting over his last observation; "and what a Babel, too, it must be! I heard French, German, and Italian in the hall; I think we can promise Irish ourselves."

"Yes," said Lionel, "it is the most amusing scene in the world. They had a ball last night in the lower gallery, where boleros and jigs succeeded each other, while the refreshments ranged from iced lemonade to burnt whiskey."

"And what did our worthy folk think of their visitors?" said Darcy, smiling.

"Not over much. Paddy Lennan looked with great contempt at the men sipping *orgeat*, and when he saw the waltzing, merely remarked, 'We've a betther way of getting round the girls in Ireland;' while old Pierre Dulange, Netherby's valet, persists in addressing the native company as 'Messieurs les Sauvages.'"

"I hope, for the sake of the public peace, they 've not got an interpreter among them."

"No, no, all's safe on that score, and freedom of speech has suggested the most perfect code of good manners; for it would seem, as they can indulge themselves in the most liberal reflections on each other, they have no necessity of proceeding to overt acts."

"Now," said the Knight, "let me not interrupt the revelry longer. To your place, Lionel, and leave me to pay my devoirs to my friends and kind neighbors."

The Knight's presence seemed alone wanting to fill up the measure of enjoyment. Most of those present were his old familiar friends, glad to see once more amongst them the great promoter of kind feeling and hospitality, while from such as were strangers he easily won golden opinions, the charm of courtesy being with him like a well-fitting garment, which graced, but did not impede, the wearer's motions.

He had a hundred questions to ask and to answer. The news of the capital travelled in those days by slow and easy stages, and the moment was sufficiently eventful to warrant curiosity; and so, as he passed from group to group, he gave the current gossip of the time as each in turn asked after this circumstance or that.

At length he took his place beside Lord Netherby, as he sat engaged at a whist-table, where the gathering crowd that gradually collected soon converted the game into a social circle of eager talkers.

Who could have suspected that easy, unconstrained manner, that winning smile, that ready laugh, the ever-present jest, to cover the working of a heart so nigh to breaking? And yet he talked pleasantly and freely, narrating with all his accustomed humor the chit-chat of the time; and while of course, the great question of the hour occupied every tongue and ear, all Lord Netherby's practised shrewdness could not enable him to detect the exact part the Knight himself had taken.

"And so they have carried the bill," said Conolly, with a sigh, as he listened to Darcy's account of the second reading. "Well, though I never was a Parliament man, nor expected to be one, I'm sorry for it. You think that strange, my Lord?"

"By no means, sir. A man may love monarchy without being the heir apparent."

"Quite true," chimed in the Knight. "I would even go further, and say that, without any warm devotion to a king, a man may hate a regicide."

Lord Netherby's eyes met Darcy's, and the wily peer smiled with a significance that seemed to say, "I know you *now*."

CHAPTER XXVIIII
THE HUNT-BREAKFAST

The ball lasted till nigh daybreak; and while the greater number of the guests departed, some few remained, by special invitation, at the abbey, to join a hunting party on the following day. For this Lionel had made every possible preparation, desiring to let his English friends witness a favorable specimen of Irish sport and horsemanship. The stud and kennel were both in high condition, the weather favorable, and, as the old huntsman said, "'It would be hard if a fox would n't be agreeable enough to give the strange gentlemen a run."

In high anticipation of the coming morning, and with many a prayer against a frost, they separated for the night. All within the abbey were soon sound asleep,—all save the Knight himself, who, the restraint of an assumed part withdrawn, threw himself on a sofa in his dressing-room, worn out and exhausted by his struggle. Ruin was inevitable,—that he well knew; but as yet the world knew it not, and for Lionel's sake he resolved to keep his own secret a few days longer. The visit was to last but eight days; two were already over; for the remaining six, then, he determined—whatever it might cost him—to preserve all the appearances of his former estate, to wear the garb and seeming of prosperity, and do the princely honors of a house that was never again to be his home.

"Poor Lionel!" thought he; "'twould break the boy's heart if such a disclosure should be made now; the high and daring promptings of his bold spirit would not quail before misfortune, although his courage might not sustain him in the very moment of the reverse. I will not risk the whole fortune of his future happiness in such a trial; he shall know nothing till they are gone; one week of triumphant pleasure he shall have, and then let him brace himself to the struggle, and breast the current manfully."

While endeavoring to persuade himself that Lionel's lot was uppermost in his mind, his heart would force the truth upon him that Lady Eleanor and Helen's fate was, in reality, a heavier stroke of fortune. Lionel was a soldier, ardent and daring, fond of his profession, and far more ambitious of distinction than attached to the life of pleasure a court and a great capital suggested; but they who had never known the want of every luxury that can embellish life, whose whole existence had been like some fairy dream of pleasure, how were they to bear up against the dreadful shock? Lady Eleanor's health was frail and delicate in the extreme; Helen's attachment to her mother such that any impression on her would invariably recoil upon herself. What might be the consequences of the disclosure to them Darcy could not, dared not, contemplate.

As he revolved all these things in his mind, and thought upon the difficulties that beset him, he was at a loss whether to deplore the necessity of wearing a false face of pleasure a few days longer, or rejoice at the occasion of even this brief reprieve from ruin. Thus passed the weary hours that preceded daybreak, and while others slept soundly, or reviewed in their dreams the pleasures of the past night, Darcy's gloomy thoughts were fixed upon the inevitable calamity of his fate, and the years, few but sad, that in all likelihood were now before him.

The stir and bustle of the servants preparing breakfast for the hunting party broke in upon his dreary revery, and he suddenly bethought him of the part he had assigned himself to play. He dreaded the possibility of an interview with Lady Eleanor, in which she would inevitably advert to Gleeson, and the circumstances of his flight; this could not be avoided, however, were he to pass the day at home, and so he resolved to join the hunting-field, where perhaps some lingering trace of his old enthusiasm for the sport might lead him to hope for a momentary relief of mind.

"Lionel, too, will be glad to see me in the saddle—it's some years since I crossed the sward at a gallop—and I am curious to know if a man's nerve is stouter when the world looks fair before him, or when the night of calamity is lowering above his head." Muttering these words to himself, he passed out into the hall, and crossing which, entered the courtyard, and took his way towards the stables. It was still dark, but many lights were moving to and fro, and the groom population were all about and stirring. Darcy opened the door and looked down the long range of stalls, where above twenty saddle-horses were now standing, the greater number of them highly bred and valuable animals, and all in the highest possible condition. Great was the astonishment of the stablemen as the Knight moved along, throwing a glance as he went at each stall, while a muttered "Welcome home to yer honor" ran from mouth to mouth.

"The bastes is looking finely, sir," said Bob Carney, who, as stud-groom and huntsman, had long presided over his department.

"So they are, Bob, but I don't know half of them; where did this strong brown horse come from?"

"That's Clipper, yer honor; I knew you wouldn't know him. He took up finely after his run last winter."

"And the fore leg, is it strong again?"

"As stout as a bar of iron; one of the boys had him out two days ago, and he took the yellow ditch flying: we measured nineteen feet between the mark of his hoofs."

"He ought to be strong enough to carry me, Bob."

"Don't ride him, sir, he's an uncertain divil; and though he 'll go straight over everything for maybe twenty minutes or half an hour, he 'll stop short at a drain not wider than a potato furrow, and the power of man would n't get him over it."

"That's a smart gray yonder,—what is she?"

"She's the one we tried as a leader one day; yer honor remembers you bid me shoot her, or get rid of her, for she kicked the traces, and nearly the wheel-horse, all to smash; and now she's the sweetest tiling to ride, for eleven stone, in the whole country. There's an English colonel to try her to-day; my only advice to him is, let her have her own way of it, for, if he begins pulling at her, 't is maybe in Donegal he 'll be before evening."

"And what have you for me?" said the Knight; "for I scarcely know any of my old friends here."

"There's the mouse-colored cob— —"

"No, no," said the Knight, laughing; "I want to keep my place, Bob. You must give me something better than that."

"Faith, an' your honor might have worse; but if it's for riding you are, take Black Peter, and you 'll never find the fence too big, or the ground too heavy for him. I was going to give him to the English lord; I suppose, after all, he 'll be better pleased with the cob."

"Well, then, Peter for me. And now let's see what Mr. Lionel has to ride."

"There she is, and a beauty!" said Bob, as, with a dexterous jerk, he chucked a sheet off her haunches, and displayed the shining flanks and splendid proportions of a thoroughbred mare. "That's Cushleen," said he, as he fixed his eyes on the Knight's face to enjoy the reflection of his own delight. "That's the darlin' can do it!—a child can hould her, but it takes a man to sit on her back—racing speed over a flat, and a jump!—'t is more like the bound of a football than anything else."

"She has the eye of a hot one, Bob."

"And why would n't she? But she knows when to be so. Let her take her place at the head of the whole field, with a light finger to guide and a stout heart to direct her, and she's a kitten; but the divil a tiger was ever as fierce if another passes her, or a cowardly hand would try to hold her back. And there's a nate tool, that black horse,—that's for another of the English gentlemen. Master Lionel calls him Sir Harry. They tell me he's a fine rider, and has a pack of hounds himself in his own place, and I am mistaken if he has the baste in his stable will give him a betther day's sport. The chestnut here is for Miss Helen, for she's coming to see them throw off, and it'll be a fine sight; we 'll be thirty-six out of your honor's stables, Mr. Conolly is bringing nine more, and all the Martins, and the Lynches, and Dalys, and Mr. Hickman O'Reilly and his son,—though, to be sure, *they* won't do much for the honor of ould Ireland."

The Knight turned away laughing, and re-entered the house.

Early as it yet was, the inmates of the abbey were stirring, and a great breakfast, laid for above thirty, was prepared in the library, for the supper-tables occupied the dining-rooms, and the débris of the magnificent entertainment of the night before still lingered there. Two cheerful fires blazed on the ample hearths, and threw a mellow lustre over that spacious room, where old Tate now busied himself in those little harmless duties he fancied indispensable to the Knight's comfort, for the poor fellow, on hearing of his master's return, had once more resumed his office.

The Knight's meeting with him was one of true friendship; difference of station interposed no barrier to affection, and Darcy shook the old man's hand as cordially as though they were brothers. Yet each was sad with a secret sorrow, which all their efforts could scarce conceal from the other. In vain the Knight endeavored to turn away old Tate's attention by inquiries after his health, questions about home, or little flatteries about his preparations, Tate's filmy eyes were fixed upon his master with a keenness that age could not dim.

"'T is maybe tired your honor is," said he, in a voice half meant as inquiry, half insinuation; "the Parliament, they tell me, destroys the health entirely."

"Very true, Tate; late hours, heated rooms, and some fatigue will not serve a man of my age; but I am tolerably well for all that."

"God be praised for it!" said Tate, piously, but in a voice that showed it was rather a wish he expressed than a conviction, when, suspecting that he had suffered some portion of his fears to escape, he added more cheerfully, "And is n't Master Lionel grown an iligant, fine young man! When I seen him comin' up the stairs, it was just as if the forty-eight years that's gone over was only a dhrame, and I was looking at your honor the day you came home from college; he has the same way with bis arms, and carries his head like you, and the same light step. Musha!" muttered he, below his breath, "the ould families never die out, but keep their looks to the last."

"He's a fine fellow, Tate!" said the Knight, turning towards the window, for, while flattered by the old man's praises of his son, a deep pang shot through his heart at the wide disparity of fortune with which life opened for both of them. At the instant an arm was drawn round him, and Helen stood at his side: she was in her riding-habit, and looking in perfect beauty. Darcy gazed at her for a few seconds, and with such evident admiration that she, as if accepting the compliment, drew herself up, and, smiling, said, "Yes, nothing short of conquest. Lionel told his friends to expect a very unformed country girl; they shall see at least she can ride."

"No harebrained risks, Helen, dearest. I'm to take the field to-day, and you must n't shake my nerve; for I want to bring no disgrace on my county."

"I was but jesting, my own dear papa," said she, drawing closer to him; "but I really felt so curious to see these English horsemen's performance that I asked Lionel to train Alice for me."

"And Lionel, of course, but too happy to show his pretty sister—"

"Nay, nay, if you will quiz, I must only confess that my head is quite turned already; our noble cousin overwhelms me with flatteries which, upon the principle the Indian accepts glass beads and spangles as gems, and gold, I take as real value. But here he comes."

And Lord Netherby, attired for the field in all the accuracy of costume, slipped towards them. After came Colonel Crofton, a well-known fashionable of the clubs and a hanger-on of the peer; then Sir Harry Beauclerk, a young baronet of vast fortune, gay, good-tempered, and extravagant; while several others of lesser note, brother officers of Lionel's and men about town, brought up the rear, one only deserving remark, a certain Captain, or, as he was better known, Tom Nolan,—a strange, ambiguous kind of fellow, always seen in the world, constantly met at the best houses, and yet nobody being able to explain why he was asked, nor—as it very often happened— who asked him.

Lady Eleanor never appeared early in the day, but there was a sprinkling of lady-visitors through the room, guests at the abbey: a very pretty, but not over-afflicted widow, a Mrs. Somerville, with several Mrs. and Miss Lynches, Brownes, and Martins, comprising the beauties of the neighborhood. Lionel was the last to make his appearance, so many directions had he to give about earth-stoppers and cover-hacks, drags, phaetons, fresh horses, and all the contingent requirements of a day's sport. Besides, he had pledged himself most faithfully to give Mrs. Somerville's horse, a very magnificent barb, a training canter himself, with a horse-sheet round his legs, for she was a timid rider,—on some occasions,—though certain calumnious people averred that, when alone, she would take any fence in the whole barony.

At length they were seated, and such a merry, happy party! There was but one sad heart in the company, and that none could guess at. And what a running fire of pleasant raillery rattled round the table! How brimful of wit and good-humor were they all! How ready each to take the jest against himself, and even heighten its flavor by some new touch of drollery. Harmless wagers respecting the places they would occupy at the finish, gentle quiz-zings about safe riding through the gaps, and joking counsels as to the peculiar difficulties of an Irish country, were heard on all sides; while the Knight recounted the Galway anecdote of Dick Perse taking an immense leap and disappearing afterwards. "'Call the ground, Dick!' cried Lord Clanricarde, who was charging up at top speed—'call the ground! What's at the other side?'

"'I *am*, thank God!' was the short reply, and the words came from the depth of a gravel-pit."

At last, venison pasties and steaks, rolls and coffee, with their due accompaniment of liqueurs, came to an end, and a very sufficient uproar without, of men, dogs, and horses commingled, bespoke the activity of preparation there, while old Bob Carney's voice topped every other, as he swore at or commended men and beasts indiscriminately.

"What a glorious morning for our sport!" said the Knight, as he threw open the sash, and let into the room the heavy perfume of the earth, borne on a southerly wind. The sea was calm as an inland lake, and the dark clouds over it were equally motionless. "We shall be unlucky, my Lord, if we do not show you some sport on such a day. Ah, there go the dogs!" And, as he spoke, the hounds issued from beneath the deep arch of the gateway, and with Bob and the whipper-in at their head, took their way across the lawn.

"To horse! to horse!" shouted Lionel, gayly, from the courtyard, for the riding party were not to proceed to the cover by the short path the hounds were gone, but to follow by a more picturesque and circuitous route.

"I hope sincerely that beast is not intended for me," said Lord Netherby, as a powerful black horse crossed the courtyard, in a series of bounds, and finished by landing the groom over his head.

"Never fear, my Lord," said Lionel, laughing; "Billy Pitt is meant for Beauclerk."

"You surely never named that animal after the minister, Knight?" said his Lordship.

"Yes, my Lord," said Darcy, with a smile; "it's just as unsafe to back one as the other. But here comes the heavy brigade. Which is your choice,— Black Peter, or Mouse?"

"If I may choose, I will confess this is more to my liking than anything I have seen yet. You know that I don't mean to take any part in the debate, so I may as well secure a quiet seat under the gallery. But, my dear Miss Darcy, what a mettlesome thing you 've got there!"

"She's only fidgety; if I can hold her when they throw off, I 'll have no trouble afterwards." And the graceful girl sat back easily in her saddle as the animal bounded and swerved with every stroke of her long riding-habit.

"There goes Beauclerk!" cried Lionel, as the young baronet shot like an arrow through the archway on the back of Billy Pitt; for no sooner had he touched the saddle than the unmanageable animal broke away from the groom's hands, and set off at full speed down the lawn.

"I say, Darcy," cried Colonel Crofton, "is n't Beauclerk a step over you in the 'Army List'?"

But Lionel never heard the question, for he was most busily occupied about Mrs. Somerville and her horse.

"Who drives the phaeton?—where's a safe whip to be found for Mrs. Martin?" said the Knight; and, seizing on a young Guardsman, he promoted him to the box, with a very pretty girl beside him. A drag, with four grays, was filling at the same instant, with a mixed population of horsemen and spectators, among whom Captain Nolan seemed the presiding spirit, as, seated beside a brother officer of Lionel's on the box, he introduced the several parties to each other, and did "the honors" of the conveyance.

Troops of horses, sheeted and hooded, now passed out with a number of grooms and stable-boys, on their way to cover; and at last the great cavalcade moved forward, the Knight, his daughter, and Lord Netherby gayly cantering on the grass, to permit the carriages to take the road. The drag came last; and although but newly met, the company were already in the full enjoyment of that intimacy which high spirits and pleasure beget, while Tom Nolan contributed his utmost to the merriment by jests which lost nothing of their poignancy from any scruples of their maker.

"There they go at last," said he, as Lionel and Mrs. Somerville cantered forth, followed by two grooms. "I never heard of a stirrup so hard to arrange as that, in all my life!"

CHAPTER XXIX
THE HUNT

The cover lay in a small valley, almost deep enough to be called a glen, watered by a stream which in winter and summer took the alternate character of torrent or rivulet; gently sloping hills rose on either side, their banks clad with low furze and fern, and behind them a wide plain extended to the foot of the great mountains of Connemara.

Both sides of the little glen were now occupied by groups on foot or horseback, as each calculated on the likelihood of the fox taking this direction or that. On the narrow road which led along the crest of the lower hill were many equipages to be seen, some of which were filled with ladies, whose waving feathers and gay colors served to heighten the effect of the landscape. The horsemen were dotted about, some on the ridge of the rising ground, some lower down on the sloping sides, and others walked their horses through the dense cover, watching as the dogs sprang and bounded from copse to copse, and made the air vibrate with their deep voices.

The arrival of the Knight's party created no slight sensation as carriages and horsemen came dashing up the hill, and took their station on an eminence, from whence all who were not mounted might have a view of the field. No sooner was he recognized, than such as had the honor of personal acquaintance moved forward to pay their respects and welcome him home again; among whom Beecham O'Reilly appeared, but with such evident diffidence of manner and reserve that Darcy, from motives of delicacy, was forced to take a more than ordinary notice of him.

"We were sorry not to have your company at the abbey last night; you 've had a cold, I hear," said the Knight.

"Yes, sir; this is the first day I've ventured out."

"Let me introduce you to Lord Netherby. One of our foremost riders, my Lord, Mr. Beecham O'Reilly. You may see that the merit is not altogether his own,—splendid horse you have there."

"He's very powerful," said the young man, accepting the praise with an air of easy indifference.

"In my country," interposed Lord Netherby, "we should value him at three hundred guineas, if his performance equal his appearance."

"I say, Lionel, come here a moment," cried the Knight. "What do you think of that horse?—but don't you know your old playfellow, Beecham? Have you both forgotten each other?"

"How are you, Beecham? I'd never have guessed you. To be sure, it is six years since we met. You were in Dublin, I think, when I was over on leave last?"

"No, at Oxford," said Beecham, with a slight flush as he spoke; for although he accepted the warm shake-hands Lionel proffered, his manner was one of constraint all through. Young Darcy was, however, too much occupied in admiring the horse to bestow much attention on the rider.

"He 'd carry you well," said Beecham, as if interpreting what was passing in his mind, "and as I have no fancy for him,—a worse horse will carry my weight as well,—I 'd sell him."

"At what price?"

"Lord Netherby has valued him at three hundred," said the young man. "I gave nearly as much myself."

The Knight, who heard this conversation, without being able to interrupt it, was in perfect misery. The full measure of his ruin rushed suddenly on his mind, and the thought that, at the very moment his son was meditating this piece of extravagance, he was himself actually a beggar, sickened him to the heart. Meanwhile, Lionel walked his horse slowly round, the better to observe the animal he coveted, and then cantered back to his place at Mrs. Somerville's side.

Beecham seemed to hesitate for a second or two, then, riding forward, he approached Lionel: "Perhaps you would try him to-day, Captain Darcy?" The words came hesitatingly and with difficulty.

"Oh, no! he 's beyond my reach," said Lionel, laughing.

"I'd really take it as a favor if you would ride him; I 'm not strong enough to hold him, consequently cannot do him justice."

"Take the offer, Darcy," said Lord Netherby, in a whisper, as he rode up to his side; "I have a great liking for that horse myself, and will buy him if you report favorably."

"In that case, my Lord, I'll do it with pleasure. I accept your kind proposal, and will change nags if you agree."

Beecham at once dismounted, and, beckoning to his servant, ordered him to change the saddles.

While this little scene was enacting, old Conolly rode up to the Knight, with a warning to keep the ladies in the road. "The fox will take the country towards Burnadarig," said he; "the start's with the wind; and as the fences are large and the ground heavy, they had better not attempt to follow the run."

"We will take your advice, Tom," said the Knight. "Come here, Helen—Colonel Crofton, will you kindly bring Mrs. Somerville up here, and tell Lord Netherby to join us—the day will be for the fast ones only. There they go,—are they off?"

"Not yet, not yet," said Conolly, as, standing in his stirrups, he looked down into the glen; "they're hunting him through the furze cover this half hour. I know that fox well; he never breaks till the dogs are actually on him."

By this time the scene in the valley was becoming highly exciting; the hounds, yelping and barking, bounded hither and thither; some, with uplifted throats, bayed deeply a long, protracted note; others, with noses to the earth, ran swiftly along, and then, stopping, burst into a sharp cry, as if of pain, while old Bob Carney's voice, encouraging this one, and cursing that, was high above the tumult.

"Tiresome work, this is," said Sir Harry Beauclerk; for his horse, mad with impatience, was white with sweat, and trembled in every limb.

"You'll have it very soon, sir," said old Conolly; "the dogs are together now. I wish that young gentleman there would move a little up the hill." This was said of a young officer who took his station at the exit of the cover. "There they go, now! Tally-ho!" cried he, in ecstasy, and the shout re-echoed from a hundred voices, as the hounds, in full cry, burst from the cover, and were seen, in one compact mass, rising the opposite hill.

In a second every horse was away, save that little group around the Knight, and which, notwithstanding all the efforts of the servants, bounded and plunged in mad impatience. Beauclerk was the first down the hill, and over the brook, which he cleared gallantly. Conolly followed close; and then came Crofton in a group of others, among whom rode O'Reilly, all riding well and safely; and last of all was Lionel, mounted on the brown thoroughbred, and holding him together, in spite of all his eagerness to get on.

The Knight forgot everything that lay heavily on his heart as he watched his son nearing the brook, which he took flying. "He knows his horse; now! see!" cried Darcy, as his whole face beamed with enthusiastic delight; "look a little this way, my dear Mrs. Somerville, Lionel's gaining on them!"

Mrs. Somerville scarcely needed the direction, for, notwithstanding her horse's plunging, she had never taken her glass from her eye.

"Is that a wall on the side of the hill? I really believe it is!" said Lord Netherby, with an accent of amazement and horror.

"A stone wall, and a stout one. I know it well," said Darcy. "There goes Sir Harry Beauclerk at it. Too fast, sir! too fast!" screamed out the Knight, as if his advice could be heard and followed at that distance.

"He's down! he's down!" cried several voices together, as horse and rider balanced for a second on the top, and rolled headlong on the opposite side, while Helen grasped her father's arm, but never uttered a word.

"His horse is away—there he goes!—but the young man is on his legs again!" called out the Knight; "see how the rest are scattering now—they 've no fancy for it;" for so it was, Beauclerk's catastrophe, mounted, as they knew him to be, on one of the most perfect of hunters, had terrified the field, and they broke up into different groups, searching an exit where they could.

"There he goes,—that's the way to take it!" cried Darcy, as Lionel, emerging from the little valley, was seen ascending the hill in a sharp canter; "see, my Lord! Do you mark how he holds his horse together? The hind legs are well forward—beautifully done!"

"Oh, beautifully done!" re-echoed Mrs. Somerville, as the young man, with one cut of his whip, rose the horse to the wall, topped, poised for an instant on its summit, and bounded down with the seeming lightness of a bird.

"They're all together again," said Helen. "Mr. Conolly has found a gap, and there they go."

For a few moments the whole field were in sight, as they rode in a waving line, only a few stragglers in their rear; but the gradual dip of the ground soon hid them from view, and nothing remained save the occasional glance of a red coat as some rider, "thrown out" for a moment, sought to recover his place by an adroit "cast."

"I suppose we are not destined to see much more of the day's sport?" said Mrs. Somerville, with a pouting look; for she would infinitely rather have braved all the hazards of the field than have remained behind with the spectators.

"I trust we shall have another peep at them," said the Knight. "By following this by-road to Burris Hill, the chances are that we see them winding along at our feet; the fox generally runs from this cover to the scrub beneath Nephin. We may go slowly, for if I be right in my calculation, they have a wide circuit to make yet."

The Knight, after a few words to the parties in the carriage, took the lead with Lord Netherby, while Mrs. Somerville and Helen followed, an indiscriminate crowd of carriages and horsemen bringing up the rear.

This was an arrangement artfully accomplished by the Earl, who had been most impatiently awaiting some opportunity of conferring with the Knight on the question of politics, and ascertaining how far he himself might adventure on claiming the merit of converting him, when he returned to England. He had already remarked that Darcy's name did not appear in the division on the second reading of the Bill of Union, and the fact seemed so far indicative of a disposition not to oppose the Government. The subject was one to be approached with skill, and it was at last by an adroit congratulation on the pleasant contrast of a country life with the fatigues of Parliament, that he opened the discussion.

"I believe, my Lord," said the Knight, laughing, "that Irish gentlemen are very likely to enjoy in future a fair proportion of that agreeable retirement you have so justly lauded. The wisdom of our rulers has thought fit to relieve us of the burden of self-government in Parliament, and left us, if we can succeed in effecting it, to govern ourselves at home."

"That will be unquestionably the lot of many, Knight. I am quite aware that men of second-rate importance will no longer possess any at all; but estated gentlemen, of high position and liberal fortunes, like yourself, for instance, will not lose their influence by the greater extent of the field in which it is exercised."

Darcy sighed, but made no reply; the thought of his utter ruin came too painfully across him to permit of an answer. Lord Netherby interpreted his silence as doubt, and continued: "You are unjust, not only to yourself, but to us, by any discredit of this point. Men of real knowledge about Ireland and her interests will have a greater position than ever they enjoyed before; no longer buried and lost among the impracticable horde of theorists and false patriots of a Dublin Parliament, they will be known and appreciated by a deliberative assembly where the greatest men of the empire hold council."

"I am forced to differ with you on every point, my Lord," said the Knight, calmly; "we are united to England, not that we may make an integral portion of your empire, but simply that we may be more easily governed. Up to this hour, you have ruled this country through the instrumentality of certain deputed individuals here amongst us; your system has had but indifferent success. You are now about to try another method, and govern us through the means of Party. Into the subdivisions of these parties Irishmen will fall,—with such success, personally, as their abilities and weight may obtain for them; but Party, I assert, will now rule Ireland, not with any regard to Irish interests or objects, but simply to put this man into power, and to put that man out. Now I, my Lord, humble as my station is, have no fancy for such contests as these,—contests in which the advantages of my country will always be subordinate to some Cabinet intrigue or Ministerial stratagem. To-day, the Government may find it suit their views to administer the affairs of Ireland ably, justly, and fearlessly; to-morrow, a powerful faction may spring up here, who, by intimidation without, and by votes within the House, shall be able to thwart the administration in their Home measures. What will happen then? This faction will be bought off. By concessions to them *in Ireland*, they will obtain all their demands, for the sake of pliancy about interests of which they care little, and know nothing. This will succeed for a time; the 'King's Government' will go well and flippantly on; you may tax the people, promote your followers, and bully your opponents to your heart's content: but, meanwhile, Ireland will be gaining on you; your allies, grown exacting by triumph, will ask more than you dare, or even have, to give; and the question will then arise, that the party who aspires to power must bid for it by further concession; and who is to vouch for the moderation of such demands, or what limit will there be to them? I see a train of such evils in the vista; and although I neither pretend to think our domestic legislature safe nor faultless, I think the dangers we have before us are even greater than such as would spring from an Irish Parliament."

Lord Netherby listened with great impatience—as perhaps the reader may have done also—to this declaration of the Knight's views, and was about to reply, when suddenly a cheer from some country people, stationed on a rocky height at a short distance, drew all eyes towards the valley, where now the hounds were seen in full cry, three horsemen alone following. One of these was the huntsman; Lionel another; the third was in plain clothes, and not known to any of the party. He was mounted on a powerful horse, and even at that distance could be seen to manage him with the address of a perfect rider. The rest of the field were far behind, some still standing on the verge of a mountain torrent, which appeared to have formed the obstacle to the run, and into which more than one seemed to have fallen.

Groups were gathered here and there along the bank, and dismounted horses galloped wildly to and fro, showing that the catastrophes had been numerous. While Lord Netherby looked with some alarm at the fearful chasm which had arrested all but three out of the entire field, the Knight followed Lionel with anxious eyes, as he led over the most desperate line of country in the West.

"I never knew a fox take that line but once," said Darcy, pointing to a wide expanse of bleak country, which stretched away to the base of the great mountain of Nephin. "I was a child at the time, but I remember the occurrence well; horse, men, and hounds tailed off one by one, some sorely injured, others dead beat, for the fellow was a most powerful dog-fox, and ran straight ahead for thirty-four miles of a desperate country. The following morning, at a little after daybreak, the fox was seen in a half trot near Ballycroy, still followed by two of the dogs, and he lived many years afterwards as a pensioner at the abbey; the dogs were never worth anything from that day."

While the Knight related this anecdote, the hounds and the hunters were gradually receding from view; and although at intervals some thought they could catch glimpses of them, at last they disappeared altogether.

"I am sorry, Helen," said the Knight, "that our visitors should have been so unfortunate in their sport."

"I am more grieved to think that Lionel should follow over such a country," said Lord Netherby.

"He's well mounted, my Lord; and though many would call him a reckless rider, he has as much judgment as he has daring. I am tolerably easy about him."

Helen did not seem so confident as her father; and as for Mrs. Somerville, she was considerably paler than usual, and managed her mettlesome horse with far less than her customary address.

As well to meet their friends who were thrown out, as to show some of the scenery of the coast, the Knight proposed they should retrace their steps for a short distance, and take a view of the bay on their way back to the abbey. Leaving them, therefore, to follow their route, and not delaying our reader by an account of the various excuses of the discomfited, or the banterings of Tom Nolan, we will turn to the wide plain, where, still in full cry, the dogs pursued their game.

The Knight had not exaggerated when calling it a dreadful country to ride over; yawning trenches, deep enough to engulf horse and rider, were cut in the bog, and frequently so close together that, in clearing one, a few strides more presented another; the ground itself, only in part reclaimed, was deep and heavy, demanding great strength both of horse and horseman. Through this dangerous and intricate track the fox serpentined and wound his way with practised cunning, while at every turning some unlucky hound would miss his spring, or lose his footing in the slippery soil, and their cries could be heard far over the plain, as they struggled in vain to escape from a deep trench. It was in such an endeavor that a hound was catching at the bank with his fore-legs, as the huntsman dashed forward to take the leap; the horse, suddenly taking fright, swerved, and, before he could recover, the frail ground gave way, and the animal plunged headlong down, fortunately flinging bis rider over the head on the opposite bank.

"All safe, Bob?" cried Lionel, as he turned in his saddle. But he had no time for more, for the strange rider was fast nearing on him, and the chase had now become a trial of speed and skill. By degrees they emerged from this unsafe tract and gained the grass country, where high ditches and stone walls presented a more fair, but scarcely less dangerous, kind of fencing. Here the stranger made an effort to pass Lionel and take the lead, and more than once they took their leaps exactly side by side.

As they rode along close to each other, Lionel from time to time caught glimpses of his companion, who was a strong-built man of five-and-thirty, frank and fresh-looking, but clearly not of the rank of gentleman. His horse was a powerful thoroughbred, with more bone than is usually found in Irish breeding, and trained to perfection.

"Now, sir," said the stranger, "we're coming near the Crumpawn river; that line of mist yonder is over the torrent. I warn you, the leap is a big one."

Lionel turned a haughty glance towards the man, for there was a tone of assumed superiority in the words he could ill brook. That instant, however, his eyes were directed to the front, where the roaring of a mountain stream mingled with the sharp cry of the hounds as they struggled in the torrent, or fell back in their efforts to climb the steep bank.

"Ride him fairly at it,—no flinching; and d——me if I care what your father was, I'll say you're a gentleman."

Lionel bit his lip almost through with passion; and, had the occasion permitted, the heavy stroke of his whip had fallen on a very different quarter from his horse's flank; but he never uttered a word.

"Badly done! Never punish your horse at the stride!" said the fellow, who seemed bent on provoking him.

Lionel bounded in his saddle at this taunt on his riding; but there was no time for bandying words of anger; the roar of rushing water, and the misty foam, proclaimed the torrent near.

"The best man is first over!" shouted the stranger, as he rushed at the terrific chasm. Lionel dashed forward; so close were they, they could have touched; when, with a wild cheer, the stranger gave his horse a tremendous cut, and the animal bounded from the earth like a stag, and, soaring over the mad torrent, descended lightly on the sward beyond.

Lionel had lifted his horse at the very same instant; but the treacherous bank gave way beneath the animal's forelegs: he struggled dreadfully to regain his footing, and, half rearing and half backing, tried to retire; but the effort was in vain, the slippery earth carried him with it, and down both horse and rider came into the stream.

"Keep his head to the current, and sit steady!" shouted the stranger, who now watched the struggle with breathless eagerness. "Well done! well done! — don't press him, he 'll do it himself."

The counsel was wise, for the noble animal needed neither spur nor whip, but breasted the white torrent with vigorous effort, sometimes plunging madly above, and again sinking, all save the head, beneath the flood. At last they reached the side, and the strong beast, with one bold spring, placed his fore-legs on the high bank. This was the most dangerous moment, for, unable to follow with his hind-legs, he stood opposed to the whole force of the current, that threatened every instant to engulf him. Lionel's efforts were tremendous; he lifted, he spurred, he strained, he shouted, but all in vain: the animal, worn out by exertion, faltered, and would have fallen back, when the stranger, springing from his saddle, leaned over the bank, and, seizing Lionel by the collar, jerked him from his horse. The beast, relieved of the weight, at once rallied and bounded up the bank, where Lionel now found himself, stunned, but not senseless.

"Let them say what they like," muttered the stranger, as he stood over him, "you 're a devilish fine young fellow! D——me if I'll ever think so much about good blood again!"

Lionel was too weak and too much exhausted to reply, and even his fingers could scarcely close upon the whip he tried to grasp; yet, for all that, the stranger's insolence sickened him to the very heart. Pride of race was the strongest feeling of his nature, and this fellow seemed determined to outrage it at every turn.

"Here, take a pull at this; you 'll be all right presently," said the man, as he presented a little leather flask to the youth's lips. But Lionel repulsed the offer rudely, and turned his head away. "The more fool you!" said he, coarsely; "your grandfather mixed many a worse-flavored one, and charged more for it;" and, so saying, he emptied the measure at a draught.

Lionel pondered on the words for some seconds, and suddenly the thought occurred to him that the stranger had mistaken him for another. "Ah! I see it all now!" thought he, and he turned his head to undeceive him; when, what was his surprise, as he looked up, to see that the fellow was gone. Mounted on his own horse, he was leading Lionel's by the bridle, and, at a smart trot, moving down the glen.

The young man sprang to his feet and shouted aloud; he even tried to follow him; but both efforts were fruitless. At the turn of the road the man halted, and, looking round, waved his hat as in sign of adieu; then, moving forward, disappeared, while Lionel, his passion giving way to his sense of the absurdity of the whole adventure, burst into a fit of hearty laughter.

"I 'll be laughed at to the day of my death about this," thought he, as he turned his steps to seek the path homeward on foot.

It was late in the evening when Lionel reached the abbey. The guests had for the most part left the dinner-room, and were dropping by twos and threes into the drawing-room, when he made his appearance in the midst of them, splashed and travel-stained from head to foot.

A burst of merry laughter rang out as they beheld his torn habiliments and mud-colored dress, in which none joined more heartily than the Knight himself, as he called aloud, "Well, Lionel, did you kill him, boy, or run him to earth below Nephin?"

"By Jove, sir! if old Carney is safe, I think nobody has been killed to-day."

"Well, Bob is all right; he came back three hours ago. He has lamed Scaltheen; but she 'll get over it."

"But your own adventures," interposed Lord Netherby; "for so they ought to be, judging from the state of your toilet. Let us hear them."

"Yes, by all means," added Beauclerk; "the huntsman says that the last he saw of you was riding by the side of some one in green, with three of the pack in front, the rest tailed off, and himself in a bog-hole."

"But there was no one in green in the field," said Crofton; "at least I did not see any one riding, except the red coats."

"Let us not be too critical about the color of the dress," said Lord Netherby; "I am sure it would puzzle any of us to pronounce on the exact hue of Lionel's at this moment."

"Well, Lionel, will you decide it?" said the Knight; "is the green man apocryphal, or not?"

"I 'll decide nothing," said Lionel, "till I get something to eat. Any one that wishes to hear my exploits must come into the dinner-room;" and, so saying, he arose, and walked into the parlor, where, under Tate's superintendence, a little table was already spread for him beside the fire. To the tempting fare before him the young man devoted all the energy of a hunter's appetite, regardless of the crowd who had followed him from the drawing-room, and stood in a circle around him.

Many were the jests, and sharp the raillery, on his singular appearance, and certainly it presented a most ludicrous contrast with the massive decorations of the table at which he sat, and the full dress of the party around him.

"I remember," said Lord Netherby, "seeing the King of France—when such a functionary existed—eat his dinner in public on the terrace of Versailles; but I confess, great as was my admiration of the monarch's powers, I think Lionel exceeds them."

"Another leg?" said Beauclerk, who, with knife and fork in hand, performed the duty of carver.

"Why don't you say another turkey?" said Nolan; then, turning to Mrs. Somerville, he added, "I am sure that negus is perfect."

The pretty widow, who had been contributing, as she thought unobserved, to Lionel's comfort, blushed deeply; and Lionel, at last roused from his apathy, said, "I am ready now, ladies and gentlemen all, to satisfy every reasonable demand upon your curiosity. But first, where is Mr. Beecham O'Reilly?"

"He went home," said the Knight; "he resisted all my efforts to detain him to dinner."

"Perhaps he only came over to sell that horse," said Nolan, in a half whisper.

"I wish I had bought him, with all my heart," said Lionel.

"Do you like him so much," said the Knight, with a meaning smile.

"I sincerely hope you do," said Lord Netherby, "for he is yours already,—at least, if you will do me the honor to accept him; I often hoped to have mounted you one day—"

"I accept him, my Lord," interposed Lionel, "most willingly and most gratefully. You have, literally speaking, mounted me 'one day,' and I very much doubt if I ever mount the same animal another."

"What! is he lame?—or staked?—did he break down?—is he a devil to ride?" broke from several of the party.

"Not one of all these; but if you'll bestow five minutes' patience on me I 'll perhaps inform you of a mode of being unhorsed, novel at least to most fox-hunters." With this, Lionel narrated the conclusion of the run, the leap of the Crumpawn river, and the singular departure of his companion at the end.

"Is this a practical joke, Knight?" said Lord Netherby.

"I think so, my Lord; one of those admirable jests which the statutes record among their own Joe Millers."

"Then you suspect he was a robber?"

"I confess it looks very like it."

"I read the riddle otherwise," said Lionel; "the fellow, whoever he was, mistook me for somebody else, and there was evidently something more like a reprisal than a theft in the whole transaction."

"But you have really lost him?" said Beanclerk.

"When I assure you that I came home on foot, I hope that question is answered."

"By Jove! you have most singular ways of doing matters in this country," cried the colonel; "but I suppose when a man is used to Ireland, he gets pretty much accustomed to hear of his horse being stolen away as well as the fox."

"Oh! we'll chance upon him one of these days yet," said the Knight; "I am half of Lionel's mind myself now,—the thing does not look like a robbery."

"There's no end of the eccentricity of these people," muttered Lord Netherby to himself; "they can get into a towering passion and become half mad about trifles, but they take a serious loss as coolly as possible." And with this reflection on national character he moved into the drawing-room, where soon afterwards the party repaired to talk over Lionel's adventure, with every turn that fancy or raillery could give it.

CHAPTER XXX
BAGENAL DALY'S VISITORS

It was at a late hour of a night, some days after this event occurred, that Bagenal Daly sat closeted with Darcy's lawyer, endeavoring, by deep and long thought, to rescue him from some at least of the perils that threatened him. Each day, since the Knight's departure, had added to the evil tidings of his fortune. While Gleeson had employed his powers of attorney to withdraw large sums from the banker's hands, no information could be had concerning the great loan he had raised from the London company, nor was there to be found among the papers left behind him the bond passed to Hickman, and which he should have received had the money been paid. That such was the case, Bagenal Daly firmly believed; the memorandum given him by Freney was corroborated by the testimony of the clerks in two separate banking-houses, who both declared that Gleeson drew these sums on the morning before he started for Kildare, and to one of Daly's rapid habits of judgment such evidence was quite conclusive. This view of the subject was, unhappily, not destined to continue undisturbed, for, on the very morning after the Knight's departure from Dublin, came a formal letter from Hickman's solicitor, demanding payment of the interest on the sum of seventy-four thousand eight hundred and twenty pounds, odd shillings, at five per cent, owing by seven weeks, and accompanying which was a notice of foreclosure of the mortgage on the ensuing 17th of March, in case the full sum aforesaid were not duly paid.

To meet these demands Daly well knew Darcy had no disposable property; the large sums raised by Gleeson, at a lower rate of interest, were intended for that purpose; and although he persisted in believing that this debt, at least, was satisfied, the lawyer's opinion was strongly opposed to that notion.

Mr. Bicknell was a shrewd man, deep not only in the lore of his professional knowledge, but a keen scrutinizer of motives, and a far-seeing observer of the world. He argued thus: Gleeson would never have parted with such a sum on the eve of his own flight; a day was of no consequence, he could easily have put off the payment to Hickman to the time of the American ship's sailing—why, then, hand over so large an amount, all in his possession? It was strange, of course, what had become of the money; but then they heard that his servant had made his escape. Why might not he have possessed himself of it after his master's suicide? Who was to interfere or prevent it? Besides, if he had paid Hickman, the bond would, in all likelihood, be forthcoming; to retain possession of it could have been no object with Gleeson; he had met with nothing but kind and friendly treatment from Darcy, and was not likely to repay him by an act of useless, gratuitous cruelty.

As to the testimony of the bank clerks, it was as applicable to one view of the case as the other. Gleeson would, of course, draw out everything at his disposal; and although the sums tallied with those in the memorandum, that signified little, as they were the full amount in each banker's hands to the Knight's credit. Lastly, as to the memorandum, it was the only real difficulty in the case; but that paper might have been in Gleeson's possession, and in the course of business discussion either might have been dropped inadvertently, or have been given to Hickman as explaining the moneys already prepared for his acceptance.

Mr. Bicknell's reasonings were confirmed by the application of Hickman's solicitors, who were men of considerable skill and great reputed caution. "Harris and Long make no such mistakes as this, depend upon that, sir; they see their case very clearly, or would never adventure on such an application."

"D— —n their caution! The question is not of their shrewdness."

"Yes, but it is, though; we are weighing probabilities: let us see to which side the balance inclines. Would they serve notice of foreclosure, not knowing whether or not we had the receipt in our possession? That is the whole matter."

"I don't pretend to say what they would do, but I know well what I should."

"And pray what may that be?"

"Hold possession of the abbey, stand fast by the old walls, call in the tenantry,—and they are ready to answer such a call at a moment, if need be,—and while I proclaimed to the wide world by what right I resisted, I 'd keep the place against any force they dared to bring. These are ticklish times, Bicknell; the Government have just cheated this country,—they 'd scarcely risk the hazard of a civil war for an old usurer,—old Hickman would be left to his remedies in Banco or Equity; and who knows what might turn up one day or other to strengthen the honest cause?"

"I scarcely concur in your suggestion, sir."

"How the devil should you? There are neither declarations to draw, nor affidavits to swear, no motions, nor rules, nor replies, no declarations, no special juries! No, Bicknell, I never suspected your approval of my plan. It would not cost a single skin of parchment."

Though Daly spoke this sarcasm bitterly, it produced no semblance of irritation in the man of law, who was composedly occupied in perusing a document before him.

"I have made memoranda," said Bicknell, "of certain points for counsel's opinion, and as soon as we can obtain some information as to the authenticity of young Darcy's signature, we shall see our way more clearly. The case is not only a complicated but a gloomy one; our antagonists are acute and wealthy, and I own to you the prospect is far from good."

"The better counsel mine," said Daly, sternly; "I have little faith in the justice that hangs upon the intelligence of what you facetiously call twelve honest men; methinks the world is scarcely so well supplied with the commodity that they are sure to answer the call of the sheriff. It is probable, however,—nay, it is more than probable,—Darcy will be of your mind, and reject my advice; if so, there is nothing for it but the judge and jury, and he will be despoiled of his property by the law of the land."

Bicknell knew too well the eccentric nature of Daly's character, in which no feature was more prominent than his hatred of everything like the recognized administration of the law, to offer him any opposition, and merely repeating his previous determination to seek the advice of able counsel, he took his leave.

"There is some deep mystery in this business," said Daly to himself, as he paced the room alone; "Bicknell is right in saying that Gleeson would not have committed an act of unnecessary cruelty, nor, if he had paid the money, would he have failed to leave the bond among his papers. Every circumstance of this fellow's flight is enveloped in doubt, and Freney, the only man who appears to have suspected his intention, by some mischance is not now to be found; Sandy has not succeeded in meeting with the boy, notwithstanding all his efforts. What can this be owing to? What machinery is at work here? Have the Hick-mans their share in this?" Such were the broken sentences he muttered, as, in turn, suspicions tracked each other in his mind.

Daly was far too rash, and too impetuous in temper, to be well qualified for an investigation of so much difficulty. Unable to weigh probabilities with calmness, he was always the victim of his own prejudices in favor of certain things and people; and to escape from the chaotic trouble of his own harassed thoughts, he was ever ready to adopt some headlong and desperate expedient, in preference to the quieter policy of more patient minds.

"Yes, faith," said he, "my plan is the best after all; and who knows but by showing the bold front we may reduce old Hickman's pretensions, or at least make a compromise with him. There are plenty of arms and ammunition, — eight stout fellows would hold the inner gate tower against a battalion, — we could raise the country from Mur-risk to Killery Harbor; and one gun fired from the Boat Quay would bring the fishermen from Clare Island and Achill to the rescue, — we 'd soon make a signal they 'd recognize; old Hickman's house, with all its porticos and verandas, would burn like tinder. If they are for law, let them begin, then."

The door opened as he spoke these words, and Sandy entered cautiously. "There is a countryman without wha says he's come a long way to see your honor, and maun see you this night."

"Where from?"

"Fra' the West, I think, for he said the roads were heavy down in them parts."

"Let him come in," said Daly; and, with his hands crossed behind his back, he continued to walk the room. "Some poor fellow for a renewal of his lease, or an abatement, or something of that kind, — they 'll never learn that I 'm no longer the owner of that estate that still bears my name, and they cling to me as though I had the power to assist them, when I'm defenceless for myself. Well, what is it? Speak out, man, — what do you want with me?"

The individual to whom this question was addressed stood with his back to the door, which he had cautiously shut close on entering, but, instead of returning an answer to the question, he cast a long and searching glance around the room, as if to ascertain whether any other person was in it. The apartment was large, and, being dimly lighted, it took some time to assure him that they were alone; but when he had so satisfied himself-, he walked slowly forward into the light, and, throwing open his loose coat of gray frieze, exhibited the well-known figure of Freney the robber.

"What, Freney! — the man of all Ireland I wish to see."

"I thought so, sir," said the other, wiping his forehead with his hand, for he was flushed and heated, and seemed to have come off a long journey. "I know you sent for me, but I was unable to meet your messenger, and I can seldom venture to send that young villain Jemmy into the capital, — the police are beginning to know him, and he 'll be caught one of these days."

"You were n't in Kildare, then?" said Daly.

"No, sir, I was in the far West,—down in Mayo. I had a little business in Ballina a short time back, and some fellow who knew me, and thought the game a safe one, stole my brown horse out of the inn-stable, in the broad noon-day, and sold him at the fair green at Ballinasloe. When I tell you that he was the best animal I ever crossed, I need n't say what the loss was to me; the nags you saw were broken-down hackneys in comparison. He was strong in bone and untiring, and I kept him for the heavy country around Boyle and down by Longford. It is not once, nor twice, but a dozen times, Matchlock has saved me from a loop and a leap in the air; but the rascal that took him well knew the theft was safe,—Freney, the highwayman, could scarcely lodge informations with a magistrate."

"And you never could hear traces of him?" "Yes, that I did, but it cost me time and trouble too. I found that he was twice sold within one week. Dean Harris bought him, and sold him the day after." Here Freney gave a low cunning laugh, while his eyes twinkled with malignant drollery.

"He did n't think as highly of him as you did, Freney?" "Perhaps he had n't as good reason," said the robber, laughing. "He was riding home from an early dinner with the bishop, and as he was cantering along the side of the road, a chaise with four horses came tearing past. Matchlock, true to his old instinct, but not knowing who was on his back, broke into a gallop, and in half a dozen strides brought the dean close up to the chaise window, when the traveller inside sent a bullet past his ear that very nearly made a vacancy in the best living of the diocese. As I said, sir, the dean had had enough of him; he sold him the next morning, and that day week he was bought by a young fellow in the West whom I found out to be a grandson of old Hickman."

"Was he able to ride a horse like this?" said Daly, doubtfully.

"Ride him?—ay; and never a man in the province brought a beast to a leap with a lighter hand and a closer seat in the saddle. We were side by side for three miles of a stiff country, and I don't believe I 'm much of a coward,—at any rate, I set very little value on my neck; but, I 'll tell you what, sir, he pushed me hard."

"How was this, then? Had you a race together?" "It was something very like it, sir," said Freney, laughing; "for when I reached Westport, I heard that young O'Reilly was to ride a new brown horse that day with the hounds, and a great hunt was expected, to show some English gentlemen who were staying at Gwynne Abbey. So I went off early to Hooley's forge, near the cross-roads, to see the meet, and look out for my man. I did n't want any one to tell me which he was, for I 'd know Matchlock at half a mile distance. There he was, in splendid condition too, and looking as I never saw him look before; by my conscience, Mr. Daly, there's a wide difference between the life of a beast in the stables of a county member, and one that has to stretch his bones in the shealing of such as myself. My plan was to go down to the cover, and the moment the fox broke away, to drive a bullet through my horse's head, and be off as hard as I could; for, to tell you the truth, it was spite more than the value of him was grieving me; so I took my own horse by the bridle, and walked down to where they were all gathered. I was scarcely there when the dogs gave tongue, and away they went,—a grand sight it was, more than a hundred red-coats, and riding close every man of them. Just then, up comes Matchlock, and takes the fence into the field where I was standing, a stone wall and a ditch, his rider handling him elegantly, and with an easy smile, sitting down in his saddle as if it was child's play. Faith, I could n't bring myself to fire the shot, partly for the sake of the horse, more too, maybe, for the sake of the rider. 'I 'll go a bit beside him,' said I to myself; for it was a real pleasure to me to watch the way how both knew their business well. I 'm making a long story of it, but the end of it was this: I took the Crumpawn river just to dare him, and divil a bit but he fell in,—no fault of his, but the bank was rotten, and down they went; the young fellow had a narrow escape of it, but he got through it at last, and, as he lay on the grass more dead than alive, I saw Matchlock grazing just close to me. Temptations are bad things, Mr. Daly, particularly when a man has never trained himself off them; so I slipped the bridle over his head, and rode away with him beside me."

Mr Freney's horse endangers a pillar of the church.

"Carried him off?"

"Clean and clever; he's at the hall-door this minute: and, by the same token, sixty-four miles he has covered this day."

"There's only one part of the whole story surprises me; it is that this fellow should have ridden so boldly and so well. I know such courage is often no more than habit: yet even that lower quality of daring I never should have given him credit for. Was he hurt by his fall?"

"Stunned, perhaps, but nothing the worse."

"Well, well, enough of him. I wanted to see you, Freney, to learn anything you may know of this fellow Gleeson's flight. It's a sad affair for my friend the Knight of Gwynne."

"So I've heard, sir. It's bad enough for myself, too."

"For you! He was not your man of business, was he?" said Daly, with a sly laugh.

"No, sir, I generally manage my money matters myself; but he happened to have a butler, one Garrett by name, who betted smartly on the turf, and played a little with the bones besides. He was a steady-going chap that knew a thing or two, but honest enough in booking up when he lost; he borrowed two hundred from me on the very day they started; he owed me nearly three besides, and I never saw him since. They say that when his master jumped overboard, Jack Garrett laid hands on all his property, and sailed for America; but I don't believe it, sir."

"Well, but, Freney, you may believe it, for I was the means of an investigation at Liverpool in which the fact transpired, and the name of John Garrett was entered in the ship-agent's books; I read it there myself."

"No matter for that, he dared not venture into the States. I know something of Jack's doings among the Yankees, and depend upon it, Mr. Daly, he's not gone; it's only a blind to stop pursuit."

Daly shook his head dubiously, for, having satisfied himself of Garrett's –escape when at Liverpool, he felt annoyed at any discredit attaching to what he deemed his own discovery.

"Take my word for it, Mr. Daly, I 'm right this time; you cannot think what an advantage a man like me possesses in guessing at the way another rogue would play his game. Why, sir, I know every turn and double such a fellow as Garrett would make. Now, I 'd wager Matchlock against a car-horse that he has not left England, and I 'd take an even bet he 'll be at the Spring Meeting at Doncaster."

"This may be all as you say, Freney," said Daly, after a pause, "and yet I see no reason to suppose it can interest me, or my friend either. He might know something of Gleeson's affairs; he might, perhaps, be able to tell something of the payment of that sum at Kildare; if so—"

"If so," interrupted Freney, "money would buy the secret; at all events, I'm determined he shall not escape me so easily. I 'll follow the fellow to the very threshold of Newgate but I 'll have my own,—it is for that purpose I 'm on my way now. A fishing-boat will sail from Howth by to-morrow's tide, and land me somewhere on the Welsh coast, and, if I can serve you, why, it's only doing two jobs at the same time. What are the points you are anxious to discover?"

Daly reflected for a few moments, and then with distinctness detailed the several matters on which he desired information, not only regarding the reasons of Gleeson's embarrassments, but the nature of his intimacy with old Hickman, of which he entertained deep suspicions.

"I see it all," said Freney. "You think that Gleeson was in league with the doctor?"

Daly nodded.

"That was my own notion, too. Ah, sir, if I 'd only the King's pardon in my pocket this night, and the power of an honest man for one month, I 'd stake my head on it, but I would have the whole mystery as clear as water."

"You 'll want some money, Freney," said Daly, as he turned to the table, and, taking up a key, unlocked the writing-case. "I 'm not as rich just now as a Member of Parliament might be after such a Bill as the Union, but I hope this may be of some service;" and he took a fifty-pound note from the desk to hand it to him, but Freney was gone. He had slipped noiselessly from the room; the bang of the hall-door was heard at the instant, and immediately after the tramp of a horse as he trotted down the street.

"The world all over!" said Daly to himself. "If the man of honor and integrity has his flaws and defects, even fellows like that have their notions of principle and delicacy too. Confound it! mankind will never let me love or hate them."

CHAPTER XXXI
"A LEAVE-TAKING"

At Gwynne Abbey, time sped fast and pleasantly; each day brought its own enjoyments, and of the Knight's guests there was not one who did not in his heart believe that Maurice Darcy was the very happiest man in the kingdom.

Lord Netherby, the frigid courtier, felt, for the first time, perhaps, in his life, how much cordiality can heighten the pleasures of social intercourse, and how the courtesy of kind feeling can add to the enjoyments of refined and cultivated tastes. Lady Eleanor had lost nothing of the powers of fascination for which her youth had been celebrated, and there was, in the very seclusion of her life, that which gave the charm of novelty to her remarks on people and events. The Knight himself, abounding in resources of every kind, was a companion the most fastidious or exacting could not weary of; and as for Helen, her captivations were acknowledged by those who, but a week before, would not have admitted the possibility of any excellence that had not received the stamp of London approval.

Crofton could never expatiate sufficiently on the delights of an establishment which, with the best cook, the best cellar, and the best stable, called not upon him for the exercise of the small talents and petty attentions by which his invitations to great houses were usually purchased; while the younger men of the party agreed in regarding their friend Lionel as the most to be envied of all their acquaintance.

Happiness, perhaps, shines more brightly by reflected light; certainly Lionel Darcy never felt more disposed to be content with the world, and, although not devoid of a natural pride at exhibiting to his English friends the style of his father's house and habits, yet was he far more delighted at the praises he heard on every side of the Knight himself. Maurice Darcy possessed that rarest of all gifts, the power of being a delightful companion to younger men, without ever detracting in the slightest degree from the most rigid tone of good taste and good principle. The observation may seem an illiberal one, but it is unhappily too true, that even among those who from right feeling would be incapable of anything mean or sordid, there often prevails a laxity in expression and a libertinism of sentiment very far remote from their real opinions, and, consequently, such as flatter this tendency are frequently the greatest favorites among them. The Knight, not less from high principle than pride, rejected every such claim; his manly, joyous temperament needed no aids to its powers of interesting and amusing; his sympathies went with young men in all their enthusiasm for sport; he gloried in the exuberance of their high spirits, and felt his own youth come back in the eager pleasure with which he listened to their plans of amusement.

It may well be believed with what sorrow to each the morning dawned that was to be the last of their visit. These last times are sad things! They are the deaths of our affections and attachments; for assuredly the memory we retain of past pleasures is only the unreal spirit of a world we are to know of no more,—not alone the records of friends lost or dead, but of ourselves, such as we once were, and can never again be; of a time when hope was fed by credulity, and could not be exhausted by disappointment. They must have had but a brief experience of life who do not see in every separation from friends the many chances against their meeting again, least of all, of meeting unchanged, with all around them as they parted.

These thoughts, and others like them, weighed heavily on the hearts of those who now assembled for the last time beneath the roof of Gwynne Abbey.

It was in vain that Lionel suggested various schemes of pleasure for the day; the remembrance that it was the last was ever present, and while every moment seemed precious, there was a fidgety impatience to be about and stirring, mingled with a desire to loiter and linger over the spot so associated with pleasant memories.

A boating party to Clare Island, long planned and talked over, could find now no advocates. All Lionel's descriptions of the shooting along the rocky shores of the bay were heard unheeded; every one clung to the abbey, as if to enjoy to the very last the sense of home happiness they had known there. Even those less likely to indulge feelings of attachment were not free from the depressing influence of a last day. Nor were these sentiments confined to the visitors only. Lady Eleanor experienced a return of her former spirits in her intercourse with those whose habits and opinions all reminded her of the past, and would gladly have prolonged a visit so full of pleasant recollections. The request was, however, in vain; the Earl was to be in waiting early in the following week, Lionel's leave was only regimental, and equally limited, and each of the others had engagements and projects no less fixed and immutable.

In little knots of two and three they spent the day wandering about from place to place, to take a last look of the great cliff, to visit for the last time the little wood path, whose every turning presented some new aspect of the bay and the shore. Lord Netherby attached himself to the Knight, devoting himself with a most laudable martyrdom to a morning in the farm-yard and the stable, where, notwithstanding all his efforts, his blunders betrayed how ill-suited were his habits to country life and its interests. He bore all, however, well and heroically, for he had an object in view, and that, with him, was always sufficient to induce any degree of endurance. Up to this moment he had scarcely enjoyed an opportunity of conversing with the Knight on the subject of politics. The few words they had exchanged at the cover side were all that passed between them, and although they conveyed sentiments very remote from his own, he did not entirely despair of gaining over one who evidently was less actuated by party motives than impressed by the force of strong personal convictions.

"Such a man will, of course," thought the Earl, "be in the Imperial Parliament, and carry with him great influence on every question connected with Ireland; his support of the Ministry will be all the more valuable that his reputation is intact from every stain of corruption. To withdraw him from his own country by the seductions of London life would not be easy, but he may be attached to England by ties still more binding." Such were some of the reasonings which the wily peer revolved in his mind, and to whose aid a fortunate accident had in some measure contributed.

"I believe I have never shown you our garden, my Lord," said the Knight, who, at last taking compassion on the suffering complaisance of the Earl, proposed this change. "The season is scarcely the most flattering, but we are early in this part of Ireland. What say you if we walk thither?"

The plan was at once approved of, and after a short circuit through a shrubbery, they crossed a large orchard, and, ascending a gentle slope, they entered the garden, which rose in successive terraces behind the abbey, and commanded a wide prospect over the bay and the sea beyond it. Lord Netherby's admiration was not feigned, as he turned his eyes around and beheld the extent and beauty of that cultivated scene, which, in the brightness of a spring morning, glittered like a gem on the mountain's side. The taste alone was not the engrossing thought of his mind, but he reflected on the immense expenditure such a caprice must have cost, terraced as the ground was into the very granite rock, and the earth all supplied artificially. The very keeping these parterres in order was a thing of no mean cost. Not all the terrors of his own approaching fate could deprive Darcy of a sense of pride as he watched the expression of the Earl's features, surprise and wonder depicted in every lineament.

"How extensive the park is," said the courtier, at length, half ashamed, as it seemed, of giving way to his amazement; "are those trees yonder within your grounds?"

"Yes, my Lord: the wood at that point where you see the foam splashing up is our limit in that direction; on this side we stretch away somewhat further."

"Whose property, then, have we yonder, where I see the village?"

"It is all the Gwynne estate," said the Knight, with difficulty repressing the sigh that rose as he spoke.

"And the town?"

"The town also. The worthy monks took a wide circuit, and, by all accounts, did not misuse their wealth. I sadly fear, my Lord, their successors were not as blameless."

"A noble possession, indeed!" said the Earl, half aloud, and not attending to Darcy's remark. "Are you certain, my dear Knight, that you have made your political influence at all commensurate with the amount of either your property or your talents? An English gentleman with an estate like this, and ability such as yours, might command any position he pleased."

"In other words, my Lord, he might barter his independence for the exercise of a precarious power, and, in ceasing to dispense the duties of a landed proprietor, he might become a very considerable ingredient in a party."

"I hope you do not deem the devoir of a country gentleman incompatible with the duties of a statesman?"

"By no means; but I greatly regret the gradual desertion of social influence in the search after political ascendency. I am not for the working of a system that spoils the gentry, and yet does not make them statesmen."

"And yet the very essence of our Constitution is to connect the power of Government with the possession of landed property."

"And justly so, too; none other offers so little in return as a mere speculation. None is so little exposed to the casualties which affect every other kind of wealth. The legitimate influence of the landed gentry is the safeguard of the State; but if, by the attractions of power, the flatteries of a Court, or the seductions of Party, you withdraw them from the rightful sphere of its exercise, you reduce them to the level of the Borough members, without, perhaps, their technical knowledge or professional acquirements. I am for giving them a higher position,—the heritage of the bold barons, from whom they are descended: but to maintain this, they must live on their own estates, dispense the influences of their wealth and their morals in their own native districts, be the friend of the poor man, the counsellor of the misguided, the encourager of the weak; know and be known to all around, not as the corrupt dispensers of Government patronage, but the guardians of those whose rights are in their keeping for defence and protection. I would have them with their rightful influence in the Senate; an influence which should preponderate in both Houses. Their rank and education would be the best guarantee for the safety and wisdom of their counsels, their property the best surety for the permanence of the institutions of the State. Suddenly acquired wealth can scarcely be intrusted with political power; it lacks the element of prudent caution, by which property is maintained as well as accumulated; it wants also the prestige of antiquity as a claim to respect; and, legislate as you will, men will look back as well as forward."

Lord Netherby made no reply; he thought the Knight, perhaps, was venting his own regrets at the downfall of a political ascendency he wished to see vested in men of his own station,—a position they had long enjoyed, and which, in some respects, had placed them above the law.

"You lay more store by such ties, Knight," said the Earl, in a low, insinuating voice, "than we are accustomed to do. Blood and birth have suffered less admixture with mere wealth here than with us."

"Perhaps we do, my Lord," said Darcy, smiling; "it is the compensation for our poverty. Unmixed descent is the boast of many who have retained nothing of their ancestors save the name."

"But you yourself can scarcely be an advocate for the maintenance of these opinions: this spirit of clan and chieftainship is opposed, not only to progress, but to liberty."

"I have given the best proof of the contrary," said Darcy, laughing, "by marrying an Englishwoman,—a dereliction, I assure you, that cost me many a warm supporter in this very country."

"Indeed! By the way, I am reminded of a subject I wished to speak of to you, and which I have been hesitating whether I should open with my cousin Eleanor or yourself; the moment seems, however, propitious,—may I broach it?"

Darcy bowed courteously, and the other resumed:—

"I will be brief, then. Young Beauclerk, a friend of your son Lionel, has been, as every one younger and older than himself must be, greatly taken by the charms of Miss Darcy. Brief as the acquaintance here has been, the poor fellow is desperately in love, and, while feeling how such an acknowledgment might prejudice his chance of success on so short an intimacy, he cannot leave this without the effort to secure for his pretensions a favorable hearing hereafter. In fact, my dear Knight, he has asked of me to be his intercessor with you,—not to receive him as a son-in-law, but to permit him to pay such attentions as, in the event of your daughter's acceptance, may enable him to make the offer of his hand and fortune. I need not tell you that in point of position and means he is unexceptionable; a very old Baronetcy,—not one of these yesterday creations made up of State Physicians and Surgeons in Ordinary,—an estate of above twelve thousand a year. Such are claims to look high with; but I confess I think he could not lay them at the feet of one more captivating than my fair Helen."

Darcy made no reply for several minutes; he pressed his hand across his eyes, and turned his head away, as if to escape observation; then, with an effort that seemed to demand all his strength, he said,—

"This is impossible, my Lord. There are reasons—there are circumstances why I cannot entertain this proposition. I am not able to explain them; a few days more, and I need not trouble myself on that subject."

The evident agitation of manner the Knight displayed astonished his companion, who, while he forebore to ask more directly for its reason, yet gently hinted that the obstacles alluded to might be less stringent than Darcy deemed them.

Darcy shook his head mournfully, and Lord Netherby, though most anxious to divine the secret of his thoughts, had too much breeding to continue the subject.

Without any abruptness, which might have left an unpleasant impression after it, the polished courtier once more adverted to Beauclerk, but rather in a tone of regret for the youth's own sake than with any reference to the Knight's refusal.

_ "There was a kind of selfishness in my advocacy, Knight," said he, smiling. "I was—I am—very much depressed at quitting a spot where I have tasted more true happiness than it has been my fortune for many years to know, and I wish to carry away with me the reflection that I had left the germ of even greater happiness behind me; if Helen, however—"

"Hush!" said Darcy; "here she comes, with her mother."

"My dear Lady Eleanor," said Lord Netherby, "you have come to see me forget all the worldliness it has cost me a life to learn, and actually confess that I cannot tear myself away from the abbey."

"Well, my Lord," interposed Tom Nolan, who had just come up with a large walking party, "I suppose it's only ordering away the posters, and staying another day."

"No, no, by Jove!" cried Crofton; "my Lord is in waiting, and I'm on duty."

While the groups now gathered together from the different parts of the garden, Lord Netherby joined Beauclerk, who awaited him in a distant alley, and soon after the youth was seen returning alone to the abbey.

The time of bustle and leave-taking—that moment when many a false smile and merry speech ill conceals the secret sorrow—was come, and each after each spoke his farewell; and Lord Netherby, kindly pledging himself to make Lionel's peace at the Horse Guards for an extended absence of some days, thus conferred upon Lady Eleanor the very greatest of favors.

"Our next meeting is to be in London, remember," said the peer, in his blandest accents. "I stand pledged to show my countrymen that I have nothing extenuated in speaking of Irish beauty;—nay, Helen, it is my last time, forgive it."

"There they go," said Darcy, as he looked after the retiring equipages. "Now, Eleanor, and my dear children, come along with me into the library. I have long been struggling against a secret sorrow; another moment would be more than I could bear."

They turned silently towards the abbey, none daring, even by a look, to interrogate him whose sad accents foreboded so much evil; yet as they walked they drew closer around him, and seemed even by that gesture to show that, come what might, they would meet their fortune boldly.

Darcy moved on for some minutes sunk in thought; but as he ascended the wide steps of the terrace, appearing to read the motives of those who clung so closely to his side, he smiled sadly, and said, "Ay! I knew it well,— in weal or woe—together!"

CHAPTER XXXII
"SAD DISCLOSURES"

The vicissitudes of life are never more palpably displayed before us than when the space of a few brief hours has converted the scene of festivity and pleasure into one of gloom and sorrow, when the same silent witnesses of our joy should be present at our affliction. Thus was it now in the richly adorned chambers of Gwynne Abbey, so lately filled with happy faces and resounding with pleasant voices,—all was silent. Iu the courtyard, but a day before crowded with brilliant equipages and gay horsemen, the long shadows lay dark and unbroken, and the plash of the fountain was the only sound in the stillness. Over that wide lawn no groups on foot or horseback were to be seen; the landscape was fair and soft to look upon; the mild radiance of a spring morning beamed on the water and the shore, the fresh budding trees, and the tall towers; and the passing traveller who might have stopped to gaze upon that princely dwelling and its swelling woods, might have thought it an earthly paradise, and that they who owned it must needs be above worldly cares and afflictions.

The scene within the walls was very unlike this impression. In a darkened room, where the close-drawn curtains excluded every ray of sunshine, sat Helen Darcy by the bedside of her mother. Lady Eleanor had fallen asleep after a night of intense suffering, both of mind and body, and her repose even yet exhibited, in short and fitful starts, the terrible traces of an agony not yet subdued. Helen was pale as death; two dark circles of almost purple hue surrounded her eyes, and her cheeks seemed wasted: yet she had not wept. The overwhelming amount of misfortune had stunned her for a moment or two, but, recalled to active exertion by her mother's illness, she addressed herself to her task, and seemed to have no thought or care save to watch and tend her. It was only at last when, wearied out by suffering, Lady Eleanor fell into a slumber that Helen's feelings found their vent, and the tears rolled heavily along her cheek, and dropped one by one upon her neck.

Her sorrow was indeed great, for it was unalloyed by one selfish feeling; her grief was for those a thousand times more dear to her than herself, nor through all her affliction did a single thought intrude of how this ruin was also her own.

The Knight was in the library, where he had passed the night, lying down at short intervals to catch some moments' rest, and again rising to walk the room and reflect upon the coming stroke of fortune. Lionel had parted from him at a late hour, promising to go to bed; but, unable to endure the gloom of his own thoughts in his chamber, he wandered out into the woods, and strolled on without knowing or caring whither, till day broke. The bodily exertion at length induced sleep, and after a few hours' deep repose he joined his father, with few traces of weariness or even sorrow.

It was not without a struggle on either side that they met on that morning, and as Darcy grasped his son's hand in both his own, his lip trembled, and his strong frame shook with agitation. Lionel's ruddy cheek and clear blue eye seemed to reassure the old man's courage; and after gazing on him steadfastly with a look where fatherly love and pride were blended, he said, "I see, my boy, the old blood of a Darcy has not degenerated—you are well to-day?"

"Never was better in my life," said Lionel, boldly; "and if I could only think that you, my mother, and Helen had no cause for sorrow, I'd almost say I never felt my spirits higher."

"My own brave-hearted boy," said Darcy, throwing his arms around the youth's neck, while the tears gushed from his eyes and a choking stopped his utterance.

"I see your letters have come," said Lionel, gently disengaging himself, and affecting a degree of calmness his heart was very far from feeling. "Do they bring us any news?"

"Nothing to hope from," said Darcy, sorrowfully. "Daly has seen Hickman's solicitors, and the matter is as I expected: Gleeson did not pay the bond debt; his journey to Kildare was, probably, undertaken to gain time until the moment of the American ship's sailing. He must have meditated this step for a considerable time, for it now appears that his losses in South America occurred several years back, though carefully screened from public knowledge. The man was a cold, calculating scoundrel, who practised peculation systematically and slowly; his resolve to escape was not a sudden notion,—these are Bagenal Daly's impressions at least, and I begin to feel their force myself."

"Does Daly offer any suggestion for our guidance, or say how we should act?" said Lionel, far more eager to meet the present than speculate on either the past or the future.

"Yes; he gives us a choice of counsels, honestly confessing that his own advice meets little support or sympathy with the lawyers. It is to hold forcible possession of the abbey, to leave Hickman to his remedy by law, and to defy him when he has even got a verdict; he enumerates very circumstantially all our means of defence, and exhibits a very hopeful array of lawless probabilities in our favor. But this is a counsel I would never follow; it would not become one who has in a long life endeavored to set the example among the people of obedience and observance to law, to obliterate by one act of rashness and folly the whole force of his teaching. No, Lionel, we are cleanhanded on this score, and if the lesson, be a heavy one for ourselves, let it not be profitless for our poor neighbors. This is your own feeling too, my boy, I'm certain."

Lionel bit his lip, and his cheek grew scarlet; when, after a pause, he said, "And the other plan, what is that?"

"The renewed offer of his cottage on the northern coast, a lonely and secluded spot, where we can remain at least until we determine on something better."

"Perhaps that may be a wiser course," muttered the youth, half aloud; "my mother and Helen are to be thought of first. And yet, father, I. cannot help thinking Daly's first counsel has something in it."

"Something in it! ay, Lionel, that it has, — the whole story of our country's misery and degradation. The owner of the soil has diffused little else among the people than the licentious terror of his own unbridled passion; he has taught lawless outrage, when he should have inculcated obedience and submission. The corruption of our people has come from above downwards; the heavy retribution will come one day; and when the vices of the peasant shall ascend to the master, the social ruin will be complete. To this dreadful consummation let us lend no aid. No, no, Lionel, sorrow may be lessened by time; but remorse is undying and eternal."

"I must leave the Guards at once," said the young man, pacing the room slowly, and endeavoring to speak with an air of calm composure, while every feature of his face betrayed the agitation he suffered; "an exchange will not be difficult to manage."

"You have some debts, too, in London: they must be cared for immediately."

"Nothing of any large amount; my horses and carriages when sold will more than meet all I owe. Have you formed any guess as to what income will be left you to live on?" said he, in a voice which anxiety made weak and tremulous.

"Without Daly's assistance, I cannot answer that point; the extent of this fellow Gleeson's iniquity seems but half explored. The likelihood is, that your mother's jointure will be the utmost we can save from the wreck. Even that, however, will be enough for all we need, although, from motives of delicacy on her part, it was originally set down at a very small sum,—not more than a thousand per annum."

A long silence now ensued. The Knight, buried in thought, sat with his arms crossed, and his eyes bent upon the ground. Lionel leaned on the window-frame and looked out upon the lawn; nothing stirred, no sound was heard save the sharp ticking of the clock upon the mantelpiece, which marked with distinctness every second, as if reminding them of the fleeting moments that were to be their last beneath that roof.

"This is the 24th, if I remember aright," said Darcy, looking up at the dial; "at noon, to-day, we are no longer masters here."

"The Hickmans will scarcely venture to push matters to such extremities; an assurance that we are willing to surrender peaceable possession will, I trust, be sufficient to prevent the indecency of a rapid flight from our own house and home."

"There are legal forms of possession to be gone through, I believe," said the Knight, sorrowfully; "certain observances the law exacts, which would be no less painful for us to witness than the actual presence of our successors."

"Who can this be? I saw a carriage disappear behind the copse yonder. There it is again, coming along by the lake."

"Daly—Bagenal Daly, I hope and trust!" exclaimed Darcy, as he stood straining his eyes to catch the moving object.

"I think not; the horses do not look like posters. Heaven grant we have no visitors at such a time as this!"

The carriage, although clearly visible the moment before, was now concealed from view by an angle of the wood, nor would it again be in sight before reaching the abbey.

"Your mother's indisposition is reason sufficient not to receive them," said Darcy, almost sternly. "I would not continue the part I have played during the last week, no, not for an hour longer, to be assured of rescue from every difficulty. The duplicity went nigh to break my heart; ay, and it would have done so, or driven me mad, had the effort been sustained any further."

"You did not expect any one, did you?" asked Lionel, eagerly.

"Not one; there's a mass of letters, with invitations and civil messages, there on the table, but no proffered visits among them."

Lionel walked to the table and turned over the various notes which lay along with newspapers and pamphlets scattered about.

"Ay," muttered the Knight, in a low tone, "they read strangely now, these plans of pleasure and festivity, when ruin is so near us; the kind pressings to spend a week here, and a fortnight there. It reminds me, Lionel," — and here a smile of sad but sweet melancholy passed across his features, — "it reminds me of the old story they tell of my grand-uncle Robert. He commanded the 'Dreadnought,' under Drake, at Cape St. Vincent, and at the close of a very sharp action was signalled to come on board the admiral's vessel to dinner. The poor 'Dreadnought' was like a sieve, the sea running in and out through her shot-holes, and her sails hanging like rags around her, her deck covered with wounded, and slippery with gore. Captain Darcy, however, hastened to obey the command of his superior, changed his dress and ordered his boat to be manned; but this was no easy matter, there was scarcely a boat's crew to be had without taking away the men necessary to work the ship. The difficulty soon became more pressing, for a plank had suddenly sprung from a double-headed shot, and all the efforts of the pumps could not keep the vessel afloat, with a heavy sea rolling at the same time.

"'The admiral's signal is repeated, sir,' said the lieutenant on duty.

"'Very well, Mr. Hay; keep her before the wind,' was the answer.

"'The ship is settling fast, sir,' said the master; 'no boat could live in that sea; they 're all damaged by shot.'

"'Signal the flag-ship,' cried out Darcy; 'signal the admiral that I am ready to obey him, but we 're sinking.'

"The bunting floated at the mast-head for a moment or two, but the waves were soon many fathoms over it, and the 'Dreadnought' was never seen more."

"So it would seem," said Lionel, with a half-bitter laugh, "we are not the first of the family who went down head foremost. But I hear a voice without. Surely old Tate is not fool enough to admit any one."

"Is it possible—" But before the Knight could finish, the old butler entered to announce Mr. Hickman O'Reilly. Advancing towards the

Knight with a most cordial air, he seemed bent on anticipating any possible expression of displeasure at his unexpected appearance.

"I am aware, Knight," said he, in an accent the most soft and conciliating, "how indelicate a visit from me at such a moment may seem; but if you accord me a few moments of private interview, I hope to dispel the unpleasant impression." He looked towards Lionel as he spoke, and though he smiled his blandest of all smiles, evidently hinted at the possibility of his leaving them alone together.

"I have no confidences apart from my son, sir," said Darcy, coldly.

"Oh, of course not—perfectly natural at Captain Darcy's age—such a thought would be absurd; still, there are circumstances which might possibly excuse my request—I mean—"

Lionel did not suffer him to finish the sentence, but, turning abruptly round, left the room, saying as he went, "I have some orders to give in the stable, but I'll not go further away if you want me."

"Now, sir," said the Knight, haughtily, "we are alone, and not likely to be interrupted; may I ask, as a great favor, that in any communication you may have to make, you will be as brief as consists with your object; for, to say truth, I have many things on my mind, and many important calls to attend to."

"In the first place, then," said Hickman, assuming a manner intended to convey the impression of perfect frankness and candor, "let me make a confession, which, however humiliating to avow, would be still more injurious to hold in reserve. I have neither act nor part in the proceedings my father has lately taken respecting your mutual dealings. Not only that he has not consulted me, but every attempt on my part to ascertain the course of events, or mitigate their rigor, has been met by a direct, not unfrequently a rude, repulse." He waited at this pause for the Knight to speak, but a cold and dignified bow was all the acknowledgment returned. "This may appear strange and inexplicable in your eyes," said O'Reilly, who mistook the Knight's indifference for incredulity, "but perhaps I can explain."

"There is not the slightest necessity to do so, Mr. O'Reilly; I have no reason to doubt one word you have stated; for not only am I ignorant of what the nature and extent of the proceedings you allude to may be, but I am equally indifferent as to the spirit that dictates or the number of advisers that suggest them; pardon me if I seem rude or uncourteous, but there are circumstances in life in which not to be selfish would be to become insensible; my present condition is, perhaps, one of them. A breach of trust on the part of one who possessed my fullest confidence has involved all, or nearly all, I had in the world. The steps by which I am to be deprived of what was once my own are, as regards myself, matters of comparative indifference; with respect to others"—here he almost faltered—"I hope they may be dictated by proper feeling and consideration."

"Be assured they shall, sir," said Mr. O'Reilly; and then, as if correcting a too hasty avowal, added, "but I have the strongest hopes that the matters are not yet in such an extremity as you speak of. It is true, sir, I will not conceal from you, my father is not free from the faults of age; his passion for money-getting has absorbed his whole heart, to the exclusion of many amiable and estimable traits; to enforce a legal right with him seems a duty, and not an option; and I may mention here that your friend, Mr. Daly, has not taken any particular pains towards conciliating him; indeed, he has scarcely acted a prudent part as regards you, by the unceasing rancor he has exhibited towards our family."

"I must interrupt you, sir," said the Knight, "and assure you that, while there are unfortunately but too many topics which could pain me at this moment, there is not one more certain to offend me than any reflection, even the slightest, on the oldest friend I have in the world."

Mr. O'Reilly denied the most remote intention of giving pain, and proceeded. "I was speaking of my father," said he, "and however unpleasant the confession from a son's lips, I must say that the legality of his acts is the extent to which they claim his observance. When his solicitors informed him that the interest was unpaid on your bond, he directed the steps to enforce the payment, and subsequently to foreclose the deed. These are, after all, mere preliminary proceedings, and in no way preclude an arrangement for a renewal."

"Such a proposition—let me interrupt you—such a proposition is wholly out of the question; the ruin that has cost us our house and home has spared nothing. I have no means by which I could anticipate the payment of so large a sum, nor is it either my intention or my wish to reside longer beneath this roof."

"I hope, sir, your determination is not unalterable; it would be the greatest affliction of my life to think that the loss to this county of its oldest family was even in the remotest degree ascribed to us. The Darcys have been the boast and pride of western Ireland for centuries; our county would be robbed of its fairest ornament by the departure of those who hold a princely state and derive a more than princely devotion among us."

"If our claims had no other foundation, Mr. O'Reilly, our altered circumstances would now obliterate them. To live here with diminished fortune—But I ask pardon for being led away in this manner; may I beg that you will now inform me to what peculiar circumstances I owe the honor of your visit?"

"I thought," said O'Reilly, insinuatingly, "that I had mentioned the difference of feeling entertained by my father and myself respecting certain proceedings at law."

"You are quite correct, you did so; but I may observe, without incivility, that however complimentary to your own sense of delicacy such a difference is, for me the matter has no immediate interest."

"Perhaps, with your kind permission, I can give it some," replied O'Reilly, drawing his chair close, and speaking in a low and confidential voice; "but in order to let my communication have the value I would wish it, may I bespeak for myself a favorable hearing and a kind construction on what I shall say? If by an error of judgment—"

"Ah!" said Darcy, sighing, while a sad smile dimpled his mouth—"ah! no man should be more lenient to such than myself."

As if reassured by the kindly tone of these few words, O'Reilly resumed:—

"Some weeks ago my father waited upon Lady Eleanor Darcy with a proposition which, whether on its own merits, or from want of proper tact in his advocacy of it, met with a most unfavorable reception. It is not because circumstances have greatly altered in that brief interval—which I deeply regret to say is the case—that I dare to augur a more propitious hearing, but simply because I hope to show that in making it we were actuated by a spirit of honorable, if not of laudable, ambition. The rank and position my son will enjoy in this county, his fortune and estate, are such as to make any alliance, save with your family, a question of no possible pretension. I am well aware, sir, of the great disparity between a new house and one ennobled by centuries of descent. I have thought long and deeply on the interval that separates the rank of the mere country gentleman from the position of him who claims even higher station than nobility itself; but we live in changeful times: the Peerage has its daily accessions of rank as humble as my own; its new creations are the conscripts drawn from wealth as well as distinction in arms or learning, and in every case the new generation obliterates the memory of its immediate origin. I see you agree with me; I rejoice to find it."

"Your observations are quite just," said Darcy, calmly, and O'Reilly went on:—

"Now, sir, I would not only reiterate my father's proposal, but I would add to it what I hope and trust will be deemed no ungenerous offer, which is, that the young lady's fortune should be this estate of Gwynne Abbey, not to be endowed by her future husband, but settled on her by her father as her marriage portion. I see your meaning,—it is no longer his to give: but we are ready to make it so; the bond we hold shall be thrown into the fire the moment your consent is uttered. We prefer a thousand times it should be thus, than that the ancient acres of this noble heritage should even for a moment cease to be the property of your house. Let me recapitulate a little—"

"I think that is unnecessary," said Darcy, calmly; "I have bestowed the most patient attention to your remarks, and have no difficulty in comprehending them. Have you anything to add?"

"Nothing of much consequence," said O'Reilly, not a little pleased by the favorable tone of the Knight's manner; "what I should suggest in addition is that my son should assume the name and arms of Darcy—"

The noise of footsteps and voices without at this moment interrupted the speaker, the door suddenly opened, and Bagenal Daly entered. He was splashed from head to foot, his high riding-boots stained with the saddle and the road, and his appearance vouching for a long and wearisome journey.

"Good morrow, Darcy," said he, grasping the Knight's hand with the grip of his iron fingers.—"Your servant, sir; I scarcely expected to see you here *so soon*."

The emphasis with which he spoke the last words brought the color to O'Reilly's cheek, who seemed very miserable at the interruption.

"You came to take possession," continued Daly, fixing his eyes on him with a steadfast stare.

"You mistake, Bagenal," said the Knight, gently; "Mr. O'Reilly is come with a very different object,—one which I trust he will deem it no breach of confidence or propriety in me if I mention it to you."

"I regret to say, sir," said O'Reilly, hastily, "that I cannot give my permission in this instance. Whatever the fate of the proposal I have made to you, I beg it to be understood as made under the seal of honorable secrecy."

Darcy bowed deeply, but made no reply.

"Confound me," cried Daly, "if I understand any compact between two such men as you to require all this privacy, unless you were hardy enough to renew your old father's proposal for my friend's daughter, and now had modesty enough to feel ashamed of your own impudence."

"I am no stranger, sir, to the indecent liberties you permit your tongue to take," said Hickman, moving towards the door; "but this is neither the time nor place to notice them."

"So then I was right," cried Daly; "I guessed well the game you would play—"

"Bagenal," interposed the Knight, "I must atop this. Mr. Hickman is now beneath my roof—"

"Is he, faith?—not in his own estimation then. Why, his fellows are taking an inventory of the furniture at this very moment."

"Is this true, sir?" said Darcy, turning a fierce look towards O'Reilly, whose face became suddenly of an ashy paleness.

"If so," muttered he, "I can only assure you that it is without any orders of mine."

"How good!" said Daly, bursting into an insolent laugh; "why, Darcy, when you meet with a fellow in your plantations with a gun in his hand and a lurcher at his heels, are you disposed to regard him as one in search of the picturesque, or a poacher? So, when a gentleman travels about the country with a sub-sheriff in his carriage and two bailiffs in the rumble, does it seem exactly the guise of one paying morning calls to his neighbors?"

"Mr. O'Reilly, I ask you to explain this proceeding."

"I confess, sir," stammered out the other, "I came accompanied by certain persons in authority, but who have acted in this matter entirely without my permission. The proposal I have made this day was the cause of my visit."

"It is a subject on which I can no longer hold any secrecy," said the Knight, haughtily. "Bagenal, you were quite correct in your surmise. Mr. O'Reilly not only intended us the honor of an alliance, but offered to merge the ancient glories of his house by assuming the more humble name and shield of Darcy."

"What! eh! did I hear aright?" said Daly, with a broken voice; while, walking to the window, he looked down into the lawn beneath, as if calculating the height from the ground. "By Heaven, Darcy, you 're the best-tempered fellow in Europe—that 's all," he muttered, as he walked away.

The door opened at this moment, and the shock bullet head of a bailiff appeared.

"That's Mr. Daly! there he is!" cried out O'Reilly, who, pale with passion and trembling all over, supported himself against the back of a chair with one hand, while with the other he pointed to where Daly stood.

"In that case," said the fellow, entering, while he drew a slip of paper from his breast, "I 'll take the opportunity of sarvin' him where he stands."

"One step nearer! one step!" said Daly, as he took a pistol from the pocket of his coat.

The man hesitated and looked at O'Reilly, as if for advice or encouragement; but terror and rage had now deprived him of all self-possession, and he neither spoke nor signed to him.

"Leave the room, sir," said the Knight, with a motion of his hand to the bailiff; and the ruffian, whose office had familiarized him long with scenes of outrage and violence, shrank back ashamed and abashed, and slipped from the room without a word.

"I believe, Mr. O'Reilly," continued Darcy, with an accent calm and unmoved,—"I believe our conference is now concluded. I will not insult your own acuteness by saying how unnecessary I feel any reply to your demand."

"In that case," said O'Reilly, "may I presume that there is no objection to proceed with those legal formalities which, although begun without my knowledge, may be effected now as well as at any other period?"

"Darcy, there is but one way of dealing with that gentleman—"

"Bagenal, I must insist upon your leaving this matter solely with me."

"Depend upon it, sir, your interests will not gain by your friend's counsels," said O'Reilly, with an insolent sneer.

"Such another remark from your lips," said Darcy, sternly, "would make me follow them, if they went so far as—"

"Throwing him neck and heels out of that window," broke in Daly; "for I own to you it's the course I'd have taken half an hour ago."

"I wish you good morning, Mr. Darcy," said O'Reilly, addressing him for the first time by the name of his family instead of his usual designation; and without vouchsafing a word to Daly, he retired from the room.

It was not until O'Reilly's carriage drove past the window that either Darcy or his friend uttered a syllable; they stood apparently lost in thought up to that moment, when the noise of wheels and the tramp of horses aroused them.

"We must lose no time, Bagenal," said the Knight, hastily; "I cannot count very far on that gentleman's delicacy or forbearance. Lady Eleanor must not be exposed to the indignities the law will permit him to practise towards us; we must, if possible, leave this to-night;" and so saying, he left the room to make arrangements in accordance with his resolve.

Bagenal Daly looked after him for a moment. "Poor fellow!" muttered he, "how manfully he bears it!" When a sudden flush that covered his cheek bespoke a rapid change of sentiment, and at the same instant he left the room, and, crossing the hall and the courtyard, walked hastily towards the stables.

"Saddle a horse for me, Carney, and as fast as may be."

"Here's a mare ready this minute, sir; she was going out to take her gallop."

"I'll give it, then," said Daly, as he buttoned up his coat; and then, breaking off a branch of the old willow that hung over the fountain, sprang in the saddle with an alertness that would not have disgraced a youth of twenty.

"There he goes," muttered the old huntsman, as he looked after him, "and there is n't the man between this and Killy-begs can take as much out of a baste as himself. 'T is quiet enough the mare will be when he turns her head into this yard again."

Whatever Daly's purpose, it seemed one which brooked little delay, for no sooner was he on the sward than he pushed the mare to a fast gallop, and was seen sweeping along the lawn at a tremendous pace. In less than ten minutes he saw O'Reilly's carriage, as, in a rapid trot, the horses advanced along the level avenue, and almost the moment after, he had stationed himself in the road, so as to prevent their proceeding further. The coachman, who knew him well, came to a stop at his signal, and before his master could ask the reason, Daly was beside the window of the chariot.

"I would wish a word with you, Mr. O'Reilly," said he, in a low, subdued voice, so as to be inaudible to the sub-sheriff, who was seated beside him. "You made use of an expression a few moments ago, which, if I understood aright, convinces me I have unwittingly done you great injustice."

O'Reilly, whose ashy cheek and affrighted air bespoke a heart but ill at ease, made no reply, and Daly went on, —

"You said, sir, that neither the time nor the place suited the notice you felt called upon to take of my remarks on your conduct. May I ask, as a very great favor, what time and what place will be more convenient to you? And I cannot better express my own sense of regret for a hasty expression than by assuring you that I shall hold myself bound to be at your service in both respects."

"A hostile meeting, sir, is that your proposition?" said O'Reilly, aloud.

"How admirably you read a riddle!" said Daly, laughing.

"There, Mr. Jones!" cried O'Reilly, turning to his companion, "I call on you to witness the words,—a provocation to a duel offered by this gentleman."

"Not at all," rejoined Daly; "the provocation came from yourself,—at least, you used a phrase which men with blood in their veins understand but one way. My error—and I 'll not forgive myself in haste for it—was the belief that an upstart need not of necessity be a poltroon.—Drive on," cried he to the coachman, with a sneering laugh; "your master is looking pale." And, with these words, he turned his horse's head, and cantered slowly back towards the abbey.

CHAPTER XXXIII
TATE SULLIVAN'S FAREWELL

The sorrows and sufferings of noble minds are melancholy themes to dwell upon; they may "point a moral," but they scarcely "adorn a tale," least of all such a tale as ours is intended to be. While, therefore, we would spare our readers and ourselves the pain of this narration, we cannot leave that old abbey, which we remember so full of happiness, without one parting look at it, in company with those about to quit it forever.

From the time of Mr. O'Reilly's leave-taking, the day, notwithstanding its gloomy presage, went over rapidly. The Knight busied himself with internal arrangements, while Lionel took into his charge all the preparations for their departure on the morrow, Bagenal Daly assisting each in turn, and displaying an amount of calm foresight and circumspection in details which few would have given him credit for. Meanwhile, Lady Eleanor slept long and heavily, and awoke, not only refreshed in body, but with an appearance of quiet energy and determination she had not shown for years past. Great indeed was the Knight's astonishment on hearing that she intended joining them at dinner; in her usual habit she dined early, and with Helen alone for her companion, so that her present resolve created the more surprise.

Dinner was ordered in the library, and poor old Tate, by some strange motive of sympathy, took a more than common pains in all the decorations of the table. The flowers which Lady Eleanor was fondest of decked the centre—alas, there was no need to husband them now! on the morrow who was to care for them?—a little bouquet of fresh violets marked her place at the table, and more than a dozen times did the old man hesitate how the light should fall through the large window, and whether it would be more soothing to his mistress to look abroad upon that fair and swelling landscape so dear to her, or more painful to gaze upon the scenes she should never see more.

"If it was myself," muttered old Tate, "I'd like to be looking at it as long as I could, and make it follow me in my dhrames after; but sure there 's no knowing how great people feels! they say they never has the same kind of thought as us!"

Poor fellow, he little knew how levelling is misfortune, and that the calamities of life evoke the same sufferings in the breast of the king and the peasant. With a delicacy one more highly born might have been proud of, the old butler alone waited at dinner, well judging that his familiar face would be less irksome to them than the prying looks of the other servants.

If there are people who can expend much eloquent indignation on those social usages which exact a certain amount of decorous observance in all the trials and crosses of life, there is a great deal to be said in favor of that system of conventional good-breeding whose aim is to repress selfish indulgence, and make the individual feel that, whatever his own griefs, the claims of the world demand a fortitude and a bearing that shall not obtrude his sorrows on his neighbors. That the code may be abused, and become occasionally hypocritical in practice, is no argument against it; we would merely speak in praise of that well-bred forbearance which always merges private afflictions in the desire to make others happy. To instance our meaning, we would speak of those who now met at dinner in the old library of Gwynne Abbey.

It would be greatly to mistake us to suppose that we uphold any show or counterfeit of kindliness where there is no substance of the feeling behind it; we merely maintain that the very highest and most acute sympathy is not inconsistent with a bearing of easy, nay, almost cheerful character. So truly was it the case here that old Tate Sullivan more than once stood still in amazement at the tranquil faces and familiar quietude of those who, in his own condition of life, could have found no accents loud or piercing enough to bewail their sorrow, and whom, even with his long knowledge of them, he could scarcely acquit of insensibility.

There is a contagion in an effort of this kind most remarkable. The light and gentle attempts made by Lady Eleanor to sustain the spirits of the party were met by sallies of manly good-humor by the Knight himself, in which Lionel and Helen were not slow to join, while Bagenal Daly could scarcely repress his enthusiastic delight at the noble and high-souled courage that sustained them one and all.

While by a tacit understanding they avoided any allusion to the painful circumstances of their late misfortune, the Knight adroitly turned the conversation to their approaching journey northwards, and drew from Daly a description of "the Corvy" that actually evoked a burst of downright laughter. From this he passed on to speak of the peasantry, so unlike in every trait those of the South and West; the calm, reflective character of their minds, uninfluenced by passion and unmarked by enthusiasm, were a strong contrast to the headlong impulse and ardent temperament of the "real Irish."

"You 'll scarcely like them at first, my dear Helen—"

"Still less on a longer acquaintance," broke in Helen. "I 'll not quarrel with the caution and reserve of the Scotchman,—the very mists of his native mountains may teach him doubt and uncertainty of purpose; but here at home, what have such frames of mind and thought in common with our less calculating natures?"

"It were far better had they met oftener," said the Knight, thoughtfully; "impulse is only noble when well directed; the passionate pilots are more frequently the cause of shipwreck than of safety."

"Nothing so wearisome as the trade-winds," said Helen, with a saucy toss of the head; "eh, Lionel, you are of my mind?"

"They do push one's temper very hard now and then," said Daly, with a stern frown; "that impassive habit they have of taking everything as in the common order of events is, I own, somewhat difficult to bear with. I remember being run away with on a blood mare from a little village called Ballintray. The beast was in high condition, and I turned her, without knowing the country, at the first hill I could see; she breasted it boldly, and, though full a quarter of a mile in length, never shortened stride to the very summit. What was my surprise, when I gained the top, to see that we were exactly over the sea. It was a cliff which, projecting for some distance out, was fissured by an immense chasm, through which the waves passed; not very wide, but deep enough to make it a very awful leap. Over it she went, and then, when I expected her to dash onwards, and was already preparing to fling myself from the saddle, she stood stock still, trembling all over, and snorting with fear at the danger around her. At the same instant, a hard-featured old fellow popped his head up from amid the tall fern which he had been cutting for thatch for his cabin, and looked at me, not the slightest sign of astonishment in his cold, rigid countenance.

"'Ye 'll no get back so easy, my bonnie mon,' said he, with the slightest possible approach to a smile.

"'Get back! no, faith, I 'll not try it,' said I, looking at the yawning gulf, through which the wild waves boiled, and the opposite bank several feet higher than the ground I stood upon.

"'I thought sae,' was the rejoinder; when, rising slowly, he leisurely walked round the mare, as she stood riveted by fear to the one spot. 'I 'll gie ye sax shilling for the hide o' her forbye the shoes,' added he, with a voice as imperturbable as though he were pricing the commonest commodity of a market.

"I confess it was fortunate that the ludicrous was stronger in me at the moment than indignation, for if I had not laughed at him I might have done worse."

"I could not endure such a peasantry," said Helen, as soon as the mirth the anecdote called forth had subsided.

"It's quite true," said Daly, "they have burlesqued Scotch prudence in the same way that the Anglo-Hibernian has travestied the Irish temperament. It is the danger of all imitators, they always transgress the limits of their model."

"It is fortunate," broke in the Knight, "that traits which conciliate so little the stranger should win their way on nearer intimacy; and such I believe to be the case with the Ulster peasant."

"You are right," said Daly; "no man can detest more cordially than I do the rudeness that is assumed to heighten a contrast with any good quality behind it. In most instances the kernel is not worth the trouble of breaking off the husk; but with the Northerner this is not the case: in his independence he neither apes the equality of the Frenchman nor the license of the Yankee. That he suffices for himself, and seeks neither patron nor protector, is the source of honest pride, and if this sometimes takes the guise of stubbornness, let us remember that the virtue was reared in poverty, without encouragement or example."

"And the gentry," said Lady Eleanor, "have they any trace of these peculiarities observable among the people?"

"Gentry!" said Daly, impetuously, "I know of none. There are some thrifty families, who, by some generations of hard saving, have risen to affluence and wealth. They are keen fellows, given to money-getting,— millers some of them, bleachers most, with a tenantry of weavers, and estates like the grass-plot of a laundry. They are as crafty and as calculating as the peasant, shrewd as stockbrokers at a bargain, and as pretentious as a Prince Palatine with a territory the size of Merrion Square. Gentry! they have neither ancestry nor tradition; they hold their estates from certain Guilds, whose very titles are a parody upon gentle breeding,—fishmongers and clothworkers!"

"I will not be their champion against you, Bagenal, but I cannot help feeling how heavily they might retort upon us. These same prudent and prosaic landlords have not spent their fortunes in wasteful extravagance and absurd display; they have not rackrented their tenantry that they might rival a neighbor."

"I am sincerely rejoiced," interposed Lady Eleanor, smiling, "that my English relative, Lord Netherby, was not a witness to this discussion, lest he should fancy that, between the wastefulness of the South and the thrift of the North, this poor island was but ill provided with a gentry. Pray, Mr. Daly, how does your sister like the North? She is our neighbor, is she not?"

"Yes,—that is to say, a few miles distant," said Daly, confusedly; for he had never acknowledged that "the Corvy" had been Miss Daly's residence. "Of the neighborhood she knows nothing; she is not free from my own prejudices, and lives a very secluded life."

The conversation now became broken and unconnected, and the party soon after retired to the drawing-room, where, while Lady Eleanor and Helen sat together, the Knight, Daly, and Lionel gathered in a little knot, and discussed, in a low tone, the various steps for the coming journey, and the probable events of the morrow.

It was agreed upon that Daly should accompany the Darcys to the North, whither Sandy was already despatched, but that Lionel should remain at the abbey for some days longer, to complete the arrangements necessary for the removal of certain family papers and the due surrender of the property to its new owner; after which he should repair to London, and procure his exchange into some regiment of the line, and, if possible, one on some foreign station,—the meeting with friends and acquaintances, under his now altered fortunes, being judged as a trial too painful and too difficult to undergo.

Again they all met around the tea-table, and once more they talked in the same vein of mutual confidence; each conscious of the effort by which he sustained his part, and wondering how the others summoned courage to do what cost himself so much. They chatted away till near midnight, and when they shook hands at separating, it was with feelings of affection to which sorrow had only added fresh and stronger ties.

Daly stood for some time alone in the library, wondering within himself at the noble fortitude with which they severally sustained their dreadful reverse. It is only the man of stout heart can truly estimate the higher attributes of courage; but even to him these efforts seemed surprising. "Ay," muttered he, "each nobly upholds the other; it is opposing a hollow square to fortune: so long as they stand firm and together, well! let but one quail and falter, let the line be broken, and they would be swept away at once and forever." Taking a caudle from the table, he left the room, and ascended the wide staircase towards his chamber. All was still and noiseless, and to prevent his footsteps being heard, he entered the little corridor which opened on the gallery of the refectory, the same from which Forester first caught sight of the party at the dinner-table.

He had scarcely, with careful hand, closed the door behind him, when, looking over the balustrades of the gallery, he beheld a figure moving slowly along in the great apartment beneath, guided by a small lamp, which threw its uncertain light rather on the wall than on the form of him who carried it. Suddenly stopping before one of the large portraits which in a long succession graced the chamber, the light was turned fully round, so as to display the broad and massive features of old Tate Sullivan. Curious to ascertain what the old man might be about in such a place at such an hour, Daly extinguished the candle to watch him unobserved. Tate was dressed in his most accurate costume: his long cravat, edged with deep lace, descended in front of his capacious white waistcoat; silver buckles, of a size that showed there was no parsimony of the precious metal, shone in his shoes; and his newly powdered wig displayed an almost snowy lustre. His gestures were in accordance with the careful observances of his toilet; he moved along the floor with a slow, sliding step, bowing deeply and reverentially as he went, and with all the courtesy he would have displayed if ushering a goodly company into the state drawing-room.

Bagenal Daly was not left long to speculate on honest Tate's intentions; and although to a stranger's eyes the motives might have seemed strange and dubious, the mystery was easily solved to him, who knew the old man well and thoroughly. He was there to take a last look, and bid farewell to those venerable portraits, who for more than half a century were enshrined in his memory like saints. Around them were associated all the little incidents of his peaceful life; they were the chroniclers of his impressions in boyhood, in manhood, and in age; he could call to mind the first moments he gazed on them in awe-struck veneration; he could remember the proud period when the duty first devolved upon him of describing them to the strangers who came to see the abbey; in the history of all and each of them he was well read, versed in their noble achievements, their triumphs in camp or cabinet. To his eyes they formed a long line of heroic characters, of which the world had produced no equal; they realized in his conception the proud eulogy of the Bayards, "where all the men were brave, and all the women virtuous;" and it is not improbable that his devotion to his master was in a great measure ascribable to that awe-struck admiration with which he regarded his glorious ancestors.

The old man stood, and, holding the lamp above his head, gazed in respectful admiration at the grim figure of a Knight in armor. There might have been little to charm the lover of painting in the execution of the picture, and the mere castle-builder could scarcely have indulged his fancy in weaving a story from the countenance of the portrait, for the vizor was down, and he stood in all the unmoved sternness of his iron prison, with his glaived hands elapsed upon the cross of a long straight sword. Tate gazed on him for some moments. Heaven knows with what qualities of mind or person the old man had endowed him, for while to others he was only Sir Gavin Darcy, first Knight of Gwynne, Tate in all likelihood had invested him with traits of character and appearance, of which that external shell was the mere envelope.

"We're going, Sir Gavin," muttered the old man, as if addressing the portrait; "'tis the ould stock is laving the place, never to see it more; 't is your own proud heart will be sorry to-day to look down upon us. Ah, ah!" muttered he, "the world is changed; there was times when a Darcy would n't quit the house of his fathers without a blow for it—aud they say we are better now!" With a heavy sigh he passed on, and stood before the next picture. "Yes, my Lady," said he, "ye may well cry that lost the two beautiful boys the same morning, fighting side by side; but there's heavier grief here now: the brave youths sleep in peace and in honor; but we have no home to shelter us!"

With a slow step and bent-down head, he tottered on, and, placing the lamp upon the floor, crossed his arms upon his breast. "'Tis you that can help us now," said he as he cast a timid and imploring glance at the goodly countenance and rotund figure of Bernhard Emmeric, fourth Abbot of Gwynne; "'tis your reverence can offer a prayer for your own blood that's in sore trouble and distress. Do it, my Lord; do it in the name of the Vargin. Smiling and happy you look, but it 's sorrowful your heart is in you to see what's going on here. Them, them was the happy days, when it was n't the cry of grief was heard beneath this roof, but the heavenly chants of holy men, and the prayers of the blessed mass." He knelt down as he said this, and with trembling lips and tearful eyes recited some verses from his breviary.

This done, he arose, and, as if with renovated courage, proceeded on his way.

"Reginald Herbert de Guyon! ah! second Baron of Gwynne, Lord Protector of Munster, Knight of Malta, Chevalier of St. John of Jerusalem, Standard-Bearer to the Queen! and well you desarve it all! 'T is yourself sits your horse like a proud nobleman!" He stood with eyes riveted upon the picture, while his face glowed with intense enthusiasm, and at last, as a bitter sneer passed across his lips, he added, "Ay, faith! and them that comes after us won't like the look of you. 'T is you that 'll never disguise from them your real mind, and every day they 'll dine in the hall, that same frown will darken, and that same hand will threaten them."

He moved on now, and passed several portraits without stopping, muttering as he went, "'T is more English than Irish blood is in your veins, and you won't feel as much for us as the rest;" then, halting suddenly, he stood before a tall figure, dressed in black velvet, with a deep collar of point lace. A connoisseur of higher pretensions than poor Tate might have gazed with even greater rapture at that splendid canvas, for it was from the hand of Vandyke, and in his very best manner. The picture represented the person of Sir Everard Darcy, Lord Privy Seal to Charles I. It was a specimen of manly beauty and high blood such as the great Fleming loved to paint; and even yet the proud and lofty forehead, the deep-set brown eyes, the thin compressed lip, the long and somewhat projecting chin, seemed to address themselves to the beholder with traits of character more than mere painting is able to convey. Tate approached the spot with an almost trembling veneration, and bowed deeply before the haughty figure. "There was a time, Sir Everard, when your word could make a duke or a marquis, — when your whisper in the king's ear could bring grief or joy to any heart in the empire. Could you do nothing for us now? They say you never were at a loss, no matter what came to pass — that you were always ready-witted to save your master from trouble — and oh! if the power hasn't left you, stand by us now. It is not because your eyes are so bright, and that quiet smile is on your lips, that your heart does not feel, for I know well that the day you were beheaded you had the same look on you as you have now. I think I see you this minute, as you lifted your head off the block to settle the lace collar that the villain, the executioner, rumpled with his bloody fingers, — I think I hear the words you spoke: 'Honest Martin, for all your practice, you are but a clumsy valet.' Weil, well! 't is a happier and a prouder day that same than to-morrow's dawn will bring to ourselves. Yes, yes, my darlings," said Tate, with a benevolent smile, as he waved his hand towards a picture where two beautiful children were represented, sitting on the grass, and playing with flowers, "be happy and amuse yourselves, in God's name; 'tis the only time for happiness your lives ever gave you. Ah! and here 's your father, with a smile on his face and a cheerful brow, for he had both till the day misfortune robbed him of his children;" and he stood in front of a portrait of an officer in an admiral's uniform. He was a distinguished member of the Darcy family; but from the nature of his services, which were all maritime, and the great number of years he had spent away from Ireland, possessed less of Tate's sympathy than most of the others.

"They say you didn't like Ireland; but I don't believe them. There never was a Darcy did n't love the ould island; but I know well whose fault it was if you did n't, — it was that dark villain that's standing at your side, ould Harry Inchiquin, the renegade, that turned many a man against his country.

Ye may frown and scowl at me; but if you were alive this minute, I'd say it to your face. It was you that first brought gambling and dicing under this blessed roof; it was you that sent the ould acres to the hammer; 'twas you that loved rioting, and duelling, and every wickedness, just like old Bagenal Daly himself, that never could sleep in his bed if he had n't a fight on hand."

"What ho! you old reprobate!" called out Daly, in a voice which, echoing under the arched roof, seemed rather to float through the atmosphere than issue from any particular quarter.

"Oh! marciful Father!" cried Tate, as, falling on his knees, the lamp dropped from his fingers, and became extinguished,—"oh! marciful Father! sure I did n't mane it; 't is what the lying books said of you,—bad luck to the villains that wrote them! O God! pardon me; I never thought you 'd hear me; and if it 's in trouble you are, I 'll say a mass for you every day till Aaster, and one every Friday as long as I live."

A hoarse burst of laughter broke from Daly, while, pacing the gallery with heavy tread, he went forth, banging the door behind him. The terror was too great for poor Tate's endurance, and, with a faint cry for mercy, he rolled down upon the floor almost insensible.

When morning broke, he was found seated in the refectory, pale and careworn; but no entreaty, nor no pressing, could elicit from him one word of a secret in which he believed were equally involved the honor of the dead and the safety of himself.

CHAPTER XXXIV
A GLANCE AT PUBLIC OPINION
IN THE YEAR 1800

Among the arrangements for the departure of the family from the abbey, all of which were confided to Bagenal Daly, was one which he pressed with a more than ordinary zeal and anxiety; this was, that they should set out at a very early hour of the morning,—at dawn of day, if possible. Lady Eleanor's habits made such a plan objectionable, and it was only by representing the great sacrifice of feeling a later departure would exact, when crowds of country people would assemble to take their farewells of them forever, that she consented. While Daly depicted the unnecessary sorrow to which they would expose themselves by the sight of their old and attached tenantry, he strenuously preserved silence on the real reason which actuated him, and to explain which a brief glance at the state of public feeling at the period is necessary.

To such a pitch of acrimony and animosity were parties borne by the agitation which preceded the carrying of the "Union," that all previous character and conduct of those who voted on the question were deemed as nothing in comparison with the line they adopted on the one absorbing subject. If none who advocated the Ministerial plan escaped the foulest animadversions, all who espoused the opposite side were exalted to the dignity of patriots; argument and reason went for little, principle for still less: a vote was deemed the touchstone of honesty. Such rash and hasty judgments suited the temper of the times, and, it may be said in extenuation, were not altogether without some show of reason. Each day revealed some desertion from the popular party of men who, up to that moment, had rejected all the seductions of the Crown; country gentlemen, hitherto supposed inaccessible to all the temptations of bribery, were found suddenly addressing speculative letters to their constituencies, wherein they ingeniously discussed all the contingencies of a measure they had once opposed without qualification. Noblemen of high rank and fortune were seen to pay long visits at the Castle, and, by a strange fatality, were found to have modified their opinions exactly at the period selected by the Crown to bestow on them designations of honor or situations of trust and dignity.

Lawyers in high practice at the bar, men esteemed by their profession, and held in honor by the public, were seen to abandon their position of proud independence, and accept Government appointments, in many cases inferior both in profit and rank to what they had surrendered.

There seemed a kind of panic abroad. Men feared to walk without the protective mantle of the Crown being extended over them; the barriers of shame were broken down by the extent to which corruption had spread. The examples of infamy were many, and several were reconciled to the ignominy of their degradation by their associates in disgrace. That in such general corruption the judgments of the public should have been equally wholesale, is little to be wondered at; the regret is rather that they were so rarely unjust and ill-bestowed.

Public confidence was utterly uprooted; there was a national bankruptcy of honor, and none were trusted; all the guarantees for high principle and rectitude a lifetime had given, all the hostages to good faith years of unimpeached honor bestowed, were forgotten in a moment, and such as opposed the Government measure with less of acrimony or activity than their neighbors, were set down "as waiting for or soliciting the bribery of the Crown."

To this indiscriminating censure the Knight of Gwynne was a victim. It may be remarked that in times of popular excitement, when passions are rife and the rude enthusiasm of the mass has beaten down the more calmly weighed opinion of the few, that there is a strange pleasure felt in the detection of any real or supposed lapse of one once esteemed. It were well if this malignant delight were limited to the mere mob, but it is not so; men of education and position are not exempt from its taint. It would seem as if society were so thoroughly disorganized that every feeling was perverted, and all the esteem for what is good and great had degenerated into a general cry of exultation over each new instance of tarnished honor.

Accustomed as we now are to the most free and unfettered criticisms of all public men and their acts, it would yet astonish any one not conversant with that period, to look back to the newspapers of the time, and see the amount of violence and personality with which every man obnoxious to a party was visited; coarse invective stood in the place of argument, a species of low humor had replaced the light brilliancy of wit. The public mind, fed on grosser materials, had lost all appetite for the piquancy of more highly flavored food, and the purveyors were not sorry to find a market for a commodity which cost them so little to procure. In this spirit was it that one of the most popular of the Opposition journals announced for the amusement of its readers a series of sketches under the title of "The

Gallery of Traitors,"—a supposed collection of portraits to be painted for the Viceroy, and destined to decorate one of the chambers of the Castle.

Not satisfied with aspersing the reputation, and mistaking the views of any who sided with the Minister, the attack went further, and actually ascribed the casualties which occurred to such persons or their families as instances of divine vengeance. In this diabolical temper the Knight of Gwynne was held up to reprobation; it was a bold thought to venture on calumniating a man every action of whose life had placed him above even slander, but its boldness was the warranty of success. The whole story of his arrival in Dublin, his dinner with the Secretary, his intimacy with Heffernan, was related circumstantially. The night on which Heffernan entrapped him by the trick already mentioned, was quoted as the eventful moment of his change. Then came the history of his appearance in the House on the evening of the second reading: his hesitation to enter, his doubts and waverings were all described, ending with a minute detail of his compact with Lord Castlereagh, by which his voting was dispensed with, and his absence from the division deemed enough.

Gleeson's flight and its consequences were soon known. The ruin of Darcy's large fortune was a circumstance not likely to lose by public discussion, particularly when the daily columns of a newspaper devoted a considerable space to the most minute details of that catastrophe. It was asserted that the Knight had sold himself for a Marqui-sate and a seat in the English peerage; that his vote was deemed so great a prize by the Minister that he might have made even higher terms, but in the confidence of possessing a large fortune he had only bargained for rank, and rejected every offer of mere emolument; and now came the dreadful retribution on his treachery, the downfall of his fortune by the villany of his agent. To assume a title when the very expense of the patent could not be borne, was an absurdity, and this explained why Maurice Darcy remained ungazetted. Such was the plausible calumny generally circulated, and, alas for the sake of charity! scarcely less generally believed.

There are epidemics of credulity as of infidelity, and such a plague raged at this period. Anything was believed, were it only bad enough. While men, therefore, went about deploring, with all the sanctity of self-esteem, the fall of Maurice Darcy, public favor, by one of those caprices all its own, adopted the cause of his colleague, Hickman O'Reilly. His noble refusal of every offer (and what a catalogue of seductions did they not enumerate!) was given in the largest type. They recounted, with all the eloquence of their calling, the glittering coronets rejected, the places of honor and profit declined, the dignities proffered in vain, preferring as he did the untitled rank of a country gentleman, and the unpurchasable station of a true friend to Ireland.

He was eulogized in capital letters, and canonized among the martyrs of patriotism; public orators belabored him with praises, and ballad-singers chanted his virtues through the streets. Nor was this turn of feeling a thing to be neglected by one so shrewd in worldly matters. His sudden accession to increased fortune and the position attendant on it, would, he well knew, draw down upon him many a sneer upon his origin, and some unpleasant allusions to the means by which the wealth was amassed. To anticipate such an ungrateful inquiry, he seized the lucky accident of his popularity, and turned it to the best account.

Whole "leaders" were devoted to the laudation of his character: the provincial journals, less scrupulous than the metropolitan, boldly asserted their knowledge of the various bribes tendered to him, and threw out dark hints of certain disclosures which, although at present refrained from out of motives of delicacy, should Mr. O'Reilly ultimately be persuaded to make, the public would be horrified at the extent to which corruption had been carried.

The O'Reilly liveries, hitherto a modest snuff color, were now changed to an emerald green; an Irish motto ornamented the garter of the family crest; while the very first act of his return to the West was a splendid donation to the chapel of Ballyraggan, or, as it was subsequently and more politely named, the Church of St. Barnabas of Treves: all measures dictated by a high-spirited independence, and a mind above the vulgar bigotry of party.

Had O'Reilly stopped here; had he contented himself with the preliminary arrangements for being a patriot, it is probable that Bagenal Daly had never noticed them, or done so merely with some passing sarcasm; but the fact was otherwise. Daly discovered, in the course of his journey westward, that the rumors of the Knight's betrayal of his party were generally disseminated in exact proportion with the new-born popularity of O'Reilly; that the very town of Westport, where Darcy's name was once adored, was actually placarded with insulting notices of the Knight's conduct, and scandalous aspersions on his character: jeering allusions to his altered fortunes were sung in the villages as he passed along, and it was plain that the whole current of popular opinion had set strong against him.

To spare his friend Darcy a mortification which Daly well knew would be one of the greatest to his feelings, the early departure was planned and decided on. It must not be inferred that because the Knight would have felt deeply the unjust censure of the masses, he was a man to care or bend beneath the angry menace of a mob; far from it. The ingratitude towards himself would have called forth the least of his regrets; it was rather a heartfelt sorrow at the hopeless ignorance and degradation of those who could be so easily deceived,—at that populace whose fickleness preferred the tinsel and trappings of patriotism to the acts and opinions of one they had known and respected for years.

Long before day broke, Daly was stirring and busied with all the preparations of the journey; the travelling carriage, covered with its various boxes and imperials, stood before the door in the courtyard; the horses were harnessed and bridled in the stables; everything was in readiness for a start; and yet, save himself and the stablemen, all within the abbey seemed buried in slumber.

Although it was scarcely more than five o'clock, Daly's impatience at the continued quietude around him began to manifest itself; he walked hastily to and fro, endeavoring to occupy his thoughts by a hundred little details, till at last he found himself returning to the same places and with the self-same objects again and again, while he muttered broken sentences of angry comments on people who could sleep so soundly at such a time.

It was in one of those fretful moods he had approached the little flower-garden of the sub-prior's house, when the twinkling of a light attracted him: it came from the window of Lady Eleanor's favorite drawing-room, and glittered like a star in the gloom of the morning. Curious to see who was stirring in that part of the house, he drew near, and, opening the wicket, noiselessly approached the window. He there beheld Lady Eleanor, who, supported by Helen's arm, moved slowly along the room, stopping at intervals, and again proceeding; she seemed to be taking a last farewell of the various well-known objects endeared to her by years of companionship; her handkerchief was often raised to her eyes as she went, but neither uttered a syllable. Ashamed to have obtruded even thus upon a scene of private sorrow, Daly turned back again to the courtyard, where now the loud voice of the Knight was heard giving his orders to the servants.

The first greetings over, the Knight took Daly's arm and walked beside him.

"I have been thinking over the matter in the night, Bagenal," said he, "and am convinced it were far better that you should remain with Lionel; we can easily make our journey alone,—the road is open, and no difficulty in following it; but that poor boy will need advice and counsel. You will probably receive letters from Dublin by the post, with some instructions how to act; in any case my heart fails me at leaving Lionel to himself."

"I 'll remain, then," replied Daly; "I'll see you the first stage out of Westport, and then return here. It is, perhaps, better as you say."

"There is another point," said Darcy, after a pause, and with evident hesitation in his manner; "it is perfectly impossible for me to walk through this labyrinth without your guidance, Bagenal,—I have neither head nor heart for it,—you must be the pilot, and if you quit the helm for a moment—"

"Trust me, Maurice, I'll not do it," said Daly, grasping his hand with a firm grip.

"I know that well," said the Knight, as his voice trembled with agitation; "I never doubted the will, Bagenal, it was the power only I suspected. I see you will not understand me. Confound it! why should old friends, such as we are, keep beating about the bush, or fencing like a pair of diplomatists? I wanted to speak to you about that bond of yours: there is something like seven thousand pounds lying to my credit at Henshaw's; take what is necessary, and get rid of that scoundrel Hickman's claim. If they should arrest you—"

"I wish he had done so yesterday,—my infernal temper, that never will let matters take due course, stopped the fellow; you can't see why, but I'll tell you. I paid the money to Hickman's law-agent, in Dublin, the morning I started from town, and they had not time to stop the execution of the writ down here. Yes, Darcy, there was one drop more in the stoup, and I drained it! The last few acres I possessed in the world, the old estate of Hardress Daly, is now in the ownership of one Samuel Kerney, grocer of Bride Street. I paid off Hickman, however, and found something like one hundred and twenty-eight pounds afterwards in my pocket—but let us talk of something else: you must not yield to these people without a struggle; Bicknell says there are abundant grounds for a trial at bar in the affair. If collusion between Hickman and Gleeson should be proved, that many of the leases were granted with false signatures annexed—"

"I 'll do whatever men of credit and character counsel me," said the Knight; "if there be any question of right, I 'll neither compromise nor surrender it: I can promise no more. But here comes Lionel,—to announce breakfast, perhaps."

And so it was; the young man came towards them with an easy smile, presenting a hand to each. If sorrow had sunk deeply into his heart, few traces of grief were apparent in his manly, handsome countenance.

Notwithstanding the efforts of the party, the breakfast did not pass over as lightly as the dinner of the previous day; the eventful moment of parting was now too near not to exclude every other subject, and even when by an exertion some allusion to a different topic would be made, a chance question, the entrance of a servant for orders, or the tramp of horses in the courtyard, would suddenly bring back the errant thoughts, and place the sad reality in all its force before them.

Breakfast was over, and yet no one stirred; a heavy, dreary revery seemed to have settled on all except Daly,—and he, from delicacy, restrained the impatience that was working within him. In vain he sought to catch Darcy's eye, and then Lionel's,—both were bent downward. Lady Eleanor at last looked up, and at once seemed to read what was passing in his mind.

"I am ready," said she, in a low, gentle voice, "and I see Mr. Daly is not sorry at it. Helen, dearest, fetch me my gloves."

She arose, and the others with her. The calmness in which she spoke on the theme that none dared approach, seemed also to electrify them, when suddenly a low sob was heard, and the mother fell, in a burst of anguish, into the arms of her son.

"Eleanor, my dearest Eleanor!" said Darcy, as his pale cheek shook and his lip trembled. As if recalled to herself by the words, she raised her head, and, with a smile of deep-meaning sorrow, said,—

"It's the first tear I have yet shed; it shall be the last." Then, taking Daly's arm, she walked steadily forward.

"I have often wondered," said she, "at the prayer of a condemned felon for a few hours longer of life; but I can understand it now. I feel as if I could give life itself for another day within these walls, where often I have pined with *ennui*. You will watch over Lionel for me, Mr. Daly. When the world went fairly with us, calamities came softened,—as the summer rain falls lighter in sunshine; but now, now that we have lost so much, we cannot afford more."

Daly's stern features grew sterner and darker; his lips were compressed more firmly; he tried to say a few words, but a low, indistinct muttering was all that came.

The next moment the carriage door was closed on the party—they were gone.

Lionel stood gazing after them till they disappeared, and then, with a slow step, re-entered the abbey.

CHAPTER XXXV
BAGENAL DALY'S RETURN

Lionel Darcy bore up manfully against his altered fortunes so long as others were around him, and that the necessity for exertion existed; but once more alone within that silent and deserted house, all his courage failed him at once, and he threw himself upon a seat and gave way to grief. Never were the brighter prospects of opening life more cruelly dashed, and yet his sorrow was for others. Every object about brought up thoughts of that dear mother and sister, to whom the refinements of life were less luxuries than wants. How were they to engage in the stern conflict with daily poverty,— to see themselves bereft of all the appliances which filled up the hours of each day? Could his mother, frail and delicate as she was, much longer sustain the effort by which she first met the stroke of fortune? Would not the reaction, whenever it came, be too terrible to be borne? And Helen, too,—his sweet and lovely sister,—she whom he had loved to think of as the admired of a splendid Court; on whose appearance in the world he had so often speculated, castle-building over the sensations her beauty and her gracefulness would excite,—what was to be her lot? Deep and heartfelt as his sorrow was for them, it was only when he thought of his father that Lionel's anguish burst its bounds, and he broke into a torrent of tears. From very boyhood he had loved and admired him; but never had the high features of his character so impressed Lionel Darcy as when the reverse of fortune called up that noble spirit whose courage displayed itself in manly submission and the generous effort to support the hearts of others. How cruel did the decrees of fate seem to him, that such a man should be visited so heavily, while vice and meanness prospered on every side. He knew not that virtue has no nobler attribute than its power of sustaining unmerited affliction, and that the destiny of the good man is never more nobly carried out than when he points the example of patience in suffering.

Immersed in such gloomy thoughts, he wandered on from room to room, feeding, as it were, the appetite for sorrow, by the sight of every object that could remind him of past happiness; nor were they few. There was the window-seat he loved to sit in as a boy, when all the charm of some high-wrought story could not keep his eyes from wandering at intervals over the green hills where the lambs were playing, or adown by that dark stream where circling eddies marked the leaping trout. Here was Helen's favorite room, a little octagon boudoir, from every window of which a different prospect opened; it seemed to breathe of her sweet presence even yet; the open desk, from which she had taken some letter, lay there upon the table, the pen she had last touched, the chair she sat upon, all, even to the little nosegay of scarce-faded flowers, the last she had plucked, teemed with her memory. He walked on with bent-down head and tardy step, and entered the little room which, opening on the lawn, was used by the Knight to receive such of the tenantry as came to him for assistance or advice; many an hour had he sat there beside his father, and, while listening with the eager curiosity of youth to the little stories of the poor man's life, his trials and his difficulties, imbibed lessons of charity and benevolence never to be forgotten.

The great square volume in which the Knight used to record his notes of the neighboring poor, lay on the table; his chair was placed near it; all was in readiness for his coming who was to come there no more! As Lionel stood in silent sorrow, surveying these objects, the shadow of a man darkened the window. He turned suddenly, and saw the tall, scarecrow figure of Flury the madman. A large placard decorated the front of his hat, on which the words "Down with the Darcys!" were written in capital letters, and he carried in his hand a bundle of papers, like handbills, which he shook with a menacing air at Lionel.

"What is this, Flury?" said the youth, opening the window, and at the same time snatching one of the papers from his hand.

"It's the full account of the grand auction of Government hacks," said Flury, with the sing-song intonation of a street-crier, "no longer needed for the services of the Crown, and to be sowld without resarve."

"And who sent you here with this?" said the young man, moderating his tone, to avoid startling the other.

"Connor Egan, Hickman's man, gave me a pint and a noggin of spirits to cry the auction, and tould me to come up here and maybe you'd like to hear of it ye'selves."

Lionel threw his eyes over the offensive lines, where in coarse ribaldry names the most venerable were held up to scorn and derision. If it was some satisfaction to find that his father was linked in the ruffianly attack with men of honor as unblemished as his own, he was not less outraged at the vindictive cowardice that had suggested this insult.

"There'll be a fine sight of people there, by all accounts," said Flury, gravely, "for the auction-bills is far and near over the country, and the Castlebar coach has one on each door."

"Is popular feeling always as corrupt a thing as this?" muttered Lionel, with a bitter sneer, while at the same time the door of the room was opened, and Daly entered. His face was marked by a severe cut on one cheek, from which the blood had flowed freely; a dark blue stain, as of a blow, was on his chin, and one hand he carried enveloped in his handkerchief; his clothes were torn besides in many places, and bore traces of a severe personal conflict.

"What has happened?" said Lionel, as he looked in alarm at the swollen and blood-stained features. "Did you fall?"

"Fall! no such thing, boy," replied Daly, sternly; "but some worthy folk in Castlebar planned a little surprise for me this morning. They heard, it seems, that we passed through the town by daybreak, but that I was to return before noon; and so they placed some cars and turf creels in the main street, opposite the inn, in such a way that, while seeming merely accident, would effectually stop a horseman from proceeding. When I arrived at the spot, I halted, and called out to the fellows to move on, and let me pass. They took no heed of my words, and then I saw in a moment what was intended. I had no arms; I had purposely left my pistols behind me, for I feared something might provoke me, though not anticipating such as this. So I got down and drew this wattle from the side of a turf creel,—you see it is a strong blackthorn, and good stuff too. Before I was in the saddle the word was passed, and the whole street was full of people, and I now perceived that, by the same manouvre as they employed in front, they had also closed the rear upon me, and cut off my retreat. 'Now for it! now for it!' they shouted. 'Where's Bully Dodd?—Where's the Bully?' I suppose you know the fellow?"

"The man that was transported?"

"The same. The greatest ruffian the country was cursed with. He came at the call, without coat or waistcoat, his shirt-sleeves tucked up to his shoulders, and a handkerchief round his waist ready for a fight. There was an old quarrel between us, for it was I captured the fellow the day after he burnt down Dawson's house. He came towards me, the mob opening a way for him, with a pewter pot of porter in his hand.

"'We want you to dhrink a toast for us, Mr. Daly,' said he, with a marked courtesy, and a grin that amused the fellows around him. 'You were always a patriot, and won't make any objections to it.'

"'What is the liquor?' said I.

"'Good porter,—divil a less,' cried the mob; 'Mol Heavyside's best.' And so I took the vessel in my hands, and before they could say a syllable, drained it to the bottom; for I was very thirsty with the ride, and in want of something to refresh myself.

"'But you did n't dhrink the toast,' said Dodd savagely.

"'Where was the toast? He didn't say the words,' shouted the mob.

"'Off with his hat, and make him drink it,' cried out several others from a distance. They saved me one part of the trouble, for they knocked off my hat with a stone.

"'Here's health and long life to Hickman O'Reilly!' cried out Dodd,— 'that's the toast.'

"'And what have I to wish him either?' said I, while at the same time I tore open the pewter measure, and then with one strong dash of my band drove it down on the ruffian's head, down to the very brows. I lost no time afterwards, but, striking right and left, plunged forwards; the mob fled as I followed, and by good luck the carthorses, getting frightened, sprang forward also, and so I rode on with a few slight cuts; a stone or two struck me, nothing more; but they 'll need a plumber to rid my friend Dodd of his helmet."

"And we used to call this town our own," said Lionel, bitterly.

"Nothing is a man's own but his honor, sir. That base cowardice yonder believes itself honest and independent, as if a single right feeling, a single good or virtuous thought, could consort with habits like theirs; but they are less base than those who instigate them. The real scoundrels are the

Hickmans of this world, the men who compensate for low birth and plebeian origin by calumniating the wellborn and the noble.—What is Flury wanting here?" said he, as, attracted by Daly's narrative, the poor fellow had drawn near to listen.

"'I 'm glad you put the pewter pot on the Bully's head, he 's a disgrace to the town," said Flury, with a laugh; and he turned away, as if enjoying the downfall of an enemy.

"Oh! I see," said Daly, taking up one of the papers that had fallen to the ground, "this is the first act of the drama. Come along, Lionel, let us talk of matters nearer to our hearts."

They walked along together to the library, each silently following his own train of thought, and for some time neither seemed disposed to speak. Lionel at length broke silence, as he said,—

"I have been thinking over it, and am convinced my father will never be able to endure this life of inactivity before him."

"That is exactly the fear I entertain myself for him; altered fortunes will impress themselves more in the diminished sphere to which his influence and utility will be reduced, than in anything else: but how to remedy this?"

"I have been considering that also; but you must advise me if the plan be a likely one. He held the rank of colonel once—"

"To be sure he did, and with good right,—he raised the regiment himself. Darcy's Light Horse were as handsome a set of fellows as the service could boast of."

"Well, then, my notion is, that although the Government did not buy his vote on the Union, there would be no just reason why they should not appoint him to some one of those hundred situations which the service includes. His former rank, his connection and position, his unmerited misfortunes, are, in some sense, claims. I can scarcely suppose his opposition in Parliament would be remembered against him at such a moment."

"I hardly think it would," said Daly, musingly; "there is much in what you propose. Would Lord Netherby support such a request if it were made?"

"He could not well decline it; almost the last thing he said at parting was, that whatever favor he enjoyed should be gladly employed in our behalf. Besides, we really seek nothing to which we may not lay fair and honest claim. My intention would be to write at once to Lord Netherby. acquainting him briefly with our altered fortunes."

"The more briefly on that topic the better," said Daly, dryly.

"To mention my father's military rank and services, to state that, having raised and equipped a company at his own expense, without accepting the slightest aid from the Government, now, in his present change of condition, he would be proud of any recognition of those services which once he was but too happy to render unrewarded by the Crown. There are many positions, more or less lucrative, which would well become him, and which no right-minded gentleman could say were ill-bestowed on such a man."

"All true," said Daly, whose eye brightened as he gazed on the youth, whose character seemed already about to develop itself under the pressure of misfortune with traits of more thoughtful meaning than yet appeared iu him.

"Then I will write to Lord Netherby at once," resumed Lionel; "there can be no indelicacy in making such a request: he is our relative, the nearest my mother has."

"He is far better, he 's a Lord in Waiting, and a very subtle courtier," said Daly. "Write this day, and, if you like it, I 'll dictate the letter."

Lionel accepted the offer with all the pleasure possible. He had been from boyhood a firm believer in the resources and skill of Daly in every possible contingency of life, and looked on him as one of those persons who invariably succeed when everybody else fails.

There is a species of promptitude in action, the fruit generally of a strong will and a quick imagination, which young men mistake for a much higher gift, and estimate at a price very far above its value. Bagenal Daly had, however, other qualities than these; but truth compels us to own that, in Lionel's eyes, his supremacy on such grounds was no small merit. He had ever found him ready for every emergency, prompt to decide, no less quick to act, and, without stopping to inquire how far success followed such rapid resolves, this very energy charmed him. It was, then, in perfect confidence in the skill and address of his adviser that Lionel sat down, pen in hand, to write at his dictation.

CHAPTER XXXVI
THE LAW AND ITS CHANCES

We left Mr. Daly at the conclusion of our last chapter in the exercise of — what to him was always a critical matter — the functions of a polite letter-writer. His faults, it is but justice to say, were much less those of style than of the individual himself; for if he rarely failed to convey a clear notion of his views and intentions, he still more rarely omitted to impart considerable insight into his own character.

His abrupt and broken sentences, his sudden outbreaks of intelligence or passion, were not inaptly conveyed by the character of a handwriting which was bold, careless, and hurried. Indifferent to everything like neatness or accuracy, generally blotted, and never very legible, these defects, if they did not palliate, they might, in a measure, explain something of his habits of thought and action; but now, when about to dictate to another, the case was different, and those interruptions which Daly would have set down by a dash of his pen, were to be conveyed by the less significant medium of mere blanks.

"I 'm ready," said Lionel, at length, as he sat for some time in silent expectation of Daly's commencement. But that gentleman was walking up and down the room with his hands behind his back, occasionally stopping to look out upon the lawn.

"Very well, begin — 'My dear Lord Netherby,' or 'My dear Lord,' — it does n't signify which, though I suppose he would be of another mind, and find a whole world of difference between the two. Have you that? — very well. Then go on to mention, in such terms as you like yourself, the sudden change of fortune that has befallen your family, — briefly, but decisively."

"Dictate it, I'll follow you," said Lionel, somewhat put out by this mode of composition.

"Oh! it doesn't matter exactly what the words are, — say, that a d — — d scoundrel, Gleeson — Honest Tom we always called him — has cut and run with something like a hundred thousand pounds, after forging and falsifying every signature to our leases for the last ten or fifteen years; we are, in consequence, ruined—obliged to leave the abbey, take to a cottage—a devilish poor one, too."

"Don't go so fast—'we are in consequence—'"

"Utterly smashed—broken up—no home, and devilish little to live upon,—my mother's jointure being barely sufficient for herself and Helen. I want, therefore, to remind you—your Lordship, that is—to remind your Lordship of the kind pledge which you so lately made us, at a time when we little anticipated the early necessity we should have to recall it. My father, some forty-five or six years back, raised the Darcy Light Horse, equipped, armed, and mounted six hundred men, at his own expense. This regiment, of which he took the head, did good service in the Low Countries, and although distinguished in many actions, he received nothing but thanks,— happily not wanting more, if so much. Times are changed now with him, and it would be a seasonable act of kindness and a suitable reward to an old officer—highly esteemed as he is and has been through life—to make up for past neglect by some appointment—the service has many such— Confound them! the pension-list shows what fellows there are—'governors and deputy-governors,' 'acting adjutants' of this, and 'deputy assistant commissaries' of that."

"I'm not to write that, I suppose?"

"No, you needn't,—it would do no harm, though, to give them a hint on the subject; but never mind it now. 'As for myself, I'll leave the Guards, and take service in the Line. I am only anxious for a regiment on a foreign station, and if in India, so much the better.' Is that down? Well—eh! that will do, I think. You may just say, that the matter ought to be arranged without any communication with your father, inasmuch as, from motives of delicacy, he might feel bound to decline what was tendered as an offer, though he would hold himself pledged to accept what was called by the name of duty. Yes, Lionel, that's the way to put the case; active service, by all means active service,—no guard-mounting at Windsor or Carlton House; no Hounslow Heath engagements."

Lionel followed, as well as he was able, the suggestions, to which sundry short interjections and broken "hems!" and "ha's!" gave no small confusion, and at last finished a letter, which, if it conveyed some part of the intention, was even a stronger exponent of the character, of him who dictated it.

"Shall I read it over to you?"

"Heaven forbid! If you did, I'd alter every word of it. I never reconsidered a note that I did not change my mind about it, and I don't believe I ever counted a sum of money over more than once without making the tot vary each time. Send it off as it is—' Yours truly, Lionel Darcy.'"

It was about ten days after the events we have just related that Bagenal Daly sat in consultation with Darcy's lawyer in the back parlor of the Knight's Dublin residence. Lionel, who had been in conclave with them for several hours, had just left the room, and they now remained in thoughtful silence, pondering over their late discussion.

"That young man," said Bicknell, at length, "is very far from being deficient in ability, but he is wayward and reckless as the rest of the family; he seems to have signed his name everywhere they told him, and to anything. Here are leases forever at nominal rents—no fines in renewal—rights of fishery disposed of—oak timber—marble quarries—property of every kind—made away with. Never was there such wasteful, ruinous expenditure coupled with peculation and actual robbery at the same time."

"What's to be done?" said Daly, interrupting a catalogue of disasters he could scarcely listen to with patience; "have you anything to propose?"

"We must move in Equity for an inquiry into the validity of these documents; many of the signatures are probably false; we can lay a case for a jury—"

"Well, I don't want to hear the details,—you mean to go to law; now, has Darcy wherewithal to sustain a suit? These Hickmans are rich."

"Very wealthy people indeed," said Bicknell, dryly. "The Knight cannot engage in a legal contest with them without adequate means. I am not sufficiently in possession of Mr. Darcy's resources to pronounce on the safety of such a step."

"I can tell you, then: they have nothing left to live upon save his wife's jointure. Lady Eleanor has something like a thousand a year in settlement,—certainly not more."

"If they can contrive to live on half this sum," said the lawyer, cautiously, "we may, perhaps, find the remainder enough for our purposes. The first expenses will be, of course, very heavy: drafts to prepare, searches to make, witnesses to examine, with opinion of high counsel, will all demand considerable outlay."

"This is a point I can give no opinion upon," said Daly; "they have been accustomed to live surrounded with luxuries of every kind: whether they can at once descend to actual poverty, or would rather cling to the remnant of their former comforts, is not in my power to tell."

"The very bond under which they have foreclosed," said Bicknell, "admits of great question. Unfortunately, that fellow Gleeson destroyed all the papers before his suicide, or we could ascertain if a clause of redemption were not inserted; there was no registry of the judgment, and we are consequently in the hands of the enemy."

"I cannot help saying," said Daly, sternly, "that if it were not for the confounded subtleties of your craft, roguery would have a less profitable sphere of employment: so many hitches, so many small crotchety conjunctures influence the mere question of right and wrong that a man is led at last to think less of justice itself than of the petty artifices to secure a superiority."

"I must assure you that you are in a great error," said Bicknell, calmly; "the complication of a suit is the necessary security the law has recourse to against the wiles and stratagems of designing men. What you call its hitches and subtleties are the provisions against craft by which mere honesty is protected: that they are sometimes employed to defeat justice, is saying no more than that they are only human contrivances; for what good institution cannot be so perverted?"

"So much the better, if you can think so. Now, what are Darcy's chances of success?—never mind recapitulating details, which remind me a great deal too much of my own misfortunes, but say, in one word, is the prospect good or bad, or has it a tinge of both?"

"It may be any of the three, according to the way in which the claim is prosecuted; if there be sufficient means—"

"Is that the great question?"

"Undoubtedly; large fees to the leading counsel, retainers, if a record be kept for trial at the Assizes, and payment to special juries: all are expensive, and all necessary."

"I 'll write to Darcy to-night, then,—or, better still, I 'll write to Lady Eleanor, repeating what you have told me, and asking her advice and opinion; meanwhile, lose no time in consulting Mr. Boyle,—you prefer him?"

"Certainly, in a case like this he cannot be surpassed; besides, he is already well acquainted with all the leading facts, and has taken a deep interest in the affair. There are classes and gradations of ability at the bar, irrespective of degrees of actual capacity; we have the heavy artillery of the Equity Court, the light field-pieces of the King's Bench, and the Congreve rockets of Assize display: to misplace or confound them would be a grave error."

"I know where I 'd put them all, if *my* pleasure were to be consulted," muttered Daly, in an undergrowl.

"Now, if we have a case for a jury, we must secure Mr. O'Halloran—"

"He who made a speech to the mob in Smithfield the other day?"

"The same. I perceive you scarcely approve of my suggestion; but his success at the bar is very considerable: he knows a good deal of law, and a great deal more about mankind. A rising man, sir, I assure you."

"It must be in a falling state of society, then," said Daly, bitterly. "Time was when the first requisite of a barrister was to be a gentleman. An habitual respect for the decorous observances of polite life was deemed an essential in one whose opinions were as often to be listened to in questions of right feeling as of right doing. His birth, his social position, and his acquirements were the guarantees he gave the world that, while discussing subtleties, he would not be seduced into anything low or unworthy. I am sorry that notion has become antiquated."

"You would not surely exclude men of high talents from a career because their origin was humble?" said Bicknell.

"And why not, sir? Upon what principle was the bodyguard of noble persons selected to surround the person of the sovereign, save that blood was deemed the best security for allegiance? And why should not the law, only second in sacred respect to the person of the monarch, be as rigidly protected? The Church excludes from her ministry all who, even by physical defect, may suggest matter of ridicule or sarcasm to the laity; for the same reason I would reject from all concern with the administration of justice those coarser minds whose habits familiarize them with vulgar tastes and low standards of opinion."

"I confess this seems to me very questionable doctrine, not to speak of the instances which the law exhibits of her brightest ornaments derived from the very humblest walks in life."

"Such cases are probably esteemed the more because of that very reason," said Daly, haughtily; "they are like the pearl in the oyster-shell, not very remarkable in itself, but one must go so low down to seek for it. I have an excuse for warmth; I have lost the greater part of a large fortune in contesting a right pronounced by high authority to be incontrovertible. Besides," added he, with a courteous smile, "if Mr. Bicknell may oppose my opinion, he has the undoubted superiority that attaches to liberality, his own family claiming alliance with the best in the land."

This happy turn seemed to divert the course of a conversation which half threatened angrily. Again the business topic was resumed, and after a short discussion, Bicknell took his leave, while Daly prepared to write his letter to Lady Eleanor.

He had not proceeded far in his task when Lionel entered with a newspaper in his hand.

"Have you heard the news of the notorious robber being taken?" said he.

"Who do you mean? Barrington, is it?"

"No; Freney."

"Freney! taken?—when—how—where?"

"It's curious enough," said Lionel, coolly, seating himself to read the paragraph, without noticing the eagerness of Daly's manner; "the fellow seems to have had a taste for sporting matters which no personal fear could eradicate. His capture took place this wise. He went over to Doncaster, to be present at the Spring Meeting, where he betted freely, and won largely. There happened, however, to come a reverse to his fortune, and on the last day of the running he lost everything, and was obliged to apply for assistance to a former companion, who, it would seem, was some hundred pounds in his debt; this worthy, having no desire to refund, threatened the police; Freney became exasperated, knocked him down on the spot, and then, turning smartly round, chucked one of the jockeys from his saddle, sprang on the horse's back, and made off like lightning. The other, only stunned for a moment, was soon on his legs again, and the cry of 'Freney! it was Freney the robber!' resounded throughout the race-course. The scene must then have been a most exciting one, for the whole mounted population, with one accord, gave chase. Noblemen and country gentlemen, fox-hunters, farmers, and blacklegs, away they went, Freney about a quarter of a mile in front, and riding splendidly."

"That I 'm sure of," said Daly, earnestly. "Go on!"

"Mellington took the lead of every one, mounted on that great steeplechase horse he is so proud of,—no fences too large for him, they say; but the robber—and what a good judge of country the fellow must be—left the heavy ground and preferred even breasting a long hill of grass-land, with several high rails, to the open country below, where the clay soil distressed his horse. By this manoeuvre, says the newspaper, he was obliged to make a circuit which again brought the great body of his pursuers close up with him; and now his dexterity as a horseman became apparent, for while riding at top speed, and handling his horse with the most perfect judgment, he actually contrived to divest himself of his heavy greatcoat. He had but just accomplished this very difficult task, when Lord Mellington once more came up. There was a heavy dike in front, with a double post and rail, and at this they rushed desperately, each, apparently, calculating on the other being thrown, or at least checked.

"Freney, now only a dozen strides in advance, turned in his saddle, and drawing a pistol from his breast, took an aim,—as steadily, too, as if firing at a mark. Lord Mellington saw the dreadful purpose of the robber; he shouted aloud, and, pulling up with all his might, he bent down to the very mane of his horse. Freney pulled the trigger, and with one mad plunge Lord Mellington's horse came headforemost to the ground, with his rider under him. Freney was not long the victor; the racer he bestrode breasted the high rail, and, unable to clear it, fell heavily forward, smashing the frail timbers before him, and pitching the rider on his head. He was up in a second and away; for about twenty yards his speed was immense, then, reeling, he staggered forwards and fell senseless; before he rallied he was taken, and in handcuffs. There is a description of the fellow," said Lionel, "and, by Jove! one would think they were describing some wild denizen of the woods, or some strange animal of savage life, so eloquent is the paragraph about his appearance and personal strength."

"A well-knit fellow, no doubt, and more than a match for most in single combat," said Daly, musing.

"You have seen him, then?"

"Ay, that I have, and must see him again. Where is he confined?"

"In Newgate."

"That is so far fortunate, because the jailer is an old acquaintance of mine."

"I have a great curiosity to see this Freney."

"Come along with me, then," said Daly, as he arose and rang the bell to order a carriage; "you shall gratify your curiosity; but I must ask you to leave us alone together afterwards, for, strange as it may seem, we have a little affair of confidence between us."

It did, indeed, appear not a little strange that any secret negotiation or understanding should exist between two such men; but Lionel did not venture to ask any explanation of the difficulty, but silently prepared to accompany him. As they went along towards Newgate, Daly related several anecdotes of Freney, all of which tended to show that the fellow had all his life felt that strange passion for danger so attractive to certain minds, and that his lawless career was more probably adopted from this tendency than any mere desire of money-getting. Many of his robberies resembled feats of daring rather than cautious schemes to obtain property. "Society," added Daly, "is truly not much benefited because the highwayman is capricious; but still, one cannot divest oneself of a certain interest for a rascal who has always shown himself ready to risk his neck, and who has never been charged with any distinct act of cruelty. When I say this much, I must caution you against indulging a sympathy for a law-breaker because he is not a perfect monster of iniquity; such fellows are very rare, and we are always too well inclined to admire the few good qualities of a bad man, just as we are astonished at a few words spoken plain by a parrot.

"'The things themselves are neither strange nor rare;
We wonder how the devil they came there.'"

While Daly wisely cautioned his young companion against the indulgence of a false and mawkish sympathy for the criminal, he in his own heart could not help feeling the strongest interest for any misfortune of a spirit so wild and so reckless.

Daly's card, passed through the iron grating of the strong door, soon procured them admission, and they were conducted into a small and neatly furnished room, where a mild-looking middle-aged man was seated, reading. He rose as they entered, and saluted them respectfully.

"Good evening, Dunn; I hope I see you well. My-friend Captain Darcy—Mr. Dunn. We have just heard that the noted Freney has taken up his lodgings here, and are curious to see him."

"I 'm afraid I must refuse your request, Mr. Daly; my orders are most positive about the admission of any one to the prisoner: there have been I can't say how many people here on the same errand since four o'clock, when he arrived."

"I think I ought to be free of the house," said Daly, laughing; "I matriculated here at least, if I didn't take out a high degree."

"So you did, sir," said Dunn, joining in the laugh. "Freney is in the very same cell you occupied for four months."

"Come, come, then, you can't refuse me paying a visit to my old quarters."

"There is another objection, and a stronger one,—. Freney himself declines seeing any one, and asked a special leave of the sheriff to refuse all comers admission to him."

"This surprises me," said Daly. "Why, the fellow has a prodigious deal of personal vanity, and I cannot conceive his having adopted such a resolution."

"Perhaps I can guess his meaning," said the jailer, shrewdly; "the greater number of those who came here, and also who tried to see him in Liverpool, were artists of one kind or other, wanting to take busts or profiles of him. Now, my surmise is, Freney would not dislike the notoriety, if it were not that it might be inconvenient one of these days. To be plain, sir, though he is doubly ironed, and in the strongest part of the strongest jail in Ireland, he is at this moment meditating on an escape, in the event of which he calculates all the trouble and annoyance it would give him to have his picture or his cast stuck up in every town and village of the kingdom. This, at least, is my reading of the mystery; but I think it is not without some show of probability."

"Well, the objection could scarcely apply to me," said Daly; "if his portrait be not taken by a more skilful artist than I am, he may be very easy on the score of recognition. Pray let me send in my name to him, and if he refuses to see me, I 'll not press the matter further."

Partly from an old feeling of kindness towards Daly, Dunn gave no further opposition, but in reality he was certain that Freney's refusal would set the matter at rest. His surprise was consequently great when the turnkey returned with a civil message from Freney that he would be very glad to see Mr. Daly.

"Your friend can remain here," said Dunn, in a voice that plainly showed he was not quite easy in his mind as to the propriety of the interview; and Daly, to alleviate suspicions natural enough in one so circumstanced, assented, and walked on after the turnkey, alone.

"That's the way he spends his time; listen to him now," whispered the turnkey, as they stopped at the door of the cell, from within which the deep tones of a man's voice were heard singing to himself, as he slowly paced the narrow chamber, his heavy fetters keeping a melancholy time to the melody:—

"'T was afther two when he quitted Naas,
But he gave the spar, and he went the pace,
'As many an like may now give chase,'
Says he, 'I give you warning.
You may raise the country far and near,
From Malin Head down to Cape Clear,
But the divil a man of ye all I fear,
I 'll be far away before morning.'

"By break of day he reach'd Kildare,
The black horse never turn'd a hair;
Says Freney, 'We 've some time to spare,
This stage we 've rather hasten'd.'
So he eat four eggs and a penny rowl,
And he mix'd of whiskey such a bowl!
The drink he shared with the beast, by my sowl,
For Jack was always dacent.

"'You might tighten the girths,' Jack Freney cried,
'For I 've soon a heavy road to ride.'
'Twas the truth he tould, for he never lied;
The way was dark and rainy.
'Good-by,' says he, 'I 'll soon be far,
And many a mile from Mullingar.'
So he kiss'd the girl behind the bar,
'T is the divil you wor, Jack Freney!"

"Sorra lie in that, any way," said the robber, as he repeated the last line over once more, with evident self-satisfaction.

"Who comes there?" cried he, sternly, as the heavy bolts were shot back, and the massive door opened.

"Why don't you say, 'Stand and deliver'?" said the turnkey, with a laugh as harsh and grating as the creak of the rusty hinges.

"And many a time I did to a better man," said Freney.

"You may leave us now," said Daly, to the turnkey.

"Mr. Daly, your sarvant," said the robber, saluting him; "you 're the only man in Ireland I wanted to see."

"I wish our meeting had been anywhere else," said Daly, sorrowfully, as he took his seat on a stool opposite the bed where Freney sat.

"Well, well, so it is, sir; it's just what every one prophesied this many a day,—as if there was much cunning in saying that I 'd be hanged some time or other; why, if they wanted to surprise me, they 'd have tould me I 'd never be taken. You heard how it was, I suppose?"

Daly nodded, and Freney went on:—

"The English horse wouldn't rise to the rail; if I was on the chestnut mare or Black Billy, I would n't be where I am now."

"I have several things to ask you about, Freney; but first, how I can serve you? You must have counsel in this business."

"No, sir, I thank you; it's only throwing good money after bad. I'll plead guilty,—it will save time with us all."

"But you give yourself no chance, man."

"Faix, I spoiled my chance long ago, Mr. Daly. Do you know, sir,"—here he spoke in a low, determined tone,—"there's not a mail in Ireland I did n't stop at one time or other. There's few country gentlemen I have n't lightened of their guineas; the court wouldn't hold the witnesses against me if I were to stand my trial."

"With all that, you must still employ a lawyer; these fellows are as crafty in *their* walk as ever you were in *yours*. Who will you have? Name the man, and leave the rest to me."

Freney seemed to deliberate for a few moments, and he threw his eyes down at the heavy irons on his legs, and he gazed at the strong stanchions of the windows, and then said, in a low voice,—

"There's a chap called Hosey M'Garry, in a cellar in Charles Street: he's an ould man with one eye, and not a tooth in his head; but he's the only man that could sarve me now."

"Hosey M'Garry," repeated Daly, "Charles Street," as he wrote down the address with his pencil: "a strange name and residence for a lawyer."

"I did n't say he was, sir," said Freney, laughing.

"And who and what is he, then?"

"The only man, now alive, that can make a cowld chisel to cut iron without noise."

"Ah! that's what you're thinking of; you'd rather trust to the flaws of the iron than of the indictment. Perhaps you are not far wrong, after all."

"If I was in the court below without the fetters," said Freney, eagerly, "I could climb the wall with a holdfast and a chisel, and get down the same way on the other side; once there, Mr. Daly, I'd sing the ould ballad,—

"For the divil a man of ye all I fear,
I'll be far away before morning."

"And how are these tools to reach you here? If they admit any of your friends, won't they search them first?"

"So they will, barrin' it was a gentleman," replied Freney, while his eyes twinkled with a peculiarly cunning lustre.

"So, then, you rely on *me* for this piece of service?" said Daly, after a pause.

"Troth, you're the only gentleman of my acquaintance," said Freney, quaintly.

"Well, I suppose I must not give you a bad impression of the order; I'll do it."

"I knew you would," rejoined Freney, calmly. "You might bring two files at the same time, and a phial of sweet oil to keep down the noise. Hush! here's Gavin coming to turn you out,—he said ten minutes."

"Well, then, you shall see me to-morrow, Freney, and I'll endeavor to see your friend in the mean time." This was said as the turnkey stood at the open door.

"This gentleman wants to have a look at you, Freney," said the jailer, — "as if he could n't see you for nothing, some Saturday morning soon."

"Maybe he 'd not know me in a nightcap," replied Freney, laughing, while he turned the lamplight full on Lionel Darcy's features.

"The very fellow that rode off with the horse!" exclaimed Lionel as he saw him.

"Young O'Reilly!" said Freney. "What signifies that charge now? Won't it satisfy you if they hang me for something else?"

"That's Captain Darcy, man," broke in Daly. "Is all your knowledge of mankind of so little use to you that you cannot distinguish between a born gentleman and an upstart?"

"By my oath," said the robber, aloud, "I 'm as glad as a ten-pound note to know that it wasn't a half-bred one that showed the spirit you did! Hurrah! there's hopes for ould Ireland yet, when the blood and bone is still left in her! And wasn't it real luck that I saw you this night? If I did n't, I 'd have done you a bad turn. One word, Mr. Daly, one word in your ear."

The robber drew Daly towards him, and whispered eagerly for some seconds.

A violent exclamation burst from Daly as he listened, and then he cried out, "What! are you sure of this? Don't deceive me, man!"

"May I never, but it's true."

"Why, then, not have told it before?"

"Because" — here he faltered — "because — faix, I 'll tell the truth — I thought that young gentleman was Hickman's grandson, and I could n't bring myself to do him a spite after what I had seen."

"The time is up, gentlemen," said the turnkey, who, out of the delicacy of his official feeling, was slowly pacing the corridor up and down while they talked together.

"If this be but true," muttered Daly to himself, "there's another cast of the dice for it yet."

"I am sorry for that fellow," said Lionel, aloud; "he did me a good turn once: I might have gone down the torrent, were it not for his aid."

"So you might, man," said Daly, speaking in a half-soliloquy; "he gives the only chance of victory I've seen yet."

These words, so evidently inapplicable to Lionel's observations, were a perfect enigma; but he did not dare to ask for any explanation, and walked on in silence beside him.

CHAPTER XXXVII
A SCENE OF HOME

If the climate of northern Ireland be habitually one of storm and severity, it must be confessed that, in the rare but happy intervals of better weather, the beauty of the coast scenery is unsurpassed. Indented with little bays, whose sides are formed of immense cliffs of chalk, or the more stately grandeur of that columnar basalt which extends for miles on either side of the Causeway, the most vivid coloring unites with forms the wildest and most fantastic; crag and precipice, sandy beach and rocky shore, alternate in endless variety; while islands are there, some, green and sheep-clad, others, dark and frowning, form the home of nothing but the sea-gull.

It was on such an evening of calm as displayed the scene to its greatest advantage, when a long column of burnished golden light floated over the sea, tipping each crested wave, and darkened into deeper beauty between them, that the Knight, Lady Eleanor, and Helen sat under the little porch of their cottage and gazed upon the fair and gorgeous picture.

If the leafy grove or the dark wood seem sweeter to our senses when the thrilling notes of the blackbird or the thrush sing in their solitude, so the deepest silence, the most unbroken stillness, has a wonderful effect of soothing to the mind beside the seashore we have so often seen terrible in the fury of the storm. A gentle calm steals over us as we listen to the long sweeping of the waves, heaving and breaking in measured melody; and our thoughts, enticed by some dreaming ecstasy, wander away over the boundless ocean, not to the far-off lands of other climes alone, but into worlds of brighter and more beauteous mould.

They sat in silence, at first only occupied by the lovely scene that stretched away before them, but at last each deeply immersed in his own thoughts,—thoughts which, unconnected with the objects around, yet by some strange mystery were tinctured by all their calm and tranquil beauty. A fisherman was mending his net upon the little beach below, and his children were playing around him, now running merrily along the strand, now dabbling in the white foam left by the retreating waves; the father looked up from time to time to watch them, but without interrupting the low monotonous chant by which he lightened his labor.

Towards the little group at length their eyes were turned. "Yes," said the Knight, as if interpreting what was passing in the minds of those at his side, "that is about as near to human happiness as life affords. I believe there would be very few abortive ambitions if men were content to see their children occupy the same station as themselves; and yet, when the time of one's own reverses arrives, how very little of true happiness is lost by the change of fortune."

"My dearest father!" said Helen, as in a transport of delight she threw her arms around him, "how happy your words make me! You are, then, contented?"

"Do I not look so, my sweet Helen? And your mother, too, when have you seen her so well?—when do you remember her walking, as she did to-day, to the top of the great cliff of Dunluce?"

"With no other ill consequence," said Lady Eleanor, smiling, "than a most acute attack of vanity; for I begin to fancy myself quite young again."

"Well, Mamma, don't forget we have a visit to pay, some of these days, to Ballintray,—that's the name of the place, I think, Miss Daly resides at."

"Yes, we really must not neglect it. There was a delicacy in her note of welcome to us here, judging that we might not be prepared for a personal visit, which prepossesses me in her favor. You promised to make our acknowledgments, but I believe you forgot all about it."

"No, not that," said the Knight, hesitatingly; "but in the midst of so many things to do and think about, I deferred it from day to day."

"Shall we go to-morrow, then?" cried Helen, eagerly.

"I think it were better if your father went first, lest the way should prove too long for us. I am so proud of my pedestrianism, Helen, I'll not risk any failure."

"Be it so," said the Knight, quietly. "And now of this other matter Bagenal presses so strongly upon us. I feel the greatest repugnance to assume any name but that I have always borne, and, I hope, not disgraced; he says we shall be objects of impertinent curiosity here to the neighborhood."

"Ruins to dispute the honors of lionship with Dunluce," said Lady Eleanor, smiling faintly.

"Just so; that might, however, be borne patiently; they will soon leave off talking of us when we give them little matter for speculative gossip. Besides, we are so far away from anything that could be called neighborhood."

"But he suggests some other reasons, if I mistake not," said Lady Eleanor.

"He does, but so darkly and mysteriously that I cannot even guess his drift. Here is his letter." And the Knight took several papers from his pocket, from among which he selected one, whose large and blotted writing unmistakably pronounced it Bagenal Daly's. "Yes, here it is: 'Bicknell says that Hickman's people are fully persuaded that you have left Ireland with the intention of never returning; that this impression should be maintained, because it will induce them to be less guarded than if they believed you were still here, directing any legal proceeding. The only case, therefore, he will prepare for trial will be one respecting the leases falsely signed. The bond and its details must be unravelled by time; here also your incognito is all-essential,—it need only be for a short time, and on scruples of delicacy so easily got over: your grandfather called himself Gwynne, and wrote it also.' That is quite true, Eleanor, so he did; his letters are signed Matthew Gwynne, Knight of——— . I remember the signature well."

"I think, with Mr. Daly," said Lady Eleanor, "it will save us a world of observant impertinence; this place is tranquil and solitary enough just now, but in summer the coast and the Causeway have many visitors, and although 'the Corvy' is out of the common track, if our names be bruited about, we shall not escape that least graceful of all attentions, the tender commiseration of mere acquaintances."

"Mamma is right," said Helen; "we should be hunted out by every tourist to report on how we bore our reverses, and tormented with anonymous condolences in prose, and short stanzas on the beauty of resignation."

"Well, and, my dear Helen, perhaps the lessons might not be so very inapplicable," said the Knight, smiling affectionately.

"But very inefficient, sir," replied Helen, with a toss of her head; "I'm not a bit resigned."

"Helen, dearest," interposed Lady Eleanor, rebukingly.

"Not a bit, Mamma; I am happy,—happier than I ever knew myself before, if you like that phrase better,—because we are together, because this life realizes to me all I ever dreamed of,—that quiet and tranquil pleasure people might, but somehow never please to, taste of; but if you ask me am I resigned to see you and my dear father in a station so much beneath your expectations and your habits, I cannot say that I am."

"Then, my dear girl, you accuse us of bearing our misfortunes badly, if we cannot partake of your enjoyments on account of our own vain regrets?"

"No, no, Papa, don't mistake me; if I grieve over the altered fortunes that limit your sphere of usefulness as well as of pleasure, it is because I know how well you understood the privileges and demands of your high station, and how little a life so humble as this is can exact of qualities that were not given to be wasted in obscurity."

"My sweet child," said the Knight, fondly, "it is a very dangerous practice to blend up affection with principle; depend upon it, the former will always coerce the latter, and bend it to its will; and as for those good gifts you speak of, had I really as many of them as your fond heart would endow me with, believe me there is no station so humble as not to admit of their exercise. There never yet was a walk in life without its sphere of duties; now I intend that not only are we to be happy here, but that we should contribute to the well-being of those about us."

There was a pause after the Knight had done speaking, during which he busied himself in turning over some letters, the seals of which were still unbroken; he knew the handwriting on most of them, and yet hesitated about inflicting on himself the pain of reading allusions to that condition he had once occupied. "Yes," muttered he to himself, "we are always flattering ourselves of how essential we are to our friends, our party, and so forth; and yet, when any events occur which despoil us of our brief importance, we see the whole business of the world go on as currently as ever. What a foretaste this gives one of death! So it is, the stream of life flows on, whether the bubble on its surface float or burst."

"That's Lord Netherby's hand, is it not?" said Lady Eleanor, as she lifted a letter which had fallen to the ground.

"Yes," said Darcy, carelessly; "written probably soon after his return to England. I have no doubt it contains a most courtly acknowledgment of our poor hospitality, and an assurance of undying regard."

"If it be of that tenor, I have no curiosity to read it," said Lady Eleanor, handing the letter to the Knight.

"Helen would like to study so great a master of epistolary flatteries," said the Knight, smiling; "and provided she will keep the whole for her private reading, I am willing to indulge her."

"I accept the favor with thanks," said Helen, receiving the letter; "you know I plead guilty to liking our noble relative. I 'm not skilled enough to distinguish between an article trebly gilded and one of pure gold, and his Lordship, to my eyes, looked as like the true metal as possible: he said so many pretty things to Mamma, and so many fine things of you and Lionel—"

"And paid so many compliments to the fair Helen herself," interposed the Knight.

"With so much of good tact—"

"And good taste, Helen," added Lady Eleanor, smiling; "why not say that?"

"Well, I see I shall have to defend myself as well as my champion, so I 'll even go and read my letter."

And so saying, she arose, and sauntered down to the shore; under the shelter of a tall rock, from whence the view extended for miles along, she sat down. "What a contrast!" said she, as she broke the seal, "a courtier's letter in such a scene as this!"

Lord Netherby's letter was, as the Knight suspected, written soon after his return to England, expressing, in his own most courtly phrase, the delightful memory he retained of his visit to Ireland. Gracefully contrasting the brilliant excitement of that brief period with the more staid quietude of the life to which he returned, he lightly suggested that none other than one native to the soil could support an existence so overflowing with pleasurable emotions. With all the artifice of a courtier, he recalled certain little incidents, too small, as mere matters of memory, to find a resting-place in the mind, but all of them indicative of the deep impression made, upon him who remarked them.

He spoke also of the delight with which his Royal Highness the Prince listened to his narrative of life in Ireland. "In truth," wrote his Lordship, "I do not believe that the exigencies of his station ever cost him more than when he reflected on the impossibility of his witnessing such perfection in the life of a country house as I feebly endeavored to convey to him. Again and again has he asked me to repeat the tale of the hunt—the brilliant ball the night of your arrival—and I have earned a character for story-telling of which Kelly and Sheridan are beginning to feel jealous, by the mere retail of your anecdotes. Lionel's return is anxiously looked for by all here, and the Prince has more than once expressed himself impatient to see him back again. My sweet favorite Helen, too,—when is she to be presented? There will be a court in the early part of next month, of which I shall not fail to apprise you, most earnestly entreating that my cousin Eleanor will not think the journey too far which shall bring her once again among those scenes she so gracefully adorned, and where her triumphs will be renewed in the admiration of her lovely daughter. I need not tell you that my house in town is entirely at her disposal, either as *my* guests, or, if you prefer it, I shall be *theirs*, whenever I am not in waiting."

Here the writer detailed, with an eloquence all his own, the advantage to Helen of making her *entrée* into life under circumstances so favorable, remarking, with that conventional philosophy just then the popular cant of the day, that the enthusiasm of the world was never long-lived, and that even his beautiful cousin Helen should not be above profiting by the favorable reception the kindly disposition of the court was sure to procure for her. This was said in a tone of half-serious banter, but at the same time the invitation was reiterated with an evident desire for its acceptance.

As the letter drew near its conclusion, the lines became more closely written, as though some circumstances hitherto forgotten had suddenly occurred to the writer; and so it proved.

"I was about, my dear Knight, to write myself, with what truth I will not say, your 'most affectionate friend, Netherby,' when I received a letter which requires some mention at my hands. It is, indeed, one of the most extraordinary documents I have ever perused; nothing very wonderful in that, when I tell you from whom it comes,—your old sweetheart, Julia Wallincourt, or, as you will better remember her, Julia d'Esterre; she is still very beautiful, and just as capricious, just as *maligne*, as when she endeavored, by every artifice of her coquetry, to make you jilt my cousin Eleanor. There 's no doubt of it, Darcy, this woman loved you! at least, as much as she could love anything, except the pleasure of torturing her fellow-creatures. Well, it would seem that a younger son of hers, popularly known as Dick Forester, paid you a visit in Ireland, and, no very unnatural occurrence, fell desperately in love with your daughter,—not so Helen with him. She probably regarded him as one of that class upon which London has so stamped its impress of habit and manner that all individualism is lost in the quiet observance of certain proprieties. He must have been a rare contrast to the high-souled enthusiasm and waywardness of her own brother! Certain it is she refused him; and he, taking the thing much more to heart than a young Guardsman usually does a similar catastrophe, hastened home, and endeavored to interest his mother in his suit. Lady Julia had an old vengeance to exact, and, like a true woman, could not forego it; she not only positively refused all intercession on her part, but went what you and I will probably feel to be a very unnecessary length, and actually declared she never would consent to such an alliance. We used to remember (some years ago), at Eton, of a certain Dido who never forgave, and we are told how, for many years after, the *lethalis arundo lateri adhosit;* but assuredly the poet was speaking less of the woes of an individual than of the sorrows of fine ladies in all ages. Unfortunately, the similitude between her ladyship and Dido ends here; the classic fair one exhibited, as we are told, the most delicate fondness for the son of her lover. But, to grow serious, Lady

Wallincourt's conduct must have been peremptory and harsh; she actually went the length of writing to the Duke of York to request an exchange for her son into a regiment serving in India: whether Forester obtained some clew to this manouvre or not, he anticipated the stroke by selling out and leaving the army altogether; whither he is gone, or what has become of him since, no one can tell. Such, my dear Knight, is the emergency in which Lady Wallincourt addresses her letter to me,—a letter so peculiarly her own, so full of reproaches against you, and vindication of herself, that I actually scruple to transmit to you this palpable evidence of still enduring affection.

"Were you both thirty years younger, I should claim great credit to my morality for the forbearance. Let that pass, however, and let me rather ask you if you know, or have heard anything, of this wayward boy? Personally, I am unacquainted with him; but his friends agree in saying that he is high-spirited, honorable, and brave; and it would be a great pity that his affection for a young lady, and his anger with an old one, should mar all the prospects of his life. Could you, by any means, find a clew to him? I do not, of course, ask you to interfere in person, lest it might seem that you encouraged an attachment which you have far more reason to discountenance for your daughter than has Lady Wallincourt for her son; however, your doing so would go far to reconcile the young man to his mother by showing that, if there was a difficulty on one side, a still greater obstacle existed on the other."

Requesting a speedy answer, and begging that the whole might be in strict confidence between them, the letter concluded.

"I do not doubt, my dear Knight," said the postscript, "that you will see in all this a reason the more for coming up to town. Helen's appearance at the Drawing-Room would be the best, if not the only, rebuke Lady Wallincourt's insolence could receive. By all means, come.

"Another complication! Lady W., on first hearing of her son's duel, and the kind treatment he met with after being wounded, wrote a letter of grateful acknowledgments, which she enclosed to her son, neither knowing nor caring for the address of his benefactor. When she did hear it at length, she was excessively angry that she had been, as she terms it, 'the first to make advances.' Ainsi, telles sont les femmes du monde!"

Such was Lord Netherby's letter. With what a succession of emotions Helen read it we confess ourselves unable to depict. If she sometimes hesitated to read on, an influence, too powerful to control, impelled her to continue, while a secret interest in Forester's fortunes—a feeling she had never known till now—induced her to learn his fate. More than once, in the alteration of her condition, had she recalled the proffer of affection she had with such determination rejected, and with what gratitude did she remember the firmness of her decision!

"Poor fellow!" thought she, "I deemed it the mere caprice of one whose gratitude for kindness had outrun his calmer convictions. And so he really loved me!"

We must avow the fact: Helen's indifference to Forester had, in the main, proceeded from a false estimate of his character; she saw in him nothing but a well-bred, good-looking youth, who, with high connections and moderate abilities, had formed certain ambitious views, to be realized rather by the adventitious aid of fortune than his own merits. He was, in her eyes, a young politician, cautions and watchful, trained up to regard Lord Castlereagh as the model of statesmen, and political intrigue as the very climax of intellectual display. To know that she had wronged him was to make a great revolution in her feelings towards him, to see that this reserved and calmly minded youth should have sacrificed everything— position, prospects, all—rather than resign his hope, faint as it was, of one day winning her affection!

If these were her first thoughts on reading that letter, those that followed were far less pleasurable. How should she ever be able to show it to her father? The circumstances alluded to were of a nature he never could be cognizant of without causing the greatest pain both to him and herself. To ask Lady Eleanor's counsel would be even more difficult. Helen witnessed the emotion the sight of Lady Wallincourt's name had occasioned her mother the day Forester first visited them; the old rivalry had, then, left its trace on her mind as well as on that of Lady Julia! What embarrassment on every hand! Where could she seek counsel, and in whom? Bagenal Daly, the only one she could have opened her heart to, was away; and was it quite certain she would have ventured to disclose, even to him, the story of that affection which already appeared so different from at first? Forester was not now in her eyes the fashionable guardsman, indulging a passing predilection, or whiling away the tedious hours of a country-house by a flirtation, in which he felt interested because repulsed; he was elevated in her esteem by his misfortunes, and the very uncertainty of his fate augmented her concern. And yet she must forego the hope of saving him, or else, by showing the letter to her father, acknowledge her acquaintance with events she should never have known, or, knowing, should never reveal.

There was no help for it, the letter could not be shown. In all likelihood neither the Knight nor Lady Eleanor would ever think more about it; and if they did, there was still enough to speak of in the courteous sentiments of the writer, and the polite attention of his invitation,—a civility which even Helen's knowledge of life informed her was rather proffered in discharge of a debt than as emanating from any real desire to play their host in London.

Thus satisfying herself that no better course offered for the present, she turned homewards, but with a heavier heart and more troubled mind than had ever been her fortune in life to have suffered.